FINAL RESORT

DISCARDED

By the same author

THE MONEY STONES
THE BALFOUR CONSPIRACY
WINNER HARRIS
THE KILLING ANNIVERSARY
COLD NEW DAWN
JUSTICE
VENGEANCE

Ian St James

FINAL RESORT

HarperCollins*Publishers*

This book was published in Great Britain in 1994 by HarperCollins Publishers.

FINAL RESORT. Copyright © 1994 by Ian St James. All rights reserved. Printed in the United States of America. No part of this book may be used or reproduced in any manner whatsoever without written permission except in the case of brief quotations embodied in critical articles and reviews. For information, address HarperCollins Publishers, Inc., 10 East 53rd Street, New York, NY 10022.

HarperCollins books may be purchased for educational, business, or sales promotional use. For information, please write: Special Markets Department, HarperCollins Publishers, Inc., 10 East 53rd Street, New York, NY 10022.

FIRST U.S. EDITION

Library of Congress Cataloging-in-Publication Data

St. James, Ian.
    Final resort / by Ian St. James. — 1st ed.
      p. cm.
    ISBN 0-06-017953-8
    I. Title
  PR6069.A423F56 1994
  823´.912—dc20   94-14335

94 95 96 97 98 HC 10 9 8 7 6 5 4 3 2 1

FINAL RESORT

CHAPTER ONE

'TRAFFIC GETS WORSE,' Herbert grumbled over his shoulder.

From the back seat, Todd glanced out at Park Lane. 'What's up? You don't like cars? I sell them, remember?'

Herbert snorted his version of a laugh.

'It's the weather,' said Todd, watching pedestrians scurry along the wet pavements. 'Traffic's always bad in the rain.'

'S'pose so. How long you going to be, Boss?'

Glancing at his watch, Todd realized he could spend only an hour with Leo. 'I promised to be home by eight. Get yourself a coffee and pick me up at seven-thirty.'

'Righto.'

For a moment, Todd wondered about taking Leo home with him. Katrina would go mad, but one day he would. One day he would *insist* upon her meeting her father; one day he would put an end to this senseless bitterness. What was done was done. Leo wouldn't live for ever. He was an old man, who yearned to be reconciled with his daughter. He deserved better, even allowing for the past – even allowing for *his* past, which was certainly colourful. The first time Todd had met him, Leo had recently returned from the borders of Afghanistan, where he had been selling guns to the insurgents. Outraged, Katrina had snorted with withering contempt. 'So now you're a gun runner!'

'Not a gun runner,' Leo had protested. 'I sold them food, too, but they won't eat unless they defend themselves. I supply whatever the market demands. I'm a dealer. You know that.'

Katrina had turned away, curling her lip. 'Dealer! You're a cheap gambler, that's all.'

The memory provoked a wry smile. *Cheap* gambler? Italian shoes, Savile Row suits, a château in France, a suite at the Ritz

– a sixty-eight-year-old man whose charm still attracted women forty years younger. Nobody with Leo's style deserved to be called cheap.

The smile faded as Todd cast his mind back to that first meeting. Six . . . no, *seven* years ago. They were still living in the flat above the garage. God, where did the time go? Leo had arrived unexpectedly. What else? Katrina would never invite him. 'Hello,' he said, when Todd opened the door. 'I'm Katrina's father.'

Katrina was furious. Hatred had distorted her features in a way Todd would not have believed. He had always thought her pretty, beautiful in some lights, and to see ugliness in her face had shocked him. She had ended the meeting within minutes, slamming off to their bedroom, eyes brimming tears, leaving him to usher Leo to the door. Leo had retained his composure, but only just. The tan had deserted his face and he had stuttered apologies. He had wanted to stay, to explain, to ask for understanding. In other circumstances Todd might have listened, but he was more concerned with Katrina at that moment. 'Not now,' he remembered saying as he pushed Leo to the door. 'Another time, eh?'

The following day, Leo had telephoned the office. After making solicitous enquiries about Katrina, he suggested, 'Maybe we could meet next time I'm in London? Just for a drink, you and me. What d'you think?'

Todd had given a vague, noncommittal reply, and what with everything else on his mind the suggestion was quickly forgotten. It was some weeks before he remembered and told Katrina. She went up like a sheet of flame. 'Why even *speak* to him? If I don't want to see him, why in God's name should you?'

Why indeed? He had every reason not to. He knew how Katrina felt. Leo had caused her untold misery, ruined her childhood, driven her mother to drink – Todd had heard all the stories. To see Leo against her wishes would be the sort of betrayal he would condemn in anyone else. 'Asking for trouble,' he would have said.

Yet when Leo telephoned six months later, Todd had agreed to a meeting. The truth was he and Katrina were going through

8

a bad patch. Their efforts to achieve parenthood were taking a toll. Closing his eyes, Todd pictured a thermometer stuck into a sumptuous backside. He pictured a chart which logged days and hours with red check-marks against vital dates. He saw taxicabs waiting to rush Katrina to the gynaecologist who would inject the magical fluid of life into her cervix. He could see the slow paddle of spermatozoa under a microscope . . . could imagine the sandblasting of Fallopian tubes . . .

'Just for a drink,' Leo had urged. 'I'm at the Ritz. Why not come round for a quick one?'

So he had gone, almost as an act of rebellion. Before he was married sex had been torrid, sweaty and passionate. Sex had been impulsive, sex had been *fun*! And so it had remained until Katrina had wanted a baby. Then the whole wretched business had started – appointments with doctors, conferences with gynaecologists, meetings with specialists – the onset of clinical, sterilized sex. Antiseptic, unadventurous sex. The physical pleasure was still to be had, if he could close his mind to thermometers and spray guns for the cervix, and the waiting taxis and knee-chest positions, and the sandblasted tubes and red-marked calendars – but closing his mind had become increasingly difficult. Even raising an erection was not always easy.

So he had gone, disgruntled, for a few drinks with Leo.

Leo had never lost an erection in the whole of his life. Not for Leo meals full of wheatgerm. He was one of the world's great adventurers. Been everywhere, done everything – traded hashish in Morocco, sold land in Alaska, mined gold in the Transvaal, hunted in Kenya, run guns into the Belgian Congo.

Conditioned to despise him, Todd had expected to dislike him. According to Katrina, he was a fraud, a con-man, a user, a womanizer, a man not to be trusted.

Yet, unexpectedly, the two had become friends. Todd had liked him from the outset, even while recognizing the differences between them. Tall and lean, Leo was eagle-eyed and noble of face. Todd was short and plump, with looks which few would consider distinguished. Leo wore clothes with the panache of a fashion plate; whereas Todd's suits always looked rumpled no matter who was his tailor. In all truth Leo was a handsome old dog. 'I wasn't even a good-looking puppy,' grunted Todd, wryly amused. What he most liked about Leo was the man's realistic approach to life. He saw things as they were. Leo had never suffered a pang of guilt about anything in his life, with the single exception of Katrina. Certainly not about his wife, nor his business affairs. If a deal went bad, it went bad. 'All business is risk,' Leo maintained. 'Win and you make a profit, lose and you take a loss.' If a creditor went unpaid, he went unpaid. 'Part of the game,' Leo would say with a shrug of dismissal.

Todd always pictured him like that – shoulders shrugged, hands upturned, that tiny deprecating smile on his face. 'Win some, lose some,' he would grin. The only loss he ever regretted was Katrina.

After that first meeting, they had met whenever Leo was in London – irregularly, never more than once or twice a year, and then only for an hour or so at a time. Usually they just had a drink at the Ritz. Gradually the friendship had developed. 'You know, Toddy old boy,' Leo would say. 'Katrina deserves someone like you. Solid, dependable, reliable –'

'Knock it off, for Christ's sake! A dead fish sounds more exciting.'

'I meant, well . . . look at the success you're making of life. A happy marriage, a growing business –'

'You're the one who jets all over the world –'

'Hah! Don't sell yourself short. Your business keeps growing. You're the type who *builds* a business. You won't gamble it away. I was slow learning that. I always reckoned what I lost today, I'd win back tomorrow.' A look of regret had crept into Leo's grey eyes. 'Take it from me, some things you never win back.'

He meant Katrina, of course. He was always seeking Todd's help in bringing about a reconciliation.

Todd had been cautious at first; after all, he had heard Katrina's stories and although sterilized sex was straining the marriage, he was unwilling to believe she had lied to him. Nor had she, for the more he heard the more aware he became that Leo's account of parenthood and Katrina's tales of childhood were mainly two points of view. Leo was unrepentant about his

10

wife. 'She always liked her tipple,' he grumbled. 'Nothing wrong with that, even in a woman, except she became a drunk. Katrina was thrown out of more schools than you can count. Always for the same reason; the fees hadn't been paid. The fees had been *drunk*, that's what, though of course Katrina never knew. I got the blame. I *always* got the blame. Sometimes I deserved it, but a woman who wasn't permanently stewed could have coped. Other women cope, don't they?' he asked, eyebrows bristling and rising like question marks. 'Army wives, people like that; women with husbands away all the time.'

He was as bitter about his dead wife as was Katrina about him.

''Course I was a bad father,' he admitted. 'Bloody awful, but that bitch made it worse. And look at the money she cost me! Private nursing homes don't come cheap, I can tell you. She went in to dry out the first time, never to touch the stuff again. Hah! Pissed as a newt the first night she came back.'

The sanatorium was permanent after that. Katrina, aged twelve, was at boarding school, and Leo arranged for her to spend her holidays with his older sister, a widow living in Harrow. 'Another mistake,' he confessed gloomily. 'You'd have thought your own kith and kin could be trusted.'

At least his sister could be trusted with money. School fees were paid on the dot – 'even when my own cheque was late, but she poisoned the kid against me. Blamed me for Miriam's drinking, never took my side in anything . . .'

Katrina was fifteen when her mother died, and her aunt died three years later. Katrina inherited the house at Harrow, together with a few thousand pounds, all administered by her aunt's solicitor. 'Snotty bastard sent me a letter six months later,' Leo exclaimed. 'Returning my cheque. Said now that Katrina had means of her own, she preferred not to take money from me. Would you believe it? My own daughter, turned against me.'

Todd had heard the story before. Katrina was twenty-three when he met her, still living in Harrow, sharing the house with two girlfriends. She had come to work for him as his bookkeeper, and one thing had led to another.

'Been a while since Mr Sinclair was in town?' said Herbert, catching Todd's eye in the mirror.

'A few months,' Todd agreed.

Herbert cocked an eyebrow. 'Still no chance of patching things up with the missus?'

'Pigs should fly,' he grunted. From time to time, he worked Leo's name into conversations, testing the water, but never with any success. There was simply no talking to Katrina. Mere mention of Leo was enough to bring a frown to her face. Bitter memories of childhood humiliations brought hot, angry words to her lips. He had *tried* to effect a reconciliation. God knows he had tried, but having kept his first meeting with Leo from her, he had become trapped into keeping the rest of them secret. Seven years of secrets. *Seven years!*

Thankfully, Leo had accepted the situation. 'I suppose there's a lot to forgive,' he admitted, grave-faced and repentant. Not that he ever remained glum for long. Setbacks were so commonplace that Leo had learned to see good news in bad. 'Things could be worse, old boy,' he shrugged. 'She's happy. Meanwhile you and I have become friends. I'm a father one step removed. If closer contact means friction, who needs it? And maybe one day, you'll bring us together?'

But Todd had his doubts.

What made it worse was that he *owed* Leo. He felt obligated. God Almighty, he *was* obligated!

'You look a bit peaky, Boss,' said Herbert, studying him in the mirror. 'You feeling okay?'

Todd grunted. What sort of a question was that? How the hell was he *supposed* to feel? Business was lousy. Two years ago nobody had talked of a recession. A temporary slowing down of the economy. That's what they had said, politicians and such people; people who wrote for the papers. Temporary? That was a joke. They should try selling cars in this market . . .

'Yesterday,' Herbert crooned. 'All my troubles seemed so far away.'

'Shut up and drive, will you?'

'Sorry, Boss. It's just the look on your face. Things can't be that bad.'

'Things could be better,' Todd grunted, remembering. Five years ago – when they had taken that holiday in Majorca – business had been booming. He had been feeling like a multi-millionaire. And the island had captivated Katrina. 'I can't believe we're only three hours from London,' she kept saying.

'You need a break,' Herbert said over his shoulder. 'Can't you get out to your boat for a few days?'

Todd winced for reasons unknown to Herbert. 'We're going out to Majorca in a couple of weeks,' he said. 'Just for a few days.'

The boat, the yacht, had come after the villa. They had bought the yacht four years ago. Even four years ago business had been good. But now the yacht had been sold to pay Aldo Moroni. Gnawing his lip, Todd tried to put it out of his mind.

'Mr Sinclair will cheer you up,' said Herbert. 'He always does. As good as a tonic is Mr Sinclair.'

There was truth in that. Leo was unfailingly cheerful. If he had problems, he made light of them. Todd recalled him laughing: 'Do yourself a favour, old boy. Never live my kind of life. The *complications*! With you, you sell a car, you get your money. With me, nothing's straightforward. I get paid when they harvest the grapes, or when the government falls, or if the oil price goes up or the dollar goes down – always *something* . . .' For a split second he had looked downcast, then had come the shrug, the upraised hands, the deprecatory grin. 'Ah, so what? We're living, ain't we? We eat well, we dress well. There's food on the table, wine in the bottle and women in our beds.'

That was another thing with Leo. Women. Like wasps to a jam-jar. Todd's lips twitched. Herbert was right. Leo *was* a tonic.

Closing his eyes, he tried to relax. He made a conscious effort to push his worries aside. Ignoring the grey London skies, he imagined the sunshine of Majorca. He remembered the feel of the sun on his face. Moistening his lips, he could almost savour the salt on the air . . . and mixed in along with it came the taste of his dreams.

*   *   *

He had always had dreams. Even as a kid. His dreams then had been to grow six feet tall, to grow into the kind of man who walks into a room and makes every woman go weak at the knees. He sweated through every stretching exercise ever invented. He even invented some of his own, but none made him taller than nature intended. Fully grown, he stood five feet five in his stockinged feet. Eventually he had decided, *Fuck it, if I can't be six feet, I'll act six feet.* A big enough challenge in itself, but what made life worse was his name. *Cyril!* He never forgave his parents. He kept it secret as far as he could. 'Call me Toddy,' he told boys at school. But inevitably it became known – and, just as inevitably, those who tormented him were bigger than he was. Not that it made any difference. He fought them all, often more than one at a time, and as a consequence had taken some terrible beatings. He might have been killed except for his solid build and strong constitution. But he had survived – and so had his dreams.

'People will look up to me one day,' he boasted to his pal Jimmy Lewis at school.

Jimmy had rolled his eyes. 'Yeah, and I'll sprout a pair of big tits.'

The same derision had come his way when he started work at Owen's. Other mechanics had scoffed, ' 'Ere, it'll save time to have you around. We'll stick you under a car instead of jacking it up.'

He had accepted their laughter. Young though he was, he had already learned one of life's saddest lessons. 'Humility has the toughest hide,' wrote Nietzsche in 'The Stillest Hour'. Todd had never read Nietzsche, but he had already learned that sometimes in life you got buried in shit. He had desperately wanted that job. Cars had been his passion even longer than girls, and where better to learn about cars than at Owen's – the biggest motor business in the district.

'Well, young man,' Mr Owen had said at the interview. 'What do you plan to do with your life?'

Todd had answered without hesitation. 'I want to become the best mechanic in London.'

Mr Owen had laughed, 'Dunno about the best, but we'll train you to be good if you work hard. That will take the next five years. What then?'

Todd's heart had thumped. Becoming a top mechanic would be an important rung on the ladder. Being five foot five would cease to matter. As a skilled man, people would look up to him. He would be *someone*. He had answered carefully, 'Seems a long way off at the moment, Mr Owen. Reckon the time to think about that is when I get there.'

A good-humoured grin of approval had appeared on Mr Owen's face. 'Right,' he had nodded before proceeding to business. 'We've six apprentices right now. Not a bad bunch of lads. You'll soon fit in. After all, you don't take up much space, do you?'

Fitting in would have been easier without Red Higgins, a tall, ginger-haired eighteen-year-old who became the bane of Todd's life, tormenting him at every opportunity. For the most part, he deflected the barbs with a wry wit which would have won the approval of even Nietzsche himself, but he knew that one day the exchanges would become more than just verbal. The day came at the end of six weeks. Red and two of his sidekicks cornered him in the paint shop. ''Ere, Shorty,' Red grinned, holding up a can of cellulose paint. 'I'm going to give you a spray job. You'd look better with my colour hair.'

While Red prised the lid from the can, the other two tried to grab Todd's arms, but past battles had sharpened his reflexes. Shaking them off, he gave them no chance. He ground his left heel into the nearest instep to send the youth hopping away, clutching his foot. His companion caught Todd's head-butt full in the face, while Red felt a knee in his groin. Red gasped and doubled over, dropping the paint and clutching himself just as Todd's clenched joined hands came down on the back of his neck. As Red pitched forward, Todd again brought up his knee, catching him hard in the chest to send him staggering backwards.

'What's going on here?' shouted a voice. Mr Owen emerged from the door to his office. 'What the devil?' he exclaimed,

15

outraged. He looked from Red on the ground to his companion clutching his nose. Turning to Todd, he demanded, 'You. What's this all about?'

Todd met his gaze. 'I think that paint can must have been greasy. It slipped in Red's hands, sir. He was trying to save it from spilling.'

A speculative look glimmered at the back of Mr Owen's eyes. He stared at Todd before turning to Joe Holmes, who was rubbing his foot. 'And you? What happened to you?'

'My fault,' Todd interrupted quickly. 'In the rush to help Red, I trod on Joe's foot.'

Mr Owen's stare returned to Todd. He seemed about to say something, then changed his mind. Instead he nodded and looked down at Red, who had heaved himself painfully on to one knee. Crimson paint dripped from his overalls to form a sticky pool on the floor. After clearing his throat, Mr Owen said severely, 'Accidents like this cost time and money. Sort this mess out and get back to work. I expect all of you to be more careful in future. Is that understood?'

'Yes, Mr Owen,' they chorused.

When work finished that day, Todd was summoned to the office. Owen looked up from his desk. 'What happened earlier?'

Todd shuffled and looked down at his feet. 'Just a bit of an accident –'

'Don't give me that, lad. I know an accident when I see one. Just as I know bullying when I see it. And I won't have it. Bit of horseplay now an' then is one thing. Put lads together and I expect it. But bullying's something else. I won't have it, understand?'

Unsure of how to respond, Todd remained silent.

'Not that they'll try it again.' Sam Owen's eyes glimmered and his face split into a grin. 'By God, that was quick thinking! The paint can was greasy. I don't know how I kept a straight face. Anyone who thinks that quick should be *selling* cars, not fixing 'em.'

*   *   *

16

'Not much of a site,' Larkins sniffed, picking his way carefully between some broken bottles. 'I mean, it's simply a patch of waste ground.'

Ignoring the criticism, Todd turned and waited for the banker. 'Watch yourself, Mr Larkins. Don't go falling over. Here, hang on to me –'

'I'm not drunk,' Larkins responded testily. 'Nor infirm. It's just that these . . .' He looked down at his mud-speckled shoes. 'I'd have worn hiking boots had I known –'

'Not far now,' Todd encouraged quickly. 'We're almost at the office.'

Adjusting his spectacles, Larkins stared ahead at the big wooden barn. 'You mean *that's* the office?'

Todd grinned. 'Only one corner. The rest is for the workshop.'

Choosing the least soggy ground, he led the way forward. 'There's room for two hundred cars out here,' he said, trying to sound confident. Beneath his breath, he cursed the weather. Overnight rain had reduced the site to a quagmire. The place had looked better last week. Last week the sun had been shining and the ground had been dust dry underfoot. Not that it had looked brilliant, it could *never* look brilliant. Larkins was right. The site was simply a patch of open ground, with a warehouse one side and a factory the other. Behind it was a row of small houses, with another mean street beyond them. But it was big, with a long frontage on to Kilburn High Road.

'This place used to be an overflow for the warehouse next door,' he explained as he turned the key in the padlock. 'It's bigger than you'd think. Stay there a minute, Mr Larkins, there's a light switch somewhere. They had to board the windows up because of vandals.'

He found a bank of switches and put them on one after another. Gradually the dark shadows receded, but the bare bulbs did little to improve the atmosphere of gloom and decay. Larkins stepped gingerly over the threshold and peered cautiously about him.

'It's a hundred and seventy foot long,' Todd said proudly. 'I measured it. And it's got a good base.' He stamped hard on the

17

floor. 'Hear that? Solid concrete. You could run a ten-ton truck over that.'

'Mmm,' Larkins murmured.

'There's a desk and chairs over here. Come and sit down a minute.' As he led the way, he took a newspaper from his pocket, unfolding it as he went. Placing one sheet over the dust-covered desk, he scrunched the rest of the paper into a ball which he used to wipe the dust from the swivel chair. Acting the role of considerate host, his cheerful grin removed any suggestion of servility. 'There you go, Mr Larkins. You sit there. Not much like your office, I'm afraid –'

'Nor yours at Owen's.'

'Ah well, that's the point. It's not my office. That's why we're here.'

Larkins gathered the skirt of his coat around him and sat down in the chair. 'I hope you know what you're doing,' he said doubtfully. 'You're giving up a great deal. How long have you worked for Sam Owen?'

'Twelve years.'

'Starting as an apprentice mechanic –'

'That was a long time ago, Mr Larkins.'

'He *still* says you're the best he's ever employed. Quite a compliment, don't you think?'

'He's been a good boss –'

'After you served your time as a mechanic, he made you a salesman. Then he made you showroom manager. Now he wants you to become general manager, with a place on the board. Not bad, for a young man of twenty-eight –'

'But that's just it. Twenty-eight! If I'm ever going to strike out on my own, now's the time.'

Larkins smiled at the urgency in Todd's voice. At fifty-six, he could scarcely remember what it was like to be twenty-eight. Not that he'd ever had an urge to strike out on his own. There was a lot to be said for security in an uncertain world. Banking had taught him that much. 'Very well,' he sighed, accepting the inevitable. 'Sam Owen and I have been friends for twenty years. I promised him I'd remind you of what you were throwing away –'

18

'We'll still do business together. Sam knows that –'

'Selling his used cars. Cars his customers trade in for new ones. I've never understood why Sam doesn't sell them himself.'

Todd laughed with surprise. 'In his showrooms? You've seen them. All those plush carpets and antique desks. Fine, when you're selling brand spanking new Jaguars. But not for old bangers.'

'You won't sell anything in this place,' Larkins said gloomily, casting a bleak look over Todd's shoulder. 'I'm not sure what I expected, but . . . I think you're making a mistake. I mean, it will cost the earth to make decent offices –'

'That's the whole point. We won't *have* decent offices. I'll level the forecourt and cover it with tarmac, but that's all.'

Larkins was astonished. 'You mean you'll work in this –'

Todd laughed, 'Let me ask you something, Mr Larkins. Why does anyone buy a second-hand car?'

Larkins took out a spotless white handkerchief and polished his glasses. His pale eyes screwed into slits of concentration while he considered the question.

Todd was too impatient to wait for an answer. 'Because they don't have the money for a new one.'

'Is that some kind of joke?' Blinking like an owl, Larkins replaced the glasses on his nose. 'I'd have thought it was perfectly obvious –'

Hearing the note of irritation, Todd hurried into his explanation. 'Look,' he said. 'People who buy second hand need a low price, but they still want the car to look good and run well . . . and, well . . . be as near perfect as possible –'

'Don't want much, do they?' Larkins interrupted sarcastically.

'They want a bargain! That's what it's about. A man comes in to buy a car. So I tell him it's a bargain. He needs convincing, right?' Pacing up and down, Todd pounded a fist into the open palm of his other hand. 'I can't say I buy cheaper because he knows I buy from the public or at the sales like any other dealer, so instead I say, look around. I've got no overheads. We don't even repair the place. Look at the rain coming through the roof. We can afford to take a small profit. What do I care if the rain comes in? We're offering you bargain prices. We could slap

19

paint on the walls, but we'd have to put a few quid on our cars. What's best for you? Come to a place like this and pay less, or go to a smart outfit and pay more? It's logic, isn't it?'

'But hardly revolutionary.'

'I'm not a revolutionary, Mr Larkins.' Todd grinned. 'I want to be a millionaire.'

Try as he would, Larkins failed to keep the smile from his lips. Sam Owens had predicted the conversation exactly. 'He's got it all worked out,' Sam had said. 'Don't be fooled by his appearance. He may look like a big lump of lard, but stupid he ain't. He's bright and ambitious and customers like him.' Larkins could understand people liking Todd. He was even a bit envious. Tall and thin himself, he knew that people were cautious around him. As usual Shakespeare had summed it up. *Yond Cassius has a lean and hungry look.* There was nothing lean and hungry about Todd. His ambition was concealed by a bulging waistline and a comfortable warmth – but ambition was there in abundance and Larkins was always ready to lend to men of ambition. 'You'll have to sell a lot of cars to become a millionaire,' he said.

'Exactly,' Todd nodded. 'Believe me, Mr Larkins, the time's right for this. It's what the Sixties were all about. Creating a consumer society. Look at what's happened in the States. So okay, now everyone's got a fridge and a washing machine and a television. The next thing's a car. Their problem is raising the money. So I take a low deposit and you write them a payment plan for the rest –'

'The bank has already started to do that –'

'Not on this scale, you haven't. I'm talking big numbers, Mr Larkins.'

When Larkins remained silent, Todd plunged on. 'Put yourself in my customer's shoes. You want to buy a car. So you see this place advertised. The biggest selection of used cars in London. Every make, every model. Britain's lowest prices. All cars sold with a three-month guarantee. Easy finance arranged. Where would you go, Mr Larkins? If you were seriously considering buying a second-hand car, wouldn't you go out of your way to come and see this place?'

Larkins had never bought a second-hand car in his life and he had serious reservations about those who did. 'We'd have to vet the credit-worthiness of your customers.'

'Sure, and some you'll reject, I know that, but I want paying the same day for those you take on —'

'The same day?'

'Too right. Every time a customer drives out with a car, I need to buy a replacement.'

'The same day?' Larkins repeated with a frown.

'Absolutely,' said Todd with a grin. 'Besides I'll have some big expenses.'

The swivel chair creaked as Larkins sat back in surprise. 'You just said you wouldn't spend much on this place.'

'Right, but I've got to tell 'em how to find us.'

The advertising broke a month later.

A double-page spread in the *Daily Express* shouted: 'The only red carpet at Todd Motors is inside our cars.'

The *Daily Mail* showed an aerial picture of the site, taken on a fine day with the sun shining down upon row upon row of cars: 'Fully air conditioned — unbeatable value at Europe's biggest car showroom.'

The word BARGAIN leapt from every page.

Herbert Spencer became Todd's most trusted employee. It was Herbert, fifteen years older than Todd, who sweated over the used cars as they came in the back door. It was Herbert who ran the workshop. Todd worked the front lot, being all things to all men: fairground barker one minute, motor mechanic the next, financial consultant later, whatever anyone wanted him to be — so long as they bought. If a potential buyer had trouble finding the deposit, Todd helped. 'You must have *something* of value? What you got at home? A piano. Okay, I'll take that as half the deposit. Get the rest in cash, and you've got a deal.' The pianos, furniture, old books, paintings and everything else, he knocked out in Petticoat Lane's Sunday market — often for less than he had allowed against the deposit on a car. 'But so what?' he said to Larkins.

21

'I still made twenty per cent, and look at the turnover I'm doing.'

A year later, he was still short and fat – but on his way to becoming someone people looked up to.

'Reckon I'm about ready to retire,' Sam Owen said, pouring a drink.

Todd laughed derisively in disbelief. 'You wouldn't know what to do with yourself.'

'Don't you believe it. I know *exactly* what I shall do.'

'Cheers,' said Todd, accepting the whisky. 'Go on. Convince me.'

'I'm going to live in the sun. I've bought a villa out in Majorca, and half share in a boat,' said Sam with an air of satisfaction. 'And I've had an offer for this place,' he waved a hand at his office.

Todd whistled. 'Seriously?'

'See for yourself.' Sam picked up a sheet of paper from the desk. 'Haslem's want to buy me out; lock, stock and barrel.'

As he studied the figures, Todd whistled again. 'You're a rich man, Sam. I'm pleased for you.' But as he handed the paper back his look was more of wistful regret than of pleasure. Sam was part of his life. 'I'll miss you, though,' he confessed with a tinge of sadness. 'It won't be the same dealing with Haslem.'

'I didn't say I'd accepted,' said Sam, tapping the paper.

Todd looked at him in surprise.

'Billy Haslem's a shit,' said Sam. 'The thought of him in this chair turns my stomach. I spent thirty years building this up, and some of 'em were bloody hard, I don't mind admitting. To think of someone like Haslem . . .' he shrugged and sipped his drink, as if to remove a bad taste from his mouth.

'I can understand that,' Todd nodded thoughtfully. He wondered how he would feel about selling Todd Motors. Could money alone recompense him for seven years of unceasing commitment? Todd Motors was his life. Just as Owen's was Sam's. Thirty years! What must it be like to give something up after thirty years? 'So don't retire,' he grinned. 'Stay here –'

'No, no,' Sam shook his head. 'I promised my wife. I've made the decision.'

'I see.'

Sam watched him across the rim of his glass. 'What about you? You going to sell used cars the rest of your life?'

'I make out okay.'

'You're making out fine, but you'll have to get into the new car business. That has to be your next step. Stands to reason. You know it, and I know it. Don't tell me you haven't thought about it.'

'I've thought about it,' Todd admitted.

He had thought of little else. After seven years of running Todd Motors, he had heard every wisecrack there was about used car salesmen. They had worn a bit thin. Without being excessively virtuous, he was no more and no less honest than any other businessman. In many cases he was more straightforward than his customers, some of whom wanted something for nothing. Seven years of working for himself had taught him a lot about people. He had become less trusting, more cautious, but no less ambitious. The effort he put into running his business was as unremitting as ever; he was making good money, but he yearned for the day when he would have an office and a smart showroom like Sam's. Then, at last, he would be *someone*! So *of course* he ached to get into the business of selling new cars, especially selling an upmarket marque. The problem was the age-old one. Manufacturers made big demands on their main distributors in terms of service facilities, stock levels, showroom space, promotion and administration. It all added up to a lot of money. And the alternative – to become a small dealer, buying cars from the distributors on narrow margins, held no appeal.

Sam waved a hand around the office. 'Why don't you take this place over?'

Todd felt the hairs rise on the back of his neck. 'You're kidding? I don't have that sort of money –'

'You've done well in the last seven years –'

'Not that well! Nothing like.'

Sam looked at him. 'Larkins will lend you the cash.'

Suddenly it all made sense. This was why Sam had invited

him over for a drink. Sam and Larkins had already discussed it.

A week later, when all the papers were signed, he took them out to dinner. He was still trying to get used to the idea. He was the new owner of Owen's. He was proud and apprehensive both at the same time. Apprehensive because running Owen's would be very different from running Todd Motors. He and Herbert ran Todd Motors with six people. Owen's had a payroll of forty. And thoughts of the bank loan brought him out in a sweat. He faced an avalanche of debt. But he tingled with pride. He was becoming *someone* . . .

'Here's to a long and happy retirement,' he said, toasting Sam at the end of the meal.

Sam thanked him and watched him light a cigarette. 'You'll have to give those up,' he said, winking at Larkins. 'You're selling to the carriage trade now. You'll have to upgrade your image.'

'Absolutely,' Larkins agreed. 'When you walk through those showrooms, I want you to exude prosperity. You'll have to smoke cigars from now on.'

'Daft pair of bastards,' Todd said fondly.

'And don't forget,' Sam chuckled. 'You're to come out to Majorca for a holiday as soon as you get time.'

Time! There was never enough. Especially with two businesses to run. He floundered badly at the outset. Everyone seemed to retire at the same moment. A week after he had moved into Sam's apartment over the showroom – luxurious compared to the tiny flat in Kilburn – Sam's bookkeeper handed in her notice. 'Sorry, Mr Todd,' she said. 'It's just not the same without Mr Sam. I'm going down to Torquay to live with my sister.'

Then the showroom manager quit, tempted away by a West End competitor.

Two of the mechanics resigned to start their own business, taking a dozen of Todd's customers with them.

A week later, Jaguar wanted to make alterations in the distributorship agreement.

And Todd felt the onset of panic . . .

*   *   *

'Take a seat, Miss Sinclair,' he said, indicating a chair in front of his desk.

'Thank you,' she said, but she remained standing.

Suddenly he realized that the chair was piled high with papers. Hurrying round the desk, he took them from the chair and stood uncertain for a moment, searching for a place to put them. Stacks of paper rose in mounds all over the carpet. Finally he found some space across the office on the cocktail cabinet.

She smiled, 'You look snowed under. The agency said you needed someone in a hurry.'

'Yesterday would be good,' he sighed as he went back to his chair. Looking at her across the desk, he liked what he saw. Without being beautiful, she was certainly attractive. Dark chestnut brown hair, amber eyes, an inch or two taller than he was — but every girl in the world was taller than he was. He pushed the silver cigarette box towards her. 'Smoke?'

She shook her head. 'Not now thanks.'

'Mind if I do?' he asked politely as he reached for a cigar. Taking it from the box, he sniffed it appreciatively. 'I'm under orders to smoke these.'

Her eyebrows rose. 'From your doctor?'

'No. My bank manager. He says they make me look prosperous.'

When she laughed, he liked the sound. It was warm and unselfconscious, confident without being pushy.

To refresh his memory, he glanced at the references supplied by the agency. 'These are good,' he admitted frankly. 'I see your present firm is moving to Scotland.'

She nodded. 'Most of them have moved already. The London office closes on Friday. They asked me and two others to stay until then. A sort of a skeleton staff.'

There was nothing skeletal about her figure. Not that she was fat, not even plump, but neither was she slim to the point of emaciation. Nor was she tall. Once when he had tried to kiss a well-grown girl he had bumped his forehead against her chin and the humiliation had stayed in his memory. Not that he had any intention of kissing Miss Sinclair, but tall women made him uncomfortable. With some reluctance he stopped admiring her and returned his attention to the references on his desk. 'The agency say your present employers have made you a good offer to go with them. What's wrong? You don't like Scotland?'

'I don't *know* Scotland, but I have a house in Harrow which I share with two friends. I know it sounds boring, but I like my house and my friends, and they . . . well, they wouldn't agree for a minute, but I think they need me.'

'You mean they're dependent upon you? Financially?'

She laughed again. 'No, Sophie earns fortunes modelling. She's full of big plans, some of them too big, that's her problem, I keep her feet on the ground. And Gloria keeps falling in love and I help pick up the pieces.' A slight blush coloured her cheeks. 'I'm the practical one, that's all. I suppose that's why I'm a bookkeeper.'

'I'm practical about cars and things, but paperwork . . .' he pulled a face, 'I mean, look at this office.'

'I expect it just needs sorting out. I've got a very orderly mind, Mr Todd.'

He grinned and pointed to the papers on the floor. 'Think you can bring order to that lot?'

'Is it all to do with bookkeeping?'

He shook his head. 'Not really. I explained to the agency. I need more than a bookkeeper or a secretary. I want someone with brains. To sort of run things while I'm out of the office. See, I've got another place over in Kilburn. Todd Motors, d'you know it?'

She smiled, 'That's where I bought my car.'

'It is?'

She nodded.

'How's it going?'

'Fine. I'm really pleased with it.'

He beamed. 'Next time you'll qualify for a staff discount.'

A moment passed until she understood his meaning. Then her eyes widened, 'You mean you'd like me to start?'

'The sooner the better,' he said, reaching a decision more quickly than he had intended. He picked up the paper from the

26

agency and searched through the details. His eyebrows rose when he saw she had been earning three hundred a year more than Sam had paid his bookkeeper. Hesitating, he realized he could find someone less expensive. But he needed a bookkeeper who could start quickly, and something about this girl's quiet manner inspired confidence. 'Er, about salary,' he said. 'I'll match what you've been getting, but I can't go higher. There's a lot to sort out here –'

'That's all right. I liked what you said about extra responsibilities, Mr Todd. Keeping books is fine, but I'd like a chance to do something more demanding. I like to be busy.'

'Don't worry,' he grinned, and extended his hand. 'You'll be busy all right.' Glancing down at the paper from the agency, he found her Christian name. 'And Katrina, being called Mr Todd makes me feel old. Everyone round here calls me Toddy.'

Within six weeks, everything at Owen's was under control and she was helping knit the two businesses together. He had never employed a bookkeeper at Todd Motors. Invoices and receipts were simply stuffed into an old biscuit tin and Manny Shiner, his accountant, sent a clerk in every month.

'I could do that work,' Katrina said one morning. 'If you brought the biscuit tin in here, I could produce accounts for Todd Motors as well. You could have the figures every week if you wanted.'

Pleased, he was about to accept the suggestion, when she added, 'The saving on accountant's fees would more than offset the extra three hundred you pay me.'

He looked at her in surprise. 'How do you know about that?'

She coloured slightly. 'I looked up last year's figures. I thought it might help you to have a system which shows comparable costs, this year on last year. You could use it as the basis for budgetary control if you wanted.'

Budgetary control was the first of many surprises. Charts began to appear on the walls of his office. Sales graphs, servicing records, revenues, costs; every fact and figure he needed was at his fingertips. When he was there. Most of the time he was downstairs in the showrooms, or in the workshops with the mechanics, or over at Todd Motors in Kilburn. He was still working every hour God sent. Saturdays were especially busy, selling new Jaguars in the showroom and used cars at Todd Motors. And although he recruited more salesmen, he was slow to make two key appointments – a replacement for himself at Kilburn, and a new manager for the showrooms at Owen's. He knew he had been lucky with Katrina. Reliable staff were rare. Until Katrina, old Herbert was the only person in whom he placed any trust. He had offered Herbert the job of works foreman at Owen's, but Herbert declined with a shake of his head. 'Not for me, Boss. Don't think I'm not grateful for the chance, I am, but honestly I'm more use to you here. See, cars we do up here are my generation. I understand 'em. But some of the technology in those new Jaguars . . .' he pursed his lips. 'Blimey, I'd 'ave to go on a course at the factory. You don't want to be sending someone my age. Get yourself a good youngster an' give him a chance.'

A year passed while Todd made his changes and watched changes occur around him – especially in the used car market. There were fewer first time buyers about than when he had started. The days of accepting pianos and furniture as part deposit on a car were almost over. It still happened – he still ran his stall in Petticoat Lane on a Sunday to turn what he had bought into cash – but now most of the people who came to Todd Motors were old customers bringing back cars they had bought a year before, to trade in for something better. Some of them were even coming to Owen's.

'It's called goodwill,' Katrina said brightly. 'It's a tribute to your reputation.'

She had become part of his life in a way he had never expected. By the time he came down in the morning, she was opening the post in the office. They had a coffee together and planned their priorities. Then he would go about his work and not see her again until the early evening. She always waited for him before going home, and that last hour became something special – sitting around discussing the events of the day, often with him in oil-stained overalls and her as crisp as a bandbox. Many a time he deliberately kept her talking to delay her departure, but eventually someone would arrive to collect her and off she would go for the evening. She had no special boyfriend as far as he could see – instead there was a whole stream of them, younger and better-looking than he was, and, of course, all had the advantage of height.

He threw himself into his work. The more he did the less he had to pay others to do, so he spent his evenings servicing cars, staying on top of things in the workshops – and trying not to be distracted by thoughts of Katrina.

But it became harder to keep her out of his mind.

One evening, he returned from Kilburn to find a stranger in the office. When he barged through the door, breathless from running up the stairs, he found her sitting behind Katrina's desk.

'Oh!' she exclaimed, startled by his sudden entrance.

He stopped, catching his breath. She was a willowy blonde with green eyes and a pert nose. He stared in surprise. She was beautiful, and what held his attention was the way she was dressed. She was wearing a strapless green silk evening gown which shimmered when she moved. *Gorgeous*, he thought, staring at the slopes of her breasts, *absolutely bloody gorgeous*.

She was the first to recover. 'You must be Mr Todd. I . . . er, Katrina's just getting changed. We're going to a party.' She dazzled him with a smile and stretched out her hand. 'I'm Sophie Bartleman. I share Katrina's house. I've heard so much about you.'

He was shaking hands when the door opened and Katrina came in. One look told him he was wrong about Sophie. *Jesus*, he thought, swallowing hard, *if a girl's wearing strapless, she's gotta have tits*. Katrina made Sophie look like a boy. He felt a rush of heat to his loins. With an effort, he dragged his gaze up from her cleavage. She had arranged her hair differently, sweeping it up from her neck into a style he had not seen her wear before. The effect was to make her look as worldly and sophisticated as a film star. As she met his gaze, a faint blush warmed her cheeks. 'Sorry about this. We'd have been late if I hadn't changed here –'

'No, no, that's all right. You . . . er, you look fabulous –'

'Thank you,' she smiled and reached for the messages on her desk. 'Carter's called,' she began as she leafed through them. 'And that man Mr Williams. And . . .'

He was deaf to every word. All he could think of was the closeness of her body and the scent she was wearing.

A horn sounded outside. Sophie went to the window and looked down into the forecourt. 'They're here,' she said. 'Shall I go down and tell them to wait?'

'It's all right,' said Katrina, handing him the last of the messages. 'I'm ready now.'

Sophie smiled on her way to the door. 'Nice to have met you, Mr Todd.'

'Yes. Er . . . and you,' he said, distracted as Katrina picked up the stole which had been draped over her desk. Taking it from her hands, he arranged it around her shoulders. A jolt of electricity passed through him as his hand brushed her body. Clearing his throat, he mumbled, 'Have a nice evening.'

She looked into his eyes. 'Thanks,' she said softly.

The car was a big Humber. Watching the young men in dinner jackets hurry forward as the girls emerged from the showroom, he felt a sharp pang as Katrina kissed her date for the evening. Hurrying around the car, the man opened the rear door with a flourish. As Katrina was about to get in, she paused and looked up, her gaze raking the windows. He stepped back into the shadows, not wanting her to think he was spying. Next moment she was in the car and he was watching it drive out of the forecourt.

He muttered as he went down to the workshops, keenly envious of Katrina's escort. 'Bloody hell! I don't even own a dinner jacket.'

The emptiness of his life came home to him that night. Since he had started on his own, he had scarcely stopped working. At thirty-six, he was beginning to be *someone* – the old boyhood dream was still driving him on – and yet . . .

Bugger it, he grumbled, *don't even think of her. Look at the life she leads . . . going to the theatre and dances, concerts and things. Besides, she's years younger than you. She probably*

30

sees you as an old man. Lay a hand on her and she'll laugh in your face. You'll lose a good bookkeeper into the bargain.

But his quandary was resolved a week later. She asked him out. Katrina asked *him* – to the opera, of all things. Late one afternoon, he returned from Kilburn and she greeted him with a look of embarrassment. 'I've just been stood up,' she said, her hand on the telephone. 'We were going to Covent Garden tonight. Tito Gobbi is doing *Don Giovanni.* There were six of us. I was supposed to go with Dave Thomas, but he's just called from Birmingham. He's stuck up there at a conference.'

He had never met Dave Thomas. He had no idea who he was. But he was glad he was stuck in a conference.

Katrina looked at him. 'I've got the tickets. You've met Gloria and Sophie, they're coming. Would you like to come too?'

The opera? He had never been. Opera had never appealed to him. He had heard of Tito Gobbi, but no more than vaguely. Music, even pop music, was not one of his interests. He doubted he would like opera, in fact he was quite sure he wouldn't, but if Katrina was asking . . .

And that was how it started.

As they sat down to dinner, she said, 'I'd like to buy you some new suits. My treat. What do you say?'

'I'd say thanks, but I don't need them. I bought a stack of new clothes when we got married.'

Something about her silence caused him to look up from his plate. 'What's up? You don't like my suits?'

She regarded him steadily.

He frowned. He had bought a Prince of Wales black and white check, and a different check in two shades of brown. 'You think they're too loud?'

'Try deafening,' she murmured.

'I'm in the car business. People expect it.'

When she remained silent, he looked at her. 'You don't think so?'

'You're a successful businessman,' she said. 'Why not look the part?'

31

'I do,' he grinned. 'That's why I smoke cigars.'

'Cigars I don't mind, but I don't like those suits. They make you look short and fat.'

'I am short and fat.'

'Not to me,' she said, reaching for his hand. 'I want others to see you the way I do.'

She had a way of looking at him that melted his insides. And she could say things which made him feel as big and important as a general commanding an army. Even now, a year after she moved into his flat, six months after they had married, he could scarcely believe what was happening. Nobody had ever been so on his side before, so supportive of all that he did. He was delighted with her effect on his life, even if he did have occasional niggles. Like her dislike of his suits. He liked his suits. What was wrong with his suits? She had never passed comment before. But in some matters he was prepared to indulge her, and two days later they went to a tailor's in Savile Row. He clutched her arm as they entered the shop. 'I don't see any prices,' he whispered. 'If they ask, say we're just looking.'

But Katrina had made up her mind. 'I'm buying,' she said. 'My treat, remember?'

While he had his measurements taken, she examined bolts of cloth on a big table. Worsteds, flannels, mohairs were squeezed tight in her hands to test them for creasing. She took them to the door to see them in daylight, and held them up against Todd to see if they suited. Finally she chose a dark grey pinstripe and a navy blue worsted with a narrow chalk stripe. 'We'll have three made up in each,' she told the assistant.

Todd had to bite his tongue to remain silent.

After accepting a cheque from Katrina, the assistant ushered them to the door. 'After a fitting, the suits will be ready in ten days,' he said. 'Would you like them delivered?'

'Too bloody right!' Todd exploded, smarting from the size of the bill. 'Under armed guard!' Outside on the pavement, he remonstrated, 'Six suits! In my whole life, I've never had six —'

'Wear a different one every day. They'll last longer.'

'At Kilburn, I sell cars for less money!'

'Oh, stop making a fuss. I'm enjoying myself. Don't spoil it,' she said with an encouraging smile. 'Come on. There's some-where else yet.'

Five minutes later, he stopped in his tracks. He stared boggle-eyed at the sign over the shop. 'This time I know you're kidding!' he exclaimed. 'What's got into you? D'you think I'm Rothschild or someone? I need custom-made shoes like a hole in the head!'

As she turned to face him, colour rose in her cheeks. She hesitated, then took a deep breath. 'Darling, we're the same height, right?'

'No we're not and you know it. You're two inches taller.'

'And it bothers you.'

'No,' he lied.

'In there . . .' she nodded at the shop door, 'is a man who can make you taller than me. Personally, I don't give a damn, except I know it worries you. So either forget it, or do something about it, but don't make me feel guilty when we walk down the street.'

'I do that?' he exclaimed, horrified.

'Sometimes.'

'Jesus! I'm sorry.' He stared at her, his eyes full of contrition. Slowly he turned to look at the shop. A wistful expression came to his face. 'D'you think anyone will know?' he asked doubtfully. 'I mean, they won't look like surgical boots or anything, will they?'

'I don't think so. Why not go in and ask?'

He could scarcely believe it. They looked like ordinary shoes. He had imagined thick platform soles, but they looked smart and stylish and comfortable, with a sole and heel no thicker than those he usually wore. Yet he was taller. He walked up and down on the thick carpet. Standing in front of an angled mirror, he stared at his feet. 'Amazing,' he muttered. Then a grin lit his face. 'Excuse us a moment,' he said to the shoemaker.

He drew Katrina towards him. For the first time her eye level was lower than his. So was the level of her nose, and her lips. Folding her into an embrace, he kissed her – and kept kissing her until she pulled away, pink with embarrassment and gasping for breath.

He grinned. 'Breathless, huh? It's the altitude. You'll get used to it.'

Smiling broadly, the shoemaker wrote out an order for three pairs of shoes.

He took her to Wheeler's for lunch. When they had started out earlier he had been anxious to go across to Todd Motors at Kilburn, but shopping had taken all morning and the discovery of built-up shoes had put him in a good mood.

'Even so,' he grumbled over coffee. 'You shouldn't have paid for everything.'

'Oh, Toddy, not again. We agreed today was my treat. Let's leave it at that.'

The frown remained on his face. He already knew she was careful with money, yet financial prudence had been thrown to the winds.

'We could have got suits for less,' he began, but she cut him short.

'That would have a false economy,' she said. 'You'll look so smart that you'll be even more successful. Call me selfish if it makes you feel better. I'm investing in my future happiness.'

A thoughtful look came to his face. 'I like that,' he said. 'Investing in future happiness. You reckon that's a good way to spend money?'

'None better,' she smiled.

Taking her elbow, he steered her out of the restaurant.

'Where are we going?' she asked, bewildered by the sudden gleam in his eye.

'You invest in your happiness,' he said. 'And I'll invest in mine.'

He was the only man in the lingerie shop, but he took it in his stride. This time the roles were reversed. It was Katrina who sat in the chair, while he inspected the merchandise. He selected a sheer black negligee, a white lace basque, three gossamer camisoles and a frothy armful of sexy silk lace-edged underwear.

Katrina was still blushing when they returned to the car. After piling his gifts on to the back seat, Todd clambered in beside her.

'Kilburn next?' she asked, trying to remember his earlier plans.

'No,' he said, shaking his head. 'Let's go home and try on our new clothes.'

She looked at him in surprise. 'You don't have yours.'

'Yeah,' he grinned. 'Ain't that a shame.'

She was cooking his Sunday breakfast when the subject arose. He came into the kitchen wearing a canary yellow pullover beneath his two-tone brown suit – the suit now designated for market use only. He glanced out of the window. 'Not a bad morning. Should be a good crowd at the market.'

'One egg or two?'

'Two, I think.'

'Much on the van this morning?'

He shrugged. 'About the usual, according to Herbert.' Herbert was his helper at Petticoat Lane. The boys loaded the van every Saturday evening, and Herbert drove it to the market on a Sunday.

Katrina carried the bacon and eggs to the table. 'I was think-ing,' she said. 'Couldn't Herbert take one of the lads with him? It would give you a day off.'

'Don't worry. I'll be finished by two o'clock.'

'That's not the point.'

He stifled a grin as he forked into his breakfast. He guessed what was coming. She had been picking around the subject for weeks. In her view it was 'inappropriate' for the Owner, Chair-man and Managing Director of Owen's to run a stall at Petticoat Lane market. 'The wrong sort of image,' she had said. 'You can't be seen selling junk one day and expensive new cars the next.' He had disagreed. 'You don't get the same sort of people at the market,' he had said. 'Besides, it all helps pay off the bank.'

Paying off the bank was a priority. The loan needed to buy Owen's had seemed monumental at the outset, but it was coming down. With the target of clearing it within three years in his sights, he had no intention of letting up.

'The point,' she persisted. 'Is you can't work every day of the week. You should have some sort of hobby.'

Glancing up, he leered at her cleavage. 'I've got a hobby.'

She smiled and pulled the housecoat around her. 'You don't have to give that up.'

'Thank Christ for that.'

'What I was thinking,' she persisted, 'is you should take up a sport.'

A look of amazement came over his face. He sat back in his chair and stared at her. 'Do I look like an athlete?' he asked, patting his paunch.

'What about golf?' she suggested.

'Golf! Golf?'

'Why not? I bet you could do a lot of business on the golf course.'

Six months later, Katrina was climbing the stairs from the show-room into the office. She carried a basket of groceries in one hand and a bulging carrier bag in the other. She glanced with approval at Sally's dark head, bent over the typewriter. Sally had been with them a month and was more than earning her keep. *Everyone* was earning their keep – Jimmy Davis, the new showroom manager, the seven salesmen, Marcia the new recep-tionist – everyone was rushed off their feet. Business was booming.

Sally looked up. Her glance took in the laden shopping bags. 'You got there in time then?'

'They were just closing, but they let me get a few bits and pieces.' Katrina glanced at the wall clock. 'It's almost six. Haven't you nearly finished?'

Standing up, Sally reached for the typewriter cover. 'I have now,' she said brightly. 'I just wanted to clear those invoices before I left.'

Suddenly a roar came from above. 'You poxy fucking thing!'

Sally jumped. She blushed and looked up at the ceiling.

'Fuck it!' bellowed a voice.

Katrina stared upwards, an expression of horror on her face.

Embarrassed, Sally said, 'He just went up –'

'Was anyone with him?'

'No.'

Shaking her head, Katrina hurried towards the stairs to the flat. 'You get off now, Sally,' she said over her shoulder. 'I'll see you in the morning.'

Another shout came from above. 'Bastard thing!' Todd bellowed.

Red-faced and angry, he was standing in the centre of the sitting-room. Arranged around the walls a number of cups were set on their side, and the carpet was strewn with golf balls. He waggled the putter in his hands as she hurried into the room. 'Bloody daft game this is! It's driving me mad.'

'People can hear you all over the building. You frightened Sally to death.'

'Rubbish! Bloody nonsense –'

'There's no need to swear.'

'Everyone swears when they're angry.'

'They don't use that sort of language.'

His eyes glimmered as he looked at her. 'What sort of language?'

'You know very well.'

'Huh,' he grunted. 'I got mad, that's all. Everyone uses bad language when they get mad.'

'I don't.'

'You must *think* it. You must say it under your breath.'

'No, I don't. Never.'

He propped himself up on the putter. 'So what do you say?' he challenged.

She flushed. 'I don't know. Damn. Blast. Things like that. Knickers.'

'Knickers!' He burst out laughing. 'A right prat I'd look shouting "knickers" all over the place.'

'Better than the words you use,' she countered ruefully, unable to stop smiling.

Setting the putter aside, he went over to her. Tenderly he brushed a hair from her forehead and kissed the tip of her nose. 'Okay. I take the point.'

'You don't *have* to swear. It's a habit, that's all. You could stop if you tried. With your determination you can do anything you put your mind to.'

He smiled and stroked the side of her face. 'You really believe that, don't you?'

'It's true.'

'Okay,' he said.

'You'll stop swearing?'

'I'll try.' Kissing the tip of her nose again, he said, 'Why don't I tidy the room while you get dinner. What we having tonight?'

'I thought Chicken Kiev if that's all right with you?'

'Chicken Kiev sounds delicious,' he smiled at her as she turned away and went out to the kitchen.

Bending down, he began to pick up the golf balls. His gaze strayed to the putter. After hesitating a moment, he walked over and took it into his hands. Stooping forward, he arranged his grip in the way he had been taught by the professional at the golf club; left hand above right, thumbs pointing down the shaft. Standing over a ball, he shuffled until his toes pointed inwards. Bending his knees, he adopted a comfortable stance. He stared at a cup on the far side of the room, drawing a line in his mind of the path the ball would take over the carpet. He shuffled into position. 'Not too hard now,' he muttered. Holding his breath, he struck the ball firmly. His heart rose. 'Straight as an arrow,' he whispered, only for his triumph to fade as the ball struck the rim of the cup and rolled back towards him. 'Fuck it!' he growled under his breath.

'You heard what they said. One in five couples have trouble making a baby,' he said gently. 'We're one in five, that's all. So we keep trying.' He lifted her chin and smiled into her eyes. 'I can stand that, can't you?'

She smiled back at him, but there was a moist look in her eyes.

He wondered if she shared the same thought – that the excitement had gone from their sex life. *Jesus*, he thought, *how can*

38

it be exciting when she gets so tense about it? Every muscle I got goes stiff except the one in my prick.

He squeezed her hand. 'We can always put in for adoption.'

'Maybe,' she shrugged doubtfully. 'We'll see how things go.'

He knew how things were going. Badly. Ever since she had said, 'Darling, I'm thirty next month. Shouldn't we start planning a family?' Ever since that first meeting with the gynae-cologist – ever since the lectures about the best time of the month, the best hour of the day, the best way to put it in and shake it all about. Ever since . . .

Even when he did get a hard on, it was testing to keep it. Sterilized sex was a turn-off. It was as if she were counting each thrust, timing him, composing a report for her doctor. And as soon as he came she jumped out of bed and rushed to the bath-room. 'It's not the same as it was,' he complained. 'You've got to enjoy it.'

'I do, I did. Just because I don't writhe and moan all the time doesn't mean I don't enjoy it. I was moist and ready for you, wasn't I?'

'I s'pose so.'

'Well, then, what more do you want? Ask Dr Clarke if you don't believe me. If I get moist it means I'm enjoying myself. I don't have to have a big fat orgasm every time. You know that.'

'I know.'

'I haven't changed. It's you. I don't know what's got into you these days. All you think about is money and sex.'

'That's the point. They go together. Making money gives us something to celebrate.'

Business was good. He had paid off the bank. Now should be a time to have some fun, except Katrina had gone all broody on him.

Always something to worry about . . .

But it was not his nature to worry. If something was a problem, do something about it. But do what?

She's bored. She doesn't even have to work in the office any more . . .

Suddenly his mind went back six years and he remembered

39

the girl who had become the woman who had turned into his wife. 'I like to be busy,' she had told him when first they had met.

She *had* been busy, frantically busy, for the first few years. But as the business had grown their lives had changed. 'You don't have to work so hard,' he had told her. 'Sally can do the typing. Barbara can keep the books. What's the point of employing staff if you still have to work all the time?'

He meant well. He had wanted the best for her. Once a week she lunched with Sophie and Gloria. On Sundays, she played tennis while he had his round of golf at the club. She read, listened to music, redecorated the apartment . . . but it still left her with time on her hands.

'I'll be down in ten minutes,' he said as he got out of the car.

'Righto, Boss. Want a hand with that?' Herbert grinned at the cardboard box.

'No. Stay and polish the car or something.'

He was still getting used to having a chauffeur. Not that Herbert was really a chauffeur. Herbert was Herbert; the best mechanic ever to work at Todd Motors. Except that ten years of fixing cars at Kilburn had given Herbert a duodenal ulcer for which the doctors advocated early retirement. 'I'll go bonkers hanging round the 'ouse all day,' he had complained mournfully when he told Todd. 'Ain't there nothing useful I could do in the garage?'

Todd puffed as he climbed the two flights of stairs to the flat. He looked down into the cardboard box. 'Stay quiet and let me do the talking. Okay?'

The fat little puppy blinked his soft brown eyes and whimpered softly.

'Katrina,' he shouted as he opened the door. 'You decent? We got a visitor.'

'But you said we were going out . . .' her voice tailed off as she came into the hall. She looked beyond Todd and then at the box in his hands. 'Visitor?'

'Here. Happy birthday.'

It took her half an hour to ask the question for which he had been waiting. Half an hour in which she cooed over the puppy, cuddled him, fussed over him, and christened him Mac because her aunt had once had a dog of that name. Then she said, 'Oh, Toddy, he's adorable, but darling . . .' she paused to cast an unhappy look around the apartment. 'Dogs need exercise. It won't be fair to keep him cooped up here. Dogs should have space –'

'I thought of that. Leave him with a saucer of milk. There's something I want you to see.'

Half an hour later, she was walking around the Hampstead house in a daze, going from one empty room to the next before returning to the front door and starting over again. 'These rooms could be beautiful,' she said. 'But everywhere's so shabby. It's such a shame. They've been so neglected –'

'I know that, but the house is structurally sound. I had it surveyed yesterday.'

The garden was an overgrown wilderness. 'Half an acre,' he announced as he opened the French doors to the terrace. 'Think Mac will be happy in that?'

She looked at him. 'Darling, it's wonderful, but we can't afford this place.'

'We can,' he grinned. 'It's all sorted out, plus the money to have it done up. And that's your job. I've got a business to run. So the sooner you start, the better. Mac won't stay a puppy much longer.'

'Come out for a holiday,' Sam said to Katrina. 'That's what I told him. He don't come the first year so I think, okay, what with buying my place and everything, he's too busy. He's got a lot on his plate. Then the second year, I hear he got married, so I say to myself, he's gone to the Bahamas on honeymoon.'

Katrina laughed. 'Honeymoon! We went out to dinner. One night! That was our honeymoon. Next day we were in the office and it was business as usual. No chance of the Bahamas!'

'That sounds like Toddy,' Sam chuckled. 'Mind you,' he

41

added, catching Todd's eye in the mirror, 'you don't look bad on it, either of you.'

'And you look like an old pirate,' Todd retorted.

Beneath a thick thatch of white hair, Sam's lined and gnarled face was a rich mahogany brown. He grinned and slowed down as they approached the traffic lights. Glancing over his shoulder, he asked, 'You been here before, Katrina?'

She craned her neck from the back seat. 'No. I've had holidays in Spain, but this is my first in Majorca.'

'Ah well,' he said with unconcealed satisfaction. 'You've saved the best place till last. I promise, once you've seen it, you'll want to come back.'

From the airport, he drove along the sea front at Palma, pointing with proprietorial pride to the centuries old cathedral and the serried ranks of boats in the yacht club. The sun blazed down from a paintbox-blue sky, and Katrina tasted the salt breeze on her lips. 'I can't believe we're only three hours from London,' she said, clutching Todd's hand. 'That's two miracles rolled into one.'

He looked at her.

She laughed. 'Just being here is a miracle. I've actually persuaded you to take a holiday!'

Sam's villa was on a hillside overlooking a small fishing village. The views from the terrace held Katrina enchanted, as did the garden. Sam's wife Pamela, as white-haired and deeply tanned as her husband, showed them around and made them feel welcome. The first two days were spent exploring. Sam and Pamela took them all over the island. They lunched at La Residencía in Deya, dined at the Palma Yacht Club, wandered through the backstreets in the old city, swam in Sam's pool, sailed on his boat – and on the third evening went to the Crow's Nest.

Afterwards, Katrina was to say: 'Everything changed after that night at the Crow's Nest.'

Even Todd agreed it was true. Everything *did* change – yet even the first forty-eight hours were wreaking changes in his subconscious. When he arrived on Majorca, he had been feeling successful. He saw himself as a prosperous businessman, taking a rare break from routine. Yet wherever he turned he seemed to see men who were *more* prosperous, men who took breaks not every few years, but every few months.

'Jesus,' he muttered to Katrina after they had dined at the yacht club. 'Hear what Sam said? Some of those boats cost a million and upwards. Imagine having that sort of money.'

He began to think about Leo, with his immaculate suits and his château in France. 'There's a guy I know,' he mused, 'who must know about this sort of life . . .'

'Oh, who?'

'What? Oh, just some guy,' he said quickly, dismissively. 'You don't know him.'

'At the golf club?'

'No. No one at the club's got this kind of money. They think *I'm* successful.'

'Oh, darling,' she turned from the balcony and came to where he sat on the bed. 'You *are* successful. Look at what you've achieved. Sam's proud of you. *I'm* proud of you –'

'Yeah, well,' he muttered. 'You're bound to be on my side.'

'And that's not enough?' she asked, taking his hand.

'It's good, but . . .' he smiled and shrugged his shoulders. 'When I was a kid, I was determined to be *someone*. Someone people looked up to . . .'

Falling back on to the bed, she pulled his face down to her own. After she kissed him, she said softly, 'I'm looking up to you.'

He smiled down at her.

A glint came into her eyes. 'Do you think if I look long enough you'll do something about it?'

The next morning, Sam told them about the Crow's Nest. 'It's the best restaurant on the island,' he said. 'It's in a little harbour, five miles down the coast. We thought we'd drive over this evening, have a drink or two on Hank's balcony, then give you a meal to remember.'

'Hank?'

'Hank Martin. He owns it. He's a friend of mine, quite a character. You'll like him.'

Todd had his doubts. In his experience, he rarely liked friends

43

of friends. But he did like the harbour when they reached it that evening. The surrounding hills seemed to shut the place off from the rest of the island, creating an air of exclusiveness which was reflected in the size and style of the villas glimpsed from the winding road as it zigzagged down to the waterfront.

As he drove, Sam talked about Hank Martin. 'He's American. Born in Connecticut, I think, though it's years since he's been in the States. He used to skipper a yacht for one of the wealthiest men in the world. He's a hell of a fine sailor. In those days he had everything he wanted. He was paid a small fortune for doing a job he loved; he was set for the rest of his life. Then one day he sailed into this harbour. Never been here before, right? Anyway, the way he tells it, as he stood at the wheel, squinting up at the hills, he had the strangest feeling of coming home. When he went ashore, the feeling grew stronger, and as he walked round the streets, it grew so powerful that he does the unthinkable. He quits his job and says goodbye to his life as a yacht captain.'

Studying the pine-covered hills, Katrina shook her head in admiration. 'It certainly is beautiful. I can understand the temptation.'

'How long ago was this?' asked Todd.

'About twelve years. Since then Hank's turned the Crow's Nest into an institution. It was just a waterfront bar when he bought it. And these hills . . .' Sam gestured airily, taking a hand from the steering wheel '. . . were empty except for a few old fincas, that's farmhouses to you. These days you won't believe the people who've got a place here – film stars, enter-tainers, top businessmen, politicians, from all over Europe. Hank was the first to see it, but twelve years ago this was the best value real estate in the Mediterranean. The harbour was just a little fishing village then. Now with its marina and everything it's become a playground for the rich and the famous. Some of the wealthiest people in Europe dine at Hank's tables . . .' Sam laughed. 'And he charges accordingly. That's why Pam and I aren't here every night.'

'A good businessman, eh?'

'Dunno about that. The thing is he knows everyone. And all

44

the guys who bought property here know him. He's a sort of go-between with them and the locals. You want a gardener, a maid, a deckhand? Hank knows the best. You want to meet a local lawyer, local banker, politician? They drive out from Palma and have dinner at the Crow's Nest. Hank makes the introductions and oils the wheels.'

After the build-up Todd was intrigued, but he was still unprepared for the magic of the harbour. As Sam drove along the sea front, the sun was setting on the horizon, bathing everywhere in a soft golden light. A gentle breeze touched the palm trees alongside the roads. Across the bay, the lights of the yacht club were just coming on, glittering like stars between the tall masts of the white boats moored along the jetties. The balmy air was full of the sea and the pines and the perfume of jasmine.

'Paradise,' murmured Katrina.

Pleased with her reaction, Sam chuckled, 'Wait till you see the view from the Crow's Nest.'

It was aptly named, because although only two storeys high, the white building rose above its neighbours, and the restaurant on the flat roof added further to the impression of height. After having a drink in the bar, they went up to the restaurant. Max, the German head waiter, greeted them and led them to a table. When they were seated, Katrina and Pamela were each presented with a corsage of orchids. 'With Mr Martin's compliments,' Max said with a bow.

'Is he here tonight?' asked Sam. 'I'd like him to meet my friends.'

'He should be back any time now.' Max glanced at his watch. 'He's been to the airport to see someone off.'

'Blonde or brunette?' Pamela asked with a look of amusement.

Max smiled and lowered his voice. 'I think one of each, madam.'

All through dinner, Todd was quiet and subdued. From time to time, he glanced around, assessing the place and the people. It was as much as he could do not to gawp. These were the chosen, he decided, the rich and successful; immaculate men in white dinner jackets, the women sleekly beautiful in skimpy dresses which showed off tanned shoulders. Conversations were being conducted in a dozen languages . . .

'That's Liza Mathews,' Sam was saying to Katrina. 'The film star. You must know her face.'

Turning in his chair, Todd watched Max conduct a glamorous blonde to a place three tables away.

Sam said, 'She's got a villa up on the point. Behind the pink walls. Remember the one?'

Todd remembered. The whole scene was etched in his memory – the properties around the harbour and Sam's potted history of the people who owned them. German industrialists, Dutch publishers, French musicians, British builders, Belgian chocolate makers . . . most of whom owned boats in the harbour as well as villas on the hillsides. And the boats! Ocean-going yachts, catamarans, trimarans, many with a permanent crew.

Todd no longer felt successful. He felt like a fat little car dealer from London.

'That's Hank now,' said Sam, nodding at a man who had just appeared in the entrance.

Todd watched as the man began to work the room, stopping at each table. Aged about forty, with dark hair, blue eyes and a deeply tanned face – and a smile which Todd guessed wreaked havoc with women.

As he approached their table, Hank extended a hand. 'Sam! How y'doing? Pamela!' He kissed her cheek. 'Dinner okay, I hope?'

'Superb, as always,' Pamela smiled.

After the introductions, he joined them for a drink and spent the next hour regaling them with stories of the harbour. From time to time, when other people finished their meals, they waved on their way to the door, and Hank beckoned them over to buy them a brandy and introduce them to Todd and Katrina – so that by the end of the evening a group of about twenty were gathered at Sam's table, all laughing and talking in differently accented English. Looking around him, Todd realized that the harbour was a sort of international club, with the Crow's Nest as the clubhouse.

He was quiet on the way home, thinking back over the

46

evening, and next day, when Sam took Katrina and Pamela into Palma, he opted for a day by the pool. But as soon as they had left, he took Pamela's car from the garage and went back to the harbour. The magic of the place was stronger than ever. In search of Hank, he lunched at the Crow's Nest and the two of them talked long into the afternoon, sitting on the balcony overlooking the sea.

'What did you think of Hank?' he asked Katrina the following morning. He had taken her back to the harbour and they were sitting in the square, having coffee in an open-air café.

'Pamela said he's slept with half the women on the island.'

'So what? He's entitled. That's what bachelors do.'

'You liked him. That was obvious.'

'You didn't?'

'No, I didn't dislike him, he was fine. Amusing, full of good stories. He runs a marvellous restaurant.'

'Terrific,' he nodded. 'The point is, Sam says we can trust him.'

She frowned. 'We don't have anything to trust him about, do we?'

Without answering, he puffed on his cigar and watched a fishing boat edge in to the quay. Gulls swooped and dived over the boat's decks. Across the bay, masts of the boats in the yacht marina reached like countless spires up into the brilliant blue sky Eventually he said, 'Ain't this harbour the greatest?'

'Heavenly.'

'I been thinking. Suppose we bought a place here?'

She smiled. 'When you retire?'

'No, no, I mean now.'

Taking off her sunglasses in order to see him more clearly, she stared at him. 'You're not serious?' she asked in astonishment.

'Sure I am.'

She raised a hand to shade her eyes from the bright sunshine. 'But we can't afford it!' A look of alarm came to her face. 'Oh, Toddy, be sensible. We spent a fortune last year on the house —'

'We can't *not* afford it. Listen,' he hissed, leaning towards her. 'Sam's place has nearly trebled in value since he bought it.

47

And the harbour's even better. Hank was telling me that properties here have –'

'Hank's a salesman!' She stared at him. 'Sometimes you
amaze me. You're such a good salesman yourself, yet you never
see when someone is selling you –'

'Hank's not selling me anything,' he retorted, nettled.

'Not directly, I'm not saying he is, but . . .' she searched for
the right words. 'He's bound to sing the harbour's praises, isn't
he? He lives here. He's got a business here –'

'And he's been all over the world. You name it, he's been
there. Yet he chose this place! That's a hell of a recommendation,
don't you think?' He glared at her. 'You're always saying I
should take more time off. That's why we're here –'

'To give you a *rest*,' she said insistently, her voice rising
again. Biting her lip, she checked her impatience. 'We came
here for a break,' she said quietly. 'You're always working –'

'Right,' he agreed. 'We should take holidays like ordinary
people.'

'Ordinary people stay in hotels.'

'Well, not ordinary. I don't mean ordinary. Who wants to
be *ordinary* for Chrissakes! I mean . . .'

'You mean rich. Like Liza Mathews –'

'No, not like her. Most of the guys here are businessmen.
Like me. They've got the same problem with holidays. We're
all tied to our business. Sometimes to get away even for a couple
of weeks can be tricky, so what's the answer? Take a break when
you can. A long weekend here, a few days there –'

She sighed and replaced her sunglasses. An exasperated
expression settled over her face. Frowning, she sipped her coffee,
then pushed the cup away. After a moment she returned to the
attack. 'And of course,' she said sarcastically, 'if we have a place
in Majorca, it *has* to be in the harbour.'

'Right.'

'The most exclusive area on the island. *And* the most
expensive –'

'That's our insurance policy. People will always pay top dollar
for something exclusive.'

'But there are other nice parts. Like where Sam and Pamela –'

'I don't like it where they are.'

'Then that other place they took us to. Deya? That was pretty –'

'Sam says it's full of writers and artists. What the hell do I know about that kind of stuff? They'd bore me to death. They're not my kind of people.'

'And these are?' She waved a hand towards the boats in the marina. 'Darling, you'd never been on a boat in your life until you went out on Sam's, and his is tiny compared to those over there.'

He puffed on his cigar and stared over the water. 'Yeah, well, the yacht can come later.'

Katrina was naked on the air mattress, her arms stretched out over her head as if she were about to dive from the springboard. Above her, the vine-covered pergola filtered the fierce Majorcan sunshine into a latticework of light which decorated her golden body like a lace shawl. Emerging on to the terrace, Todd finished buttoning his shirt. His hair was still damp from his shower and his cheeks stung from the application of aftershave.

'Sure you've got enough of that on?' Katrina murmured into the mattress. 'I can smell you from here.'

He grinned and walked over to her. Bending forward, he cupped his hand over her buttocks and squeezed. 'Can't have too much of a good thing.'

Groaning softly, she pressed herself deeper into the mattress. He slid his hand down until he felt her heat in his fingers. 'Don't touch unless you're buying,' she warned softly.

Reluctantly he took his hand away. 'Can't. Hank's on his way up. Otherwise . . .'

'Promises, promises,' she mumbled drowsily. 'You going out on the boat?'

'Not today. He wants to show me something.'

'Last time he showed you something you spent a hundred thousand buying the boat. We can't afford it, whatever it is.'

'Don't get your knickers in a twist –'

'I'm not wearing any.'

49

'I need telling?' he grunted as the heat rose in his loins. Turning away, he cursed his appointment with Hank. Without that, he could have stripped off and joined her on the mattress. Yesterday she had fed him grapes from the vine before making love. What more could a man ask for? The Spanish siesta was the most civilized custom ever invented.

'What's he showing you this time?'

'Dunno. He says it's a secret.'

She pushed herself up from the mattress. A look of concern came to her face. 'You promised, remember? This villa, the boat, then you consolidate. No more big spending –'

'Yeah, yeah, stop worrying. Okay?'

As she stared at him her worried expression faded. A rueful smile came to her lips. 'Sorry. I didn't mean to nag. It's just . . . well, sometimes you get carried away.'

'Only with naked women,' he grinned, and turned for the staircase. 'Can I get you a drink or something?'

She shook her head the merest fraction. 'Thanks, I don't think so. I'll just doze for a while. You have a nice time.'

'Sure.'

He used the outside staircase to descend to the lower terrace. Passing the swimming pool, he paused to inspect one of the filters. Satisfied, he walked over to the refrigerator built into the outside bar. Uncapping an ice-cold San Miguel, he took a drink from the bottle, sank into a wickerwork chair and looked down into the bay. He never tired of the view of the harbour. It always filled him with satisfaction and a sense of achievement. A moment later, he was puffing contentedly on a Monte Cristo, counting his blessings and thinking of Hank.

Hank had found the villa for him, taught him to sail, found him a boat . . . Hank had become his man in the harbour. In two years the friendship had come to mean more to Todd than any of his friendships in London. Men at the club with whom he played golf lacked Hank's worldly experience. They were provincial by comparison, grey as shadows compared to the colourful people he met at the Crow's Nest. The only exception in London was Leo. Leo and Hank were kindred spirits. Todd liked nothing better than to share a drink with Leo at the Ritz,

50

or with Hank at the Crow's Nest, listening to tales of business deals struck in different parts of the world. Hank gleaned a fund of such stories at the Crow's Nest which he was always eager to share. Todd had learned to read Hank's expressions. Those blue eyes conveyed a glint of excitement for only one of two reasons – a new woman or some new gossip about a business deal – and Hank knew his views about women. Hank had teased him at the outset. 'Know something,' he said once. 'You're the only guy here not looking to get his leg over.'

'I'm married,' Todd had retorted.

'So are the others, but that don't stop them. Don't you ever feel like getting some spare?'

'Nah.' Todd had shrugged uncomfortably, reluctant to discuss the subject. In truth, he had looked. Jesus, it was impossible not to look, impossible not to become aroused; some of the women at the Crow's Nest would give a brass monkey an erection. But Katrina was always around, and anyway, he had never been forward with women. Besides, deep in his heart, he was a bit apprehensive, not so much of women, but of losing Katrina. In many ways she had taught him a lot. She had smoothed his rough edges. Without being superstitious, he knew she had been good for him, and at the back of his mind lurked a small fear that his luck would run out if ever she ceased to be part of his life. Anyway, he was getting all the sex he could handle. With the house in Hampstead and their new holiday home, sterilized sex had become a thing of the past. None of which he had said to Hank. All he said to Hank was, 'I like things the way they are. Let's leave it at that.'

And Hank had.

'What's up?' Todd had asked on the phone earlier.

'I got something to show you. I'll pick you up at around three.'

He had heard the excitement in Hank's voice. 'What is it?'

'That's the surprise, ole buddy. But it will blow your mind when you see it.' Hank chuckled. 'Paloma Blanca will blow everyone's mind.'

As Todd puffed his cigar and waited, a pleasurable anticipation merged with his contentment.

He was still short and fat.

He was still just a car dealer from London.

But with two businesses, two homes, a yacht and a permanent tan . . . he was becoming someone people looked up to.

CHAPTER TWO

'TODDY!' LEO EXCLAIMED, breaking away from a group at the bar. A smile lit his face and he extended both hands as he hurried forward. 'Good to see you, old boy.' Pumping Todd's hand, he stepped back to appraise him. 'You're looking well. As successful as ever.'

'Yeah? You're kidding? I could be an actor with such talent. Business is lousy.'

Leo chuckled. He was the one who looked well. He always did. He carried his years lightly. The tan helped. So did his trim figure and the superbly tailored suit, but most of all it was in the look of amusement which shone from his eyes. He always gave the impression of verging on laughter. Even when his face was in repose – when he was talking seriously or listening intently to what someone was saying – the gleam of good humour lurked in his grey eyes. 'How's Katrina?' he asked.

It was always his first question.

'Fine.' Todd wished he could say, *she sends her love – she's joining us later – she's looking forward to seeing you again.* Unable to say any such thing, he retreated, as always, behind a rueful look of apology.

'How about things in Majorca?' asked Leo. 'You're keeping Moroni happy, I hope?'

'As a matter of fact –'

'Hang on,' Leo interrupted, turning his back to the group at the bar. 'I'm afraid things are a bit awkward this evening,' he said softly. 'You see, I've met up with some people. Any chance of you staying for dinner? I bumped into an old friend –'

'I can't, I'm afraid –'

'Oh surely?' Leo interrupted with a look of disappointment.

'I promised I'd be home at eight –'

'Can't you get round it?' Leo pressed. Searching Todd's face, he found the answer. 'What a bloody nuisance. We won't have much chance for a chat.'

Todd cursed silently. It had been on his mind to talk to Leo about Moroni. 'Can't be helped,' he shrugged, disappointed.

'You'll like Frank,' said Leo, still trying to persuade. 'He's a lot of fun. And I've got a customer for you. The girl wants to buy a new car.'

Todd had noticed her as soon as he stepped through the door. She had been standing next to Leo at the bar, her head thrown back in laughter. Smartly dressed, wearing a severely tailored moss green suit with a froth of white lace at the throat. He had noticed her figure. She was nicely built and scarcely taller than he was himself.

'Anyway, come and meet them,' Leo urged. 'Maybe they'll persuade you.'

She smiled hello as Leo led him to the bar, blinding him with a dazzle of teeth. Her bright red-gold hair was cut short and close to her head, brushed and burnished, gleaming like a helmet. Her eyes were emerald green against very white skin. As Todd drew closer, he noticed a scatter of freckles across her snub nose. The corners of her mouth twitched with puckish good humour.

Leo introduced the men first. 'This is Frank Stapleton, an old friend of mine. And Bob Levit.'

Todd shook hands.

'And this delightful young thing is your first customer tomorrow.'

She smiled again as Todd extended his hand. 'Hello,' she said. 'Leo's been telling me all about you.'

'All I said,' Leo interrupted hastily, 'was you're just the man to make her dreams come true. Isn't that right, Frank?' He glanced at Stapleton for agreement.

Her name was Charlotte. 'But my friends call me Charlie,' she said, adding a quizzical look of amusement. 'Are you a friend? Is Leo to be believed? Will you make my dreams come true?'

He struggled to invent a brilliant response – something witty to keep the eyes crinkled and her mouth upturned. But all he could think of was the banal, 'If your dreams include a car, I will. What sort do you want?'

'A Jaguar sports. You know, the pretty one?'

'The XJS.'

'Is that what it's called?' The wide, humorous mouth pouted with disapproval. 'What a waste to call something so beautiful by a string of letters.'

'You could give it a nickname,' he suggested, recovering.

A speculative gleam lit her eye as she looked at him. 'Mmm,' she murmured, 'I'll think of something. Do you have one in your showroom?'

Leo laughed. 'Toddy's the biggest Jaguar dealer in London.'

Which was not true, but Charlie seemed impressed. Watching her eyes widen, Todd was grateful for the exaggeration.

'I want a bright red one,' she said decisively. 'Upholstered in sexy black leather.'

Levit chuckled. 'Trust Charlie to know what she wants.'

Todd's effort to recall colour combinations was hampered by Charlie's use of the word sexy. If anything was sexy, it was Charlie herself. Not even the severely tailored suit could disguise the svelte lines of her figure. Resisting an urge to step backwards to get a better look at her legs, he suggested, 'Maybe you could call in at the showroom?'

'Depends.'

'On what?' he asked, wondering if she were with Leo. They had been laughing together when he arrived, and a sideways glance was enough to glimpse Leo's look of approval. What the hell was it with Leo and women? Where did he find them? Todd tried to suck in his stomach and grow an inch taller.

Charlie smiled. 'On whether you've got what I want.'

'I'm bound to,' he answered, feeling like a boastful nineteen-year-old. He wondered if she set out to tease? 'Here's where we are,' he said, giving her a card. 'Or I'll have someone collect you if you like? Are you staying here?'

Her huge green eyes threatened to engulf him. 'No, I have a flat in London. I come here for R and R.' The teasing look held for a moment. 'Rest and recreation,' she explained, and burst out laughing. 'Sorry,' she giggled. 'I'm in the most peculiar mood –'

'Charlie's celebrating,' Levit cut in, grinning hugely. 'She's painting the town tonight.'

'The mood she's in,' Leo laughed, 'she'll get us all arrested.'

Then everyone started talking at once, and it took him some minutes to piece the conversations together. The first thing he realized was that they had not started out as one party. Leo had never met Levit or Charlie before. Stapleton was the link, he and Leo were old friends and Stapleton knew Levit. 'Bob and I did some business a few years back,' Stapleton explained. 'We were having a reunion drink, when in walked Leo –'

'So we're all set for an impromptu party,' Charlie declared. 'They're always the best.'

Todd had been feeling down in the mouth when he arrived. Business was bad, the wet autumn night was depressing, and worries about Moroni smouldered away at the back of his mind. He had looked forward to spending an hour with Leo. It had promised to be the one bright spot in the day, and he was disappointed to find him in company. But his disappointment faded in the face of their collective high spirits. Bob Levit was a quick little man with an india-rubber face and a fund of good stories. Stapleton was taller, as tall as Leo and about the same age, with similar grey hair, except his was stubble-short in a crew cut. They vied with each other to tell tales of their days in Afghanistan. And, of course, there was Charlie, turning her dazzling smile from one to the other, encouraging them with a laugh and a nod. Whether her laughter was more infectious than Leo's – who threw his head back and bellowed – or Stapleton's – he bent forward and slapped his knee – was hard to say, but hers was certainly the most musical, throaty and bubbly, denoting a sense of fun and high spirits which quite captivated Todd. He would have liked to ask what she was celebrating, but what with Leo and Stapleton reminiscing, and Bob Levit telling a story, it was some time before he could put the question. Even then it was Levit who answered. 'Success,' he said, beaming at Charlie and raising his glass. 'Here's to the island's golden girl.'

Of all things, Charlie was an accountant. Todd would have been less surprised to learn that she was a circus performer. Or a dancer. Or a stripper. She had the body for it. Accountants of his acquaintance were male, middle-aged and boring. But Charlie was no ordinary accountant. She worked in Jersey, in the Channel Islands, with Bob Levit who had started an accountancy practice there ten years before. 'Offshore banking has come a long way since then,' said Levit, with some satisfaction. 'These days we're more an investment house than a firm of accountants. We manage clients' investments all over the world.'

'Nothing to it, really,' Charlie said with a bright smile. 'We just move money around.'

'In very large quantities,' Levit grinned.

It was neither the time nor the place to elaborate, not that they would have: confidentiality was their stock in trade, and they were obviously good at it. When it came to financial matters, wealthy clients demanded the utmost discretion, and Todd didn't doubt they received it from Levit and Charlie. Even Charlie's cause for celebration was dismissed under the heading of 'a very big deal'.

'Do you know Jersey?' she asked him.

He shook his head, acutely aware of her mischievous green eyes.

'It's a goldfish bowl,' said Levit. 'Everyone knows everyone, especially among the financial community.'

'That's the problem,' said Charlie, nodding emphatically. 'Oh, it's pretty enough. Gets a bit crowded with tourists in summer —'

'Trouble is, it's so *small*,' Levit interrupted. 'Charlie gets claustrophobic after four weeks —'

'I go stir crazy!' Charlie exclaimed. 'Wouldn't you?' She put a hand on Todd's arm and he felt a shock of excitement run through his whole body. 'Seeing the same old faces, going to the same dreary dinner parties . . .' she shook her head and crinkled her nose. 'Oh, I don't know. Some of them are okay, but others are so *pleased* with themselves. You'd think it was paradise, their tight little island.' She laughed. 'I have to break out now and then. Take tonight. A night on the town to celebrate. I can't let my hair down on Jersey! I can't even *wash* it without everyone knowing next morning!'

When she laughed everyone laughed with her; it was impossible not to, her high spirits were infectious.

'Why don't you come with us?' she asked Todd enthusiastically, reinforcing her invitation with a smile which quickened his pulse. 'My treat. We'll have another few drinks here then go to the Ivy or somewhere. After that we're off to this new nightclub Frank's found. I'll have a stinking hangover in the morning, but hell, that's tomorrow.' Her green eyes grew large and shone with excitement. 'Tonight I feel like kicking cans down the street, knocking policemen's helmets off their fat heads, and generally making whoopee!'

'Terrific!' grinned Leo.

'Fantastic!' exclaimed Levit.

'I'm in,' said Stapleton.

Silence reigned during the journey home. From time to time street lamps cast a light into the car, affording Herbert a glimpse of Todd's face in the mirror. The scowl was enough for Herbert to know better than to utter a word. *Blimey*, he thought, *nothing will cheer him up. Not even a few drinks with old Leo. Not like the Boss. Not like him at all . . .*

Todd seethed with frustration on the back seat. Even on the way to the Ritz, he had been feeling out of sorts. He had put it down to the state of business, but it was more than that. Business was bad, but he had survived bad patches before. He was a natural survivor. He *always* coped. He was a natural-born coper. Katrina was always saying, 'Nothing fazes Toddy, he could cope with the end of the world.' Yet what was the point? What was the point if there was no fun to be had? What was the point of becoming *someone* if all there was to life was going home every night?

He had been enjoying himself. He always did with Leo. And Charlie was something else! High-spirited, good-looking, sexy. *By God, fancy having that in bed!* And bright, too, bright as a button. Look at the way she had organized the evening. They'd have a bloody good night. And he could have gone. He might have sent Herbert home to collect Katrina. They could have joined in the party. Except Katrina refused to speak to her father. Except Katrina would never give Leo a chance. Except . . .

His spirits plunged even deeper as he remembered his reason for getting home early. Dinner with the Middletons. During the day he had shut the thought from his mind. 'Don't be late, darling,' Katrina had said as he left. 'Julie needs us there early to help break the ice.' The bloody Middletons! The most boring couple on God's earth, who surrounded themselves with the most objectionable, stuck-up bunch of creeps he'd ever met. Break the ice! Blow torches would fail! Jesus! What a sacrifice! And for why? Because of this thing . . . this absurd, monstrous, stupid complex she had about Leo! It was ridiculous, bloody ridiculous!

His fingers drummed on the padded armrest. This couldn't go on. Why *should* it? Leo might be her father, but he was also a good friend. *I need Leo! I need his help, I need his advice – and look at tonight, for God's sake – he's even selling my cars!*

'Bloody Middletons!' He ground his teeth.

The car swept on, through Camden Town and up Hampstead High Street to the private road in which the Todds had their home. The leafy lane usually lifted his spirits and filled him with an unmistakable tingle of pride. Sometimes he marvelled at his own success, casting his mind back to his early beginnings. How far he had come since those days. Now, to live in such a fine house. He remembered the details sent out by the estate agent. *Only three miles from London's West End . . . secluded, but not isolated . . . rare opportunity to purchase one of the most distinctive addresses in London.*

Not a word about the Middletons. The estate agent had kept bloody quiet about them.

His house was the last of twelve. Secluded and set in the middle of a tree-studded half-acre, it was fronted by a high brick wall which spanned the width of the cul-de-sac. The Middletons owned the next plot – of similar size and with an identical curving gravel drive sweeping up to the front door. Todd scowled balefully as they swept past and on through the wrought iron gates to his home.

After bringing the car to a halt at the foot of the steps, Herbert leapt out and opened the rear door. 'Usual time in the morning, Boss?'

'S'pose so,' Todd grunted as he clambered out. He knew it was unfair to vent his feelings on Herbert, but *life* was unfair. Dinner with the Middletons was unfair. Katrina was unfair about Leo. And what fuelled his guilt was that *he* was being unfair about Leo. Loyalty was a two-way street, or it should be. For favours rendered, Leo deserved better . . .

Mac came bounding down the hall, woofing a welcome. Usually Todd crouched down and fussed over the labrador, patting his big golden head, stroking his ears. Usually the exchange of greetings took fully five minutes . . . but usually Todd was in much better mood.

'Katrina,' he called, glancing through the open door to his study. Not finding her there, he went on to the drawing-room.

It was a pleasing room, well-proportioned, with big sofas flanking the genuine Adam fireplace. The pale green walls were adorned by Katrina's art collection, mostly landscapes lovingly assembled over the years. A gleaming black grand piano bore a dozen silver-framed photographs, several picturing Todd at the wheel of *The Sea Princess* with the coast of Majorca in the background. The pale Indian rugs on the moss green carpet added to the quiet luxury. Behind the drawn curtains, leaded glass doors led out on to the terrace.

'Katrina,' he repeated, turning on his heel and going into the kitchen.

Lights were on all over the house. In the dining-room, the big chandelier blazed down on to the mahogany table; the snug was cosily lit, the breakfast-room was bright and inviting. Mac padded along on heavy feet, wagging his tail as he followed Todd back to the drawing-room. The ormulu clock on the mantelpiece showed ten past eight. Katrina would be upstairs, getting ready, but Todd was in no mood to be hurried. After pouring a large whisky, to add to the several consumed at the Ritz, he sat down to contemplate the evening ahead. 'What a bore,' he grumbled aloud. 'What a stupid waste of an evening.'

He rose, picked up his glass, went out to the hall and climbed the stairs with the heavy tread of a man on his way to the scaffold. Every step he took fuelled his resentment. *What a damn silly waste of time.* Entering their bedroom, he crossed the room with scarcely a glance, his brow furrowed in gloomy concentration.

On the far side of the bedroom, an open door revealed Katrina at her dressing-room mirror. 'Darling!' She paused in the act of applying mascara. 'Thank goodness you're home. Hurry now. We'll be late for the Middletons.'

Her sense of priorities filled him with sudden outrage. He stared at her, seeing her almost impersonally, as if through the eyes of a stranger. She was still pretty, he thought. She was sitting in her slip, the sexy black one with the lace top. A glass half-filled with gin and tonic stood at her elbow. A cigarette, red-smeared at the tip, smouldered gently in an ashtray. Her chestnut brown hair, cut and styled that afternoon, gleamed like polished mahogany in the light cast by the lamp. She waggled the fingers of her left hand, the quicker to dry the coral pink varnish applied to her nails. Her smart black dinner frock was carefully laid out on the midnight-blue chaise longue behind her.

'Oh, Toddy, don't just stand there,' she scolded, catching his eye in the glass. 'We're late as it is. Do get a move on.'

Without answering, he went through to his own dressing-room and slumped into the chair by the window. The curtains were still undrawn and he looked out into the rose garden. He sat awkwardly, hunched and uncomfortable, as if ready-ing himself to ward off a blow. He was feeling most peculiar. Staring with sightless eyes, resentment boiled up within him. He wanted to swear, to curse . . . to lash out in frustration. He wanted . . . he wanted . . . he did not know what he *did* want! But he knew what he did *not* want. He did not want to go to the Middletons.

Katrina finished her eyes and dabbed a powder puff over her chin. Rising hurriedly, she turned to the couch and drew the little black dress over her head, using a tissue to avoid lipstick marking the fabric.

'I'm not going,' Todd called out, more truculent by the minute. 'I am *definitely*, *positively*, bloody well not going.'

Giving another push to her hair, Katrina drew in her lips to spread the lipstick evenly. 'Sorry,' she said, cocking her head. 'I missed what you said.' But the half-heard words were enough to wrinkle the smooth, creamy skin of her forehead. Stooping, she slipped the black and gold evening shoes on her feet, and hurried into his dressing-room.

Turning from the window, he looked at her. Something was happening inside his head – as if by rebelling against the prospect of the Middletons, he was somehow seeing his wife from a distance. She stood before him, a healthy woman in her thirties, the black frock moulding over her firm breasts and delicious backside. Very bedworthy, he decided, subconsciously admiring her creamy complexion and dark amber eyes.

At that moment her looks were marred by a frown. 'Oh, darling, do hurry up. You know what they're like. Julie dreads these evenings with Mark's friends. She *relies* on us –'

'*Everyone* dreads Mark's friends. With good reason. In fact, I dread them so much I'm staying here.'

Opening his wardrobe, she took a hanger down from the rail and held out a hand for his jacket. 'I know it's a dreadful bore,' she purred, as if coaxing a child.

Mechanically he passed her his jacket and loosened his tie. 'Mark's a shit!'

'But you like Julie,' she pleaded, slipping the jacket on the hanger. 'You're always saying –'

'I'm sorry for the poor bitch, that's all, married to that –'

'Every woman can't be as lucky as I am,' Katrina countered sweetly, hurrying into the bathroom. 'Besides,' she called above the sound of water gushing into the bath. 'I persuaded Gloria and Sophie to come to lend moral support. You like them –'

'I don't care,' he shouted. 'I am *not* going to the Middletons.'

Hurrying back into the dressing-room, Katrina dropped to her knees in front of the wardrobe. 'These shoes?' she suggested, holding up a pair of soft leather casuals.

Stepping out of his trousers, he tossed them over a chair and picked up his glass before walking into the bathroom. It was one of his favourite places. This part of the house had been remodelled even more extensively than the rest; two other bedrooms had been sacrificed to create the master suite of bedroom, his and her dressing-rooms, and a bathroom glittering with bevelled-edged mirrors.

'Don't settle in for a soak,' she warned from the open door, raising her voice above the sound of running water. 'Just in and out. Oh, *do* hurry. You're always the same. You did know we were going. I reminded you this morning –'

'You *told* me this morning.'

'I told you last week. I *reminded* you this morning.'

Testing the temperature with his toe, he found it to his satisfaction and lowered himself into the water.

'What's up with you, anyway?' she asked, her voice still raised above the torrent tumbling out of the taps. 'Did you have a bad –' she broke off, turning her head to the bedroom. 'Oh, damn and blast! There's the phone.'

Left to himself, he turned off the taps and lay back in the bath. Life should be better than this. He should make his own arrangements. The Middletons wouldn't be included, he'd make damn sure of that. He'd not suffer them at the end of a day. No sir, not bloody likely. He wanted some *fun* at the end of the day. Sit around, have a few drinks, go out for a meal, share a few laughs with people like Leo and Charlie . . .

Katrina's voice floated in from the bedroom. 'Julie! Yes, yes, we'll be along shortly. Toddy's just this minute come in –'

He shouted with uncontrollable frustration, 'You don't listen, do you? I am not, repeat *not* bloody well going.'

'See you soon,' Katrina reassured into the telephone. Next minute, back at the door, her voice sharpened. 'Oh, Toddy –'

'Guess who I met tonight?' he interrupted angrily, water lapping his chin.

Snatching a bathtowel from the heated rail, she advanced across the bathroom. 'Can't you tell me while you get dressed?'

'Your father,' he said, looking up, his head on the same level as her shoes.

'Good God!' For a split second the Middletons went clear out of her head. 'Did you speak to him?'

'Of course I spoke to him. We had a drink at the Ritz.' Craning his neck, he drew spiteful satisfaction from her shocked expression.

'The Ritz?' she repeated, wide-eyed.

He began to feel better. He had spent the journey home telling himself to bring things to a head. And he would. Right now. There was no time like the present. 'I like him –'

'Rubbish! You don't even *know* him –'

'You're the one who doesn't know him. You won't give him a chance –'

'Please, Toddy –'

'Okay, you had a bad time as a kid, but for Christ's sake –'

'Will you get *ready*!' Katrina pleaded, her voice rising. 'We can talk about this –'

'Now.'

'There's no time now,' she retorted with bewildered frustration.

'We've got the whole evening.'

'At the Middletons? Oh darling, don't be impossible.'

Pulling himself upright, he rose in the tub. Water cascaded over his paunch and streamed down his legs. He stood for a moment, gloomily regarding his stomach. 'I could have had a good time tonight,' he said petulantly. 'Correction. *We* could have had a good time. You and me and Leo and some people he knows –'

'Not me. I can imagine his sort –'

'No you can't! You've no idea of the people –'

'Thugs, I should think!'

Like magic, Aldo Moroni's face came into his mind. Moroni looked like a thug. Moroni *was* a thug. But Bob Levit wasn't. Neither was Stapleton. And there was nothing thug-like about Charlie.

Throwing down the bathtowel, Katrina turned on her heel.

He climbed out of the tub and reached for the towel. Slowly he began to dry himself. For a moment he was uncertain of his own intentions. Championing Leo had become vitally important. This nonsense must end once and for all. Katrina must be *made* to understand. But his conscience was uneasy about the

64

Middletons. Of course he *should* go . . . Katrina had made the arrangements . . . Katrina had promised . . .

'No,' he muttered fiercely, wrapping himself into the towel. 'I won't go! I bloody well won't.'

In Todd's dressing-room, Katrina waited like a gentleman's gentleman. She had already taken underwear and socks from the drawer in the tallboy. Bemused by Todd's mood, her thoughts were in turmoil. *Good God, what's the matter with him? Showing off like an overgrown schoolkid!* Unbuttoning the front of a clean shirt, she took it down from a hanger. Her hands trembled slightly as she stifled her temper. *What a performance!* Hurriedly, she began to flick through his collection of ties, while under her breath, she counted the minutes. *Oh, hurry up! Do hurry up . . .*

He padded in from the bathroom. 'Whether you like it or not,' he announced portentously. 'Your father and I have become good friends.'

Her head jerked as if pulled by a string. 'Over a couple of drinks? Great! That's about his mark. How much did you lend him?'

'Nothing, he doesn't need money from me. On the contrary, he's done very well for himself –'

'That takes some believing –'

'Besides, it wasn't just over a couple of drinks. He calls me whenever he's in London.'

'Since when?' she snorted dismissively.

'Since ages.'

'Oh, stop it! You're just trying to provoke me. Which tie do you want?'

'No, seriously, ages. Six or seven years. I worked it out earlier.'

Katrina's eyes widened. 'Six or seven *years?*' Her voice rose incredulously. 'You're not serious?'

'Oh yes I am.'

'You've been seeing my father for six or seven years?'

'It's not a crime!'

'You must be joking!' She stared at him, searching for give-away laughter. 'I don't believe this. Six or seven years?'

He nodded.

Suddenly she knew it was true. She could see it in his eyes, in his earnest expression. She *did* believe him. 'My God! And you didn't tell me?'

'What's the point. Whenever I try –'

'*Try?* What do you mean, try? All that time . . . six or seven years . . . and you didn't get a *chance?* It slipped your mind to tell me?' Even to her own ear her voice was shrill, but it rose with a will of its own.

'Right!' he retorted angrily. 'Exactly. Look at you now –'

'Oh no!' Involuntarily, her head began to shake from side to side. 'Oh no!' she repeated, throwing his ties on to the floor. 'You're saying this is *my* fault? I'm not having that. You sneak behind my back then have the brass nerve to blame *me*?'

He groaned, 'I knew it would be like this.' Dropping the towel, he stepped into his underwear. 'It's always the same –'

'How can it be the *same*?' she demanded, going red in the face. 'You never told me before.'

Sighing, he reached for his shirt. 'You know what I mean –'

'No I don't!' She shook her head, stuttering from temper and shock. 'I don't know anything. I'm not sure I even know *you* any more. You come home here and . . . and announce something like that . . . seven *years*!' She gulped and took a deep breath. 'I can't believe it.' Her hands trembled, her knees shook. She had to move to release some of the tension in her limbs. Turning to the door, she was unsure of where she was going for a moment. Then she remembered. *Oh God! The Middletons. Julie would be in a panic.* 'I'm going,' she said.

'Wait a minute. I'm nearly ready.'

'Don't bother. You don't want to come anyway.'

He plunged one leg into his trousers. 'Hang on,' he called as she went through the door.

'No!' She hurried across the bedroom. 'I'll make some excuse.'

'You can't go without me.'

'I'd *rather* go without you. I don't *want* you there.' Katrina whirled around on the landing. Her amber eyes glistened, her colour was high, her voice sounded strange. She nodded furiously as if convincing herself. 'After all, it's only an evening out with your *wife*! You won't enjoy it. You said so. You won't enjoy it at all.'

By the time he reached the landing, she was running down the stairs. 'Wait!' he shouted.

But she did not wait.

He reached the bottom of the stairs as the front door slammed with a deafening bang. Mac raced out from the kitchen, barking furiously, bounding down the hall to sniff at the gap beneath the front door. Turning, growling and muttering, he padded back to Todd and licked his bare feet.

'Shit!' Todd groaned. 'Shit!'

CHAPTER THREE

HE ALMOST FOLLOWED HER to the Middletons. He ran back upstairs, flung on his clothes, stepped into his shoes, and was half-way down again when he stopped. *Why should I run after her? This is her fault! Any reasonable woman would patch things up with her father. Any reasonable woman would avoid the Middletons like the plague . . .*

Returning to his dressing-room, he kicked off his shoes and hung up his jacket. Smouldering with indignation, he took a sweater from a drawer, pulled it over his head, and after a moment's hesitation, padded downstairs in his stockinged feet.

He had no idea what to do with himself, or with the evening ahead. The house felt strange. Katrina's absence was disconcerting. He felt disoriented. She was always here when he came home . . . always in the house with him. With a shock of surprise he realized that never before, not even once, had he been in the house without her.

In the hall, Mac waited, with his head cocked to one side and an enquiring look in his eyes.

Todd sat on the bottom stair and beckoned him over. 'Yeah, you're right,' he said softly. 'Another stupid argument. One more to add to the list.'

He fondled the dog for a moment, then rose with a sigh. 'Come on, let's see what we can find to eat.'

He had never learned to cook. What was the point? Katrina was a *cordon bleu*. Most nights she enjoyed cooking. On the nights she baulked at the prospect they dined out. As it happened they dined out a good deal, what with business and social engagements, but even without them, learning to cook would never have entered his head. The kitchen was foreign territory.

Opening cupboards, he inspected the contents with eyes blank with incomprehension. Finally he found some bread, made a cheese sandwich, set it on a dinner plate with a side portion of pickles, and carried it back to the drawing-room. As he poured out a Scotch, his thoughts strayed enviously to Leo at the Ivy. *Crazy*, he thought, *I could be enjoying myself. I could have gone out with Leo and that girl Charlie and the others ... I could even go next door and get a decent meal. Instead here I am eating a sandwich.*

'It's the principle,' he announced, watching Mac curl himself into a ball on the rug.

The dog regarded him quizzically before lowering its head on to its paws.

'Bullshit, huh? Yeah, you're right.' He swung his legs up on to the sofa, sipped his drink and munched his sandwich. He pondered the reasons for the latest quarrel. Not the Middletons. Who gave a shit about them? In the old days, he and Katrina would have bust a gut laughing. But lately . . .

'What happened to the laughter?' he frowned.

But he knew, he knew where the laughter had gone.

It had started to go the day he set eyes on Paloma Blanca.

Bouncing along in Hank's open jeep, they drove up over the hill and out of the harbour.

'Where we off to?'

'Ah! Like I said, that's the surprise.'

'I don't like surprises.'

'You'll like this one.'

'Yeah? How far we going?'

'About six miles.'

Sensing Hank's excitement, he tried to guess their destination. Two years had done nothing to widen his knowledge of Majorca. Whenever Katrina suggested exploring, he had a standard response. *What's the point? We got everything we need in the harbour.* And he had. The villa, the boat, the Crow's Nest, his circle of friends. *Door to door in five hours,* he boasted to people in London. Thanks to Katrina's efficiency, to fly from

London to Majorca was to transfer from the comforts of one home to the pleasures of another. They travelled without luggage, confident that wardrobes at each end contained all their needs. Arriving at Palma they took a cab from the airport, reversed the procedure at the end of their stay, and saw little or nothing of the rest of the island. They came not to Majorca but to stay in the harbour – which suited Todd fine until he tried to guess Hank's destination.

'Bit off the beaten track, isn't it?' He frowned at the unfamiliar road.

They were following one of the roads along the coast, and not striking inland. He groaned. 'Don't tell me you've found me a new boat. Katrina's still going bananas –'

'No, nothing like that.'

He took out a handkerchief and mopped his brow. 'Phew, today's a scorcher. Aren't you sweltering? Don't you feel the heat? Why don't you get air-conditioned wheels for God's sake! I'll do you a special deal.'

'I like the sun. That's why I live here.'

Todd grunted and watched the deserted road curve around to the left. The jeep's tyres crunched over the dry road to billow white dust up in their wake. After about a mile, Hank turned off into a narrow lane. Todd glimpsed the shimmering sea over his shoulder; then his view was blocked by a high brick wall which became such a permanent feature that it ran alongside for the next couple of miles. The lane narrowed and then narrowed again. Todd winced as the jeep bounced over ruts and craters. Finally Hank drew to a halt, pulling so close to the wall that he left himself no room to alight. 'I'll climb out your side,' he said.

Todd got out and looked up and down the empty lane. 'Welcome to the middle of nowhere,' he announced dryly.

'You're an impatient bastard at times. It's along here.' Hank pointed to a wooden door in the wall. 'There's another way in, but I want you to see it from here.'

'See what?'

'You'll find out,' said Hank, unlocking the door. 'Come on.'

Stepping through the opening was like entering a forest.

70

Dense trees crowded to within a few yards of the wall, growing so close together that the narrow path between them was scarcely visible. Hank locked the door and put the key back in his pocket. 'Come on, ole buddy,' he said again as he set off down the path.

The shadowy coolness came as a relief after the scorching sunshine outside. Glancing up at the tall dark green spires, Todd was reminded of the vaulted roof of a cathedral, an impression strengthened by the peaceful solitude of the place. The air was pungent with the scent of the pines, and beneath his feet the path was springy with needles. 'Is this private land?' he asked suspiciously.

'In spades. Been in the same family for two hundred years.'

'You mean we're trespassing?'

'I had a key, didn't I?'

'If you had a gun it wouldn't make you a soldier.'

Hank grinned and his teeth showed white in the gloom. 'Don't worry, we got permission. Come on,' he repeated with such obvious eagerness that once again Todd felt his excitement.

The path was so narrow that they had to walk in file. Hank led and Todd followed, hurrying to keep pace. After fifty yards, he became more breathless than ever. 'What's the rush?' he protested. 'Whoever she is, she'll wait. Did you tell her to bring a friend?'

'For you? Are you kidding? You'd run a mile. Anyway, this is more exciting than sex.'

Hank grinned as Todd rolled his eyes in mock amazement. 'Quit horsing around,' he urged impatiently. 'You'll see. Not far now.'

Nor was it. After twisting to the left, the path began to fall away. The ground descended into a significant slope. The pines began to thin out, gaps widened between them to allow sunlight through the branches, and Todd could again feel the warmth of the sun on his skin. Moments later he followed Hank into a clearing. Hank stopped, half-turned and swept his arm forward theatrically. 'Behold,' he said. 'Feast your eyes.'

The pines curved away, hundreds of them, sentinels on the crest of hillsides which descended to form three sides of a basin.

Almost two hundred yards ahead and much lower down, sited at the centre of the basin, an old finca sprawled in the sunshine, its mellow stone walls conveying an air of contentment. Todd could see terracotta pots on the paved terraces and geraniums spilling over a balcony. And beyond that – at least another two hundred yards beyond – a sliver of golden sand separated the land from the sea.

He stood staring, absorbing overall impressions – the blue of the sky, the deeper blue-green of the sea, the verdant grandeur on all sides. Sheer beauty and ageless tranquillity held him entranced for a moment. Then he began to dwell on details. Like the way terraces had been cut into the hillsides. Where the pines stopped, the terraces began – different widths, some wide, some narrow, hugging the contours of the hillsides, and all planted with vines. Row upon row of vines, neglected and over-grown. Lower down was a grove of almond trees, with orange trees beyond, bright with fruit on their branches. And lemon trees. To the right of the finca, he saw what he imagined had once been a flower garden, for that too was overgrown and badly neglected. And up the slope to the left – more vine-covered terraces. Gulls swooped in from the sea, their shrill cries con-trasting with the cooing of some white doves perched in the twisted branches of an olive tree nearby.

Hank watched him, impatient for a reaction. 'Beautiful, eh?'

Todd nodded, still staring.

'I've got an option to buy it,' Hank said quietly.

Todd's head jerked round in amazement. His voice rose. 'You're buying this? What is it? A farm or a vineyard or something?'

'Or something,' Hank nodded. 'Have you ever seen anything so beautiful?'

Todd turned his gaze back to the finca and the sea beyond. The empty beach was at least a hundred yards long, tapering off at each end as the hillsides came around to embrace the shoreline. His gaze traversed the basin. 'It's paradise,' he said. Looking up at the pines on the skyline, he felt a tingle of excite-ment. 'Fancy owning this,' he muttered softly, shaking his head enviously. 'You're right. It's beautiful.'

Hank beamed.

Walking to the edge of the clearing, Todd cupped his hands to his eyes and turned around as he walked, craning his neck. 'It goes on for ever. How big is it for God's sake?'

'About twelve hectares.'

'What's that in English?'

'Thirty acres, give or take a few square yards.'

'Thirty acres,' Todd repeated excitedly as he walked back. 'Bloody hell! It's fantastic. Imagine waking up to this every morning? It'd be like dying and waking up in heaven.' He stopped with a sudden realization. 'You say you've got an option to *buy* this? How come? If it's been in the same family two hundred years —'

'The old man died last year. I'm dealing with his son.'

'Yeah? What's up? He hates the place?'

'He's a gambler. Dropped a bundle at the casino and owes money all over.'

Todd stared down at the old finca and imagined the cool comfort of its rooms and the lifestyle which went with them. Thinking of a family living there for generations caused him an unaccountable moment of sadness.

'What do you think?'

Todd grunted, 'I'm glad I don't have kids.'

'I mean about the site?'

Todd shook his head in wonder. 'What can I say? It's the most beautiful spot I've ever seen. I really mean that. Seriously. It's paradise. Like a country estate . . . a country estate in the sun, yet with the sea and everything else —'

'Glorious, right?'

'And how.'

'Good,' Hank grinned. 'Now use your imagination. See over there . . .' he pointed to the extreme left end of the beach. 'See where those rocks jut out into the sea. That's where we put the jetty.'

'You're building a marina?'

'Nothing big, but very exclusive. Say about two hundred berths.'

Todd whistled softly. He paid four thousand a year for his

73

berth and knew others paid more. 'That's useful dough.'

'That's peanuts,' Hank interrupted, pointing again. 'Along there, we'll have the yacht club —'

'Yacht club?'

'With a clubhouse, cocktail bar, swank restaurant, international cuisine, the lot.'

'Wow! Something like the Crow's Nest?'

'Better than the Crow's Nest. Non-residents will pay a premium to get in.'

'Non-residents? You mean foreigners?'

Hank laughed, 'No, people who aren't staying at the hotel.'

'What hotel?'

'The one we're going to build! Wake up, Toddy, I said use your imagination, didn't I? What's up with you?' Grabbing Todd's shoulder, he pointed again. 'See over there? Take a line from those orange trees through to the finca. Got it? That's where we build the hotel.'

'Hotel,' echoed Todd.

'Not some concrete monstrosity but a thing of beauty. Very old world Spanish. Wide Moorish arches, high vaulted ceilings, marble floors, Italian mosaic swimming pools; it'll be like a palace. I've taken on the most fantastic architect. You should hear him on the subject. His idea is to harmonize with the natural beauty of the site. All the high-tec stuff will be there, but hidden away —'

'You've got an architect?' Todd's head was spinning. 'Boy, you're really moving on this.'

'One of the best architects in the world. Back at the office I've got plans, elevations, provisional costings, everything.' Hank paused, his eyes shining. 'This guy's talking about shipping blocks of stone in from Barcelona, tons of the stuff. But it'll be worth it. We're talking exclusive, right? The height of luxury. I reckon two hundred and fifty suites, not rooms, *suites*, all with their own private terrace with a plunge pool and everything, all overlooking the sea. And behind it, up here on these terraces, we'll site tennis courts and swimming pools, all linked by walkways lined with palm trees, walls dripping with mesembryanthemum and stuff. We'll have discreet little bars set into

74

clearings, with fairy lights coming on at night. Down there we'll have the yacht club –'

Todd sank down on to the ground. 'Jesus H. Christ!' he exclaimed. 'Some hotel.'

Hank threw himself down beside him. 'More than a hotel. That's the whole point. This site's so unique we've got a chance to create something spectacular. A standard of luxury never seen in the Balearics, maybe in the Mediterranean. Christ, I dunno, maybe in the whole world. Paloma Blanca will become –'

'Paloma Blanca? What's Paloma Blanca?'

'That's what it's called. There's a story attached to this place. See over there.' He pointed towards the olive trees. 'A hundred years ago, a man planted olive trees and vines up here. He cut out the terraces, tended his vines, cherished and watered them, worked night and day for a year. The poor bastard did everything right, but one by one the vines shrivelled and died. So he cleared the site and started all over again, using the last of his money. But when the new vines started to grow they looked as bad as the first lot. He thought they were doomed to die. He was in despair. Then he woke up one morning, and there was a white dove outside his window. Until then he had seen only sea birds and gulls. The white dove had a broken wing and the other birds would have killed it for sure. Anyway, the story goes that this guy put a splint on the wing and fed the dove and nursed it until it could fly again. But it stayed, and the sickness left the vines and they grew strong. The man prospered, and since that day if you come up here you'll always find a white dove. La Paloma Blanca.'

Todd realized that Hank was pointing not at the olive tree but at a dove sitting on a branch. 'So that's what it means? White Dove?'

Hank nodded. 'Paloma Blanca. I thought I'd keep the name. It's a lucky omen, and there's all sorts of connotations associated with the image of a white dove. I can see it on the logo . . .'

'It's fine. Got a good ring to it,' Todd agreed hastily, too bemused by the scenery to pay much attention to the name. 'I'm still trying to take this place in.' He shook his head with wonder. 'Jesus!' he exclaimed softly as he stared down the slope to the finca. When he squinted, he could almost see the hotel.

'What d'you think?'

'The whole thing blows my mind, that's what I think! You've gotta be the luckiest guy under the sun to stumble on this.'

Hank laughed. 'I nearly called you four weeks ago to tell you to get over here, but Don Antonio was playing hard to get –'

'Is he the gambler?'

Hank looked surprised. 'You've never heard of Don Antonio?'

Todd shook his head.

'He's the architect. He's a big name in Spain and Europe, probably the world over for all I know.'

'I dunno about architects,' Todd confessed with a shrug.

'Believe me, he's up there with the best. He was the man I wanted. So I went over to Barcelona and pleaded with him to come and look at the site. To begin with he said he was too busy, so I went to his office every morning and just sat there.' Hank grinned. 'I figured there was no point calling you while I was sitting in Barcelona.'

'But he came in the end?'

Hank nodded, still smiling. 'After I'd begged for a week. He flipped when he saw the place. We went back to the Crow's Nest to call his office, and next day two of his assistants were here. They were here three days, taking photographs, surveying the site and God knows what else. He promised to get some ideas over to me by this week, and I knew you were coming, so I waited. It's all back at the office, sketches and drawings and provisional costings. He's got a lot more work to do, but there's enough for us to knock some ideas about.' Hank looked at him. 'That is, if you want to come in as my partner?'

Todd's heart thumped in his chest. He swallowed hard. 'Partner?'

'Fifty-fifty.'

'Dear God,' Todd said softly. He felt the same mixture of fear and excitement that he had felt when Sam Owens had so casually asked, *Why don't you take this place over?* Stunned by the prospect, he remained silent for a long moment. Then he echoed, 'Partner?'

Hank nodded again.

Feeling dizzy, Todd said, 'We're talking millions here, right?'

Another nod. 'Millions to build, millions in turnover and millions in profit.'

Todd moistened his lips. Taking a deep breath, he said, 'I gotta be honest with you. All I do is sell cars. I mean, that's all I know about, right? Basically I'm just a mechanic. That's how I started.'

'So? I started as a deck hand.'

'I don't know the first thing about hotels.'

'What's to know? They're restaurants with rooms, that's all. I know restaurants and you know business. I figured we'd manage between us.'

A weak smile came to Todd's face. 'But why me?' he asked, his pulse racing and his heart still thumping.

'Why not you? I thought we were buddies?'

'Sure, but . . . let's be honest, plenty of guys in the harbour have got —'

'More dough than you,' Hank finished. 'I know, but I need someone I can trust. Most of those old bastards would rob their own mothers. Besides,' he smiled. 'I figured you've still got the urge to climb mountains.'

Todd raised his head and looked at the pines on the hilltops. 'And how,' he said softly.

'This is the big one, Toddy,' said Hank. An earnest expression came to his face. 'I remember coming to Europe for the first time in the Sixties. Hell, that was great. St Tropez, Cannes, all that stuff down the French Riviera. Then in the Seventies . . .' his eyes brightened at the memory. 'You should have seen Marbella then, but now . . .' he pulled a face. 'They've lost that exclusiveness. People still go there, of course — that's the trouble, too many people. I don't want us to make that mistake. We've got a chance here to make Paloma Blanca the new watering-hole for the jet set.' He stared out to sea. 'Know something?' he said softly. 'I'm getting tired of running a restaurant. This is what my life's been about. Waiting for this to happen. I tell you, Toddy, this is the right idea in the right place at the right time.'

The words took him back to the day he had started. *The right idea in the right place at the right time.* Exactly what he had said to Larkins all those years ago. Now Hank was saying the same thing. Tingling with excitement, he stared at Hank and realized that the usual smile had deserted him. Every mental image he had of Hank was of him smiling. But now his wide mouth was set in a straight line and tiny beads of sweat had collected on his upper lip.

'I don't reckon on blowing this,' Hank said in the same soft voice as before. 'And I don't want to put you under pressure, but I can't hang about. This deal I got on the site was a sixty-day option. Half the cash down, half in sixty days. I put the half down, now I got twenty-two days left to find a partner.'

'Twenty-two days?' Todd yelped with surprise. 'Three weeks?'

Hank nodded. 'I wanted you to have first chance. No harm done if you say no. I've still got time to find someone else, but I can't hang about. I want you to know that.'

'What happens if you don't find someone?'

'I lose the deal and a hundred million pesetas.'

Frowning, Todd converted a hundred million pesetas to sterling. A startled look came to his eyes. 'That's more than a quarter of a million pounds. Is that right?'

Hank nodded. 'Everything I could raise. I put the Crow's Nest in hock.'

'You'd lose the Crow's Nest? Whew!' Todd swallowed hard. 'I thought the other guy was the gambler.'

'I'll find the money somewhere. And it's not a gamble.'

Todd moistened his lips as he calculated his cash reserves. He *could* raise a quarter of a million. Just. Things would be tight for a couple of months, but business was booming. He was still stunned that Hank had put his restaurant on the line. Hank's entire life was invested in the Crow's Nest. His entire life! He wouldn't risk that unless he was stone cold certain . . .

'Twelve million pounds!' Katrina's voice rang through the villa. 'You're going to borrow twelve million pounds?'

Todd looked up from the plans spread over the coffee table.

Red-faced and angry, he retorted, 'This is the biggest chance of my life!'

'Your life! I don't count. That's obvious. You didn't even discuss it –'

'I told you, didn't I? I'll take you to see it in the morning.'

'I won't go. I don't want anything to do with it.'

Sighing heavily, he rose and went to the bar for a drink. 'Be reasonable, will you? All I told Hank was –'

'You'd pay him a quarter of a million by the end of the month.'

'Not definitely,' he lied. 'I said *probably*. I wanted to sleep on it, and talk things over with you.'

'That's not what you said when you came back. It was all cut and dried. You came rushing in here, all excited, carrying those plans, and . . . and suddenly you're in the hotel business. Suddenly . . .' she gulped. 'Oh Toddy, why? *Why?* You don't need –'

'Over a million a year!' he interrupted angrily. 'That's the profit in this. Every year! For each of us!'

He carried her glass over to the table next to her. 'We're made for the rest of our lives. Can't you understand that?'

Turning away, he returned to the bar for his own glass.

Katrina watched him with frightened eyes. Childhood had turned her into a prudent bookkeeper. Where other girls had dreamed of glamorous lives, she had yearned only for a settled existence. Her earliest memories were of her mother dealing with bailiffs. She had grown up frightened by men who came to the house. Dozens of men, all looking for her father after the failure of one of his speculative schemes. Her mother had cracked under the strain. Every knock at the door had become a signal to drink.

Ignoring her own drink on the table, she pleaded, 'Let Hank find someone else. You don't *need* it. We have a wonderful life –'

'And a million a year makes it worse?'

'We come here to enjoy ourselves. I don't want you working the minute we get off the plane –'

'Work at what? It'll take two years to build, for God's sake!

After that Hank's going to run it. We'll just come over to have a good time.' He sat down, grinning broadly. 'And rake in the loot.'

'So Hank does all the work and you get half the profit?'

'I raise the money to build it. That's my end of it.'

'Twelve million? How d'you think you'll raise twelve million?'

A look of surprise came into his face. 'The bank lent me the money for Sam's place, didn't they? They've got no complaints –'

'That wasn't anything like twelve million! Besides, that's the car business. They lent it on your record with Todd Motors. You'd *proved* yourself –'

'So that's all I do? Sell cars?' Indignant and hurt, he went red in the face. 'That's all I'm good for?'

Heedless of what she was doing, Katrina emptied her glass. Her mind was in turmoil. To begin with his excitement had bewildered her. Then she was frightened. Automatically her bookkeeper's brain began to add up their debts – the villa was only half paid for – they still owed fifty thousand on the boat – all manageable if business continued to boom. But now he was spending the cash reserve and was full of wild talk of borrowing millions . . .

'What you don't understand,' he was saying, 'is a project like this brings enormous prestige, terrific respect –'

'People respect you now. Everyone who knows you –'

'Nah.' He shook his head. 'Not some of the crowd at the Crow's Nest. Take that guy Hans Ginsberg. Know what he paid for that yacht? One point seven million.'

'Who cares? The man's a creep.'

'Okay, so what about Dutch Harry? Know what he made from his nightclubs last year? The other day he was telling me –'

'A pack of lies, I expect.'

'How can it be lies? You've seen the way they live. The Hicksons arrive in their own jet, for Godsakes! Last year Billy Thompson made enough to buy a string of racehorses. I read that in the paper.'

'I thought we came here to relax,' she interrupted sharply. 'I was wrong. You come to count people's money.'

'We're mixing with rich people. They're *all* interested in money. And I'm sick and tired of them seeing me as that fat little car dealer from London! This'll make 'em sit up. This'll prove I'm as good as they are.'

They stared at each other, aware of the gulf opening between them. Finishing his drink at a gulp, he went to the bar for another. As he poured the whisky, he said, 'This is my chance to be someone. To really count. I mean, this is big time! This is *international*, for Christ's sake!'

Dismay was written in every line of her face. 'You've worked so hard,' she protested fearfully. 'All your life. That's all you do. Work, work, work. How can you risk –'

'Where's the risk? People won't stop taking holidays. These days they take two or three a year. It's the business to be in.'

'And yours isn't? Toddy, think about it! You don't *have* a quarter of a million to invest in some half-baked –'

'I'll manage. Delay paying a few people, juggle the cash flow –'

'Suppose you hit a bad patch? Suppose business goes flat?'

'"Suppose, suppose?"' he echoed sarcastically. 'Why should it? We broke records last quarter, and the quarter before.'

'But just suppose?'

'So okay, worse comes to the worse, we'll sell this place.'

'Sell the villa?' Her eyes rounded with disbelief. She loved the villa. The thought of losing it . . .

'Why not? We won't need it. We'll have a permanent suite in Paloma Blanca.'

'But . . .' She drew in a sharp breath. 'We've made this our home. Everything here . . .' She gulped in dismay. 'We've poured ourselves into this place. This is *us*!' She gestured about her. 'Our furniture, our glasses –'

'Glasses! You want glasses? We'll have five bars, three restaurants and a yacht club. Glasses by the gross you can have!'

*   *   *

81

'Harry Larkins would've lent me the money,' he said bitterly. 'What is it with you guys? You don't have vision, that's what. Harry had vision.'

'It's a totally different situation,' Smithson explained patiently. 'When Mr Larkins was manager and made that loan, his lending was secured by a mortgage on Owen's. He had asset cover. He also had Sam Owen's trading accounts. So with a record of past profits, he could see how you'd repay the loan.'

'I paid it off faster than your people expected.'

'You did indeed, Mr Todd.' Smithson smiled across the desk. 'None of us doubt your ability to make profits in the motor business. You've been in it all your life. You're an expert. But this . . . er, this hotel scheme . . .' He frowned at the plans on the desk. 'It is speculative, I'm sure you'll agree.'

'No, I don't,' Todd said bluntly. 'That's the whole point.'

He had already been an hour at the bank and the discussion was going badly. In his opinion Smithson was a poor substitute for Larkins. Old Harry would have loaned him the money. Harry trusted his instincts and backed his own judgement. Not for him slavish adherence to head office directives. 'I'm the man at the rock face,' he would say. 'I know my customers better than some stuffed shirt at head office. If they don't like the way I do things they can sack me. Failing which they can stay off my back.'

Smithson would never dare say that to head office. Smithson did things by the book. Smithson spoke with a plum in his mouth and had a protruding Adam's apple which bobbed up and down above the old school tie knotted around his neck. Todd had as much in common with him as he did with the man in the moon. Sighing under his breath, he marshalled his arguments and began all over again. 'Take what you just said about asset cover. We don't want all the money at once. We'll pay the builder as work goes along. At each stage we get an architect's certificate, so you don't pay until the work's done. The value increases in step with the loan.' Raising his hands, he sat back in his chair. 'You're covered every step of the way.'

Smithson smiled. 'If only it were that simple −'

'What's so hard about it?'

'Difficulties invariably arise with this type of large development, especially with builders.'

'We got the best builder in Majorca lined up.'

Smithson ignored him. 'And at the end of two years you'll owe us twelve million plus interest –'

'Secured by a mortgage.'

'I agree, but will the finished building be worth it?'

Todd was so exasperated that his hands bunched into fists. 'What d'you mean, will it be worth it? I just explained! Architect's certificates will prove –'

'What it cost, not what it can earn. Your ability to repay the loan is totally dependent upon what it will earn.'

Todd glared across the desk. His voice was harsh when he spoke. 'I don't think you understand what we've got here, Mr Smithson. You're underestimating this whole proposition. We're talking about the finest hotel in the Mediterranean! You've seen the projections –'

'Yes, but that's just it. They're just projections. There's no track record.'

'Hank's got a track record. The Crow's Nest is the best restaurant on the island.'

'This is more demanding than running a restaurant,' Smithson said dismissively. 'And you'll be totally reliant on his management skills. It's not even as if your own background qualifies you to make a contribution.'

'Hank will do fine.'

'What about existing hoteliers? If this is such a winner, why aren't they building this hotel?'

'We've got the site,' Todd exclaimed, smugly triumphant. 'That's the whole point! That's our trump card. It beats every other card in the pack. Sure, new hotels are going up. The point is, they're just hotels. See one and you've seen 'em all. Paloma Blanca will be totally different. That's why we got Don Antonio to design a beautiful building. We're going to furnish it with antiques. That's why we can charge top dollar –'

'That's another thing. You assume people will pay some very high prices –'

'Absolutely. Paloma Blanca is for *la crème de la crème*. Very exclusive.'

'But these prices?' Frowning, Smithson searched through Todd's proposal. 'Will people really pay –'

'Let me tell you something, Mr Smithson,' said Todd angrily, pointing a stubby finger across the desk. 'Millions of people holiday in Majorca every year. Millions! All we got is two hundred and fifty suites. So we can afford to be exclusive. I mean, it's a drop in the ocean!'

'Bad day?' Katrina asked over dinner.

He grunted as he reached for the salt. 'Not good.'

Bad would have been a better description. Disastrous would have been more accurate. Another bank had said no. That made seven in ten weeks.

She watched him shake salt all over his meal. 'I seasoned it in the cooking. You don't need all that. Too much is bad for you.'

'Everything's bad for me,' he mumbled.

She stared at him for a moment, then making a great effort to ignore his bad mood, she said brightly, 'Jimmy Davis phoned. He said to tell you Holloway's confirmed their order for two more XJs. That's good, isn't it?'

'Yeah,' he said, sounding uninterested.

'Jimmy was thrilled.'

'Any other messages?'

Deep down, he was ashamed of his surliness. Part of him regretted his behaviour, but to his mind she left him no option. She was the one who was being unreasonable. The subject he most wanted to discuss was banned from their conversation. Paloma Blanca was on his mind morning, noon and night. It was all he wanted to talk about. But she had screamed at him – *I don't want anything to do with it*. So it had become a taboo subject. They talked of other things. Instead of a dialogue conversations had become two separate monologues.

'Well?' He looked up. 'Anyone else call?'

She hesitated, pointlessly because she knew she would tell him. 'Hank, to ask if you had any news.'

'What did you say?'

'I said you'd probably call him back after dinner.'

'Uh huh.' He nodded absently and picked up his knife and fork. He ate in silence, brooding over the day and the weeks which had gone before. One thing Paloma Blanca had taught him. Apart from being the biggest shits under the sun, bankers were downright stupid. They wouldn't know a good business proposition if it jumped up and bit them. No imagination, no vision . . .

Katrina made another attempt at conversation. 'Gloria came round for lunch.'

'Oh?' he said, feigning interest. 'What's she doing?'

'Celebrating. She gets to keep the house now the divorce has gone through.'

'Poor old Peter.'

'It was his fault.'

He doubted it. Without disliking Gloria, it seemed wrong to defend her. Her first marriage had lasted two years, now this one had gone belly up. 'Seems to me she's making a good living out of divorce,' he said between mouthfuls. 'What's she doing now? Looking for another mark?'

'I think she's off men for the moment.'

'Yeah, and the Pope's off religion.'

'That's unfair,' Katrina said sniffily. 'You quite like her, really.'

'Mmm,' he murmured, not in the least interested in Gloria. Withdrawing from the conversation, his thoughts reverted to business. Hank would be devastated by the bad news, especially now that he and Don Antonio had concluded their negotiations with the builders. Everything had been agreed – a firm price, guaranteed completion date, penalty clauses, everything – but only if the builders could start almost immediately. The trouble was that no start date could be sanctioned until he raised the money, and there was no telling when that would happen.

'Oh, I nearly forgot,' said Katrina. 'Sally called. She said the

Jaguar people were upset about you cancelling that meeting again. She said –'

'Right, I'll talk to them in the morning.'

'And she said Manny Shiner's been trying to get you all week.'

Digesting the information in stony silence, he wondered how to cut the link between Katrina and Sally. He had to do something. It was like an unholy alliance. The bond they had formed when working together meant that at times Sally reported more to her than to him.

Katrina read his mind. 'She only phoned because you didn't get back to the office this afternoon. She's just passing on messages, that's all.'

'Okay,' he said, nettled. 'I'll deal with them.'

Some almost forgotten advice of Sam's came into his mind. Sam had once said, 'A business is like a vegetable patch. Tend it every day and you'll live like a king.' The memory made him fidget. He was *not* tending his business. Chasing the money for Paloma Blanca was consuming weeks of his time and all of his energy. He was *neglecting* his business. He knew it, and, from her thinly veiled reproach, so did Katrina. Finishing his meal, he pushed his plate away. 'That was fine,' he said. 'I'd better call Hank before he gets tied up in the restaurant.'

'Don't you want coffee?'

'I'll have it in the study.'

Lighting a cigar, he sat down at his desk. He delayed dialling for a moment, trying to think of the best way to break the bad news. But there was no best way, only the blunt, unvarnished, unpalatable truth. With a sigh, he reached for the telephone and within minutes was deep in conversation with Hank.

Katrina came in while he was still talking. 'That's right, Hank,' he said. 'The sticking point's the same every time. Yeah, right, the projections. They don't believe we'll do that volume of business.'

To his surprise, Katrina had brought in a full pot of coffee. Usually she poured it in the kitchen, bringing him a cup before taking her own into the drawing-room. He watched as she set the tray on his desk.

'. . . I know that, but we can't *prove* it,' he said. 'Like we've never run a hotel. We can't give 'em a list of names and say these people were here this year and they'll be back next year, this is what they pay for their rooms, this is what they spend in the bar . . .'

Katrina went to the sideboard and poured out their drinks, Scotch for him and brandy for her.

'. . . You bet,' he said, watching her bring the glass to his desk. 'That's right, Hank. I'll keep trying. Don't worry, we're not beaten yet.'

But he felt beaten when he hung up. His confident tone was belied by the defeat on his face.

He felt crushed and frustrated and downright miserable.

Katrina poured coffee into their cups and took her own to an armchair next to the hearth. Putting it next to her brandy on the low table, she sat down and faced him. 'Can we talk about this?' she asked quietly.

His eyebrows climbed as his expression changed to one of surprise. 'Why? You said you wanted nothing to do with it.'

'No more I did, but I didn't expect a succession of strained silences.'

He stared at her with eyes full of resentment. 'What did you expect? I'm trying to put together the biggest deal of my life, and you don't want to know about it.'

A flush came to her face which she tried to hide by glancing down at her lap. After a long moment she looked up, her eyes meeting his. 'I was wrong to say that and I'm sorry. I just thought . . . hoped . . . it might make you realize you had enough on your plate . . . prompt you to have second thoughts.'

'Well it didn't,' he retorted, biting his tongue as he saw the hurt spring into her eyes.

Silence descended. They stared at each other, pain on her face and resentment in his. Eventually she said quietly, 'Let's call a truce. This isn't like us. We've always talked to each other, ever since we met —'

'I know,' he interrupted, his voice softening. What she said was perfectly true. Sometimes in a restaurant they would catch sight of other couples, obviously married, who could go through a whole meal without exchanging a word, as if everything they had to say to each other had been said long ago. Whereas the Todds were always talking. True, a great deal of the talk concerned business, but so what? Katrina had once worked in the business; she was still interested, still had a point of view. Apart from the time she had got broody their only real arguments had been about Leo. Until Paloma Blanca.

'I'm sorry,' he said. Taking a breath, he tried to explain. 'I know you can't understand, but you must let me do this. I can't walk away from it. It's the biggest chance of my life. I'd always regret it if I let it slip through my fingers. Ten, twenty years, I'll look back and think – Jesus, you should have gone for that. You blew it. You could have been up there with the big boys. You could have been someone –'

'But you don't need it.'

His eyes flashed angrily. 'If I don't make it now, I'll never make it.'

'Make what? More money?'

'It's not just money. It's proving yourself. You know, the way . . .' Frowning furiously, he sought an example. 'Take a racing driver. He wants to prove he's the best. His performance is measured by how fast he can go. In business the measurement is money, that's all, it's a way of keeping score, proving how good you are.' He paused, watching her face. Her lack of comprehension was so disheartening that he knew it was futile to try to explain further. What was the point?

'I thought we were happy as we were.'

'We are happy. We'll *stay* happy. I swear –'

'No! We'll end up facing a huge pile of debts, worried sick . . .' her voice creaked in desperation. 'Oh, Toddy, it's a pipe dream. The banks won't lend you that sort of money. And it's taking up all of your time. You've a business to run. We've bills to pay! We owe for the villa, the boat –'

'We're paying them. For Christ's sake, anyone would think we're overdue. We're not.'

'So far. But it all comes out of the business. Unless you look after the business, it can't look after us.'

'Oh, for Christ's sake! Stop talking like a bookkeeper.' Stung, he spoke more sharply than he had intended. Reaching for his glass, he swallowed some Scotch. Then he took a puff of his cigar in an effort to calm himself. 'Look,' he began persuasively, 'Hank was telling me something just now. If this doesn't prove we're right, nothing will. Are you ready for this?'

She shrugged.

Undaunted by her lack of enthusiasm, he pressed on, 'He was telling me just now, there was a guy in the Crow's Nest last night who runs Suntours. You know Suntours?'

She nodded. 'The travel firm.'

'Right. I mean, Suntours are *big*. Hank says they're the biggest in Europe. Anyway, this guy is having a drink and guess what? *He's* telling Hank that Majorca needs another luxury hotel. He's telling *Hank*! Can you believe it? This guy can't get enough luxury accommodation at peak season. For Christ's sake! If that don't prove we're right, nothing will. That's what's so crazy. I've got bankers saying I won't fill Paloma Blanca, and there's this guy telling Hank —'

'Crazy,' she admitted softly, shaking her head.

'Yeah, well, proves we're on the right track. That's the main thing. I've just got to keep flogging round the banks and Hank's got to hang in there. It'll come right in the end, believe me.'

'I hope so,' she said fervently. 'Honestly, Toddy, I really do hope so.'

Mistaking her tone for encouragement, his look of surprise turned to pleasure. 'See? Now you're coming round to the idea. That's what happens. It grows on you.' He puffed on the cigar. 'To begin with you think — Christ, this is big. Will it work? What happens if it goes wrong? All that stuff. Then you figure it out and think — Hell, let's go for it!' He laughed, his enthusiasm rekindled by her apparent approval. 'Of course, proving it to the banks is something else! You'd need to be a courtroom lawyer to persuade those guys.'

'Or a hotelier.'

'Yeah,' he nodded. Then he looked at her. 'What makes you say that?'

'Something you were saying to Hank when I came in. Something about if you owned a hotel you could tell the bank that these people spent this much on their rooms, this much in the bar and so on. So I thought . . .' she crossed her fingers '. . . why not sell the site to a hotel group? Let them borrow the money.'

He stared at her.

Hope sounded in her voice as she plunged on. 'You'd make a big profit, wouldn't you? It's the best site on the island, you've done all the development work, you've got the architect's drawings –'

'Why would a bank lend to a hotel?' he asked, his heart pounding with rising excitement.

'But . . .' A puzzled note sounded in her voice and she looked at him in surprise. 'You said it yourself; track record, forward bookings, that sort of thing. Not many, perhaps.' She paused, confused by the way he was looking at her. 'I expect it's like those wall charts I did at the office, only hotels would use them for booking rooms . . .' Her voice faded and she went pink in the face. 'You could probably tell how busy you'll be in the summer by the number of rooms you've got booked in January. I know I'm explaining this badly –'

'No. Of course! That's the answer. Forward bookings!'

'Sell the site to a hotel?'

He felt dizzy with excitement. 'Not bloody likely. Not now I know how to raise the money.' He snatched up the telephone. 'Wait till I tell Hank. I wonder if this guy from Suntours is still in Majorca?'

With a puzzled look on his face, Leo shook his head. 'I don't get it, old boy. They still won't go for it? Even with the Suntours deal? What more do they want?'

Todd's expression was one of disgust. He had arrived at the Ritz directly from meeting his bankers. Instead of celebrating, he was plunged into the depths of despair. 'Damned if I know,' he said bitterly. 'I really thought the Suntours contract would clinch it. I was *sure* it would!'

They had met downstairs in the bar, but after one look at Todd's face Leo had steered him out to the lobby and into the elevator. Scowling furiously and weighed down by a bulging briefcase, Todd had arrived carrying the troubles of the world on his shoulders. Up in Leo's suite, he dropped the briefcase on the floor, slung his coat on a chair and stared sightlessly out over Green Park. He was half-way through his first whisky before he could stop swearing. 'I dunno,' he sighed wearily. 'Maybe I'm explaining things badly? The whole deal is crystal clear to me, but those dummies get the wrong end of the stick every time.'

'Happens sometimes, old boy,' said Leo sympathetically.

Todd fell silent for a moment, angrily thinking back over his meeting. 'Stupid bastards,' he muttered, reaching into an inside pocket for his cigar case. 'Tell you what,' he said. 'Let me go through it with you. Okay? You be the banker. See what you think.'

'Fine, but calm down first. Finish your drink and light your cigar.'

Todd loosened his tie. He had been so pleased with himself when first he had told Leo about Paloma Blanca. He had tingled with pride. Until then Leo had made him feel provincial, with his tales of deals all over the world. Now he had a deal of his own, bigger than anything Leo had ever talked about, a deal which would make him a millionaire many times over, a deal that would make him *someone*.

'Okay,' he said, recovered enough to puff on the cigar. 'This is how it stacks up. We spent two whole days with Tommy Hastings, he's the guy who runs Suntours. We showed him the site, the plans, everything. He loved it. The biggest problem I had was with Hank. He got dead worried that dealing with someone like Suntours would bracket Paloma Blanca with cheap package holidays. Anyway, Tommy gets so sold on the site and Don Antonio's sketches that he pitches in on my side. He promises to print a special brochure, run a big advertising campaign and do such a classy job that eventually Hank drops his objections.' A wry smile came to Todd's face. 'Then the horse trading starts. Eventually, when all the haggling's over, what it comes down to is we give Suntours a special exclusive price on Paloma Blanca for two years. In return they guarantee us

91

seventy per cent occupancy for nine months each year. Plus . . .' His pause added emphasis to his words. 'This is the clincher. They pay us up front at the start of each year.'

Leo whistled softly with approval. 'That helps the cash flow.'

'It *secures* the cash flow. That's the whole point. I had all these bankers sneering at our estimated volume of business, so I reckoned they'd turn green if I slapped this guarantee on the table.'

'And they didn't?'

'They did to start with. Their eyes popped when they saw the contract with Suntours. They were all over me for ten minutes. I was sure it was sewn up. Then they began to go through the figures all over again.' Todd's expression changed to one of disgust. 'You won't believe this. Suntours pay us seven and a half million a year. Right?'

Leo nodded.

'So then they say — "But Mr Todd, you don't make a profit on this deal with Suntours. Your annual overheads come to seven and a half million. How do you repay us our money?"' Rocking back in his chair, Todd cast a beseeching look upwards. 'I say — what d'you mean, *I don't make a profit?* I got all our costs covered, so everything else is the profit. All the cash from the bars and the restaurant, revenue from the yacht club, fees from the berths, everything! And . . .' he held up a hand '. . . I also point out that although Suntours only *guarantee* seventy per cent for nine months a year, Tommy reckons that's his absolute minimum, so we'll get more from Suntours! When you add that lot up you're looking at another seven million, maybe more. So I say to these knuckleheads, "Listen, for fuck's sake! There's easily enough there to pay you off over three years!"' He glared at Leo. 'Know what they say? "In that case, it takes us back to projections!"'

'I don't believe it,' Leo grunted, shaking his head.

'Half the forecast is secured, for God's sake!' Todd's voice rose in a howl of angry disbelief. His frustration knew no limits. 'How come it's back to projections?' He slapped a meaty hand to his forehead. 'I told 'em, they're out of their minds. Their fucking brain cells have gone!'

Shaking his head in sympathy, Leo got up to freshen their drinks.

Todd glared at the back of his head. 'So? What d'you think? I am nuts or are they crazy?'

'They're bankers. They hand out umbrellas when the sun shines.'

'Fuck 'em,' Todd grunted, accepting the drink. 'They'll eat their hearts out when Paloma Blanca is up and running.'

'I'll drink to that,' said Leo as he returned to his chair. He sat down and raised his glass.

Scowling furiously, Todd swallowed his whisky in silence.

'What will you do now?'

'Do the rounds all over again. Keep going. What else can I do? Hank keeps bitching about the delay, but . . .'

'It's easy for him.'

Todd shook his head. 'To be fair, he's got his worries. He's put some local politicians on his payroll. You can lose months if you don't grease the right palms. And he and the architects have got the best firm of builders in Majorca standing by. That's the big worry. If we get started now, these guys can complete in time for the season after next. We need that to tie in with the contract with Suntours. So right now time's critical and it's slipping away.' The scowl returned to his face and the bitterness to his voice, 'Thanks to these bastard bankers!'

Leo regarded him steadily. 'You've set your heart on this, haven't you? I mean you're so *sure* it will work. You're absolutely certain.'

Todd was so surprised that he slopped his drink over his tie. Putting the glass on the table, he dabbed the stain with a handkerchief. 'You think I'd have wasted all this time without being certain?' he asked angrily. 'One,' he said, holding up a finger. 'We've got the best site in the Mediterranean. That's not just my opinion. That's Hank's opinion, and he's been everywhere, and Tommy Hastings who knows every resort in the –'

'Things can still go wrong, old boy. That's a lesson I've learned.'

'Such as?' Todd challenged, heat rising into his face.

'Suppose the builder lets you down?'

'He gets crucified! Don Antonio's set this contract in concrete. There are penalty clauses like you won't believe. I tell you –'

'But suppose?'

'Don Antonio will have his guts. Besides Hank will be on site every day! Kicking arse –'

'He's not a builder.'

'He's got eyes. If the schedule starts to slip, he can draft in other builders.'

'At extra expense.'

'Not down to us. That's the builder's liability. It's in the contract. If he fouls up, he pays all extra expenses.'

'But you haven't signed the contract with the builders yet.'

'We can't sign the bloody contract!' Todd bounced up on his chair. 'That's the whole point. We can't sign until I'm sure of the money.'

They exchanged looks; Todd still flushed and belligerent, Leo frowning and pensive. Then Leo smiled, 'Katrina must be excited?'

Mention of Katrina wrong-footed Todd for a moment. He had no wish to explain Katrina's thoughts on the matter. Recovering, he avoided the question. 'If I pull this off, your daughter will become a very wealthy woman. And we will pull it off. If I can raise the twelve million.'

'If,' Leo repeated heavily.

For a moment they just looked at each other.

Something in Leo's eyes heightened Todd's expectations. He found himself holding his breath.

Leo said quietly, 'If the banks turn you down, I might know of someone.'

Todd's breath escaped with what sounded like a sigh of relief.

'But I want you to be totally sure about repaying the loan.'

'You've seen the figures. There's no problem.'

Leo's nod did nothing to disguise his uncertainty – as if having raised the possibility, he wished he had remained silent.

A note of urgency crept into Todd's voice. 'I don't have the right contacts for this. Know what I mean? Sometimes it's who you know, not what you know. So I'd be really grateful –'

'This someone I know,' Leo interrupted with a thin smile, 'isn't with Barclays or Chase Manhattan or any of the big banks.'

'Thank God for that! I'm pissed off with big banks. Do you know a smaller one with that kind of money?'

'It's not a bank at all,' said Leo with a shake of his head. 'It's an individual.'

'Jesus!' Todd exclaimed, impressed. 'We're talking millions here. Who is he? Rothschild or someone?'

Leo smiled. 'His name is Aldo Moroni.'

'Never heard of him. What is he? Italian or something?'

Leo shrugged. 'Corsican, I think. The point is he's not the sort you'd want to upset. He has a certain reputation.'

Todd blinked, unsure of his response. Leo's serious expression gave him no clue. He was reminded, not for the first time, of Leo's life and background. On the surface, he was urbane, successful, charming, friendly, approachable – but some of the stories he told indicated that he had survived some tough times. During which he must have met some tough people.

Moistening his lips, Todd asked bluntly, 'You mean he's a crook?'

Leo laughed. 'Some people say he is, but they say that about me, old boy. No, he's not a crook, at least in my opinion.'

'So what's the problem?'

Leo said, 'He's absolutely ruthless. Very tough. The thing is he sticks to a bargain. And he expects other people to do the same.'

'Can't complain about that.'

Leo gave him a curious look.

Todd frowned. 'What's up?'

'Look.' Leo sighed and began to fidget. 'I hope you find some-one else, but if all else fails –'

'All else *is* failing, Leo. I just told –'

'I don't know him that well.'

'You wouldn't have thought of him unless you felt he might lend me the money. And I grew up in the motor business, remember? I've met some sharks in my time.'

'Not like Moroni.'

'So what's special about him?'

Leo hesitated for a long moment. Then he said, 'Maybe if I tell you how I first came across him. You can judge for yourself.'

'Fine.'

'This was a long time ago, at the start of the Sixties. Moroni was a mercenary in the Belgian Congo. That's how he started.'

'You were a mercenary?'

'Not me, old boy, not bloody likely, and certainly not in the Congo.' Leo shook his head. A wistful look came into his eyes. 'That was my first experience of Africa. The Congo is huge, you know, as big as India, but a hell of a sight richer in minerals, especially copper. There was so much potential, still is I suppose, but it was a mess then − the end of colonialism, the beginning of self-government. I was working for a Belgian, a man called Van Rooen who was clinging on to vast tracts of land in the north. I always suspected he had some secret deal going with Lumumba for the mineral rights, my guess was he was paying him off in a Swiss bank.' Leo shrugged. 'The usual political corruption, civil war and blood baths while the fat cats lined their own pockets.'

Todd nodded, though he had no concept of the Congo and had never heard of Lumumba.

'Some of the Europeans had got out by then, me included, but a lot of Belgians stayed on, Van Rooen's son among them. Most of them had businesses to run or investments to protect, but others stayed simply because they couldn't leave the life they had there. I tell you, those old colonialists knew how to live.' Leo paused to sip from his glass. 'Jojo Van Rooen lived in this huge mansion just outside Elisabethville, with his wife and young family, waited on hand and foot by an army of servants. I guess he thought he was safe with Lumumba in his back pocket. Anyway, a fortnight after independence, civil war erupted all over again. Lumumba was arrested and killed. Elisabethville went up in flames. An orgy of rioting and raping and killing filled the streets. It was a blood bath. Belgians fled in their thousands over the River Congo to Brazzaville. Belgian paratroops were flown in. The United Nations sent in a so-called peace-keeping force −'

'But you weren't there?'

96

'Not bloody likely. No, I was in Brussels with old man Van Rooen. We thought Jojo had got away to Brazzaville, then we heard he was being held in Katanga. It was all rumour, you could never find out anything definite, the country was in chaos with the Congolese fighting each other and the UN troops caught in between. We kept hearing stories of Europeans raped and killed. Old man Van Rooen was frantic about Jojo and Annette and their kids. He called everyone he could think of – people he knew in the government, men he knew in the army – but still Jojo and his family remained missing. Finally some colonel in the paratroops came up with Aldo Moroni's name. Moroni was ex-French Foreign Legion. Then he was a mercenary in the Congo right up until independence, so knew the territory and all that went with it. Van Rooen had got this address in Paris so he sent me there to persuade Moroni to go in and get Jojo out, money no object.'

Todd whistled softly.

'I remember being surprised by how young he was,' said Leo. 'I wasn't that old myself, but Moroni looked about nineteen. Afterwards I found out he was twenty-six. Mind you, he looked like a soldier; strongly built, muscular shoulders. He had a very penetrating stare. I remember sitting in this bar, explaining everything, and for a long time he just looked at me without saying a word. Then he gave a shrug of indifference and said they'd already be dead so we were wasting our money. I told him Van Rooen knew that was possible, but there was a chance they'd still be alive because they were known to be rich and could be used as hostages – so he wanted Moroni to go ahead at full speed. Moroni went to a phone and made some calls. He said he'd only take the job if he could get the right men to go with him. When he returned he said they'd do it for ten million Swiss francs, half for expenses and equipment up front, the rest when they got back, with or without Jojo and the family. I told him I had to get authority, so I got Van Rooen on the phone, explained everything, and then Moroni took the phone from my hand and spoke to Van Rooen himself . . .' Leo's lips twitched into a smile. 'I was a bit put out, being relegated to messenger boy, but I was damn glad later.'

'Why, what happened?'

'Moroni got them out. All of them, Jojo, Annette and the three kids. It took him five weeks. I don't know much about it, except afterwards Jojo told me they were being held in a village when Moroni's boys stormed in and slaughtered half the inhabitants.' Leo shrugged. 'But that's not the story. The point is Van Rooen ratted on the deal.'

'You mean he didn't pay the rest of the money?'

Leo nodded. 'Thankfully, I had nothing to do with it. Moroni and Van Rooen had arranged the money between them. I didn't even know it hadn't been paid until a month later. One night, just as I was leaving a restaurant, a car pulled up alongside me. Next minute I was bundled into the back and held down on the floor. We didn't go far, about twelve kilometres to a little village outside Brussels. We pulled off the road into a little wood, where another car waited, and inside was Moroni. I wasn't hurt, but I was bloody scared, old boy, I don't mind admitting.'

'Who wouldn't be?'

'There was no need, actually. Moroni treated me all right. He said he realized I was just the messenger, so he had a message I was to deliver to old Van Rooen. It was then I realized we were in Jojo's car, it was an Aston Martin and there weren't many in Brussels. I was to take it to the old man and tell him to look in the boot. That was all. Except I was to drive directly to the old man's house without going anywhere first. I did as I was told, and I arrived at Van Rooen's place to find them in panic. Jojo and his two sons had disappeared. Annette and her daughter were there, verging on hysteria when I drove up in Jojo's Aston. The old man was on the point of calling the police. I half guessed what had happened, but even that didn't prepare me for what we found in the boot. Jojo's head. Not his body. Just his severed head.'

'Dear God!'

'Luckily Annette never saw, neither did her daughter. Just me and the old man. I'll say this for old Van Rooen, he was made of granite. After locking the car, he took me off to his study. He had a couple of brandies to pull himself together, then he questioned me about what had happened. When I told him, he swore me to secrecy. I was due to go to Amsterdam the next morning and he told me to stick to my plans. And to be honest, that's all I know. I was in Amsterdam for about ten days. When I got back to Brussels there had been a funeral for Jojo who apparently had been killed in a traffic accident. That was the story.'

'What about the kids? The two boys?'

'They were back with Annette, and about three weeks later she went to live in the States, taking her three children with her.'

'So this guy Moroni got away with it? He got away with murder?'

Leo shrugged. 'I've told you all I know. I never saw Annette again, and old Van Rooen and I grew uncomfortable with each other, so we parted company. He's long dead, of course, and until now I've never told anyone.'

'But it was murder. Come to think of it, it was everything. Kidnap, extortion *and* murder.'

Leo looked at him. 'I honestly don't know what it was. I've told you everything I know, and it was all a long time ago. Perhaps I shouldn't have told you.'

'No, I mean yes, I'm glad you did, but . . .' He swallowed hard. 'So what about Moroni? I mean, what happened to him?'

'It was years before I met him again. Someone I know was looking for some money for a project . . . a shipment of arms, actually . . . and he happened to mention Moroni. I didn't make the connection at first, but it turned out to be the same man. These days I suppose you'd call him a financier, for want of a better description.'

'Have you dealt with him?'

'Once. And I made very sure that nothing went wrong.'

'And he remembered you?'

Leo smiled. 'I think that's why he did it. My deal was small beer by his standards. His lawyer was surprised when he agreed to do it.'

'His lawyer?'

'He has a lawyer in Paris. Fellow by the name of Lapiere. You go and see him, explain everything, he puts the proposition up, and Moroni makes a decision. I had my money in forty-eight hours.'

Todd felt awed as he reflected on the fourteen weeks he had spent going from one bank to another.

Fourteen wasted, frustrating weeks – with Hank becoming more desperate every day. Three and a half months stolen from his business.

Katrina was right to worry . . .

He looked at Leo. 'What would you do?'

Leo smiled. 'Raise the money elsewhere.'

'And if you couldn't?'

Leo shrugged. 'I'll give you the lawyer's address in Paris, if you like. You could give him a try. But remember what happened to Jojo.' He grinned cheerfully. 'No point losing your head over this, Toddy old boy.'

Without his contract with Suntours, Todd might have admitted defeat, but winning the approval of a man like Tommy Hastings added even more fuel to his determination. 'Tommy's an expert,' he told himself fiercely. 'What do bankers know about the holiday business?'

Bankers were even blind to the value of the design work. Don Antonio was predicting at least one architectural award for Paloma Blanca, in which case magazines would want to write features, they would clamour to take pictures and publish articles – the whole world would sit up and take notice.

Todd fumed. 'What do bankers know about fine buildings?' The experts were all on his side. 'Look at Hank!' he would explode to anyone willing to listen. 'Hank's been to every watering hole in the Mediterranean. He knows all there is to know about running a restaurant, and what's a hotel but a restaurant with rooms?'

His emotional commitment to Paloma Blanca had become total. To encourage himself he recited instances of setbacks suffered by other successful men – Edison, Henry Ford, Brunel, Conrad Hilton, Charles Forte and a host of others – all of whom had persevered and had gone on to become household names, internationally respected and immensely wealthy. In his interminable meetings with bankers he buoyed himself up with one thought. 'It's like selling a house,' he told himself. 'All I need is one man to say yes. All I need is one buyer.'

Not that he immediately rushed over to Paris. Leo's warning had induced a certain caution. So he persevered with his contacts in London. He followed up every meeting, even with bankers whose reactions had been doubtful, who said, 'It doesn't look our kind of thing, but we'll think about it. Give us time.'

But time ran out when the builders issued an ultimatum. They would only guarantee the completion date if they had a firm contract within ten days. Ten days! Unless he could raise the money in ten days his dream of becoming *someone* would be over. Moroni was the end of the line. Todd had nowhere else to go. By then he had put the proposition to every major bank in London, plus most of the minor ones, with conspicuous lack of success.

After making an appointment over the phone, he travelled to Paris, feeling worried and anxious with no idea of what to expect. But he was soon reassured. Lapiere turned out to be a neat little man in a neat little office – a suite of rooms in Montmartre. No taller than Todd, he was as thin as a matchstick. He was courteous, attentive and extremely professional. Meeting him put things into perspective. It settled Todd's nerves. So what if Moroni had been a mercenary in the Congo? That was thirty years ago. These days he was a conventional businessman who conducted his affairs through his lawyer.

Lapiere asked dozens of questions and made endless notes. He was very encouraging, nodding approval as Todd outlined his plans. But by the end of the meeting it was obvious that he lacked the power of decision. The real negotiations would take place with Moroni himself. 'How quickly can you arrange a meeting?' asked Todd.

Looking up from the papers all over his desk, Lapiere shrugged. 'It is up to my client. Personally I like what I see. The project will carry my recommendations. I'll call you as soon as I can.'

The call came through two days later, so late in the evening that Todd was on his way up to bed. 'Monsieur Todd? Claude Lapiere here. My client can see you tomorrow afternoon.'

'Tomorrow?' Todd echoed, his heart leaping.

'*Oui*. In Rome.'

Taken by surprise, his reaction was a startled laugh. 'Rome? Tomorrow? Why there? Is that where he lives?'

'*Non*.'

'That's where he has an office?'

Lapiere's reply was curiously vague. 'My client is there at present,' he said carefully. 'When I explained it was urgent, he said he would see you at five o'clock.'

'Well, great . . . but hang on a minute, I'm not even sure I can get a flight –'

'I have checked already. Seats are available on a BA flight and back again in the evening.' Lapiere paused before concluding, 'Shall I tell my client to expect you?'

'Well, er . . . yes, I suppose –'

'*Bon*. You will be met at the airport.'

He spent the whole of the following morning preparing for the meeting. After a sandwich at his desk, he left for the airport, his briefcase bulging with notes and photographs of the site, all additional to the file of papers he had given Lapiere in Paris. During the flight, while he nibbled the airline's uninteresting food and sipped his way through a half-bottle of wine, he tried to imagine Moroni. Ex-soldier, ex-mercenary-cum-financier. Leo had described him as tough. *But he sticks to a bargain*, Leo had said. *He keeps his word and expects others to do the same.* 'Suits me fine,' Todd exulted, confident of his own integrity. He had built a business with that as his motto. Even now the sign above Todd Motors in Kilburn read, *Bargain cars at bargain prices from people whose word you can trust.*

Full of hope, itching with nervous anticipation, he pored over his notes, honing his presentation until every word he planned to say was crystal clear in his mind. For the most important negotiations of his life, he rehearsed as never before.

*　　*　　*

Had he known more about Aldo Moroni, he would have realized he was wasting his time. Moroni did not negotiate in the normal sense of the word. It was not the way he did business. He did not *ask* men to borrow from him, he did not seek to *persuade* them, they could either accept or reject any arrangements he offered. That every man would act in his own interests was a fact as basic as breathing – so therefore it followed that any man who borrowed from Aldo Moroni did so because it suited him and for no other reason. Consequently any attempt to negotiate terms was seen by Moroni as an insult. He saw himself as a benefactor. He was for ever saying, 'Is'sa my nature to help people.' It was something which he truly believed.

Born poor on the outskirts of Ajaccio in Corsica fifty-five years earlier, Moroni was self-taught in everything except soldiering. Soldiering had given him his start in life, first as a Legionnaire, then as a mercenary, and although many years had passed since he had followed that trade, lessons learned then were never forgotten. He had found a set of rules to last him the rest of his life.

One of the most important related to theft. Young Moroni had been in the Legion scarcely a month when he witnessed an event which burned itself into his memory. A sergeant had been caught stealing from the soldiers in his troop: the sums involved were not vast – how could they be when Legionnaires were so poorly paid – but to steal from comrades was a heinous offence. Taken on to the barrack square, the sergeant was stripped of his chevrons and reduced to the ranks. Then he was tied to a post and lashed until he was unconscious. After which he was revived and beaten again. When passing judgement the colonel quoted from a Persian proverb: 'An egg thief becomes a camel thief.' And in the desert a camel was a man's most precious possession.

Standing to attention under the fierce Algerian sun, young Moroni's heart had warmed with approval. A cruel smile had lit his face as he watched the lashes strip the flesh from the sergeant's back. It was not enough for a thief to be punished, he realized, what was important was that the thief be *seen* to be punished to deter others – and the more vicious the punishment, the stronger the deterrent.

The Legion was Moroni's university in more ways than soldiering. By the time he left he could speak all the major languages of Europe. He spoke them with such a thick Corsican accent that many people had trouble understanding him, but that was their problem not his. Certainly he never tried to conceal his Corsican origins, for he was as proud of his birthplace as of being a soldier. It had been soldiering which led him into the arms business – first on his own account, then as a financier – and financing arms had led him into lending money for other business ventures until eventually he had become wealthy. But the caution of a man who had known hard times was bred into his bones. Trusting nobody, he surrounded himself with ex-mercenaries; tough, sometimes brutal men, accustomed to discipline. He lived comfortably, but not extravagantly. He had homes in Corsica, Paris and Basle. The home in Corsica was a farm, managed by his wife who was expected to run it at a profit. He was just as frugal with his mistress Nicole, who although housed in his sumptuous Paris apartment was still required to earn her keep by running a flower shop in Montmartre. He shared his home in Basle with no one, using it as a place where he conferred with his bankers. The clue to his character was that he still thought as a Legionnaire. If a man failed to repay money, his failure made him a thief, and it was right and proper that thieves should be punished. If a man dishonoured a bargain, his failure made him an enemy, and soldiering had taught Moroni to remove any enemy who stood in his way.

He prospered mightily, yet stood aloof from the two biggest money earners of all time. Having learned to distrust drugs in the Legion, he refused to finance traffic in drugs, turning his back on millions in profit. And as a Legionnaire he had come to despise pimps, so he would have nothing to do with the lucrative prostitution rackets of Marseilles, even though they were the traditional province of the Corsicans. Some people admired his restraint, while others of a less charitable nature pointed to the benefits won by such sacrifices. By not infringing on the activities of the Mafia, or on business controlled by the Corsican Millieu, he was treated as a friend, so that from time to time they did business together; business conducted between men of honour. Which was how he saw himself – as an honourable and reasonable man. He never thought of the men he had gunned down in his youth, the three he had blown up, the one whose head he had hacked from his body, the one he had strangled and dismembered with his own hands, the scores of others whose executions he had ordered – instead he thought of the men who had wronged him in smaller ways and whose lives he had *spared*.

'Is'sa my nature to help people,' he would say, and believe every word.

This then was the man Todd went to see. Todd was not a fool. For years he had dealt with rogues in the car business. He was an experienced negotiator, but nothing in his past had prepared him for a man like Aldo Moroni.

As the plane began its descent over Rome, he returned his notes to his case, confident that he had mastered his brief. Looking out of the window, he wondered where the meeting would be held. Lapiere had merely said, *You will be met at the airport.* Did that mean they would meet in an apartment, a villa, an office? Whatever and wherever, it would have to be nearby because of the return flight in three hours. Three hours! The knowledge that the fate of Paloma Blanca would be sealed in the next three hours filled him with nervous anticipation.

He saw the man immediately upon passing through Customs. Bare-headed, dark-suited, bronze-faced; holding a placard across his chest bearing Todd's name. He smiled briefly as Todd approached.

'Signor Todd?'

Todd nodded.

'This way.'

'Hang on a minute.' Todd put down his briefcase and reached into his pocket for his cigar case.

Whenever he flew, he cursed the regulations which forbade him to smoke cigars. He had long since lost the taste for cigarettes. 'That's better,' he said, blowing a column of blue smoke into the air.

Nodding impassively, the man turned on his heel. Falling into step, Todd tried to guess who he was? Chauffeur? Assistant?

Messenger? He had not offered to carry the briefcase, although he had stared at it as if trying to imagine the contents. He walked briskly enough to compel Todd to hurry along on his short legs. The concourse was crowded and repeatedly Todd had to dodge around people to avoid a collision. He was glad when they reached the escalators. 'Do we have far to go?' he asked breathlessly.

As the staircase descended, the man stared intently at the people below, his sharp eyes traversing the crowds as if searching for a recognizable face. In absent-minded response, he pointed to a sign at the foot of the escalators. Seeing the outline of a motor car, Todd recognized the universal sign for a car park.

'I meant is it far from the airport?' he asked.

Before the man could reply, they reached the ground floor. Stepping off the escalator, he walked briskly ahead, jerking his head impatiently, silently urging Todd to keep up. Hastening after him, Todd collided with a woman who berated him for his clumsiness. Apologizing, he hurried onwards and drew level as the man entered the car park, whereupon the man took his elbow and steered him towards a pair of swing doors. Another man was leaning against the wall next to the doors. Instinctively Todd felt a moment's alarm. Most of the other passengers were walking towards the elevators on the far side of the car park. The grip on his elbow tightened. The man slouching against the wall straightened up as they approached. He opened one of the doors. Beyond, Todd saw the foot of some concrete steps. Once through the doors, they stopped. After a furtive look up at the empty stairs, they turned to Todd. 'Excuse,' said the man who had met him. His companion began to run his hands over Todd's clothes, patting him down with more expertise than had been displayed by the staff in the airport. Then he held a hand out for Todd's case. Without a word Todd handed it over. His heart pounded. His mouth became dry. He began to perspire. Inwardly he felt the stir of misgivings. Meeting Lapiere in Paris had been nothing like this. Meeting Lapiere had been a business meeting like any other, but these grim-faced men . . .

'Okay,' said the man, closing the briefcase and handing it back. They climbed the staircase to the next floor where yet a third man was waiting. He turned and led the way across the car park. Todd and the others followed, along an avenue of parked vehicles. At the far end three cars were backed up against the wall – a large Citroën, flanked by a Fiat and an Opel. Propped against the Citroën was a man reading a newspaper. As they approached, he folded his paper and went to the rear of the vehicle to open the door. Suddenly the man next to Todd reached out and with a deft movement took his cigar from his fingers. As Todd opened his mouth to protest, he was nudged forward so that instinctively he lowered his head to duck into the limousine's open door. In the shadowy interior, he saw a small fold-away table upon which stood a bottle of red wine, two glasses and the file of papers he had left with Lapiere in Paris. Behind the table in the corner of the rear seat sat a large man who reached forward and held out a hand. 'Mist' Todd?' His voice rasped like coarse sandpaper drawn across stone. 'Aldo Moroni.'

Shaking hands across the table restricted Todd's first impressions. He saw a broad face above wide shoulders, a powerfully built body clad in a pale grey suit and a dark blue silk shirt open at the neck. He felt the man's strength in the handshake.

'Sit here, Mist' Todd.' Moroni indicated the seat beside him. 'Is'sa more comfortable.' He wheezed as if to cough but instead cleared his throat noisily.

Todd squeezed past the table and on to the rear seat.

'Was'a you' flight okay?' Moroni enquired in the same gravelly whisper.

'Fine, thanks,' Todd managed to reply as he sank into the velour upholstery. Still alarmed by the body search, he tried to compose himself. Looking at Moroni he saw a dark-skinned, fleshy face, pitted with the craters of acne. A Mediterranean face weathered by a life spent in the sun. The dark eyes were very intense, reminding him of Leo's comment about a penetrating stare. The nose was broad and slightly crooked. The man's bulk was commanding, making Todd feel shorter than ever. He watched the big hands with square-tipped fingers pour dark red wine into two glasses and slide one towards him.

'Salute,' Moroni grunted, raising his own glass.

As he reached for his wine, Todd was distracted by a

107

movement outside. The man who had met him was talking to the driver of the Fiat, gesticulating as if conveying directions. Then both men laughed and relaxed into desultory conversation. Wondering where they were going, Todd turned to Moroni with a look of enquiry, but Moroni was engrossed in his wine. Beyond him, Todd glimpsed the driver of the Opel. Meeting Todd's gaze, the man looked away, causing Todd to realize that there was at least six men surrounding the Citroën who, for all their apparent casualness, were carefully surveying the car park. In front of him, beyond the smoked glass partition, the driver of the Citroën conversed with the others without a word reaching the deeply padded back seat.

'Cheers,' he said uncertainly, trying to maintain his composure.

Moroni smacked his lips as he returned his glass to the table. Placing a meaty hand on the folder, he bent the cover back with his thumb and riffled the pages. 'Was'sa matter, Mist' Todd?' he murmured with sly humour. 'You don' wanta sell cars no more? You think the 'otel business is better?'

Todd laughed. 'No, it's not that. It's just that . . . well, this is a chance in a lifetime. A one-off, something quite exceptional.'

Moroni regarded him steadily. 'You get rich, huh? Make'a plenty of money?'

'I hope we can both make money, Mr Moroni.'

Moroni nodded and transferred his gaze back to the folder. 'Is'sa big,' he said almost mournfully, his breath rasping. 'Lotta money.'

'Yes,' Todd agreed.

'Is'sa lotta money no one will len' you. So you come to me,' said Moroni abruptly, his voice suddenly hardening, his face becoming stern.

Todd blinked, taken aback by the sudden note of aggression. The uncompromising opening was another trick learned in the Legion. The first rule of command is to gain ascendancy. Later, when Moroni was ready, would come the opportunity to suggest that beneath this tough exterior beat a heart of gold. Later, when he had gained his advantage, he would say, *Is'sa my nature to help people* – but first he had to underline that his help could never be taken for granted. His voice softened a fraction. 'Tell me your plan, Mist' Todd. We see if we do business.'

Todd had imagined a conversation in a villa, or an office, even in an hotel – not in a car park. To come all this way at short notice, then to discuss the matter like this? He wondered if they were meant to talk as they travelled, but when Moroni topped up his glass and sat back in his seat, it became obvious that the Citroën would remain where it was.

Disconcerted and wrong-footed, he tried to bluff. After admitting that the loan was proving 'quite difficult to arrange', he pretended to have an alternative. 'Some friends of mine want to form a consortium,' he lied.

Moroni read the bluff as easily as a newspaper. 'Does he take me for a fool?' he asked himself. He wiped the air in front of his nose as if brushing a fly away from his face.

The gesture so clearly implied disbelief that Todd was unsettled. 'It is a possibility, er, something we've considered,' he said uneasily. 'But . . . er . . . my partner and I would prefer to raise a loan.'

'Sure. Is'sa more better for you, huh? You don' have to share,' Moroni said drily, reprimanding Todd for his greed when in fact his own was monumental. *This is a man with a dream*, Lapiere had said on the telephone. Moroni had been pleased. Men with dreams were bad negotiators. They went through the motions, but in reality would sacrifice everything for the sake of their dreams. Moroni had made a lot of money from dreamers.

Still trying to collect himself, Todd reached for his briefcase, only to feel Moroni's hand on his arm. 'No paper,' said Moroni, shaking his head. 'Lapiere he'sa lawyer, he lika lotta paper. I lika talk. Just you an' me. We talk things through, see if we become frien', okay?'

It was the strangest meeting Todd had ever attended. The dark-suited men outside added an indefinable tension. Moroni's bulk made him intimidating, and the bizarre circumstances of the car park removed any lingering doubts in Todd's mind. *These men are thugs, gangsters, crooks!* A chill crept up the back of his neck. He was seized by a desire to rush downstairs to the airport concourse, to mix with the crowds, to mingle with law-abiding citizens as they went about their business. But then he thought, *You're not doing anything wrong. Nothing illegal. You're here on legitimate business. There's nothing crooked in discussing a loan.* And another thought flashed through his mind – a memory of Leo saying that Moroni always honoured his side of a bargain.

So, with pounding heart, he began to talk about Paloma Blanca and once started his nervousness faded. When he described the project he became fluent, even eloquent. He knew the words by heart – when to pause, what to emphasize, when to expect a question – he had told the story so many times: and if the circumstances were unusual, they ceased to matter. All the preparation in London paid off. He was word perfect, a salesman at the top of his form, and he was vastly encouraged by Moroni's reaction.

Moroni was certainly attentive. Most of the time his dark eyes were fixed on Todd's face with the unblinking gaze of a lizard. Now and then he nodded encouragement, even conferring apparent agreement, while all the time thinking: *Lapiere was right. This Englishman is consumed by ideas of grandeur. A pathetic little car dealer, a fat little man who sees himself as an international tycoon. Poof! But there is profit in his dreaming for me.*

Finally, when Todd finished, Moroni nodded approvingly as he replenished their glasses. He had made up his mind to make the loan, even about the terms and conditions, which he had no doubt would be accepted. But when he spoke it was as if thinking aloud. 'Lapiere says is'sa good business for me.'

Todd's heart thumped, but he remained silent, concentrating on understanding the difficult accent. He watched Moroni's face, seeking clues from the man's expression.

'But . . .' Moroni patted the file of papers and pulled a face of disapproval. 'I don' like'a the way is'sa putta together. Some'a money now, some'a money in six months, some'a in eight months . . . busy, busy. Like a bee. Always'a comin' an' goin'.'

Relieved that the objection was so easy to answer, Todd

smiled. He explained about the architect's certificates and paying the builder in stages. 'It's a way of ensuring that your money is always protected.'

'Huh?'

'Secured. You'll have a charge on the building work.'

The dark eyes glimmered half-way between contempt and amusement. 'Is'sa lesson I learn. I tell you. If I trust, I do business. If I don', I don'. Is'sa good lesson. Huh?'

'Absolutely,' Todd nodded enthusiastically.

'You're a serious man, Mist' Todd. A frien' of Leo Sinclair's. A man of honour, huh? If I do business is'sa because'a we frien's, eh? Because'a I think you no let me down.' He fixed Todd with his unwavering gaze. 'If I take'a charge on this building, is'sa look like I trust you? Is'sa insult, not trust. You want'a me to insult you?'

Todd sat still enough to have stopped breathing. Was it possible that this man would lend so much money without security?

'Man borrows some money,' Moroni shrugged, lifting his hands palm upwards. 'So he gotta let the lender sleep with his wife? Is'sa right?'

Baffled as how to answer, Todd shrugged.

Moroni growled in disgust. 'Is'sa not right. Is'sa insult. Why run to me with these pieces of paper? If the builder does good work, you pay him. If his work is bad, you don'. Simple. Huh?'

Not daring to speak, Todd nodded and wondered where it was all leading. Despite the wine, his mouth had turned dry.

Moroni tapped the papers on the table. 'Is'sa my nature to help people. We make'a arrangement we both understan'. I read'a all that stuff. You need'a six'a million the first year an' the same in the second. Pounds. Is'sa right?'

'In total, yes. That's what it adds up to.'

Extending a finger, Moroni poked Todd in the chest. 'We do business as frien'. Eh? You an' me. I lenda the money. Go to Paris an' see Lapiere. Fix everything up. Is'sa six million now. A year from now is'sa same. Huh? Twelve million. Pounds. Two years from now you pay me six million back. Three years from now, you pay the rest.' Moroni smiled. 'See? Simple. No complications.'

111

Todd's heart thumped. His spirits soared. He imagined Hank's reaction. Hank would be ecstatic. They could sign the contract with the builders, work could start, the project would cease to be a dream and become reality. Bursting with excitement, he struggled to contain his feelings. Inwardly he exulted. It had been so easy! What he'd said to Leo was true: *It's not what you know but who you know!* His brain whirred like an over-wound clock. The rate of repayment was faster than ideal, but it was manageable thanks to his agreement with Suntours.

A look of benign satisfaction came to Moroni's face. 'Is'sa deal?'

Todd grinned and held out his hand. 'You won't regret it, Mr Moroni.'

Moroni had no intention of regretting anything. 'An' you pay interest at'a twenty per cent,' he said.

The smile faded on Todd's face. 'Twenty?' He had expected twelve, perhaps even fourteen or fifteen, but twenty! He shook his head. 'That's, er . . . well, that's a bit high, it's way above market rate –'

'So go to the market. Go to these men who wanna sleep with your wife. Huh? What'a they do for you? You gotta no market.' Moroni stared at the Englishman, rebuking this show of impertinence.

Staring into those dark eyes, Todd sensed an implacable will.

'My terms are my terms,' said Moroni, looking severe. 'I don' argue.' He allowed a long moment to pass, then relaxed his face muscles a fraction. 'Is'sa only right you want the best deal. But remember, my frien', you get my money now. Make it work for you. Do what you like. Is'sa your business. I don' interfere.'

Nodding slowly, Todd realized the truth of what had been said. It would be possible to invest the money until the stage payments were due to the builder. He could earn interest on the money he retained. That would reduce the impact of twenty per cent . . .

Moroni said, 'An' interest will be pay every half year.'

Again Todd betrayed his dismay. 'But we haven't an income until we open Paloma Blanca.'

With a bored look, Moroni sat back in his corner and closed his eyes as if wishing to commune with himself in private.

Fearful of interrupting, Todd said hesitantly, 'I suggested to Monsieur Lapiere that interest be allowed to accrue until we get our money from Suntours. Then we can begin repayment of capital plus accrued interest.'

Frowning with concentration, Moroni remained silent for a long moment. Finally he opened his eyes. 'Is'sa no possible,' he sighed with a shrug. 'I took'a you for a reasonable man. My frien'?' His reproachful look suggested that a mistake had been made.

'I don't wish to be unreasonable,' Todd protested.

'I have to eat. I have bills. Huh? These people . . .' Moroni gestured towards the men surrounding the car '. . . have wives, *bambini*.' He shook his head to signal his last words on the matter, 'Is'sa no possible,' he said, hardening his voice. 'Interest must be paid every six months. There is no more to say.'

Todd's spirits plunged. To have come so close! He wondered if he could finance the interest from his motor business? That would be the only possibility. It would be a heavy burden, but it *might* be possible. Given a bit of expansion, say a fifteen or twenty per cent increase in sales. Frowning with dismay, he said, 'It needs thinking about.'

Moroni's eyes seemed devoid of curiosity. His expression was a study in indifference, as if the four point eight million pounds he would make if Todd said yes was of no consequence. Inwardly he had no doubt that Todd would say yes.

The intense stare made Todd uncomfortable. Apologetically he said, 'It won't be easy to pay interest every six months. Perhaps I should discuss it with my accountant? Er . . . could I contact you tomorrow, perhaps?'

Moroni shook his head. 'Is'sa not possible. Tomorrow I go away for six week.'

'Six weeks!'

Moroni raised his hands palm upwards. 'You frien' of Leo Sinclair,' he said in the injured tone of a man who was trying to be reasonable. 'Is'sa urgent, you say. So I see you at once. Now is'sa not so urgent.' He shrugged. 'You wanna do business,

I 'ave to tell Lapiere. He fix'a the money tomorrow. Now you wanna wait six weeks!'

'No, I mean . . .' Todd interrupted fearfully. Six weeks was out of the question. 'I mean . . .' he took a deep breath as he realized what Moroni had said. 'You mean I could fix everything up tomorrow?'

Moroni shrugged. 'Go to Paris an' see Lapiere. Sure, fix everything up. But you pay'a interest on time. You pay'a on the day. Understand? Every six months. Is'sa important. You don' pay an' . . .' he drew a finger across his throat. 'Huh? Our arrangement is finished.'

'Like an overdraft.' Todd nodded, swallowing hard. 'The full sum becomes repayable on demand.'

Moroni studied him for a moment. '*Si*, I demand,' he said darkly, then his sternness disappeared into a smile. 'Is'sa no problem, huh? You hones' man, frien' of Leo Sinclair. You won' let me down. Go to Paris an'' he stopped, struck by a sudden thought. 'One more thin'. Your health is'sa important to me, yes? Somethin' bad happen to you, and . . .' he puffed out his cheeks. 'Poof. I lose'a my money. So you take'a out insurance. Eh? No problem. Somethin' happen to you, the insurance pay me.' He smiled broadly. 'Is'sa give me enough to send flowers to your funeral.'

He kept it from Katrina. She knew he had been to Rome because he bought her some perfume in the duty free shop, just as the week before he had bought her a present at Charles de Gaulle airport – but he said nothing about Moroni. What was the point? She would only nag about him taking time off from his business. And if he told her about Moroni he would have to tell her about Leo, which would lead to another argument. Besides, any description of Moroni would scare her to death. So he said not a word. Even to Hank on the telephone, he simply said he thought he could raise the money from 'a small outfit in Paris'. But he had to disclose at least some of the details to Manny. Manny had been his accountant ever since he had started. He liked Manny. He respected Manny. Manny had been the source of much good advice. He had to explain quite a lot to Manny, including his urgent need to insure his life for twelve million pounds.

They argued for hours. A whole morning. 'Why?' Manny shouted. 'You've got a good business here. Why take the risk?'

'It's the challenge. I've still got an urge to climb mountains.'

Manny threw up his hands. 'A mountaineer all of a sudden. Read the papers, why don't you? Men break their necks climbing mountains. How long have I been your accountant? Did I ever give you bad advice? Would I tell you to jump off a cliff? Or put your head in an oven? So now I say this. Don't do this, Toddy! Don't do it!'

'But if we tighten our belts for two years –'

'A noose!' Manny shouted insistently. 'You tighten a noose. You gotta be nuts to do this! Out of your mind!' Jumping to his feet, he began to pace the office in a state of agitation. Physically he was not dissimilar to Todd; an inch or two taller, ten years older, his round face more florid, but his waistline betrayed a similar comfortable plumpness. Not that he was at all comfortable at that moment. He was decidedly uncomfortable. 'Twenty per cent!' he shouted, his face mottled with temper. 'This is your idea of making money? I'll tell you how to get rich. Find some schmuck and lend him twelve million at twenty per cent.'

'But it's *not* twenty per cent. I told you. I worked it out. I'll get a safe twelve per cent on the overnight money market –'

'Correction!' Mannie interrupted, wagging a finger as he returned to his chair. '*I* get a safe twelve per cent –'

'Okay, thanks to you, I'll get twelve per cent. So we deposit this six million and pay the builder in dribs and drabs. Stage payments, remember? We'll earn enough to reduce the real cost to about fourteen per cent –'

Manny slapped a hand to his head. 'Only for the first year. Anyway, how you going to pay? You don't get any money until you open Paloma Blanca.'

'I just told you. We'll fund the interest from here.'

Manny groaned. His facial muscles twitched into a grimace of pain. His eyes bulged. 'Know what it adds up to?' he asked angrily. 'In the first year? Even after you've played put and take with the overnight market. Eight hundred and forty thousand –'

'We'll manage.'

'Oh yeah?' Slumped in his chair, Manny's voice became hoarse. 'You got a special way of adding up? Like some system I don't know about? Last year you made seven hundred grand. Both businesses combined. So how's it possible to pay eight hundred and forty thousand? You already used your cash reserves buying the site –'

'We were fifteen per cent up last year. If we get the same increase this year –'

'If,' Manny sneered.

'But it's possible!'

'So's swimming the Channel. Most people drown. And look at the second year. Know what you need? Over two million –'

'In two instalments,' Todd interrupted. 'We get the money from Suntours by the time the second instalment comes due. Seven and a half million, remember? I know it's tight, but –'

'You won't make it. Okay, the first year, it's possible. And when you get the money from Suntours, you can make the last payment. That's possible too. But you won't get that far. Don't you understand? That third payment – the one a year and a half from now – that one will kill you!'

'I think you're wrong,' Todd retorted, white-faced and determined. 'Anyway, it's a risk I'm going to take.'

'Yeah? Well I think you're crazy. And this insurance you asked me about. I spoke to my client the broker. Abe Katzman. You met him, remember, that day at the races?'

'So can he fix me up?'

'You're talking big money, you know that? Insuring your life for so much. You think we're talking petty cash here?'

'So how much?'

'First you get a medical. Abe's fixing that for tomorrow. Lucky it's only a physical.' Manny tapped his head. 'A shrink would say you were nuts.'

'So, okay, I'll have a medical. I'm feeling okay.'

'You're overweight. For that they charge extra.'

'I'll diet.'

'And you smoke. They charge more –'

'I smoke cigars. It's cigarettes they worry about.'

'For twelve million!' Manny cast his eyes upwards in a plea to God to give him patience. 'Believe me, for twelve million they worry about everything.'

'So? What did Abe say it would cost?'

'You don't wanna know,' Manny snorted and then paused for effect. 'I'll tell you the cost of this madness. At least fifty grand. See? Your overheads are soaring already.'

Todd whistled. 'So's my blood pressure.'

'Well don't tell Abe. The premium will go up.' Manny snorted again as he began to stuff his papers back into his brief-case. 'Oh and by the way, this medical. Did I tell you? These days they test for HIV. You leading an active sex life?'

Taken by surprise, Todd pulled a face and managed a sarcastic response. 'Oh sure,' he said drily. 'I'm about as active as Errol Flynn.'

'The movie star? Boy, he was active.'

'Not for the last twenty years,' Todd said gloomily. 'I think I stopped the same time he did.'

CHAPTER FOUR

RESTLESSLY HE TOSSED AND TURNED. Bedclothes rode up over his face, causing him to snort and to utter a shuddering groan. He clawed at the linen which had become tangled around his neck.

Coughing and choking, he could feel his head being torn from his shoulders. Blood was soaking his pillow. He cried out and sat bolt upright. Staring into the grey early morning light, he clutched his throat before patting the pillow; searching for blood, and finding only the damp patch of sweat.

Moroni! He had been dreaming about Aldo Moroni. He fell back, his breath coming in gasps as his terror subsided. The dream had been so vivid, so real! Turning on to his side, he reached for the comforting warmth of Katrina, only to discover the bed empty beside him. Startled and disoriented, his mind stalled for a moment. Then it came back to him. He began piecing together the events of the previous evening. He recalled their quarrel and her storming off to the Middletons. He remembered drinking all night, then going late to bed, and later still the noise she had made when she returned to slam her way into the guest suite.

'Oh, Jesus!' he moaned into the pillow. 'Why do we fight all the time?'

Last night he had dined on cheese and pickles and a great deal of whisky. Now as the taste of bile rose rank in his mouth, he wished he had eaten more wisely.

A shower helped, but only marginally; his head still ached, and dizziness engulfed him when he put on his shoes. Downstairs, dressed and ready for the office, he opened the kitchen door and sucked in lungfuls of air. He made some coffee and carried his cup over to the open door where he watched Mac bound across the lawn, barking at starlings. The din cut through his head like a buzz saw. To escape the noise he shuffled back into the kitchen where he sat on a stool, grumbling under his breath, pinching the bridge of his nose, opening and closing his eyes as if testing his eyelids.

Dimly he recalled the previous evening. He cocked an ear, half-expecting to hear sounds of Katrina. He went out to the hall. At the foot of the stairs, he looked upwards, thinking to see her on the way down. But the stairs were empty and the landing deserted. Crooking his head, he stared at the guest suite, hoping the door might open. When it remained firmly shut, he retreated to the kitchen to consider their quarrel.

He had been *partly* to blame, he was fair-minded enough to admit that – it was *partly* his fault – but it took two to argue and Katrina was impossible about Leo, bloody impossible. Sipping his coffee, he remembered them arguing about the Middletons. 'Better you don't come,' she had shouted. 'I don't want you to come.'

'Your decision,' he grumbled aloud. 'I was getting ready.'

He listened again, but the only noise he could hear was Mac barking outside. 'If she comes down now,' he muttered under his breath. 'We can put an end to it.' In his mind he saw her apologizing, he imagined tears on her part and forgiveness on his. He saw himself being coaxed into a good-natured acceptance of her shortcomings, he could almost hear her pleading for him to forgive and forget . . .

'Fat chance,' he thought drily. Katrina did not plead for anything, least of all for forgiveness. She was a woman with strong opinions. Like her opinion of Paloma Blanca. Even now she had not been to the site. She refused. Even now, with Paloma Blanca more than half finished, with the builder coming in on schedule, with the project looking more glorious by the month. The scenic grandeur of the place took his breath away whenever he saw it, and he saw it every time he went to Marjorca. *He* saw it, not Katrina. She declined with a shake of her head. 'We'll only argue,' she would say. 'Best you go by yourself.' So while she remained at the villa or drove into Santa Ponza to visit Sam and

Pamela, he went with Hank to inspect progress at Paloma Blanca. Just to walk over the site made them as excited as schoolboys. The thrill of ownership was as powerful as their anticipation of the profits. 'Not bad, eh,' Hank would say, slapping his shoulders. 'An old salt like me and a grease monkey like you, owners of one of the finest hotels in the world! Won't be long now, Toddy ole buddy, won't be long now!'

Nor would it be. Sixteen months into the project they were eight months from completion. Horrendously over budget, but exactly on schedule. And *still* Katrina refused to look at the place.

Her attitude marred his enjoyment. He lived for the completion of Paloma Blanca. It was the one scrap of hope floating on a sea of misery which politicians had dubbed a recession. Recession! It was a full-blown slump as far as he was concerned. People had stopped buying cars; customers were delaying decisions, making old models last longer, haggling for discounts and generally being a pain in the arse. His business projections had been cut to ribbons. Profits were down, the cash flow was tight, bankers were behaving like frightened old women. Meanwhile he had to meet the interest payments to Aldo Moroni. He had to find money from *somewhere*.

His gloom was interrupted by the ringing of the door bell, heralding the arrival of Herbert. Swallowing the last of his coffee, he picked up his jacket and slipped it on as he walked into the hall. He paused at the foot of the stairs. 'One last chance,' he thought hopefully as he looked upwards. 'Come down now and Herbert can wait while we have a coffee together.'

But Katrina remained silent upstairs and he turned and went out to the car, slamming the front door behind him.

'Morning, Boss.'

'Morning, Herbert.'

He glared as they passed the Middletons' house. 'Dickheads,' he muttered. 'Arseholes!'

He gazed with distaste at the well-known streets as they set off along the familiar route.

Grey skies, as grey as Welsh slate, reflected his mood.

'Forecast says it will clear up later,' said Herbert, uncomfortable with the bleak silence.

'Bloody well needs to,' Todd muttered, glaring balefully at the rain-slicked streets.

Herbert eyed Todd's unhealthy pallor. 'Heavy night last night?'

It could have been a *good* night. They could have joined Leo's party at the Ivy. With that girl Charlie. They could have had some fun for a change. Mumbling under his breath, he picked up the newspaper which Herbert always brought with him. With sightless eyes he stared at the headlines. His thoughts were elsewhere. He tried to remember when he'd last had some fun. The past eighteen months had been one unremitting slog. He had cut costs in his motor businesses, stretched resources, watched the pennies. Every day was a battle. Day after bloody day . . .

All of Moroni's twelve million had gone. All of it! The total cost would be nearer fourteen million by the time Paloma Blanca was finished. Not that he blamed Hank. Hank was doing a marvellous job in keeping the project on schedule. And he had made the ultimate sacrifice when Don Antonio's *extras* had soared over budget. The regulars at the Crow's Nest had been astounded. Hank's life had been one long procession of women, here today and gone tomorrow, the departure of none of them had caused him much heartache . . . but to part with his boat! The sale of his ocean-going sloop, *The American Dream*, had made headlines throughout the Balearics. Buyers had come from Barcelona, Nice, Southampton, the Adriatic, even from Sydney, Australia. Hank had attended the auction, looking grim-faced and shaken, but he had gone through with it – all for the sake of Paloma Blanca.

Todd's own boat had raised a pittance by comparison, but he had sold it as well. 'Who gets time to go sailing?' he had said to Katrina. 'I won't even miss it.'

Liar. He did miss it. But what sickened him most was they might have coped with one disaster. It was the two together which had crippled him; Paloma Blanca costing much more than expected *and* the recession. Manny's words came back to haunt him. *Do this and it will kill you.* It *was* killing him. The first two interest payments had bled him dry. Now the third payment loomed on the horizon. In two months, unless a miracle happened, the third payment would defeat him.

He knew the figures by heart. The next interest payment was for one point two million. He had expected, forecast, *relied* upon the motor businesses to earn at least six hundred thousand. Instead the best he could hope for was four hundred thousand. Hank was throwing in the profit from the Crow's Nest; that could be another two hundred thousand. He had arranged a mortgage on his house for three hundred thousand. Katrina would go spare if she found out. 'Ignorance is bliss,' he told himself glumly, as he calculated that he was still three hundred thousand short.

'Bloody recession,' he cursed under his breath. He might have pulled it off without the recession. Even Manny admitted he was surviving better than most. But the cash flow got tighter all the time. More and more was going out, less and less was coming in . . .

And Katrina was no help. She was no fun. They still made love, but less often. When was the last time she made the first move? It's always left to me. Our sex life is worse now than when she had that broody patch. Worse than when she used to cry, *We're supposed to be making a baby, not just enjoying ourselves.* Too bloody right! But that phase had passed. Her appetite had returned with the house, with holidays in the sun, and above all, with the villa in the harbour. Regular and joyful sexual congress had returned. Married bliss had returned – until Paloma Blanca had become a bone of contention.

His frustrated ponderings were interrupted by their arrival.

'Here you go, Boss,' said Herbert, with attempted cheerfulness. Rebuffed earlier, he had completed the journey in silence, deciding it was a bad day for small talk. Others were quick to reach the same conclusion. As Todd walked through the doors, Jimmy Davis, the showroom manager, looked up and remembered an urgent telephone call. Jill Daniels, the receptionist, busied herself arranging some showcards. And upstairs in the office, Sally hurried off to make some coffee. She met Bill

Hawkins, the workshop foreman at the top of the stairs. 'Is it urgent?' she asked with a warning look. 'If not, I'd leave him for a while.'

'Oh? Like that is it? He was a bit touchy yesterday.'

'And the day before. I don't know what's up with him lately.'

Todd knew exactly what was up. He scowled as he settled at his desk. His brow knitted as he stared at the colour photographs of Paloma Blanca on the opposite wall. Like a man serving a prison sentence, he had no escape. Of course everything would come right in the end – his confidence in the future was undented, everything would come right when they got their money from Suntours – it was the everyday grind of *now* that was getting him down. The relentless pressure. The robbing of Peter to pay Paul. It was being hemmed in by worries that was making him claustrophobic, making him want to break out, creating a yearning restlessness which he might have associated with the onset of spring had he been younger.

Sally opened the door and brought in his coffee. 'You're not looking too well,' she said as she put the cup on his desk.

He managed a weak smile. 'One too many last night, that's all.'

'Oh,' she said softly with sudden understanding. 'Can I get you anything? Aspirin –'

'Thanks, just coffee.'

The coffee helped. Black and sweet, hot and strong. Exactly to his taste. The dull pounding in his temples lessened and he began to concentrate on his problems. The villa would have to be sold. It was the only way of raising the extra three hundred thousand. He had tried to avoid it, but he had pledged and hocked everything else. The bank refused to lend him another penny. He had planned to discuss the matter with Leo last night, hoping he might have some ideas.

Katrina would go ape. His heart sank at the prospect of another quarrel. If only she would see it for what it was. A short-term cash flow difficulty. It would be worth it in the end. In eight months Paloma Blanca would be finished, they'd get their money from Suntours and their problems were over. If only she would see it in that light, it would lessen his guilt. If she relaxed, he could relax. They could take it in their stride, have some fun for a change.

He should have told her weeks ago. It had been on his mind. He would have to tell her soon. Time was getting short. Hank was already looking for a buyer, keeping his ears open, asking around. If that failed he would have to put the villa in the hands of the real estate people in the harbour.

Gnawing his lip, he wondered if the real reason for their quarrel last night was simply that he had been steeling himself to raise the matter. Raising it now would be harder than ever.

'Lunch,' he decided. 'Ring her up and take her to lunch.'

Rare were their lunches together. In the past lunches had usually been celebrations of birthdays or anniversaries, often ending with a cab ride home and straight into bed. Lunches were full of good connotations, and if this was to be different at least she'd be in a good mood at the outset.

Apologize for last night, eat humble pie, then break the news gently . . .

As he chewed on a fingernail, making his plans, the telephone rang. Frowning, he picked it up. 'Who? Mr Sinclair? Oh, Leo. Right, put him through.'

'Toddy, old boy!' Leo boomed down the line.

Todd winced and held the phone away from his ear.

'Just wanted to say sorry about last night. Bit of a nuisance.'

'Yeah, I wish I could have come with you. You have a good time?'

'Absolute ball! You should have been there,' Leo laughed. 'You made a great hit with Charlie.'

'I did? You mean the redhead?'

'As if you'd forgotten,' Leo chuckled, amused by Todd's pretended nonchalance. 'You should have seen her last night. I tell you, she's one hell of a woman . . .'

By the sound of it, they'd had one hell of a night. Cradling the receiver under his chin, Todd reached for the first cigar of the day and listened enviously as Leo described dinner at the Ivy, more drinks at the Meridien, and gambling at Blatchfords. Leo laughed. 'We're going in and Charlie says, "Okay, fellers, I limit myself to five hundred in these places. That's my mad

124

money. Once I lose that, I'm off home to hit the sack. Usually takes me an hour."' He laughed again. 'We finally left at three this morning. She kept winning and winning. Everyone's around her table, watching and cheering her on, betting along with her. Guess how much she walked out with? Nineteen thousand!'

Todd whistled softly.

'She's on a roll,' Leo laughed. 'And she's got the hots for you. Take it from me, old boy, I know the signs. She said so herself. She described you, listen to this, as the sexiest thing she's seen in a long time.'

'You're kidding.'

'I'm not. Have you heard from her yet?'

'No.'

'You will. She was talking about her new car all through dinner, that was when she wasn't asking about you. I tell you, she's very attracted.'

The black coffee, the cigar, being told that a good-looking woman had found him attractive, were all doing their bit to dispel Todd's black clouds of depression. He was feeling immensely better than a few minutes before.

'Anyway,' said Leo. 'I gathered you wanted a chat? Trouble is I'm tied up all day, and I'm leaving midday tomorrow. Can you make breakfast in the morning? Here at the Ritz. Say at about eight?'

'Sure. I wanted your advice about our friend in Paris. The next payment's due in two months and . . . well, what with business being so lousy . . . you know, sales down and everything, I'm a bit worried. Naturally, everything will come right when we get the Suntours money –'

'Absolutely. Nothing like an ace up your sleeve. Let's go through it in the morning, old boy. And try not to *worry*. You were looking really down last night. Do yourself a favour. Sell the delicious Charlie a car and take her out for a drink or something. That'll cheer you up.'

The conversation left Todd feeling better than for days past. Leo was always a tonic. Nothing got him down. And his comments about Charlie . . .

The door opened and Sally came in. 'My word, you're looking brighter. I came to see if you wanted more coffee?'

'I'm okay.'

'You're certainly looking better. In fact, you look quite cheerful for once.'

'Don't you start.'

'It's a welcome change, that's all. I'll organize the balloons and the dancing girls, shall I?'

A picture of Charlie leapt into his mind. He saw her at the Ritz, felt her hand on his arm, heard her warm laughter – *Why don't you come with us? My treat. We'll have a few drinks here then go to the Ivy or somewhere.* He had sensed her disappointment when he had shaken his head.

'Leave the dancing girls to me, but tell Jim to make sure there's a red XJS in the showroom.'

'A red one.'

'Right, with sexy black upholstery,' he said.

And all thoughts of taking Katrina to lunch went out of his head.

In fact Katrina already had a lunch date. She was lunching at the Vineyard. It was the third Wednesday in the month, and she lunched there every third Wednesday with Sophie and Gloria. Experiences shared when they had lived together at Harrow had made them closer than sisters. They had met boys, dated together, compared notes, borrowed clothes, given parties, watched films, read books, lost their virginities and compared notes even about that. 'How was it for *you*?' Gloria had shrieked at the time. Even after the Swinging Sixties, at the start of the more sober Seventies, London had been fun. Being nineteen had been fun – twenty-one in Sophie's case – full of plans for the future. And the future, now the past and the present, had given them more or less what they wanted, although at the time only Sophie had known what she did want. Then, as now, she was a model – except that now she was also owner of the Bartleman Model School and the Bartleman Agency for Fashion Models, both started in the past ten years and both producing good profits. Intent on her career, Sophie indulged in countless relationships, whereas Gloria's joke was that marriage made her more money.

What had started as a regular get-together had become institutionalized into the rules of a club. Not that the Vineyard *was* a club, merely the smartest French restaurant in Hampstead, and the rules were less those invented by the proprietor than those devised by the women themselves. Unwritten and unspoken, but rules for all that – and strictest of all was the rule of attendance. Quite simply, unless any of them were sick, or on vacation, or had business commitments or house guests, they *had* to attend. Generally it was no hardship. The food was good, they enjoyed each other's company, there was always plenty to gossip about – they had no reason *not* to attend. But for Katrina, that Wednesday was different. That Wednesday she would have swapped a bowl of solitary gruel for the culinary delights of the Vineyard, for even as Pierre hovered to take their orders, questions were writ large in the eyes of her friends.

'How was Toddy *feeling* this morning?' Sophie asked in a voice warm with concern.

'Okay,' Katrina said, her voice carefully neutral.

'He went to the office, then?'

'Yes.'

'So he must have been feeling better?'

Katrina had no idea how he was feeling. She hadn't set eyes upon him since storming out the previous evening. When she returned, late and the tiniest bit tipsy, he was in bed and she had slept in the guest suite. Not that she had slept. Most of the night was spent tossing and turning, worrying about their quarrel, and the excuses she had made at the Middletons. 'Toddy's coming down with flu,' she had announced upon arrival. 'Eyes streaming and all the rest of it. Sweating buckets, poor lamb. I couldn't inflict him on you . . .' Despite the odd looks, she had been reasonably satisfied with her performance. For Julie's sake, she had worked hard to break the ice and make a success of the evening. Except that now, contending with the faint buzz of a mild hangover and facing her friends, she knew that her performance had failed to convince. 'Yes, well . . .' she said. 'You know Toddy. Nothing keeps him from work.'

'You're sure work is the only attraction?' asked Sophie, turning to Pierre. 'I'll have a steak tartare, please, Pierre, with lots of tabasco. But let's have one more bloody mary, all right, girls?'

Gloria nodded with happy acceptance. 'And make mine steak tartare too.'

As Pierre's gold pen raced over his pad, he cocked an enquiring eyebrow. 'With a delicious non-fattening salad, madame?'

'Please. Tossed, with plenty of dressing. But let's have the other drink first.'

'Very good, madame,' he nodded, taking Katrina's order for veal, before suggesting, 'Shall I send the *sommelier?*'

'God, no,' groaned the ladies in a chorus. 'Just Perrier.'

'What I mean,' Gloria said sweetly, returning to Katrina, 'is, don't you think Toddy spends an awful lot of time at the office?'

Katrina flushed. *Compared to whom?* she wanted to ask. Compared to Gloria's last husband who inherited a fortune and dabbled in antiques with little success? Born with an entire silver tea service in his mouth, he was always ready to take time off from business. Katrina's lips felt suddenly stiff. 'Toddy's always worked hard.'

'Mmm,' Gloria mused thoughtfully. 'When Peter worked *that* hard it was on a little blonde number who called herself his secretary. Needless to say, I had another name for her. The point is, lovey, nobody makes the entrance you made last night straight from a sick bed. Not unless you were responsible for hospitalizing the patient. Honey, you were *steaming* –'

'I was late,' Katrina countered, in an attempt to stem the inevitable.

'Boy,' Gloria giggled. 'Did you make up for it? I thought you'd drink the *men* under the table.'

Katrina set her empty glass down very carefully. Lighting a cigarette, she was relieved to see the steadiness of her hand. Inside she was churning. *Where was Pierre with that second drink? I could do with a double.* Clearing her throat, her voice came; false, brittle and bright. 'It was a party, wasn't it? Besides, I was on my own, without Toddy –'

'And didn't that guy Alec appreciate it? He had plans to enjoy you all night.'

Katrina flushed. Alec Jepson was a pain, like most of Mark's friends. She shared Todd's views about Julie's husband. Mark Middleton was a creep. Why Julie put up with him was a mystery. After all, she was not unattractive; a bit empty-headed perhaps, but quite amusing at times. She had a generous spirit and was unfailingly kind. Liking her, it made Katrina's blood boil to watch Mark walk all over her. 'Anyway,' she said lightly. 'Thanks for coming and helping out. Julie gets in such a flap —'

'She should shoot that husband of hers,' said Gloria.

Sophie pulled a face. 'Never again. Not even for you. I know they're neighbours and everything, but why on earth do you bother?'

Katrina frowned and tried to explain, 'It's just that Julie so obviously needs a friend —'

'What she *needs*,' Gloria interrupted, with a touch of impatience, 'is a good lawyer. Get her to call me. Anyway, enough about that bubble-brain. I want to hear about Toddy. What happened last night? One minute you're on the phone saying he's home and you'll be round in five minutes, then wham, bang, you arrive with smoke steaming out of your nostrils.'

'I told you, I was late, that's all. I hate being late.'

'Sure, and Toddy's fine and dandy one minute and at death's door the next? Come on, we know you from way back, remember?'

Pierre's return gave Katrina a moment's respite, but she knew she was losing the battle. Gloria was right, they *did* know her from way back.

'You'll tell us in the end,' Sophie urged. 'You can't kid a kidder. We've been at it too long.'

And so the story came out; that Todd had returned home in a foul mood, refused to go to the party, then confessed to seeing her father.

'It's the deception that hurts,' said Katrina miserably. 'Seven years! I mean, can you believe that? All this time and he's not told me. How could he *do* that?'

Instantly sympathetic, Gloria reached across the table to squeeze her hand. Sophie did the same in a gesture which seemed entirely instinctive. They were her friends, good friends from way back. They pursed their lips, tut-tutted at appropriate times, murmured mournfully and commiserated gently. They were compassionate, tender-hearted and caring as only true friends can be. To begin with. Then, when they moved to their table, they began to analyse the situation with the thoroughness of detectives searching for clues.

'Toddy does have a point, you know.' Sophie dabbed her mouth with a napkin. 'I remember now. You are a bit paranoid about your father.'

'So would you be, with a father like mine. He's a liar and a cheat and totally unreliable.'

'Just like a man,' Gloria commented drily.

'But Toddy's not like that,' Katrina said hotly. 'They're complete opposites. I can't imagine what they even find to talk about.'

'You, probably. You brought them together,' said Sophie. 'What I don't get is Toddy refusing to come to the Middletons *before* you argued. He'd already *decided*. Or did I get that wrong?'

'No, that's right.'

'There.' Gloria sighed and jutted her lower lip out in a pout. 'And I thought he liked me.'

'Of course he likes you. It had nothing to do with you, us . . . it was just he came home in this impossible mood.'

Sophie and Gloria exchanged knowing looks. Sophie cleared her throat and chose her words carefully. 'Well . . .' she said doubtfully, 'I have wondered lately. You two don't seem to be hitting it off as you used to.'

'Exactly,' agreed Gloria. 'I can remember when it was impossible to get a word in edgeways. Talk, talk, talk, that's all you did, and always to each other. We practically ceased to exist.'

'Nonsense,' Katrina interrupted crisply.

'No,' Sophie contradicted. 'That's how you were.'

Katrina fixed her with a resentful stare. 'We're the same as always. A bit older that's all –'

'Ah!' Gloria interrupted. 'Maybe that's it. How's your sex life?'

Katrina felt the colour rush to her face. 'None of your business.'

Unabashed, Gloria smirked. 'Okay, if it's nothing to write home about don't tell us, but –'

'It's . . . quite satisfactory, thank you.'

'Satisfactory? What sort of word's that? I'm talking about good old-fashioned humping, not the state of the drawing-room curtains.'

'Tell us to mind our own business if you like,' said Sophie. 'But we do *care* about you. Both of you. Toddy as well. And something's wrong –'

'Nothing's wrong. He just came home in a bad mood, that's all.'

'In that case,' said Sophie, with the slightest shrug of her shoulders, 'there's only one question.'

Katrina looked puzzled.

'Who is she?' said Gloria, nodding.

'Who's *who*?' Katrina's eyes rounded.

'The woman. There *has* to be a woman. Toddy's not the kind to behave badly unless there's a reason.'

'Oh, no.' Katrina shook her head. 'There isn't a woman. I'd know if there was. He's been working hard, worrying a lot, that's all. Business isn't good at the moment. This recession –'

'We know about the recession,' Sophie interrupted. 'We also know Toddy. Kind, generous, considerate. We love him dearly. But when this kind, generous, considerate man spends more and more time at the office, then flips his lid over a simple thing like going to dinner –'

'I don't believe it,' Katrina said sharply. 'Toddy's not that sort.'

'They're *all* that sort, lovey,' Gloria sighed with an air of resignation.

'But I'd have *known*.'

'Like you knew about him seeing your father?'

Katrina had not been feeling hungry when she sat down. Now

her appetite vanished entirely. Setting her knife and fork on the plate, she looked askance at Sophie.

Sophie said, 'Darling, face up to it. You've had a good run. How long have you been married?'

'Ten years.' Pushing her plate away, Katrina turned in her chair and searched for Pierre. 'Ten years and five months.'

'Is it really ten years?' Gloria asked, almost in awe. 'That must be some sort of record. Men get tired of the same trade, same thing, day in and day out. They figure they deserve a little variety to put the spring back in their step.'

'How old is Toddy?' asked Sophie.

'Forty-five,' Katrina answered absently as she caught Pierre's eye. 'Pierre, I'll have another of your bloody marys.' She glanced across the table. 'Any other takers?'

Gloria and Sophie shook their heads, regret on their faces.

Pierre inspected Katrina's plate. He looked pained and sounded faintly offended. 'Did madame not enjoy her lunch today?'

'I'm more thirsty than hungry.'

Sophie watched Pierre retreat to the bar. 'Dangerous age, forty-five. Male menopause and all that.'

'Oh, shut up!' Katrina flushed with irritation. 'It's all very well to joke —'

'Steady on,' Gloria soothed gently. 'Something's wrong, you said so yourself. Toddy's acting strangely. We're asking why? That's all. I mean last night was unprovoked, wasn't it? I bet you were running around as usual, the way you always do when he comes home —'

'You *do* pamper him, Katrina, you know you do. I've said so before.' Sophie's mild disapproval made clear that she expected her men to pamper her, never the other way about. And they usually did.

Katrina opened her handbag, took out her cigarettes, and was fumbling for her little gold Dupont when Pierre returned. 'Allow me, madame.' After lighting her cigarette, he set the bloody mary in front of her and cleared the plates from the table.

Sophie watched the eagerness with which Katrina reached for

her glass. 'Hair of the dog? Sweetie, you do put it away, you know,' she said in the cautioning tone of a hospital matron. 'How much *are* we drinking these days?'

'Most of this is tomato juice,' Katrina muttered defensively, her nerves jangling as she waited for the vodka to bite.

'Maybe,' Sophie sounded doubtful, 'but I bet you have a couple before dinner, then wine with the meal and brandy afterwards. Then a nightcap because you can't sleep. Aren't I right?'

Katrina sipped her drink while she considered the question. She *was* drinking too much. She knew it. A couple of drinks while preparing dinner had become habit, and then, because Toddy was late getting home, one, maybe two more while she waited.

'It all mounts up, honey. I have to be terribly strict.' Gloria's eyes narrowed as she studied Katrina. 'You *are* beginning to get a little heavy in the upper arms, you know. Once that sort of weight gets a grip, it's the devil's own job to shake off. And you've always been a big girl.'

'I'm not fat,' Katrina retorted, patting her arms. 'You can't call me fat.'

'No one's saying that. It's just that it's best to be careful at our age.'

Katrina felt something shrivel inside, as if her body were trying to escape. A shudder ran up her spine.

Sophie said, 'Darling, I don't want to be crass or anything, but didn't your mother have some sort of problem . . .' Her voice died with the look of pain in Katrina's face. 'Oh honey, I'm sorry. Really. I'm not being bitchy. It's just that booze can get such a hold.'

'Sophie's right,' Gloria said, sitting upright in the armchair. 'Why don't you go to Broadlands with her tomorrow? A week would work wonders.'

Set in eighty acres of Sussex countryside, Broadlands was the most exclusive health club in England. Sophie went every year and returned as radiant as a bride.

'Tomorrow?' Katrina exclaimed, shaking her head. 'I can't drop everything just like that.'

'Why not?'

'Don't be silly. It's out of the question. Toddy would be lost without me. Besides we're off to Majorca in a week or so's time.'

'Screw Majorca.'

'No, I can't. I want to see Pamela and Sam, and besides there are things to do at the villa. We need to shut the pool down, things like that.'

'Let Toddy fix it. That's your trouble. He takes you for granted. Shake him up. He needs it. Go to Broadlands and get yourself a new body, a new hairstyle –'

'I'm not sure. It's so expensive.'

'Good! That *will* shake him up. In fact that's the answer. Spend some serious money! Get yourself a new wardrobe, the whole works.'

'I don't know. One way and another, we spend an awful lot –'

'Does he care? I bet he's not counting money with this girl-friend of his.'

'You don't *know* there's –'

'Oh, sure,' Gloria interrupted scornfully. 'We don't *know*, but believe me, something's on a man's conscience when he can't stand ordinary pressures. Why else would he blow his stack like that? You haven't been fighting lately, have you?'

'Fighting?' In a different mood, Katrina might have laughed. 'We haven't been doing anything. He's hardly home –'

'Exactly!'

In all fairness, Todd's behaviour that day was unusual. He was not a promiscuous man. His background – his early life working long hours in the garage, the pressures of running a business, not to mention a marriage that worked for most of the time – all conspired to make him unusually faithful. To look at other women was one thing, to do something about it another.

But he had been restless for days. For weeks, even months he had been burdened by worries.

And he had enjoyed meeting Charlie at the Ritz. He had sensed her disappointment when he had not joined them for the evening. He felt she had *liked* him and he'd *liked* her, but for

God's sake – what Leo had suggested was stronger than liking . . .

So he spent the morning anticipating her visit. His hangover lifted and went. He even cracked jokes when discussing workshop matters with Bill Hawkins. But when lunchtime arrived without bringing Charlie, he felt a pang of disappointment. For some reason he had expected her at midday. He had seen himself taking her to his local Italian restaurant; imagined the other customers, most of whom he knew, craning their necks to see who he was with and had revelled in their envious looks. However, at one-forty, when there was no sign of her, he was compelled to make a decision. To go out for a late lunch meant he might miss her, so Sally was despatched to the shop on the corner in search of a sandwich.

By two-thirty his expectations had greatly diminished.

An hour later he had given up hope, which was when the telephone rang and Jill Daniels, the showroom receptionist, said, 'There's a lady here to see you. A Miss Charlotte Saunders.'

His heart pounded. 'Okay,' he said, careful to keep the excitement out of his voice. 'I'll be right there.'

He went to his washroom, combed his hair, straightened his tie and hurried downstairs.

Davis was drooling all over her by the time he entered the showroom. Charlie was admiring the car and Davis was admiring Charlie. Not that he blamed him. As she twisted and turned to inspect the car, her unbuttoned coat swirled like a cloak, revealing a short-skirted black dress and long, shapely legs. The fluorescent lights gave an extra sparkle to her coppery hair, and she moved with an energy which belied someone who had been up until the small hours. She turned to greet him with a dazzling smile. 'Hi! Isn't this great? It's exactly what I want.'

She was even more glamorous than he remembered. A grin came over his face.

'That's better,' she said approvingly. 'You look pleased to see me.'

'Of course I'm pleased –'

'No, I mean *really* pleased. I wasn't sure last night. You were

135

sort of grouchy. I thought you disapproved of me letting my hair down.'

'No, no. I wish I could have joined you. I gather you had quite a night.'

'It was great! Sensational. Hey?' Her green eyes rounded with surprise. 'How did you know?'

'Leo called me.'

'Oh, I see. For a minute I thought we'd made the papers. You know, Casino Owners complain to Gambling Board or whoever. I imagined them calling a Steward's Enquiry or something,' she giggled. 'Did Leo tell you how much I came out with?'

'He did. Congratulations.'

She laughed. 'Boy, I could have fallen in the Thames and come out dry. Every number came up. You should have seen their expressions. Croupiers had smiles screwed to their faces. When the floor manager congratulated me, I swear he spoke without moving his lips.'

Her laughter was wonderfully infectious. When she laughed, he laughed, gripped by a growing excitement.

Stepping backwards, she gave him a quizzical look. 'Know something? You look really good when you laugh. It suits you. You've got a nice happy face.' She turned to Davis for confirmation. 'See the way his eyes go all crinkly? Cute. Don't you think?'

Davis choked and gulped hard.

Todd felt ten feet high.

'And isn't this gorgeous?' Charlie turned back to the car. 'It's exactly what I want. Wrap it up, I'll take it. Second thoughts, don't bother to wrap it, I'll take it as it is,' she laughed again with unrestrained exuberance. 'I think I'm still celebrating. I feel like it's Christmas. You enjoy Christmas?'

'Sure —'

'Last night was Christmas Eve, today's Christmas Day and . . .' she placed a hand on the roof of the car '. . . and this is my present.'

She was as effervescent as champagne. He remembered thinking the same about her at the Ritz. And everything she said, indeed her entire manner, suggested she was as pleased to see

136

him as he was to see her. 'You're right,' he laughed. 'It *does* feel like Christmas.' Opening the car door, he asked, 'Why not try it behind the wheel?'

As she stepped in, her heel caught the hem of her coat. 'Oh heck! I get it. Rule number one. Don't wear a coat.' Within a minute she had discarded it and was wriggling behind the wheel. 'Wow! Smell that leather. I love it! Couldn't you get off on that smell? Who needs coke? I've got goose bumps all over.'

Not that he could see any on her shimmering thigh.

Once he had explained the layout of the dashboard and everything else, he suggested that they go for a test drive.

'Great,' she smiled. 'Let's do that. It's a lovely afternoon.'

And so it was. Looking through the showroom windows, he realized that the sun had come out, exactly as Herbert had predicted. Patches of blue had appeared amid the grey. The heavy overcast was giving way to puffy white clouds. The streets were drying out, leaving puddles glinting in the afternoon sun.

'Not just round the houses,' she warned, putting a hand on his arm. 'I want to get the feel of that engine. I've been cooped up on Jersey. Did you ever drive over there? Of course not, I remember, you've never been. Well, I can tell you, the longest straight road's only about a hundred yards long.'

'Right, we'll go for a *proper* drive,' agreed Todd who, having spent most of the day waiting for her, had no intention of doing anything less.

Indecision makes bad drivers. There was nothing indecisive about Charlie. Kicking off her high heels, she drove in her stockinged feet. Within minutes she had mastered the feel of the car, her hands were sure on the wheel, and her road sense was perfect. He directed her to the motorway without hesitation. They talked as she drove, exchanging sideways glances, full of smiles, already enjoying each other's company. In an expectant mood before she arrived, Todd's spirits rose. The rapport which he had sensed at the Ritz grew stronger than ever. Sitting close together, side by side, set them apart from the rest of the world. At one point, when he reached across to indicate how to switch

137

into overdrive, their foreheads touched and as they drew back they both smiled contentedly, their faces lit up by the mutual pleasure of being together.

For the first ten miles or so their conversation was about the car, but gradually the talk shifted to matters more general, and inevitably, since they had met through Leo, it was with Leo they started.

'He was fun last night. Really good company. He helped make the evening.'

'He's a good friend of mine,' Todd said warmly.

'Isn't he your father-in-law?' she asked with a quick sideways glance.

'Right. His daughter won't talk to him, so I'm a sort of go-between.'

'His daughter? You mean your wife?'

He wondered if he had avoided saying *wife*. Had it been deliberate? 'Yes,' he agreed cautiously, glancing at her, searching for a clue, but her eyes were on the road.

The corners of her mouth puckered. 'Must make it awkward for you.'

'And how,' he agreed heavily, staring at her knees as if they held the answer to the mystery of life.

'What's she got against him?'

'She claims he's the source of all evil.'

'Wonderful,' she giggled, accelerating into the fast lane. Her laughter drew his attention to her lips, soft and fresh with a mere smear of lipstick, reminding him that a discussion about Katrina was the last thing he wanted. 'Tell me about Jersey,' he said quickly. 'What is it you do exactly?'

Charlie answered with a laugh, 'Make money. It's the abiding passion on Jersey.'

She had been there for two and a half years. 'I signed a three-year contract with Bob Levit. It seemed a good idea at the time. What am I *saying*?' she exclaimed, horrified. 'It *was* a good idea. I've gained a lot of experience, made plenty of contacts, that sort of thing. The money's fantastic but the island's a bore. I can't wait to get back to London next year.'

'To do what?'

'They need a London office and I'm going to run it. At least that's the plan, but just lately . . .'

His heart pounded as he watched her skirt ride up over her knees. He stole little sideways glances at her face. *Vibrant*, he thought, *that's the word for her.*

'Just lately what?' he asked, trying to concentrate on what she was saying.

'Maybe I'm getting bored? You know? Moving money around for rich people is pretty easy once you get the hang of it. I need a new sort of challenge. Something where I meet more people. You know, face to face, not just on the phone . . .'

He admired the tilt of her nose and the way in which her mouth puckered at the corners. All sorts of descriptions came into his mind. *Vivacious. Desirable. Very desirable.*

Her sheer zest was exhilarating. He found himself comparing her with other women – Katrina's friends, customers, acquaintances made in Majorca – and found her unique in his experience. He probed into her private life, suspecting a liaison with Bob Levit, and was oddly relieved when she laughed at the notion. Amazingly she seemed not to have any man in her life.

'The last one of any consequence,' she said, 'was three years ago. Then it broke up and I had this offer to go to Jersey, and since then . . .' she turned to give him a quick smile. 'I could do with some new friends. Like I come over to celebrate and there's no one here to share a good time. Look at last night. Thank God we bumped into Leo and Frank like that. They were great. The whole night turned into a party . . .'

The talk flowed as the miles sped past. The sun slid towards the horizon, but neither of them heeded the lengthening shadows. There seemed so much to talk about. They talked as close friends, not new acquaintances, a fact due less to the enforced intimacy of the car than to her directness. Dispensing with small talk, she cut through normal convention. He thought it impossible that he had only just met her. And the more he told her, the more she responded. She was so *interested*, so enthusiastic about his plans for the future. He found himself boasting about Paloma Blanca, telling her about Hank and their contract with Suntours – revealing details which he would never have discussed with anyone else.

'Sounds marvellous,' she said. 'Paloma Blanca. Great name for it. Move over Conrad Hilton. Make way for Hank and . . .' she stopped in mid-sentence. 'I just realized, I don't know your first name.'

'Toddy,' he said quickly. 'Everyone calls me Toddy.'

'Everyone?'

'Sure.'

'Surely not *everyone*?'

She means Katrina, he thought. *She stopped short of saying 'your wife'. Why? Was that deliberate? And why am I pleased?*

'But you must have a Christian name?'

'I don't use it.'

'I don't use Charlotte but it's *there*. Charlotte Anne Marjory Saunders. It's all over the place; cheque books, passports, tax returns. You can't stop using your name.'

He shifted in his seat and stared at the road.

She slid him another look. 'I don't believe this. You're not going to tell me, are you?'

'It's not that. It's just . . . well, like I said, everyone calls me Toddy.'

'Why?'

'Because I hate the name I was given, that's why. I haven't used it in years. Not since I had any choice in the matter.'

'How intriguing,' she laughed. 'You may as well tell me. I'll worm it out of you in the end. I'm the curious sort.'

Rejecting one response, he thought of another, but before he could give it expression, she said, 'Give me a clue. What's it begin with?'

'C,' he said.

Idiot! Why did I tell her? I should have thought more quickly. I should have avoided . . .

'So it's the same as me. Charlie?'

'No, no, Charlie's okay. I like Charlie –'

'Claude?'

'No. I don't think –'

'Cedric?'

140

'No!' he exclaimed.

'Cecil?'

'For Christ's sake!'

'Cyril?'

He was on the point of inventing a lie when she interrupted him with a gurgle of laughter. 'It is, isn't it? It's Cyril!' A sideways glance at his dismay set her off into a fit of the giggles. She trembled with laughter. Her chest heaved and her hands shook on the wheel. Easing her foot on the accelerator, she moved into the slow lane, spluttering 'Sorry' between spasms of laughter.

'It's not that funny,' he protested.

'Cyril!' she shrieked.

Unable to stop himself, he started to grin.

'Cyril!' she snorted.

He laughed, and once started was helpless. He brayed like a maniac.

Halting the car on the hard shoulder, she collapsed over the wheel, tears streaming down her cheeks. 'You're right,' she spluttered eventually, gesturing an apology by putting a hand on his shoulder. 'I'm sorry. It's really not that funny.'

But every sideways glance provoked another outburst of mirth. Minutes passed before they fell into a gasping, panting sort of silence. Finally she eased back into her seat. Dabbing her eyes with a handkerchief, she inspected her mascara in the mirror. 'Whew,' she gasped softly. 'Oh, golly, I am sorry, honestly —'

'It's all right —'

'I didn't mean to be rude —'

'I told you,' he said ruefully. 'It's a bloody silly name, that's all.'

'Don't start me off again. I haven't the strength. Anyway, I take it all back. You're right. Toddy's a good name for you. You're like a cuddly teddy bear.'

His heart pounded when she looked at him. He sensed a new intimacy. The companionable warmth had already developed to something far deeper. It seemed to him that some sort of threshold had been crossed. He was sure of it when she leaned toward him and kissed him briefly on the cheek before turning away to look in the mirror.

He needed no further encouragement. Vague plans began to form in his mind as, with admiring eyes, he watched her dab the smears on her cheeks. For a moment, neither said a word. Traffic thundered past in the late afternoon sunlight, and with a start of surprise he realized that the clock on the dashboard registered six o'clock. Good God, was it that late already?

She peered through the windscreen. 'Where are we? Do you know?'

He had only an approximate idea. They must have driven at least sixty miles. As he began to place where they were, he felt a stab of alarm. He glanced at the fuel gauge. Cars taken from the showroom never had a full tank.

'What's up?'

Indicating the gauge, he said, 'We're almost empty.'

'Oh?' A teasing look came to her eyes. 'Now that's really corny. You'll have to do better than that. I was sixteen when I last heard that line.'

'What?' Colour rushed into his face. 'No, I mean, it's true –'

Cutting short his protestations, she reached over and put her hand on his arm. 'It's okay, I believe you,' she laughed. 'Although come to mention it, *I'm* empty. Know something? I haven't eaten since last night. I've just realized, I'm starving.'

Suddenly his ideas stopped being vague. He knew exactly what he would do, or at least what he would *try* to do, what he would *hope* to do. A sudden gleam came to his eye. 'You still feel like celebrating?'

'I'm not stopping now. Look at my record. I wiped them out at the casino, bought a new car, met a new friend. Celebrating's good for me.'

'Me too. I can't offer you the Ivy in this neck of the woods, but if we get off the motorway I know an old country inn where they serve fabulous food. Things like pheasant and venison and –'

'Stop!' She placed her fingers on his lips. 'You've got a date. My mouth's watering already. Let's go find your old country inn in . . .' she glanced through the window '. . . in whichever county we happen to be. Where the hell is this anyway?'

'Just north of Rugby,' he said, peering up the motorway and placing their whereabouts exactly. 'We'll take the next exit.

142

First we need a garage. Then I'll take you to a gourmet's paradise.'

'You're the boss,' she said, with a sideways glance which raised hairs on his neck.

A sudden excitement drove all other thoughts from his head. He could still taste her fingers on his lips. And before that, what had she said? *You're like a cuddly teddy bear.* And earlier, in the showrooms . . . *cute*, she had said. And Leo had said . . . *Oh, Jesus!*

The traffic noise faded when they turned off the motorway. As did the light. Dusk was settling, bringing a light downfall of rain. Street lamps on the rural secondary roads were few and far between. Driving on headlights, Charlie switched on the wipers. Beneath the companionable silence, he concentrated upon working out directions. The Jaguar people had once given him lunch at a place called Brislington Manor, near Rugby. They must be quite close to it. An old country hotel. Well-appointed and comfortable. He imagined the bedrooms; timbered ceilings over big four-poster beds. He gnawed his lip.

'Penny for them?' she asked suddenly, sliding him a sideways glance.

'I . . . er . . . was just thinking, I'm sure this is the right road. We must reach a garage soon.'

'There's no sign of one.'

'Keep going. We must come across one.'

But another five miles passed and they did not reach a garage. The sky darkened, the rain came on harder; beyond the hedgerows the empty fields stretched for miles, without even the lights of a farmhouse.

The gauge on the dashboard showed empty.

Suddenly they came upon a fork in the road. 'Turn left,' he commanded triumphantly. 'See that signpost? Four and a half miles to Brislington village. I knew we were near it.'

The road narrowed into a tree-lined lane. Branches joined over their heads, obliterating the fading light. 'It's as black as pitch,' cried Charlie, peering into the darkness. 'Really creepy. If we run out here, I'm staying put.'

'Me too. We'll spend the night in the car.'

'That could be fun,' she laughed.

Hear that! Oh, Jesus!

'What an adventure!' she laughed, her voice lifting with excitement.

He saw Brislington Manor in his mind's eye. He imagined Hank in the same situation. Hank the master seducer. Hank would have worked out an angle. Concentrating furiously, he imagined their arrival at the hotel . . . then it came to him exactly . . .

The lane twisted and turned. It rose and fell over a hump-backed bridge. Trees crowded to the edge of the road which narrowed until it was wide enough for only one lane of traffic.

He was wondering if somehow they had missed a turning, when the road curved around to the left and then widened before them.

'Ah!' Charlie exclaimed. 'Civilization.'

Looking ahead, he saw the lights of a village. They passed a pub, a church, and three or four shops before reaching the garage. 'Hang on,' he said when she stopped. 'I won't be a minute.'

He hurried across the forecourt. A bell tinkled as he opened the door to the office. An old man looked up from behind the counter. A teenage boy put down the paper he was reading and rose to his feet. 'Petrol, sir?'

'Fill her up, would you? And d'you know the best way to Brislington Manor?'

The old man nodded. 'Up the road, sir. About three miles. Big place, set back on the left.'

Triumphantly he returned to the car and strapped himself in. 'Just up the road,' he said, and minutes later, when she drove into the car park, he looked at the ivy-clad walls and exulted. Brislington Manor was every bit as impressive as he remembered. Squares of yellow light fell from big mullioned windows. Huge wooden doors, twenty feet high, stood open beneath massive stone lintels.

'This is a find!' Charlie exclaimed, stopping the car.

Peering out, she twisted with a movement which drew up her skirt.

As his gaze went to her legs, she turned back and caught the direction of his eyes. Her own lit with amusement. Without hurrying, she pulled down her skirt and looked at the huge wooden doors. 'Looks an interesting place,' she murmured.

'Too right,' said Todd with a growing ache in his groin.

Deliberately, he took her in by a side entrance. His memory served him well. The small bar in which they found themselves was heavy with oak and gleaming with brass. An unexpected but welcoming fire blazed in a stone hearth. The scent of pine logs mingled with furniture polish. Hunting prints decorated fine panelled walls. Deep armchairs were covered in chintz, and – best of all – although the buzz of conversation floated in from an adjoining bar, they had the place to themselves.

She had thrown her coat around her shoulders on her way from the car. As he reached to take it, she lifted her hand to her collar. When their fingers touched, he felt a shock through his body. He heard her quick intake of breath. Colouring slightly, she turned away, to stand in front of the fire, crossing her hands in front of her, rubbing her upper arms as if feeling cold.

'I'll go and find the dining-room,' he said, his voice sounding strangely husky.

She turned to look at him. Something in her eyes put a more powerful thought into his head. He remembered her saying, *I came over to London to celebrate and there's no one here to share a good time.* His heart pounded.

'You okay?' she asked.

He jumped. Avoiding her gaze, he turned to the small brass bell on the counter. Next to it a card bore a hand written inscription: *Please ring for service.*

'You looked sort of pensive.'

'No, er . . . I was wondering what to get you to drink.'

'A pink gin would be nice, but let me get the drinks while you check out the rest of the place.'

'Fine,' he said, wondering whether by *rest of the place* she meant the dining-room or something more intimate. He was already at the door when she called him. He turned with a guilty look on his face.

'What are you having?' she asked as she reached for the bell.

'Oh!' He laughed, a strangulated laugh, not at all his normal laugh. 'Scotch,' he said. 'A large Scotch.'

His pulse was racing when he went through the door. He wished he had learned from Hank, picked up some tips.

'Can I help you, sir?'

He had come into the lobby of the hotel. He remembered the wide oak staircase with ornate carved banisters which curved around to his left. To his right were a pair of large doors, while in front of him was a desk behind which sat a middle-aged woman with an expectant look on her face.

'What? Ah, yes . . .' he peered about him. 'We seem to have come in – '

'From the car park,' she nodded with an air of understanding. 'It often happens. Our main entrance is on the London Road. If you'd come that way you would have driven through the grounds to the front door.' She indicated the large doors with a smile and a wave of her hand. Then, with a smile, she asked, 'Will you be staying tonight?'

He almost lost his nerve. He was about to answer when he saw the leather-covered menus. 'Er . . . depends,' he muttered. Opening the folder, he cast his eye down a list of excellent dishes – pheasant, venison, game pie. Turning to the wine list he saw an excellent Beaune, a Nuits St Georges, a very good Montrachet . . .

It took him fifteen minutes to complete the arrangements, which included time spent searching for the machine on the wall in the gentlemen's toilet. Then, with a menu tucked under his arm and his heart thumping wildly, he returned to the cosy little bar.

Charlie was in an armchair at the fireside, sipping a drink. He saw his Scotch on the table next to her. Looking up, she smiled as he came in. 'You've been a long time?'

'I've been making arrangements.'

'Oh?'

Nodding, he flourished a menu. 'Having conferred with the chef, I can promise you something quite special.'

146

Her green eyes glimmered with amusement.

'I suggest oysters to begin with. That is, of course, if Madam likes oysters?'

'I adore oysters.'

'Then oysters and champagne, followed by . . .' he consulted the menu. 'Perhaps the pheasant with a bread sauce and game chips and –'

'Sounds mouthwatering.'

'Accompanied by at least one bottle of Nuits St Georges.'

'Oh, *at least* one,' she nodded, entering into the game. 'Two would be better.'

'An excellent suggestion –'

'And to finish,' she interrupted enthusiastically, 'large brandies in front of the fire.'

'Mmm,' he murmured, pretending to sound doubtful. 'But I do see a problem.'

She looked at him.

'After so much to drink, Madam would be ill-advised to drive her new car.'

Her eyes lit with amusement as she watched him over the rim of her glass. Setting her drink on the table, she folded her hands in her lap. 'Oh dear. So what would you suggest?'

His brow crinkled as he considered. 'I suppose,' he said, sounding disappointed, 'if I abstained, I could act as chauffeur?'

'That won't do,' she said with a shake of her head. 'Madam hates drinking alone.'

'Then if Madam insists –'

'Absolutely!'

'Then neither of us should drive.'

'Oh.'

The perfect oval of her lips reminded him so strongly of a particular sexual act that his penis threatened to burst through his pants.

'Ought we to enquire about room at the inn?' she asked coyly.

He bowed as much as his erection would allow. 'I've already taken that liberty, Madam.'

Her right eyebrow arched. 'With a view to taking further liberties?'

147

'If Madam permits.'

The long look which passed between them ended the banter. She studied his face intently for several seconds which to him seemed like hours. Then, softly, she said, 'Madam looks forward to it, on certain conditions.'

'Oh?' he exclaimed, too excited to imagine what she would say.

The glint of amusement faded from her green eyes. Her face became serious. 'You must know you attract me, otherwise you wouldn't have suggested it – you're not a letch, thank heavens, I wouldn't be here if you were. If we go to bed, fine, I think I'd like it, but I don't want to fall in love. That would be silly. Don't you agree?'

Lost for a response, he fumbled for words which might make him sound gallant. 'I . . . er, don't think I'd thought that far ahead, but I'm sure it's not just sexual.'

'Oh dear. Then we'd better call it off.'

'What?' he yelped in a horrified whisper.

'All I'm saying is I don't want to fall for a married man, and if you're honest you don't want to fall in love either. This is not an affair.'

'Oh,' he said in total confusion.

The smile returned to her face and she tilted her head to one side. 'So if we're honest with each other, I don't see a problem. Do you?'

He swallowed. 'No. No problem.'

'Did you get the key to our room?'

It was burning a hole in his pocket. 'It's a suite. Overlooking the lake, apparently.'

She held out her hand. 'Give me ten minutes,' she murmured with a heart-stopping smile.

Lunch had been ghastly. And to think Gloria and Sophie were friends! Some friends. Katrina had never known them so bitchy. On reaching home, she had marched up the stairs, slammed through the bedroom, flung herself into her dressing-room and kicked off her shoes. Mac had followed, to sit in the corner from where he watched with curious eyes, his head to one side and his tongue lolling out.

Flinging her coat over the couch, she stripped off her clothes until they were all piled on the couch.

Mac dribbled and panted.

'Atta boy,' she said drily. 'At least I get the right reaction from you.'

Naked before her mirror, she twisted one way, then the other, inspecting her body with critical eyes. Her legs were still good. Her breasts still firm. Her bottom had not sagged. Fat! Only a clothes-horse like Sophie would consider her fat. At least she had a bust line. She remembered Sophie's lack of inches from when they had lived in Harrow. Thirty-two! *Now* it might be thirty-two, it wasn't thirty-two then. Katrina had filled a thirty-six cup since her eighteenth birthday.

Pinching her upper arms, she squeezed them against her body, as if expecting to see flesh expand into biceps. Turning sideways, she stared at her stomach. She sighed, knowing she was not as flat as once she had been. 'Gently rounded,' she admitted, feeling defeated.

'But not *fat*!' Certainly not fat.

Dressed again, she sat in front of her dressing-table mirror and inspected her skin. *Even kids have laugh lines.* Laugh lines are different from wrinkles. Her forehead was still smooth. Drawing back her lips, she inspected her teeth. Good, white and even. Wearing a brace had mortified her as a child, but she had lived to bless the results. Tilting her head, she inspected her hair . . .

Her panic receded. Examining herself, she felt reassured. She was realistic enough to know she was not beautiful, but it was sensible to make the most of her looks and as far as she could see she was the same as the three-year-old photograph on her dressing-table.

'Come on,' she said to Mac as he followed her out on to the landing. Dutifully he padded downstairs.

She went from room to room, examining furnishings with a critical eye, searching for she knew not what. She had *tried* to create a comfortable home, a place to enjoy, an oasis in which Toddy could relax . . .

In his study she inspected the bottles in the cabinet. Scotch, gin, vodka, everything was there. She knew study was the wrong name for the room. Books lined the shelves, but Toddy's most avid reading was of balance sheets and technical journals. The room functioned more as a bar, used for drinks when people came to dinner, so that after the meal they could adjourn without finding the drawing-room full of used glasses and ashtrays. The desk belonged more to her than to him. It was where she did her accounts, where she wrote the cheques which kept the household running so smoothly. *And I do run a good house*, she told herself firmly.

Making tea in the kitchen, she carried her cup through to the snug – a large-windowed, south-facing room which took on the appearance of a conservatory in high summer. Even now it was rampant with greenery. Sinking into the sofa, she watched Mac clamber up beside her on to the only sofa in the house on which he was allowed. As she stroked him, she thought – *Things would have been different if we'd had children. But different might not have been better. Toddy had never wanted children, not really . . .*

'You're my baby, aren't you?' she cooed, playing with Mac's ear, allowing him to turn to lick her fingers. 'Perhaps I should go out to work? What do you think, Mac? Shall I leave you at home and take up a career?'

But what career? She could type and keep a set of books, but so could hundreds of others. And her typing had been on a typewriter, not the computers everyone used these days. Besides, Toddy *was* her career! Running two homes was a full-time job. Of course she had help – Mrs Bridges came in four times a week, old Tucker did the garden, Maria cleaned the villa in Majorca, Manuel looked after the pool – but *someone* had to organize them. *Someone* had to book the flights, do the shopping, stock the bar, cook meals, act as social secretary, fill in the forms, renew club memberships, pay the mooring fees, answer the phone . . .

'It's a dog's life,' she sighed to Mac.

150

He wagged his tail, making her laugh. 'Not true, is it? Anyway, what's wrong with a dog's life?'

Her perspective had been distorted over lunch. She had confided too much. Sophie's ideas and Gloria's views had been shaped by their own experiences, some of which left a lot to be desired in her opinion. Especially with men. Neither of them had sustained a lasting relationship. Sophie's string of boyfriends stretched back to the Ark, and Gloria had made a mess of her marriages. They were old friends and good friends, but sometimes she grew somewhat resentful. 'Damned cheek,' she complained out loud. 'Who do they think they are? Passing judgement like a pair of agony aunts.'

Mac snuffled and flopped his tail in agreement.

Indignation dispelled the last remnants of self-pity. She flushed as she returned to the kitchen. *We had a tiff. So what? It isn't the first. It won't be the last. But to think of another woman is ridiculous!*

She knew perfectly well what was wrong. Who would know better? Business was bad and had been for months. And on top of everything he had Paloma Blanca to worry about. Her lips tightened as she rinsed the cup under the tap. He knew her views. She blamed Hank. It seemed madness to her. Having a holiday home was one thing. They could just about afford that. But to borrow so much, twelve million pounds . . . *twelve million!* The very thought made her shiver. 'Speculate to accumulate,' he had grinned. She could have strangled him. He had worked so *hard*. They had a good life. Why risk everything? What was the need to accumulate more?

She knew what had shaken her. She had known last night. She had known over lunch. Him seeing her father. What on earth about? And why keep it secret?

But at least her nerves had stopped jangling. Lunch had thrown her into confusion. She smiled, almost laughed. Another woman would have presented a *real* problem. She had been fighting her father all her life.

Glancing at the clock, she started with surprise. *So much for long lunches! The day almost over and not a thing done.* Gathering herself, she thought first of their evening meal and wondered what time he would be home. Using the kitchen telephone, she called the office.

'He's out,' said Sally. 'And we're about to lock up.'

'Oh? Do you know where he is?'

'He took a customer off for a test drive. They've been gone all afternoon.'

Katrina frowned. 'Isn't Jim Davis in today? Doesn't he usually —'

'Usually he does, but this woman arrived and asked for him in person. She had one of his cards so he must know her from somewhere.'

'Yes, I see . . .' absorbing the information, she saw no reason to worry. Toddy was always handing out cards; half the people in Majorca had his card, *everyone* at the golf club had his card. 'So you don't know when I can expect him?'

'No, I don't. Herbert was just asking the same thing.' Sally sounded cross. 'There are letters to sign and goodness knows what. I've never known a test drive take this long.'

'Mmm,' mused Katrina, thinking to have dinner ready for eight. 'I expect he'll be back any minute, but you lock up and go home.'

'And Herbert? What about him?'

'Him too. There's no need for him to hang on. Toddy won't mind driving himself home for once.'

All was activity after that. She prided herself on her cooking. It had never seemed difficult to her. Most of it was just common sense. Like bookkeeping. A few basic rules. *Bookkeeping and cooking. Keep the brute solvent and feed him.* The practical tools of a practical woman. Was that all she was? No charm or allure? Her heart sank. Then a faint smile touched her lips. Alec had been charmed last night. He had wanted her. Had she encouraged him? A bit, but not much. To flirt with someone you had to like them, and she felt no liking for Alec Jepson. She had only bothered for Julie's sake, to help the evening go with a swing, and then . . . her smile widened . . . she had flirted because Sophie tried to take over.

Her eyes smarted as she sliced onions and tossed them into the pan. She snorted an unladylike sniff. Sophie *always* tried

152

to take over. Yes, she was good-looking . . . yes, men found her attractive . . . but for God's sake, she had no monopoly. *And I saw her off!* The sense of satisfaction came as a surprise. Adding shreds of bacon to the onions, she prodded them with a spatula, tilting the pan over the heat. *My God, fancy competing for a jerk like Alec Jepson! It was only because of my mood, because Toddy wasn't there, because . . .*

But Alec's attentions had made her feel better. More attractive. More desirable. As she chopped beef into cubes, she wondered how she rated in bed? Perhaps Alec would have been disappointed? Probably. Sophie had slept with more men. Sophie would be more accomplished. Emptying the pan, she tossed in the beef and went to a shelf for the brandy.

Cooking was therapy. She had never thought of it as such before, but she knew it was so. The fact that the smells were right and her hands were busy encouraged her peace of mind. She could never cook when she was angry. No more than she could eat. The gastric juices refused to flow. Pouring brandy into a ladle, she put down the bottle and picked up her lighter. The brandy caught with a lazy blue flame which she allowed to build before pouring over the meat. Hearing Mac snuffle behind her, she said, 'Yes, yes. Don't worry, I've made some for you.'

Stirring the ingredients into the casserole dish, she splashed in some burgundy, gauging the amount. Too much and Toddy would become sleepy. Not enough and it would cease to be his favourite dish. But just right, and . . .

After checking the dining-room, she went upstairs to run her bath. Plenty of time to bathe, to put on her face and decide on her dress. She wondered if he would bring her some flowers. He often did after a quarrel. The traditional peace offering. Handed over with a shamefaced grin which she pretended not to notice. *A sort of code,* she smiled to herself. *He brings me roses and I cook his favourite meal — we each say we're sorry without using the word.*

Contemplating the evening filled her with pleasurable anticipation. Past quarrels had been mended in the same way, a long lingering meal served as a prelude to love-making. *But before we kiss and make up,* she vowed, *I want to know about him meeting my father.*

She was downstairs in less than an hour, bathed and perfumed and wearing a yellow dress with a low neckline. In the kitchen, the *boeuf bourguignon* simmered gently. Opening a bottle of burgundy, she left it to breathe. And throughout it all, she resisted the temptation to pour herself a drink. She mimicked Sophie's voice – *Booze can take such a hold. We have to be careful at our age.* She snorted. *Good God! What does she mean, our age? Anyone would think I was sixty!*

She tried to occupy her mind while she waited. For a while she watched television, but even after flicking through the channels, nothing engaged her attention. Fidgeting, she read the paper from cover to cover, while all the time listening for sounds of the car. Twice she went into the study to peer out of the front windows.

At eight o'clock, she permitted herself the first drink of the evening; a gin and tonic, with plenty of tonic.

'Where is he?' she asked Mac, beginning to worry.

At eight-thirty she telephoned the office.

He might be back, clearing his desk, signing his letters.

But the only reply was provided by the out-of-hours answering machine.

By nine o'clock she was back in the kitchen, trying to salvage the dinner.

By nine-thirty, she was genuinely worried about an accident.

At nine-forty, the telephone rang.

The sounds of a trolley being wheeled down the corridor had seeped into his consciousness. Propping himself up on one elbow, he looked down at her face and marvelled about what had happened. With his finger he gently traced the curve of her nose. 'You sure oysters are enough? You were starving earlier.'

Opening her eyes, she smiled up at him. 'Oysters will do fine. I only want to build up your strength. You've a long night ahead of you.'

He grinned, quickly kissed her and rolled out of bed. 'Stay there. Let me go and sort things out.' Hurrying into the bath-room, he snatched up a robe, wrapped it around himself and crossed the bedroom to the sitting-room. 'I'll give you a shout when we're ready.'

Closing the door, he stood undecided for a moment. His heart thumped. For the past few hours, entranced and captivated, he had thought only of Charlie. Lust had taken control of his senses. But now . . . he could delay it no longer, now he would *have* to call Katrina. Hurriedly he scanned the sitting-room in search of the telephone. His conscience assailed him. Panic set in. *What can I say? Think! Think! What excuse can I make? You'll have to phone, you'll have to let her know, you'll have to say something!*

His mounting alarm was interrupted by a discreet knock from the corridor. He crossed the room and opened the door. A waiter wheeled a trolley over the threshold. 'Good evening, sir. Your oysters and champagne.'

'Fine. Set it up in the window, would you?'

'Certainly, sir.'

The big bay window overlooked the lake, now a shimmering blackness relieved by the reflections of lights strung through the branches of overhanging trees. Not that Todd took much notice. At that moment he was distracted by the sound of the shower from the bathroom. His heart lurched. Sensing his chance, he tried to hurry the waiter along. 'Thank you,' he said, as the man spread a linen cloth over the trolley. 'Thank you,' he repeated, looking at the two platters of oysters on beds of crushed ice. 'I'll open the wine,' he volunteered, looking at the champagne in the ice bucket. 'That's fine, fine, thank you.' Patting the empty pockets of his robe, he shrugged an apology for his lack of small change. 'I'll see you in the morning, all right?'

Closing the door, he took a deep breath. The shower was still running in the bathroom. Hurriedly he reached for the tele-phone and dialled his home number. Turning his back to the bedroom, he trailed the cord behind him and walked to the farthest corner of the room.

Katrina sounded anxious when she answered. 'Where are you? I've been worried –'

'Sorry, I couldn't call before, I'm up in the Midlands. Got some trouble with a car I've been testing. The only thing to do is to stay over and come back in the morning . . .'

'Stay over?'

He tried to ignore the dismay in her voice. 'Yeah, well,' he mumbled. 'The local garage is closed. If they've got the spare, I can fit it first thing in the morning. Won't take me a minute, I'll be in town by –'

'Stay over?' she repeated.

'It's all I can do,' he said helplessly.

'I see,' she said, sounding bewildered. 'Will you come home first? In the morning, I mean. Before you go to the office?'

He groaned as he remembered. 'Er . . . no, I can't do that . . . er . . . you see, I've got an early meeting with . . . er . . . someone.'

'Someone?' she enquired sharply, sounding more suspicious with every word.

'Well . . . er,' he squirmed.

'Who's someone?'

His capacity for deception was temporarily exhausted. 'Leo, actually.'

He heard her quick intake of breath.

'You're seeing him *again*?' she cried in alarm. 'What is this?'

'Only for breakfast.'

'Oh, Toddy, what's going on?'

Straining his ears, he heard the shower suddenly stop in the bathroom. Hairs rose on the back of his neck. Instinctively he lowered his voice. 'Nothing's *going on*,' he hissed into the telephone. 'I'm seeing him before he leaves, that's all. Don't make a big thing of it. Look, I must go now. Okay?'

Suddenly Charlie's voice rang out. 'Toddy, darling. You've got the only robe, did you know?'

He froze. Horror held his limbs in a vice. Then he slapped his hand over the mouthpiece and turned to the bedroom. 'Be with you in a minute,' he croaked in a loud whisper.

'Toddy?' Katrina's voice queried from the phone.

156

He snatched his hand away from the mouthpiece. 'I'll call you in the morning.'

'But —'

Charlie sang out from the bedroom. 'Don't worry. I'll manage.'

He almost dropped the telephone. Heedless of what Katrina was saying, he hissed, 'I'll call you from the office tomorrow, okay? 'Bye for now.' Before she had a chance to respond, he broke the connection. Beads of sweat stood out on his forehead. *Jesus! Did she hear?* With shaking hands he carried the instrument back to the table. *That was awful! Worse than I imagined.*

For the first time in his life he disliked himself. The realization came as a shock. The concept of self-esteem was something he had never considered. There had been times in his life when he had been pleased with himself — even proud of himself — but self-analysis was not something he went in for. Lies he had told Katrina in the past had been lies of omission, or exaggerations, or embellishments to add fun to a story . . .

'Is the coast clear?' Charlie called.

Guilt-stricken eyes turned to the bedroom. 'What?'

'Has room service gone?'

'Oh, yeah, sure,' he said, trying to recover.

His heart missed a beat as she came through the door. Dressed in his shirt, shaking her red hair loose from a shower cap, she was the stuff of erotic dreams, a centrefold come true, as luscious and sweet-smelling as a peach. Pecking his cheek, she twirled around in front of him. 'Will this do?'

'Oh, Jesus,' he groaned in guilty confusion. Dragging his gaze away from her tight little buttocks, he sank into the sofa.

As she laughed, she caught sight of the oysters. 'Mmm. Don't they look gorgeous? Come on, let's eat. Making love always makes me ravenous . . .' she lifted the bottle of champagne from the bucket '. . . and thirsty. Will you do the honours?'

Taking the bottle from her hands, he began to untwist the wire from the cork.

'Look at that view,' she exclaimed, squeezing alongside the trolley in the bay window. 'Do you bring all your mistresses here?'

'Huh,' he grunted, twisting the bottle.

Picking up a napkin, she reached for an oyster. 'Come on,' she encouraged. 'Tell the truth.'

'To tell the truth,' he echoed. 'I've never done this before.'

Her hands flew to her mouth in mock horror. 'You mean you were a virgin?'

He burst out laughing. For a moment all guilt was forgotten. Charlie erupted into giggles, and they were still laughing when the cork flew from the bottle. 'Whoops!' she laughed, seizing a glass. 'Cheers! Here's to celebrations.' Pulling a chair out from the table, she sat down, raising her glass to him as she did so. 'Then I'm very flattered,' she said as she reached for her oyster. 'Not that I needed to be told. I guessed. Faithful husband is written all over you. Trouble was, I fancied you as soon as I saw you –'

'Why on earth –'

'Why does anyone fancy anyone? Besides I was feeling unbelievably horny. That's what being cooped up on Jersey does for you.' She smiled. 'I'm feeling much better now, thank you, kind sir. You're a wonderful lover.'

He shook his head in dazed disbelief. 'Now it's my turn to be flattered.'

'So you should be. I don't usually behave like a sailor on shore leave. As a matter of fact it's my first time, too. With a married man, I mean. Well almost, and the circumstances were quite different before.' She stared at him, struck by a sudden thought. 'Oh,' she exclaimed. 'I forgot to ask. Did you call home?'

The sheer unexpectedness of the question defeated him.

'If you haven't, you'd better,' she continued, her hand poised to scoop up another oyster. 'I'll wait in the bedroom if you like.'

'No . . . I mean, yes, I phoned.'

'Good. Was she okay? I expect she was worried.'

He stared at her in amazement, 'You're concerned?'

'Of course I'm concerned. That's not a kind thing to say,' she exclaimed, sounding offended. 'What sort of person do you take me for?'

'Sorry, I didn't mean . . .' Unsure of what he did mean, he started again. 'It's not as if you know her –'

'I know you. That's enough. You're nice.' Cocking her head, she looked at him, suddenly thoughtful. 'Funny word, "nice". I remember my English teacher calling it a word without meaning. Never understood that. Some people *are* nice. Even some men. You're nice, so I expect you have a nice wife.'

'Well . . . er, thanks.'

'You're welcome. So how do you feel?'

He stared at her. 'About what?'

'About committing adultery. Full of regrets, riddled with guilt, that sort of thing?'

'Er . . .' he began, taken aback.

'Truth, remember,' she reminded him.

'Confused, I suppose.'

She regarded him thoughtfully for a moment and then reached for an oyster. 'You're not eating. I'll wolf all of these if you let me.'

Dutifully he took one. He *was* confused. Too confused to eat.

'Pity,' she said.

'What is?'

'You being nice. You should have been a shit. Then whenever I came over, we could have spent the night together without your conscience playing up.' Her green eyes sparkled with amusement. 'On the other hand, if I ask myself would I allow a shit to make love to me, the answer's no, so that generates confusion on my part. Even more confusing is you're not the only one with a conscience. Still, if I really thought tonight would damage your marriage, I wouldn't have said yes in the first place.'

He shook his head in bewildered admiration. 'You are extraordinary, d'you know that?'

'No, I'm not. Just honest, that's all.' She stared at the oysters left on his plate. 'Are you going to finish those?'

With a smile, he pushed his plate across the table. 'You were hungry. I should have ordered the –'

'Now don't feel guilty about *that*!' Pushing her own plate

aside, she looked up and grinned. 'For heaven's sake! Do you always worry so much?'

'It's just . . .' he began and then realized that he did not know what to say. He started again. 'It's crazy. Feeling guilty. I dunno. I must be absolutely bloody mad. Guys at the club have affairs all the time.'

'Shits,' she said, dabbing her mouth with her napkin.

'Hank would laugh himself sick.'

'So don't tell him.'

'Don't worry, I won't, but . . .' staring across the table, he was momentarily overcome by her beauty. 'Christ, you're lovely! I mean, this is totally bloody ridiculous. I must be old enough to be your father.'

'Nonsense. I'm twenty-eight and you're what? Mid-forties. You'd have to have been sixteen or seventeen –'

'Even so,' he interrupted sorrowfully, shaking his head. 'Twenty-eight. I was starting my business when I was twenty-eight. Girls like you weren't around then.'

'Think what you missed,' she laughed, finishing the last oyster. Dabbing her mouth, she reached for her wine. 'Oh Toddy, don't look like that. Besides I'm not a girl, I'm an adult. So let's behave like adults. No strings, no regrets, and no guilt. I thought we agreed that downstairs. Let's enjoy each other and end up as friends. Okay?'

'Right,' he agreed.

'So don't go all serious on me. You're all tensed up.'

'No, no, I'm fine,' he protested, as he pushed back his chair. 'I just need a cigar, that's all.'

She crinkled her nose. 'Stay there. Tobacco's bad for you, don't you know that? I know how to relax you.'

His heart thumped as she brushed past him. 'I am relaxed,' he protested. As the shirt lifted, he caught a glimpse of the dark triangle at the top of her legs, then the taut little buttocks, and before he could check himself a groan escaped from his lips.

She was opening her handbag as she returned to the room. 'Here,' she said.

He looked at her hand. 'I don't smoke cigarettes.'

'It's not a cigarette.'

'Oh,' he said.

'Oh?' she echoed to tease him. Standing behind him, she kneaded his shoulders. 'My God, you *are* tense! You're as stiff as a board. Come on, you can smoke that later. Come back to the bedroom. I'll give you a massage.'

Feeling slightly bemused, he allowed her to lead him back to the bed.

'Take your robe off,' she said.

As he disrobed, his awakening erection became obvious.

'Save that for later, too,' she smiled. 'First let's get your shoulders unknotted.'

'But —'

'No buts,' she said, turning him round. 'Lie face downwards, that's right. Get yourself comfortable. Here, put this pillow under your head. That's right. Good. I'm an expert at this, really. Now relax.'

He groaned into the pillow as she straddled him, and groaned again as the tips of her breasts brushed across his back.

'Sorry, that was unintentional,' she murmured as she started to massage. 'Think pure thoughts for a while. You're in bad shape, did you know? There! Feel that?'

'Umph,' he grunted as her fingers explored his shoulder muscles.

'Relax,' she coaxed. 'Don't fight me.'

A pleasing warmth invaded his muscles as she worked up and down his spine. His erection faded beneath him, and above him the occasional stabs of pain diminished. A pleasurable glow tingled through his entire body. Her hands were surprisingly strong, although after a while he seemed not to feel them at all, instead he felt caressed by the waves of a warm sea, so gentle and relaxing that gradually and imperceptibly he drifted into a state of drowsiness. Vaguely, he was aware that she had moved from him, but it was merely a shadowy thought, secondary to a wonderful sense of well-being. When finally he roused himself, he realized she was lying naked beside him. As he turned to her, she put the half-smoked joint between his lips.

'Feel better?'

'Fantastic.' Closing his eyes, he inhaled deeply without thinking. 'Mmm,' he murmured. 'Like I'm on a cloud floating.'

'Sssh,' she hushed, taking the joint from his fingers. 'Just relax. You were really all knotted up, d'you know that?'

'I'm not now,' he said. It was true. He had never felt so relaxed. 'Can I have another puff of that thing?'

She passed it back to him. 'Just one.' Her hand hovered while he inhaled. Taking it from him, she drew on it herself before turning to the bedside table to extinguish it in the ashtray. As she came back into his arms he shifted his weight. For a long moment he caressed her shoulder, at peace with the world.

'Doesn't your wife ever give you a massage?'

In his drowsy state, the idea seemed mildly amusing. 'No,' he smiled lazily. 'No massage, no sharing a joint. Nothing like that about Katrina.'

Katrina's mind lurched as she went back over the conversation. She had listened as with special antennae. A wife's sixth sense, honed and developed by time, and fuelled by suspicions born in the minds of her friends.

His tone was all wrong. He sounded guilty. Something was wrong . . . but not with a car. The car hasn't been built that Toddy can't fix.

She had scarcely been able to speak to him, her throat had gone so dry. And he had seemed to whisper, not his normal voice at all.

Last night was bad enough – finding out he's been keeping things from me. But this is worse. I just don't believe this. He's telling lies. Oh Toddy, what's happening to us?

She felt lost. Aspects of her life which she had taken for granted, no longer seemed permanent. The ground seemed to shift beneath her feet. He had sounded impatient to be rid of her; totally and utterly uninterested. Throwing herself face down on the sofa, she sobbed uncontrollably. Mac came and snuggled close to her, but her weeping drowned his encouraging snuffles. Minutes passed before she was aware of his presence. Even when she realized he was there, she still wept, cradling his head in her lap, while rocking back and forth on the sofa.

Twenty minutes passed before she gathered herself. Drained and wrung-out, she walked to the sideboard. With shaking hands, she poured a large brandy. Fumbling for a handkerchief, she glimpsed herself in the mirror. Her white face was streaked with mascara.

Mac tilted his head and uttered soft whimpers of concern.

'Oh, Mac,' she sighed as she returned to the sofa. 'What's going on?'

The unexpectedness of events had left her stunned. Her mind struggled to interpret what was happening. She recalled Sally saying, 'He took a customer for a test drive . . . she arrived and asked for him in person.'

She remembered the knowing looks exchanged between Sophie and Gloria. Gloria gloating, 'There *has* to be a woman.'

Why? Who said so? Apart from Gloria. Gloria's an absolute bitch . . .

Her empty glass took her by surprise. At the sideboard, she poured another drink, took a cigarette from the box and returned to the sofa in search of her lighter. Thoughts without order whirled through her mind. He had sounded so strange on the phone. Different. How different? She frowned, concentrating. Not a word about my day. Not a word about me at all. He couldn't wait to hang up . . .

To call Sally at home was unusual, but not without precedent. 'Sorry to bother you,' she said, making her voice bright and conversational. 'Did Toddy say anything about going on some- where? After he took this customer for a test drive?'

'Isn't he home yet?'

'No, but . . . er, I was in the bath, and he left a message on the machine.' Katrina covered the lie with a brittle laugh. 'It's a bit garbled, I'm afraid. I wondered if you knew any of the details.'

'No, just that he went off with this customer.'

'A woman, you said? Someone from the club, I expect. What was she like, I must know her?'

'Very dolly. Jim Davis was green with envy.'

163

As her memory searched through the faces of acquaintances, her brain scrambled and staggered. 'Blonde? Brunette?'

'Redhead. Good figure, green eyes, smartly dressed. Quite a looker.'

Not from the club. *Definitely* not from the club. Her stomach contracted. Her heart pounded. 'Ahh . . .' She turned her dismay into what she hoped sounded like a cry of recognition. 'Pauline . . . er . . . Dickinson, I should think. Of course. She did say something about a new car. You thought she was pretty, did you?'

'Don't you?' Sally sounded baffled.

'I suppose so, if you like that type.'

Her hand was shaking when she put down the phone. 'The bastard!'

Recognizing anger, Mac whimpered and retreated to the door.

'Bastard!' she repeated as she jumped up from the sofa. Pouring another brandy, she began to pace the room, too agitated to sit down. As she passed the piano, her gaze fell upon a framed photograph of Toddy and Hank at the Crow's Nest. With a great sideways swipe, she knocked it to the floor. She ground her stiletto heel into it, using her weight to splinter the glass. Finishing her drink at a gulp, she retreated to the sideboard with a sense of satisfaction.

Her face was no longer white. Anger and brandy combined to bring a flush to her cheeks. *I'll kill him!* Walking across to the photograph on the floor, she stamped upon it with her other foot. *How could he do this to me?*

She carried her glass back to the sofa. *I wish I had slept with Alec. Two can play at that game. That would have shown him. I wish . . .* But she had no idea what she wished. Anger kept other thoughts at bay. Pictures of him making love were swamped by the red rage of temper. 'Bastard!' she spat the word out like a bullet.

Fifteen minutes later, she was on the phone to Sophie. 'Changed my mind,' she said. 'To hell with expense. I wanna come to this fat farm with you.'

'Broadlands is not a fat farm,' Sophie corrected snootily. 'It's the most exclusive health club in the country.'

'Thash what I said,' Katrina began, and to her horror realized she was slurring her words.

'Have you been drinking?'

Katrina stared at the decanter and hiccuped.

CHAPTER FIVE

RARE ARE DAYS WHEN EVENTS conspire to change so many lives, but such was the day about to begin. In London, oblivious of what was to happen, Katrina awoke slowly. Fuddled by brandy fumes, her brain stumbled and fumbled over the events of the night. God, what a night. Drinking too much, yet again. Feeding *boeuf bourguignon* to Mac at midnight. Weeping and gnashing her teeth. And look at the night before? The mood he was in. Coming home late, spoiling for trouble, refusing to go to dinner at the Middletons. Closing her eyes against the morning light, she snuffled under her breath and attempted to take stock of her life.

Similar thoughts occurred to Charlie when she woke at Brislington Manor. Not that she had any immediate complaints. Her trip to London had turned into enormous fun. Winning at the casino, buying her car, meeting Toddy. A sideways glance at his sleeping figure was enough to bring a smile to her lips. He was a breath of fresh air. In her world of financial schemers, nice guys were thin on the ground. Not that she would allow things to get out of hand. She had meant what she said about married men. She had played that game before and once was enough. 'Except this one's got scruples,' she thought, trying to calculate the odds of finding a car salesman with scruples. Smiling at the irony, she was surprised to realize she was rather pleased with his scruples. 'A decent guy in a world full of shits,' she concluded, which is what reminded her of her career and where it was going. In all truth she was bored in Jersey; been there, done that, and done it well, but it was not what she wanted. She had always seen her qualifications as a stepping stone into general management, and although handling big investment portfolios had widened her experience, the prudence demanded by the work was stifling her initiative. 'You don't need new ideas to play safe,' she thought, and not for the first time wondered how to transfer her energies to something more creative, something more challenging, more *exciting*! 'Is that why I'm here?' she asked herself. 'In search of a challenge, in search of excitement?'

She knew what she wanted. Start something new and build it up. And do it soon. She was twenty-eight. Toddy had been twenty-eight when he had started in business, and he seemed to be doing well for himself. Not that she was so sure about his hotel venture. She had almost blurted out her misgivings. To her mind, for a mass-market operator like Suntours to be handling an up-market resort hotel seemed like asking Woolworths to sell Christian Dior. Not that she had said so. After all, his business was his business. Tomorrow she would drive her brand spanking new Jaguar down to the coast, board the ferry and get on with her life. 'Me in Jersey,' she thought wistfully. 'And him in sunny Majorca with friend Hank.'

Friend Hank would have been staggered. Like many men who lived with a succession of women, he felt something akin to reverence when confronted by an enduring marriage. 'A guy who don't cheat on his wife, won't cheat on his partner,' was the way he saw it, and he would have been alarmed to think of Todd making love to a glamorous redhead.

Later that day it seemed to Todd that making love to Charlie was the only good thing to have happened, but at the time he was so busy enjoying her that he wouldn't have believed his luck could run out.

After they had made love, in fact as soon as orange juice, coffee and croissants had arrived at their room, he broke the news about meeting Leo in London.

'Eight o'clock?' Charlie cried in dismay.

'Afraid so. We ought to leave right away.'

'You don't mind if I dress first?' she demanded, as his apologies brought a rueful smile to her face. 'Oh well,' she shrugged. 'Business is business. But I hate early mornings. You drive and wake me up when we get there.'

In the car, she reclined the seat, strapped herself in, curled her legs under her, gave him a sleepy grin, closed her eyes and went back to sleep with a smile on her face.

He made up the lost time on the road, concentrating so intently that all other thoughts went out of his head – but as the motorway ended and he drove into the outskirts of London, familiar anxieties returned to plague him. Each well-known landmark was a reminder of problems. Last night had been an escape; a wonderful release from everyday tension, but every mile nearer to his office tied another knot in his stomach.

Waiting at traffic lights, he glanced at the figure beside him. His gaze lingered on the hem of her skirt which had ridden up almost to her thigh. *Jesus! She's got sensational legs.*

But in all fairness, he thought, so has Katrina.

He had a thing about legs. Maybe because his own were so short. Katrina's had held him enchanted for as long as he could remember. He groaned under his breath. *What do I tell her?*

She must never find out. She'd never be unfaithful to me. Never!

'You're scowling,' Charlie said, so suddenly that he jumped.

'What? Oh, hello. Had a good sleep?'

She stretched her arms and adjusted her seat. 'You look like a man with a conscience.'

For a moment he was lost for a reply. Then he grinned, slightly shamefaced. 'Do you always know what people are thinking?'

'Only when it's obvious. Anyway, I'm glad. You *should* have a conscience. It means you won't turn into a shit and cheat on a regular basis. Look at it that way. Okay?'

'Er . . . if –'

'But no regrets.'

'Regrets? Are you kidding? No . . . I mean I had a . . . I mean, it was marvellous. *You* were marvellous –'

She laughed and rested her hand on his arm. 'And I've never enjoyed a celebration more,' she said, giving his arm a quick squeeze. 'And we end up good friends, right?'

'Absolutely.'

'Good. Now then. Can you sort the car by about five? You know, tax, insurance and everything?'

'Sure.'

'Good, I'll collect it then. Okay?'

'Fine. We'll have a drink or something.'

'Not something,' she teased him with a smile. 'Just a drink. You'd better go home to your wife and I need some rest. I'm driving down to Weymouth in the morning to get the ferry over to Jersey.' She pulled a face. 'Back to the salt mines.'

He laughed.

Removing her hand from his arm, she patted her hair and inspected herself in the mirror. 'We're almost there, aren't we?'

'Not far.'

'Is that a cab rank? Why not drop me off? You can't drive into your forecourt with me beside you, can you?'

'I could drop you off at your apartment first.'

'For heaven's sake! That's behind Baker Street. You've a meeting to get to. No, a cab will do fine. I'm only going home to crash out.' She smiled, 'I'll sleep until lunchtime, do some shopping and see you around five. Okay?'

She leaned over and kissed him. Then she was gone, opening the passenger door before he could get out and open it for her. He sat for a moment, watching her step into the cab, and he waved back as she fluttered her hand at the rear window. Then as the cab swung round and set off, he let in the clutch, feeling a bit dazed and thinking how the world had changed since he was twenty-eight. But as he edged into the traffic and joined the approach road to his office he stopped marvelling about Charlie. What came to mind was his meeting with Leo. He wondered how to begin? Perhaps by emphasizing that the first payment to Moroni had been made on time. The *second* was paid on time. And they'd have nine hundred thousand towards the third. Almost a million! Which was a miracle in the midst of this recession.

Perhaps Moroni would wait for the rest until the money came in from Suntours?

Perhaps I should go over to Paris and see Lapiere?

Perhaps . . .

He was the first at the office. The postman was at the door, on the point of feeding the mail through the letter box. Taking the bundle of letters, Todd hurried up the stairs and dumped them on Sally's desk. Then he went into his washroom. Although he had shaved with a razor purchased at the hotel, he hastily ran his electric shaver over his chin to improve the effect, and had almost finished when he saw the mark on his shirt. A small patch of make-up, half-way down the front, the size of a small coin.

Cursing in his annoyance, he held some tissues under the tap. Dabbing furiously, he rubbed at the mark. His eyes widened in dismay. The stain grew larger. Unable to do more, he abandoned the effort. Thankfully the mark was on the chest, not the collar, and was invisible under his jacket. Later he could buy a new shirt. 'Jesus, I'll *have* to buy one before I go home.' Meanwhile there was breakfast with Leo. Hurrying downstairs, he was on the point of walking round the corner to the cab rank, when Herbert pulled into the forecourt.

'Stay in the car,' he shouted, locking the door.

Not hearing the instruction, Herbert got out. 'Morning, Boss. I went out to the house –'

'Yeah, sorry about that. I got held up last night. The Ritz, Herbert. Fast as you can. I'm due there at eight.'

'Blimey,' Herbert exclaimed, glancing at his watch as he hurried to open the rear door. 'That only gives us ten minutes. You seen the traffic?'

He could feel Herbert's curiosity. Even when they set off, he could sense his eyes in the rearview mirror.

'Problems, last night?' Herbert enquired, lifting an eyebrow.

'What? Oh, I sorted it out.'

To avoid further discussion, he reached for the newspaper which Herbert always collected on his way to meet him. He sat back and opened it out. Then his eyes widened as the headlines came out to greet him. He caught his breath. His stomach lurched.

TRAVEL FIRM GOES BUST

The recession claimed another victim today when Suntours, the largest travel business in Europe, called in the receivers.

He stared with disbelieving eyes. His pulse raced. His brain rejected what he was reading. Perhaps it was *another* Suntours? Not his Suntours. That was it. It couldn't possibly be *his* Suntours. But there was a picture of Tommy Hastings, obviously taken in happier times because the smile on his face was at odds with the caption.

Chairman blames recession for holiday slump.

His hands shook so violently that the newsprint became a blur. He felt sick. He redoubled his efforts to comprehend what he was reading. But again the photograph swam out of focus. Instead of Tommy Hastings, he saw another face – the fleshy features of Aldo Moroni.

It was obvious when Leo opened the door that he had heard the news. He looked old and tired and somehow less elegant; unusually crumpled, as if his grey pinstripe needed pressing. Not that Todd took much notice. He almost stumbled over the threshold.

'Steady, old boy.' Leo put out a hand. 'You're white as a sheet. You'd better sit down before you fall down.'

Todd's glance took in the newspapers spread over the breakfast table. 'Christ, Leo! You've seen the news. I mean . . . I can't believe it! Suntours are *big*, for God's sake! The biggest in Europe.'

On rubbery legs, he allowed himself to be led across to the armchairs facing the window. He stared sightlessly out at the park. On other occasions, he had admired the view. Many an evening he and Leo had gazed down upon the trees, nursing their drinks as they talked. He remembered when he had first shown Leo the plans of Paloma Blanca . . .

'I'll get you some coffee,' said Leo with a look of concern. 'And something stronger by the look on your face.'

Todd sank into an armchair. Another newspaper lay open on the coffee table. Headlines leapt up at him. *SUNTOURS IN LIQUIDATION. Travel firm goes bust. Thousands of holiday-makers stranded.* His hands felt clammy. A vein pulsed in his neck. Sucking in a deep breath, he struggled to concentrate. 'It says they announced it last night,' he said as he read.

'Yes,' said Leo, pouring the coffee.

Last night he had been enjoying himself with Charlie. Groaning aloud, he felt a sudden longing for normality, a craving for domesticity, even a perverse irrational desire to see the Middletons. Forty-eight hours before, the thought of wasting time under their roof had induced a blinding red rage. Now he would give his soul to step back in time. A way of life taken for granted suddenly gained the allure of the unattainable.

Leo stood before him with the coffee and a bottle of Scotch. 'Here you go, old boy. Get this down you. You'll feel better.'

Todd held the cup with both hands and watched as Leo added some whisky.

'It was on the news earlier,' said Leo, with a nod towards the television.

'Was it? I didn't know until I saw the paper.' Todd coughed as he drank. The hot coffee and whisky warmed him, causing him to realize how cold he had become. Wiping his mouth, he said, 'I feel gutted. I still can't believe it.'

'Neither could I at first. Hell of a shock. It's this bloody recession. Fewer people are taking holidays –'

'But Suntours are big –'

'Were,' Leo corrected as he set the bottle down on the table. 'They've gone belly up now, and apparently there's no chance of a rescue. There was a chap on the box just now, some business analyst, who said it was the sort of deal they made with you that landed them in trouble.'

'He mentioned Paloma Blanca?'

'Not specifically, but to get the best hotels they were guaranteeing occupancy to hoteliers all over the world. Fine when business was booming. It gave them an edge over their competition, but when holidays slumped they were faced with millions of claims. They simply ran out of cash.'

The cup rattled in the saucer as Todd put them on the table. The magnitude of what was happening – *had happened* – was still sinking in. 'Let me call Tommy Hastings,' he exclaimed suddenly. 'He must be able to do *something*. We've got a contract, for God's sake!'

'Humph.' Leo shrugged dismissively. 'Not worth the paper it's written on now.'

Letting the newspaper fall to the floor, Todd rose and went to the telephone. Some of the colour returned to his face, and he coughed to clear his throat. 'Operator, could you get me a company called Suntours. That's right, the travel firm. They're in Pall Mall. Thanks.' Replacing the receiver, he walked to the window. Gripped by panic, he stared blindly out at Green Park. He had seen failure overtake other men; men he had known at the club, suddenly faced by mountains of debt, hitherto prosperous men who had seemed set for the rest of their days. He had seen the bleak despair in their eyes; listened to talk of marriages falling apart under the strain. 'My God, Leo,' he exclaimed miserably. 'Without Suntours I'm wiped out. Even if . . . even if . . .' he sucked in a breath. 'This will take everything . . . the business, the house, everything I've built up over the years.'

When the telephone rang, it was Leo who answered it. 'Yes, I'm not surprised,' he said. 'Try again later, will you?' Looking at Todd, he said, 'No joy with Suntours, old boy. Their switchboard is jammed. Stranded holidaymakers I expect, worried about how they'll get home.

'Anyway, there's no point in talking to Hastings. He's no longer in control. They've appointed a liquidator. You're better off staying here and talking it through. Suntours are finished. Kaput. Get the picture?'

The only picture Todd got was of himself in the bankruptcy courts. Returning to the armchair, he sank into the upholstery and closed his eyes until the dizziness passed. He took deep breaths to regain control, then, with his head in his hands, he plunged into his story. He told Leo what he would have told him two nights before – that even without this latest blow he was already in trouble, that he would be unable to meet the next interest payment . . . that he had been considering going to Paris to see Lapiere, and why he had delayed selling the villa: '. . . property prices have fallen so it's a bad time to sell, but the real reason I've held off is Katrina. I swear she thinks more of the villa than our place in Hampstead.'

Unusually, Leo showed no interest in mention of Katrina. Instead he said sternly, 'You must pay Moroni. He won't mess about. I did warn you –'

'But Lapiere will understand. Especially now, with Suntours down the tube.'

'You can't go to Lapiere. Not on top of this news. This will have shaken their confidence –'

'*Their* confidence! It's not done a bundle for mine,' yelped Todd, squirming in his seat.

'If you miss an interest payment they'll call in the loan.'

'There's no point. I can't pay fifteen million, nothing like.' Hot and bothered, Todd looked disgusted at having to explain the obvious. 'We'll have to reschedule the loan, that's all.'

The matter-of-fact words brought a strange look to Leo's face. He stared at Todd for a long moment, then went to the coffee jug, half-filled their cups which he topped up with whisky, and finally took the chair opposite Todd, so that several moments passed before he spoke. 'I think you're missing the point,' he said in a calm, level voice. 'I did warn you. You're not dealing with a conventional banker. To say you *can't* pay won't do you any good. Moroni will still want his money.'

'He can't have what's not there.'

'Then he'll use his insurance.'

Todd stared at him. 'What does that mean?'

'He made you insure your life, remember? His company is the beneficiary.'

''Course I remember. I had a row with Manny about that. In the end even he admitted it was a fairly standard requirement. It's bloody expensive, but not unusual. It's protection for Katrina. The loan gets paid off if anything happens to me.'

174

Leo's grey-eyed stare was unblinking. 'Moroni wasn't concerned about Katrina. He was protecting himself.'

Todd stared for a long moment. 'I don't get it. I'm going bust, not kicking the bucket.'

Leo regarded him with a curious look.

Growing realization brought a look of horror to Todd's face. His voice rose with incredulity. 'You mean Moroni will *make* something happen to me? You mean he'd *kill* me? For the insurance money?' It was true. He could see it in Leo's face.

Leo shrugged. 'He wouldn't want to. The insurance only covers the capital sum. He only makes money if you stay alive to pay his interest. On the other hand . . .' he paused meaningfully. 'If you don't pay the interest –'

Covering his ears with his hands, Todd shook his head. He stared dumbfounded. Finally he found his voice. 'He'd *kill* me! Dear God! I don't believe this! Jesus! He'd actually *kill* me? You mean he'd murder me? Oh, my God!' He shuddered as a shiver ran up his spine. He felt suddenly cold. Swallowing hard, he fixed Leo with a look of accusation. 'And you knew this? You let me sign –'

'Steady, old boy. That's not fair. I did warn you –'

'Not about this, you didn't. You told me about that Belgian . . . what was his name . . . the guy who tried to cheat him?'

'The point was Moroni can be ruthless –'

'With anyone who *cheats* him!' Todd interrupted, nodding his head emphatically. 'Fine. Okay. I got the point. I can understand that. But I'm not trying to cheat him. I'm asking for a bit more time, that's all –'

'He won't see it that way.'

'But that's how it is!' Todd retorted, his voice rising. Thoroughly frightened, he wished he had never set eyes on Paloma Blanca. Katrina had been right all along. So had Manny. Even Smithson at the bank had been right. They had all said the same thing: *Stick to selling cars, stick to what you know about . . .*

'You're okay so long as you pay the interest,' Leo repeated.

Todd was beyond listening. His usual resilience had deserted him. Worn out by the pressures of the past months, reeling from the news about Suntours, he was completely unnerved. Loosening his tie with shaking hands, he unbuttoned his collar and sucked air into his lungs as if suddenly suffocating. Cold only a moment before, now he felt hot. He even looked hot. A glassy sheen glistened on his forehead, his cheeks were flushed and his palms felt greasy with sweat.

Full of concern, Leo tried to pacify him. 'It's okay. It won't come to that. Calm down. This is a setback, that's all. It needn't be a disaster.'

'How can you say that?' Todd howled. 'I'm dead and it's not a disaster? I should take it in my stride? Is that it? You don't shrug off something like that!'

'But it won't come to that! I promise. I'm saying what he could do, not what he *will* do.'

'God Almighty,' Todd groaned with his head in his hands.

'He won't do anything if he gets his interest. Believe me, I know the man.'

Ignoring him, Todd jumped to his feet and began to pace the room, going to the window and peering down into the park as if expecting to see Moroni under the trees. Leo carried Todd's cup from the table. 'Drink this and sit down. I've worked out an answer to this, really I have.'

With a doubtful look, Todd allowed himself to be led back to his chair. He sank down like a man who had lost the use of his legs.

'First things first,' Leo said crisply as he sat down. 'You must meet the interest payment. How much will you have, do you think?'

Still in shock, a moment or two passed while Todd collected himself. His hands shook as he sipped his mixture of coffee and whisky. Concentrating on Leo's question, he was not sure how much he would have. The interest payment was not due until the first of December. 'We've still got seven or eight weeks,' he said finally, gathering his wits. 'I think we'll have about nine hundred grand.' He looked at Leo as if expecting criticism. 'That's a miracle, considering the state of business.' He waited for Leo to comment, but when the older man remained silent he continued, 'So if I sell the villa, even on this market I *should*

176

get about three hundred thousand for it, so you see, I *should* just about make it. Moroni can have his money.'

Leo nodded. He seemed to consider for a moment, then he said, 'I could be good for three or four hundred thousand by December.'

Todd looked at him in surprise.

'I'll cover the shortfall.'

Such was his lingering shock that Todd could only continue to stare.

Leo laughed. 'I'll be in funds at the end of the month, and it's a mug's game to sell property on a weak market.'

'You mean you'd lend it to me? Three hundred grand?' Todd was overwhelmed.

'Of course. After all, I'm partly responsible. What with Moroni being my contact –'

'No. That's not fair,' Todd interrupted, shaking his head, immediately shamefaced as he recovered his nerve. 'It's not your fault. You did warn me. What I said earlier . . . I'm sorry . . . I didn't mean –'

Leo brushed the apology aside. 'You were shocked, that's all.'

'But . . .' Todd swallowed. 'I mean, it's great . . . thanks, it's really generous of you, but . . . well, let's be honest. There's no telling when you'd get it back.'

'Nonsense. Paloma Blanca will come good. I still have every confidence in the project, and in you, so I don't see anything to worry about.'

When Todd opened his mouth to protest, Leo held up a hand. 'If it bothers you,' he said. 'Let's say I'm lending you the money for Katrina's sake. After all, if she loves the villa so much there's no point in upsetting her, is there?'

Todd felt too numb to respond.

'The point,' Leo continued, 'is, that if I cover the shortfall you're totally safe. Moroni won't do a thing if you honour your end of the bargain. And that gives you time to sort something out. You've still got Paloma Blanca. You'll have the best hotel in the Mediterranean, finished and ready in eight months. What you've got to do now is find another Suntours.'

Todd stared at him.

'There are plenty of other travel firms,' Leo said breezily. 'You only offered Paloma Blanca to Suntours, remember? And what happened? They snapped it up. Right?' He laughed. 'You never know, you might get a better deal from another outfit. This could be a blessing in disguise.'

Badly in need of blessings, disguised or otherwise, Todd felt some of the strength flow back through his veins. He watched in silence as Leo topped up their cups with his mixture of coffee and scotch.

'Think about it,' Leo said insistently. 'Paloma Blanca wasn't even *started* when you clinched the deal with Suntours. Now it's half finished. You've a hell of a lot more going for you than you had then. True or not true?'

'True, I suppose.' Todd was beginning to feel better. 'By God, you're a good man in a crisis, I'll say that for you, Leo.'

Leo accepted the compliment with a wry smile. 'I've had enough practice,' he said drily. 'Besides, I heard the news earlier. I've had time to think. And . . .' he pointed to his cup. 'I had two of these before you arrived. I find that half and half is about the right mixture for shock.'

'Life savers,' Todd admitted gratefully.

'And don't forget,' Leo added. 'I know the way Moroni operates. He won't touch you if you make that next payment. That gives you until next summer to find a replacement for Suntours.'

Stifling a shudder at the thought of being *touched* by Moroni, Todd began to make a mental list of people to call.

'After all,' said Leo. 'Hank must have plenty of contacts in the travel business.'

'Hank!' Todd exclaimed guiltily. Until that moment he had given no thought to Hank. 'Oh my God, I'd better call him –'

'No, no, sit still,' Leo commanded. 'Let's talk this through before we call anyone.' Getting up from his chair, he turned to the table. 'And let's have breakfast before it's totally cold.' He began lifting silver covers and peering underneath. 'Got your appetite back now? There's bacon and eggs . . .'

And so they breakfasted. Half an hour before Todd would have choked, but encouraged by Leo he managed quite well.

And of course, when he thought about the problem calmly and rationally, he realized that Leo was right. He *had* offered Paloma Blanca only to Suntours, and they *had* snapped it up.

'Bloody hell,' he exclaimed. 'You're an absolute tonic, Leo, you really are. You're right. This is a setback, that's all. And I've got eight months to find another Suntours. Eight months. I bet I can find a dozen in that time.'

He felt warm with gratitude. Over the years he had been lucky with friends; Sam, old Larkins, Hank, and now Leo. With breakfast finished he felt recovered enough to smoke a cigar, and they sat at the table for another hour, talking through again what they had already discussed, and although Leo mentioned Moroni again, to Todd's relief, it was only in passing. After all, Moroni was no longer the problem. With Leo making up the shortfall, the next interest payment was covered.

Afterwards, Leo refused the offer of a lift to the airport. 'No, I'll get a cab. You've no time to waste seeing me off. Get Herbert to take you back to the office. The sooner you're talking to people in the travel business, the better.'

So they said goodbye on the pavement outside the Ritz. Leo's last words were to confirm his promise about the shortfall. 'I'll be in touch about the money early next month,' he said as he climbed aboard his taxi.

Waving goodbye, Todd felt a conflict of emotions; an enormous surge of gratitude towards Leo, but also a surprising flash of anger with himself. He guessed that Leo's offer of the loan had been prompted by concern for his daughter. Leo had said as much. It made Todd's blood boil. Even worse, it made him feel guilty. He knew perfectly well that Leo still hoped for a reconciliation. 'All this time,' he muttered to himself. 'Seven years, and all I've done is sit on my arse!' Indignation rose within him. 'Well not any more. Not after this. I'll bring them together if it's the last thing I do!'

Such were his thoughts as he watched Leo's taxi disappear along Piccadilly. He had quite forgotten how frightened he had been of Moroni. After all, now he had no reason for fear. Leo would help make the payment and that would be an end to the matter.

'Good God,' he thought fondly. 'How can I possibly fail with someone like Leo behind me.'

There was a tinge of hero-worship in his attitude which might have evaporated had he realized he would never see Leo again.

Katrina, of course, knew nothing of all this. She had never even *heard* of Moroni. She had no knowledge of the insurance policy on Todd's life, an insurance policy which under certain circumstances was tantamount to a death warrant. Even the news about Suntours had passed her by, for she had looked at neither a newspaper nor the television that morning. Her thoughts and concerns were quite different, and at the moment that Todd was on the kerbside outside the Ritz, she was in her dressing-room with Sophie.

The open suitcase was half-packed and Sophie was supervising last-minute additions while delivering a lecture. 'You brought this on yourself, you know,' she said sternly. 'I saw it coming. The way you run around after him. You've always been the same. He takes you for granted. You're doing absolutely the right thing.'

'I wish I could be sure.'

Sophie's eyes widened in alarm. 'You can't change your mind now. Not now I've phoned Broadlands. I had to go down on bended knees to get you in. You know what they're like –'

'I'm *not* changing my mind,' Katrina exclaimed defensively. 'We're going and that's that, but I wish you'd stop nagging about doing the right thing. Something had to be done and I'm doing it. But I can't just go without telling him –'

'Leave him a note or something,' said Sophie, her mind more on their packing. 'You'll need your tennis stuff, by the way. They've got the best indoor courts in the country. Wait until you meet Steve. The money's worth it just for –'

'Steve?'

'The tennis coach.' Sophie gave her a look of surprise. 'Honestly, I don't think you're listening half the time.'

More accurately, Katrina was half listening. 'I can't just leave a note,' she said miserably. 'I wouldn't feel right. I must see him before I go. The thing is he's not at the office –'

'He *will* be. Isn't that what Sally said? She's expecting him shortly. Herbert checked in on the car phone.'

'I know, but –'

'We'll call round there, if you like. On the way out of town. I drive right past it.' Solving one problem gave Sophie the impetus to solve another. 'Come on, let's get this finished. I should pack that magenta top if I were you. Everyone dresses up in the evenings . . .'

Fifteen minutes later, they were downstairs in the kitchen. Sophie sat and drank coffee while Katrina went through lists of things to do with Mrs Bridges. 'Yes, I know it's short notice,' she said, irritated by Mrs Bridges' manner: her looks of enquiry verged on outright suspicion. 'I only decided last night,' she said crisply, while thinking, *Why should I explain to her? Good God, she works for me, not the other way around.*

Sophie smiled sweetly from the other side of the table. 'You won't recognize her when she comes back, Mrs Bridges.'

'Oh?' said Mrs Bridges, raising an eyebrow. 'That's nice.'

Katrina said, 'When you leave every day, can you make sure Mac's in his basket –'

'You're not taking him to the kennels then?'

Katrina bit her lip. *That,* she thought, *is perfectly obvious.* Aloud, she said, 'The kennels will have him while we're in Majorca, but he can stay here this week. He's no trouble. Just make sure he's indoors when you leave.'

'What about Tuesday?' asked Mrs Bridges in case she was being asked to come in on her day off.

'Toddy will have to send Herbert round or something. I'll tell him, don't worry.'

With her head in a spin, Katrina inspected the larder. *Not that there's any point. He'll eat at the club every night. Or will he?* Panic rose within her. *Perhaps he'll be out with whoever he was with last night? What was it Sally had said – Red hair, good figure, quite a looker! Davis was green with envy. Davis would be. Typical! Anything in a skirt . . .*

'How we doing, then?' Sophie asked impatiently with a glance at her watch.

'I'm ready,' said Katrina, feeling distinctly unready, feeling distinctly unsure about the wisdom of what she was doing. Last night's crystal clear certainties were dissolving into wishy-washy doubts. And Sophie was no help – making her rush as though the house was on fire! Somewhere at the back of her mind nagged an old saw about deciding in haste and repenting at leisure. 'Now you be a good boy,' she said, crouching over Mac and fondling his ears.

'Right,' said Sophie briskly. 'Goodbye, Mrs Bridges.'

In Sophie's car, giving her friend a sideways look, Katrina's thoughts verged on the resentful. *It's all right for you. You haven't a husband to worry about . . . a dog to leave . . . a house to run. You have a serviced apartment. No one to consider but yourself. Free to make instant decisions . . . to come and go as you please . . .*

'We should have done this ages ago,' Sophie exclaimed with a quick smile of excitement. 'I can't think why you haven't been to Broadlands before. You'll love it. And the people! Honestly, I've never been there without meeting someone really interesting . . .'

That's why you go, thought Katrina. *To pick someone up. Another affair. A fling for a month, or two months, or three months. Never much longer . . .*

'We'll be down there for lunch. I can show you over the grounds this afternoon. They're lovely this time of year, beautiful, a mass of autumn colours, then we'll have a sauna and a swim and a massage . . .'

I might not go, Katrina thought rebelliously. *Even now, I might not. This whole thing is stupid; rushing off, jumping to conclusions. If Gloria hadn't needled me yesterday . . . God, she's a bitch . . . she knows exactly how to wind me up. How to get me going. She always has, ever since I've known her. That's what started this. All that stupid talk of another woman, then last night Toddy sounding strange on the phone and not coming home. Coincidence, that's all. There's me adding two and two and making God knows what, meanwhile poor old*

Toddy's stuck up in the Midlands with a car broken down. I bet he was fuming. If I told him, he'd laugh. We'll both laugh. Clear the air, get back to normal – Sophie can go down to her bloody fat farm all by herself . . .

'Here we are,' Sophie said brightly as she drove into the forecourt at Owen's. 'Shall I come up to see Toddy with you?'

'What? No, I don't think so. There's no need. I shan't be a minute.'

She felt that she was looking good. Well, at least smart. He had always liked this blue suit. 'You should wear that more often,' he had said in the past. As if she would. He'd be sick of it then. Men! He was just the same with his own things. To compliment him about something was fatal. He'd wear it for ever.

'Morning, Mrs Todd,' said Davis, opening the door with a cheerful grin.

I could spit in your eye! she thought angrily. 'Morning,' she smiled, sweeping past and on up the stairs.

'Hello, Katrina,' said Sally, smiling as she looked up from her desk.

Katrina looked at the frosted glass panelled door to his office. 'Is anyone with him?'

'No, but he's frantically busy,' said Sally, as she reached for the telephone.

'Don't bother to announce me.' Katrina smiled as she advanced to the door. 'I'll surprise him.' Unconsciously she was crossing her fingers. She was aware of feeling nervous. *What's to be nervous about! Good God, it's your husband, not the dentist! He's in the wrong, not you. All you're doing is trying to get life back to normal . . . to restore things to the way they were . . . when you were happy . . .*

Opening the door, her face broke into a smile. 'Surprise!' she cried as she breezed into his office.

'Jesus Christ!' Startled, he jumped up from his desk. 'What are you doing here?' The question was blurted out without thought. He was not even concerned with her answer. What concerned him was the conversations buzzing around in his head. Having spoken to a dozen people in the travel business, his earlier talk with Leo was beginning to seem hopelessly optimistic. Faced with falling bookings, travel operators were in a state of collective hysteria. Thanks to advance publicity, they had all heard of Paloma Blanca. They liked what they heard. There was plenty of interest. But no one was making forward commitments. The collapse of Suntours had taught them a lesson. Worried by the future, they were avoiding obligations even to established hotels, let alone new projects like Paloma Blanca.

Jolted by his manner, Katrina stopped in her tracks. 'Oh,' she exclaimed, going pink in the face. 'Yes, well,' she said, as disappointment prompted a tart rejoinder. 'It's nice to see you, too.'

'What?' he frowned, looking baffled.

'You were going to phone me, remember? That's what you said. You said you'd call me first thing. I'm just making sure you're still alive.'

He groaned. 'Look, I'm really sorry, honestly I am, I forgot, but you won't believe, all hell broke loose this morning . . .' he paused as the telephone rang. Distracted, his harassed gaze returned to the desk. He ran a hand through his hair. 'Get Sally to give you a coffee and we'll talk in a minute.'

'No,' she said as he picked up the receiver.

His hand stopped in mid-air. 'What?'

'I haven't time. Sophie's outside in her car. We're going down to Broadlands for a few days.'

A look of astonishment came into his face. 'Since when?' Raising the receiver to his ear, he said, 'Tell 'em I'll call back.' He stared at her. 'I didn't know. You didn't tell me –'

'Chance would be a fine thing. The point is you'll have to look after yourself for a week –'

'A week?'

'Or longer. Sophie's going for ten days. And I've booked the flights to go out to the villa. We did say we'd go on the twelfth, didn't we?'

'I dunno. Christ, I don't believe any of this! I'm up to my neck –'

'And Mrs Bridges finishes at two every day, so Mac will be

shut in until you get back in the evening. Then there's Tuesday, of course, she doesn't come in on Tuesdays, so you'll have to send Herbert round at lunchtime or something.' Taking malicious pleasure from his confusion, she went on, 'All of which I'd have told you last night if you'd been there.' Emphasizing the point by nodding her head, she was about to say more when she realized that something about him was different. Something jarred her eye. As usual, his jacket was draped over the back of his chair. But usually his white shirt was spotless. There was a mark on it. Her heart lurched as she stared. Her eyes narrowed. *I can't quite make it out . . . but is that . . . can it be?*

'About last night . . .' he started to say and then froze as she advanced to the desk.

'What's that?' she asked, pointing to the mark on his shirt.

'What's what?'

'That's make-up.' Convinced, she stepped closer to peer at the spot. Her nostrils twitched. 'And perfume,' she exclaimed, looking up to see the colour rush to his face. 'My God! You smell like a . . . a –'

'Nonsense,' he protested shakily. 'It's aftershave, that's all.'

'You bastard! That settles it!'

'Settles what?' His brain stalled as he slumped in his chair.

'You lied to me! All that garbage about a car breaking down . . .' She gulped and stepped away from the desk. 'What sort of a fool do you take me for?'

'I dunno what you're talking about.'

'Not much!'

'Listen,' he blustered. 'I'm in the middle of the biggest crisis of my life –'

'You and me both,' she retorted turning on her heel. 'Well, you have your crisis here and I'll have mine at Broadlands.'

He stared at her with disbelief. 'What's got into you? What's this about?'

'Us. You and me,' she laughed, a brittle echo of scratched nerves.

The telephone on his desk rang again as she crossed the office.

'Katrina!' he shouted above the ringing, but by then she had gone through the door.

Sally looked up. 'Katrina?' she said in surprise, with her eyes full of queries.

But Katrina kept going, chin up, her gaze fixed straight ahead, through the outer office and down the stairs, her heart pounding as hot tears pricked her eyelids.

' 'Bye, Mrs Todd,' Davis smiled respectfully, opening the door of the showroom.

She grimaced a smile. Speech was beyond her. Tight-lipped, she stifled a sob as she ran out to Sophie's car. Wrenching open the door, she flung herself on to the seat.

'All set?' Sophie asked brightly.

Todd was punch-drunk. It was the most miserable day of his life. Propped up by Leo, he had been doing his best to pick himself up, only to be floored by Katrina. He might have chased after her had Sally not rung through at that moment. 'I've got Hank on the line. He sounds in a bit of a state.'

A bit of a state was an understatement. Hank sounded suicidal. 'Have you heard about Suntours?' he cried without preamble.

'Don't be bloody daft! Of course I've heard.'

'Holy Christ! What a disaster. People out here are slashing their wrists. Every fifth tourist who came out here was booked in by Suntours. Twenty per cent! Imagine! Just now a guy from Palma called me, wanting to know if we'd buy *his* hotel . . .'

Too dazed to dwell on Katrina's stormy departure, the best Todd could think of was to call her later at Broadlands. 'God knows what I'll say,' he thought miserably. 'But I'd better call and say *something*.'

It took him half an hour to calm Hank. The news about Suntours had cast a pall over the whole of Majorca. With an economy dependent upon tourism, the island was threatened by an absence of tourists. 'It won't happen,' Todd insisted. 'Just calm down and think about it sensibly. People will still take holidays. The beaches are still there, the mountains are still there . . .'

Finally he quietened Hank enough to tell him about his meeting with Leo, and Leo's offer to lend them three hundred thousand. 'Would he do that if he had any doubts? Think about it. This guy's been around. He's as shrewd as they come. I ask you? He *knows* we're on to a winner.'

He sounded more confident than he was. The reaction of travel operators had shaken him badly, but he saw no point in burdening Hank. That could wait until later. Meanwhile he suggested that Hank sound out his own contacts in the travel business, and then catch the afternoon flight to London. 'I'll have Herbert pick you up at the airport. We'll get together tonight and knock some ideas around.'

After which he went back to what he had been doing. With a travel trade directory open in front of him, he started on a succession of calls. For two years he and Hank had sacrificed their all for Paloma Blanca. Everything they owned had been thrown into the pot. Now the pot had been knocked over by this bloody recession.

He made call after call.

He talked until his voice rasped.

Sustained by coffee and sandwiches, he worked through lunch and into the afternoon.

His head buzzed from hundreds of conversations, most of them bad, until finally, defeated, he slumped in his chair and stared into space – which is what he was doing when Sally announced that a Charlotte Saunders had arrived to see him.

He looked at his watch in disbelief. Charlie? Five o'clock! Already? Where had the time gone?

The irony escaped him. With his wife in the country, he had every chance to plan another night of sexual excitement, but the thought never even entered his head. His mood was all wrong. Impending disaster had dampened his ardour. Fear is the most powerful sexual depressant known to man, and amazingly the pleasures of last night were almost forgotten.

'Okay,' he said as he gathered himself. 'Jim should have her car ready. Get him to sort out the paperwork. You and Jim explain everything to . . . er Miss Saunders. Then bring her up here for a drink. Give me . . . er, ten minutes . . . okay?'

Galvanized into action, he hurried into his washroom,

splashed his face with water, dried himself, and tried to rub the creases out of his forehead. Patting cologne on his cheeks, he unrolled his shirt sleeves, buttoned his cuffs and hurried back into his office, where he threw the remains of his lunch into the waste bin.

'What a day,' he moaned. 'What a bloody awful poxy day!' He was still muttering and shrugging into his jacket when Sally opened the door and ushered Charlie over the threshold.

'Ta ra!' Charlie cried as she entered, twirling around and dangling her key ring at arm's length for him to see. 'Guess who's the proud owner of a shining new Jaguar!'

Despite his misery, his depression lifted a fraction. Her smiling face came as a relief. A beautiful face smiling over a beautiful body, dressed in a yellow silk suit. Managing to respond with a smile of his own, he ushered her over to the sofa before turning to Sally. 'Thanks, Sally, there's no need to wait. Herbert can bring Hank up when they arrive.'

'Yes, well . . .' Sally eyed Charlie with disapproval. 'I'll see you in the morning, then.'

Charlie's response was a radiant smile. 'Thanks, Sally,' she said sweetly. 'It was nice meeting you.'

'Mmm,' Sally murmured doubtfully as she closed the door.

Charlie giggled and lowered her voice to a whisper. 'Wow! If she had her way she'd shave my head and parade me through the streets.'

'Rubbish.'

'It most certainly isn't,' she contradicted confidently as she advanced around his desk. 'Either she's jealous or she's a spy for your wife. Both, I should think.' Giving him a glowing smile, she brushed her lips against his cheek and turned away to inspect his office. 'This is rather grand, isn't it? I must say, Toddy, you do yourself proud.'

Her approval lifted his spirits.

'I can see this pictured in *Business* magazine,' she said, waving a hand at his desk and beyond. 'Hub of a commercial empire. Motor cars to hotels magnate, the mysteriously named Mister C for my first name's confidential Todd, sits at his desk –'

'Don't start that again,' he warned, unable to stifle a grin.

188

'That's better. You're looking more cheerful.'

'By God,' he said with genuine admiration. 'You'd cheer anyone up. Are you always like this?'

'Only when a sweet man promises me a drink.' Laughing, her eyes continued to traverse his office. 'Paloma Blanca! That's it, isn't it?' Pointing to the coloured photographs on the far wall, she went over to study them at close range. 'Oh, Toddy, it's fantastic. Really enchanting.' Turning to face him, her smile faded. 'What's up? You haven't forgotten already, have you? A pink gin would be nice, but you'd best make it a small one.'

'It's not that.'

'You've gone all glum again. I told you. It doesn't suit you.'

'Yeah, well,' he shrugged as he turned to the drinks cabinet. 'It's you looking at that photograph. I've had a pig of a day. Just about the worst of my life. Suntours have gone bust.'

'Oh, no! They were the people you were dealing with. You had a contract with them.' She was at his side in an instant, her eyes full of concern. 'You poor darling. You must be shattered. I'm surprised you're still on your feet.' Taking his arm, she led him to the sofa. 'Whatever you're on beats Valium, that's for sure. Sit down, I'll get the drinks. Oh, how awful. That's it, sit there and tell me about it.'

Gratefully, he did as he was told. He felt like an invalid being tended by a considerate nurse.

'There's not much to tell,' he confessed gloomily. 'Without Suntours we're wiped out unless I find a replacement, and there's not much chance of that the way the market is now. Hank should be here soon. We're having a council of war tonight, then he's flying to Germany tomorrow. He's got some contacts in the travel business in Berlin —'

'There,' she interrupted to hand him a whisky.

'Then he might go on to Copenhagen. A lot of Scandinavians holiday in Majorca. Danes, Swedes —'

'I know who Scandinavians are,' she said brightly, bringing the water jug to top up his whisky. 'You'll find someone. I'm sure of it. More than ever now I've seen those pictures. It really is an incredibly beautiful place. Is that enough water?'

Returning to the cabinet, she swirled Angostura around in a

glass before adding gin. 'Cheers,' she said as she joined him on the sofa. 'Don't worry. You'll find a *better* solution than Suntours. I know you will. There's something indestructible about you. Resolution chipped in granite.' She laughed at his look of protest. 'No, seriously, I mean it.'

To his vast surprise, he was reminded of Katrina. Not the Katrina who had stormed out of his office, but the Katrina of years before. There was something special about a woman's encouragement and he realized then how much he missed it.

'Besides . . .' Charlie continued as her gaze returned to the photographs on the wall. 'That's too good to fail.' She went back to admire them from close range. 'Can I say something? Um . . .' she hesitated for a second. 'I feel funny about this. You mightn't like it. I don't mean to be rude or anything, but it's something I thought when you were telling me about it yesterday. I'm sure I'm right, more than ever now I've seen it . . .' She took a deep breath. 'I do wonder if Suntours were the right people? Aren't they a bit down-market for this?'

'They were planning a separate marketing campaign,' he said resentfully.

Concentrating on the photographs, she missed his sulky expression. 'Maybe,' she said doubtfully. 'But Ford are still Ford. They're not Rolls-Royce or Ferrari are they? That's the image you want for Paloma Blanca.'

It was Hank's point all over again. Todd had heard it all day. Travel operators had been shocked at the prices he quoted. 'Too much for our clientele,' Global Travel had said. 'And another thing. Paloma Blanca looks terrific, but no one outside the trade has heard of it. Punters can pick and choose these days . . .'

'Paloma Blanca's for the rich,' said Charlie. 'Not the very rich. They have their own holiday islands or they can borrow one, so you won't get them, but there's enough of the ordinary rich to fill Paloma Blanca –'

'You're an expert, I suppose?' he interrupted with a sarcastic edge to his voice. Selling was something he knew about and he was in no mood to be lectured.

'Only about the rich. And I know a bit about boats and marinas and . . .' Her voice faded as she turned around and saw the look on his face. 'Oops. I've put my foot in it, haven't I?'

She was at his side in an instant. 'Me and my big mouth,' she said, full of contrition.

But even as he reassured her that he had not taken offence, he realized she had identified a worry that had been growing all day. Without Suntours, or a replacement for Suntours, the only hope of saving Paloma Blanca was to go into the holiday business and take over the marketing themselves. With a wry smile, he said, 'There were sound commercial reasons for dealing with Suntours.'

'I don't doubt it. I only meant that the short-term benefits might conflict with your longer-term interests.'

He knew she was right. He had linked the income from Suntours to his repayments to Moroni and stood back to count the profits. Now there would be no profits unless he did something fast. The conversation with Global came back to haunt him: *Paloma Blanca looks terrific, but no one's heard of it.*

'If no one's heard of it, how do I fill it?' he muttered.

'Sorry?' said Charlie, cocking her head.

He had spoken aloud, or at least partly aloud, but having started felt a need to go on. And talking to Charlie opened the floodgates. Prowling around his office, he found himself telling her about the travel operators and their reluctance to take risks in the present market. 'Which means we'll have to deal with the public ourselves. It would be a damn sight easier if we'd had time to launch Paloma Blanca. At least people would have heard of it . . .'

The more they talked, the more he liked her answers and her ideas. The points she made were all sound, all businesslike. He was seeing a different woman from his bedmate of last night. He had known she was bright, but yesterday he had been mesmerized by a different kind of brightness.

When the telephone rang at seven o'clock they were deep into a discussion about the marina and the big-spending customers it would bring. Always stimulated by business discussions, Todd's depressed mood had lifted. He had even had the idea of staging a regatta by then, which is what he was thinking about when he picked up the phone. He listened with half an ear as Herbert explained that after being delayed Hank's flight was due any minute, but his concentration was still on the discussion. A grin came to his face as he replaced the receiver. 'I've got it,' he said. 'We need more than a regatta. Suppose we stage a race round the Balearics? Make it an annual event. Call it the Paloma Blanca Gold Cup or something?'

Charlie's eyes lit with excitement. 'That would get the name known! It will give us terrific publicity with exactly the right people. The big spenders.'

Once the idea had been aired, they seized upon it, and after that there was no turning back. Whatever one said, the other took further. What Todd improved upon, Charlie expanded.

The meeting of minds was as powerful as the meeting of bodies twenty-four hours earlier. And almost as exciting. Soon they were talking about mailing details of their race to yacht clubs all over Europe. 'And even beyond,' Charlie said excitedly. 'I can get details of clubs in the States from the Royal Jersey Yacht Club. Besides, I know a few guys on Long Island . . .'

She certainly had a mass of wealthy contacts. She dealt with the rich every day, all over the world. 'Oh sure,' she said in answer to one of his questions. 'I can lend six million off my own bat, without referring to anyone.'

'I wish I'd met you two years ago.'

She laughed. 'It wouldn't have done you any good. Projects like Paloma Blanca aren't our kind of thing. Our stuff is short-term. A hundred and twenty days maximum and fully secured.'

But the conversation rarely strayed far from Paloma Blanca, and gradually an idea took hold in Todd's mind. The more he thought about it, the more it made sense. The pressures on his time were already enormous. And Hank had the same problem, what with running the Crow's Nest and spending every spare minute chasing the builders. If they were to take over the marketing of Paloma Blanca, the pressures on their time would become greater than ever. They would need help. And who better than Charlie? She had looks and personality. Her ideas were impressive. All of her comments were pertinent. She had a mass of wealthy contacts . . .

He broached the subject when they were discussing the casino.

'You're banned from our place by the way,' he joked. 'I'm not letting you in after the way you cleaned up at Blatchfords.'

'It's the only time I've won anything. I *always* lose in those places.'

'That's what they all say. But I've got another idea. Why don't you join us to run it?'

She looked at him. Cocking her head, her excitement gave way to a quizzical look. 'Now there's a thought. Pay me enough and I might even take you up on that. How d'you fancy me as your Entertainments Director?'

'I fancy you period,' he joked, and on impulse leaned forward and kissed her.

'Nice,' she murmured after the embrace. 'But no nooky if we work together. It never works out. Agreed?'

Even though it was a thump to his ego, he was oddly relieved. He knew she was right, and taking her hands into his, he was about to say so when he heard a noise at the door. Turning his head he saw Hank on the threshold. 'Hank! Hi! Come in, come in.'

He was too absorbed to take note of Hank's startled expression. He was too anxious to explain about the Paloma Blanca Gold Cup, and to work out a way in which Charlie might join them. Invariably optimistic, always busy, never one to sit back, it was his nature to go forward. The day had been a succession of shocks – the demise of Suntours, Leo talking about a possible threat to his life, Katrina slamming off to Broadlands – but look what had happened? Leo had come on board with three hundred thousand. And after three hours of exchanging ideas with Charlie, they had hit upon a project to make Paloma Blanca famous. And what was more, it involved yachts, Hank's big passion in life. So after making hurried introductions, Todd sat Hank in a chair, poured him a drink, and brought him up to date on their discussion.

Hank was unexpectedly cool to begin with. And his attitude towards Charlie was odd. After seeing him with any number of women, Todd knew the power of Hank's charm. But he made no effort to charm Charlie. Instead he was reserved and polite. 'Businesslike,' Todd thought with approval. Aloud, he said,

193

'When you've finished your drink, let's take Charlie out to dinner while we talk more about this.'

Even Charlie knew it was the wrong thing to say. Nothing would have pleased her more, but the surprise on Hank's face was warning enough. 'Er . . .' she mumbled, shaking her head. 'Didn't you say you were going home? Won't your wife be expecting you?'

'She's not there. She's gone to a health farm.'

'Katrina's gone away?' Hank looked bewildered. His gaze went from Todd to Charlie and then back to Todd.

'Yeah, well . . .' Todd shrugged with pretended indifference. 'She went for a week or ten days, something like that, depends if she likes it, I suppose. So you see, we've got to go out and get something to eat.'

And so it was settled. After promising Charlie that Herbert would deliver her car to her apartment first thing in the morning, Todd ushered them down the stairs and, after locking up, across the road to the Italian restaurant on the corner.

Hank thawed out a bit over the meal. And, of course, as a sailor himself, he liked the idea of the Paloma Blanca Gold Cup. 'The publicity will be tremendous,' he agreed with a rueful smile. 'I should have thought of it myself.'

Todd immediately sprang to his defence. 'Come on,' he said. 'Be fair to yourself. You've had enough to do, what with chasing progress on the site and running the Crow's Nest. You're working twenty-four hours a day as it is. Besides, we didn't need ideas until now. We had Suntours.'

'I suppose,' Hank admitted. 'Mind you, you know what I think about Suntours.'

'Charlie's the same,' said Todd, looking at her. 'Isn't that right?'

Listening to them agree with each other made him realize how much they had in common. Hank was a sailor. Charlie had sailed all her life. She and Hank knew far more about wealthy people than he did. When he had been selling used cars, Hank had been skippering a billionaire's yacht across the Aegean. And Charlie had all the right contacts. They would make a marvellous team.

194

Charlie was in tremendous form. Captivated by the photographs of Paloma Blanca, she could see a new life for herself – a life of colour and excitement compared to the routine of moving chunks of money around in Jersey. What Toddy and Hank had started, she saw herself taking further. The world had moved on and she was the new generation; well-trained, ambitious, and her job of handling the investments of the wealthy had given her every chance to study their thinking. She was sure of one thing. The 'haves' did not want to live cheek by jowl with the 'have nots', especially when on vacation.

'More expensive is better,' she said. 'Let's go really up-market with this. The more we charge, the more exclusive Paloma Blanca becomes. The more cachet we create, the more profit we make.'

Which was music to Todd's ears, and he was feeling very much better by the end of the evening. He remembered Leo saying, 'It's a setback, not a disaster.' As he sat there with Hank and Charlie, even 'setback' seemed too strong an expression. 'A blessing in disguise,' Leo had said, and that seemed more like it. So by the time he paid the bill and led the way out of the restaurant, Todd had recovered his usual good spirits – little knowing that the shocks of the day were far from over.

The row erupted within minutes of their reaching home. Hank had fallen into a smouldering silence from the moment they left Charlie at her Baker Street apartment. He had glowered every mile of the way during the journey to Hampstead, composing his onslaught . Now, zipping his fly from his trip to the bathroom, he hurried into the kitchen. 'So come on. Give. What's going on?'

His truculence caught Todd at a bad moment. Returning to an empty house had been worse than he had imagined. It had been easy to forget Katrina earlier, easy during the day with a million calls to make, easy over dinner discussing regattas and yacht races – but coming into an empty home had set him back on his heels. He had already been all over the house, leaving lights on in his wake. He had let Mac out for a run, fed him, fussed over him, and tried to pretend that things were normal. But things were *not* normal. The house was no longer home without Katrina.

'This is where she should be,' he seethed to himself. 'Not off gallivanting with Sophie! She should be here. She's *always* here!'

'So?' Hank repeated. 'What's going on?'

Todd turned from taking cups down from the dresser. 'How d'you mean?'

'You know. With you and Charlie?'

'I thought you liked her.'

'I didn't dash across here to watch you play footsie! We're down the tubes an' suddenly you start playing Casanova. What's up with you? And what's this rubbish about Katrina going to a health club? Since when have you two been leading separate lives?'

Todd went red in the face. 'That's my business.'

'Oh no it's not! We're partners, remember? If I'd wanted someone with a brain in his dick, I'd have asked one of the old farts in the harbour. At least they've got plenty of dough.'

'Bollocks!'

'That's what I thought!' Hank retorted furiously.

Clenching his fists, Todd took a deep breath to control his temper. Unclenching them, he wagged a finger in Hank's face. 'Don't you talk to me about going down the tube. You think I don't know? And I'll tell you something else I found out today. We won't find another travel firm to take over from Suntours. They've all lost their bottle. Our only hope is to do the selling ourselves and we need someone like Charlie for that. She's got some great ideas and plenty of contacts –'

'Sure. She's great. Okay? Satisfied? Sweetest piece of ass I've seen in years. Bright too, quick as a fish. I think we can use her, but not if you're giving her one.'

Todd glowered but said nothing. Charlie had already made her views on their future relationship perfectly clear, but he saw no reason to go into that. He scowled as he poured the coffee. 'You want sugar in this?'

Hank shook his head.

'Come on, bring it with you, let's get a drink.'

He led the way, switching on every table lamp in the drawing-room as if flooding the place with light would prove he had nothing to hide.

'So?' Hank persisted in a challenging voice.

Helping himself to a Scotch, Todd poured Hank a brandy and set the decanter in front of him.

Hank watched and waited. 'So how long's this been going on?'

'Nothing's going on.'

'Oh sure. You're out screwing and Katrina's gone into hiding. That's normal? Since when?

'You're an item, you and Katrina. You're always together. You *like* each other, for fuck's sake! You're not the type to play around. You're one of the world's great married men and there ain't a thing you can do about it. Anything else and you'd be like a fish out of water.'

'I wasn't tonight.'

'You were when you got back here. I saw the look on your face.'

Todd was unwilling to admit the truth, which was that he felt deserted, abandoned, let down. Katrina had never gone off before. She was always here at the end of the day. His resentment simmered, but biting his tongue he kept such thoughts to himself. His marriage was his business. Past conversations with Hank had been about Paloma Blanca, about harbour gossip and tales of faraway places; about rates of exchange, and cars, and who owned what and how they'd come by their money.

Hank said, 'Meeting someone like Charlie was the last thing I expected.'

'You spent the evening agreeing with her.'

'Sure, I *liked* her for Chrissakes! I said so, didn't I? I'd even like her involved in Paloma Blanca. You're right, she's got a lot of good contacts and her ideas are terrific. But we're in the shit, right? This ain't the time for screwing around. I just didn't expect . . . what I expected was . . .' Shaking his head, he started over again. 'I thought we'd have dinner with Katrina, then kick some ideas around.'

It was the last straw for Todd. 'With Katrina?' He snorted in disbelief. His pent-up resentment boiled over. 'You've gotta be joking!'

'Why's that?'

'She won't even *talk* about Paloma Blanca. The subject's banned. Taboo! It doesn't exist. Like Leo. He's lending us three hundred grand and she won't even *speak* to the man! Her own father!'

Hank sat back with a startled look on his face.

Jumping up, Todd went back to the whisky bottle. Frustration swamped his inhibitions. Guilt and drink loosened his tongue. 'She's being totally unreasonable! Bloody impossible! I don't know what's up with her these days.'

His sense of injustice boiled over. Katrina was showing a total lack of consideration. In a fury, he paced up and down.

'To just up and leave at a time like this!' he exclaimed, losing his temper completely. 'This is Sophie's fault! And Gloria's. They're a menace with all that woman's lib crap. It's a load of bollocks. What good's it done them? Either of them? Katrina has a far better life, but oh no, according to them she's a down-trodden woman!' Pausing for breath, he went red in the face. 'It's bound to have an effect. Them bleating on all the time. I've heard them. They think I don't know, but I do. It's all bollocks. Bollocks,' he repeated as the telephone rang. He stopped and listened. 'That'll be her now,' he said hotly as he crossed the room. 'About bloody time too! Here I am, worrying myself sick about staying in business, while she's out spending money. It'll blow your mind if I told you what they charge at this bloody fat farm!' He snatched up the telephone. 'Yes!' he bellowed.

'Mist' Todd?'

'Yes!'

'Is'sa Aldo Moroni.'

'Right! What d'you want?'

'Just'a say I heard the news.'

The call came at the wrong moment. Staring at the mantel-piece clock, Todd realized it was midnight! Bloody midnight! Katrina even lacked the decency to let him know if she had arrived safely. A red mist of anger seized his brain. 'We've all heard the sodding news,' he snapped. 'I'm working my bollocks off to sort things out. Okay! The last thing I need is you bleating about your money. You'll get your fucking twenty per cent when it's due and not before. Understand?'

The shocked silence brought him to his senses. Red-hot rage turned to ice-cold fear. Colour drained from his flushed face. His mouth went dry. He had to cough to clear his throat. 'Mr Moroni,' he croaked.

Silence.

'Mr Moroni?'

There was a sudden click as Moroni hung up.

'You still there?' Todd rattled the receiver rest. 'Mr Moroni!'

His eyes widened as he looked at Hank, and his hands shook as he replaced the telephone.

'Moroni?' Hank mused, frowning in thought. 'That name rings a bell. Isn't he the guy in Paris?'

On unsteady legs, Todd returned to his chair. Overcome by horror, he realized that he had committed an act of monumental stupidity.

'You sure told him, ole buddy,' Hank said with a dry laugh.

Todd felt sick. 'Oh Christ,' he groaned. 'Oh fuck.'

A little outfit in Paris. That was all he had told Hank. That was all he had told anyone. He had glossed over the details. He had always felt that anyone who was *someone* should have been able to borrow from a proper bank. He was ashamed of having to deal with a man like Moroni. Besides, there had been no need for explanations. Everything had been buttoned up, thanks to Suntours.

Swallowing his drink, he returned the glass unsteadily to the table. 'Hank,' he said, 'I think there's something I'd better tell you about this guy Moroni.'

CHAPTER SIX

IF THERE WAS A SINGLE ACT which sealed Todd's fate it was his ill-timed outburst on the telephone. It unsettled Moroni, it unsettled him badly. Not that he emulated Todd by flying into a rage; ranting and raving were not his style. The Legion had taught him to avoid rushing into action before considering his options, and life as a financier had taught him that men with quick tempers were unreliable in matters of money, especially when the money belonged to Aldo Moroni. So the telephone call caused him anxiety more than anger, and the following morning he took his worries to the suite of rooms which Claude Lapiere used as an office.

Lapiere rearranged the pencils on his desk as he listened. He knew Moroni to be exceptionally cool-headed, remarkably so for a Corsican. He also knew that his innermost thoughts were more often revealed by his tone than by what he said. Nuances were important, especially as the dark eyes and impassive, pock-marked face gave no hint whatsoever. The only clues were revealed in the gravelly voice, and even then Lapiere had to concentrate as he tried to gauge how much Moroni had been insulted.

When Moroni finished, Lapiere set the pencils aside, cleared his throat and marshalled his thoughts. He had a vested interest in painting a bright picture. After all, he had recommended the loan. A loan which went bad reflected on his judgement. So he tried to make light of the incident. 'Don't forget he's English. He's not used to our ways. The English are too arrogant to understand respect. Either that or too stupid.' He cocked his head and watched Moroni with the sharp-eyed look of a sparrow. When that failed to draw a response, he continued, 'After all, what is this Todd but a mechanic, a jumped-up car salesman? He has no manners, I agree, but I can't believe he meant to insult you. He wouldn't dare.'

Moroni nodded ponderously as if the explanation were the only one which made sense.

'The point,' Lapiere continued, 'is, that he said he'd pay the interest on time.'

Moroni hoped so. It had been a difficult year. The recession had brought worry to bankers all over the world, Moroni included. Loans made when times were good were proving hard to collect now that times had turned bad. When he had made the loan to Todd, the economies of Europe had been booming. Now Europe was plunged into recession. When he had made the loan, Suntours were part of the picture. Now Suntours had gone. And to cap it all Todd had been abusive on the telephone. The man had shown no respect.

'His payments have been on time so far,' said Lapiere encouragingly.

Moroni dismissed the point with a shrug of his shoulders. It had no relevance. He expected people to meet their payments; that was the whole reason for making an arrangement. Besides yesterday was history. It was the future which concerned him, especially now that Todd faced a future without Suntours.

Slouched in his chair, he knitted his brows in concentration. Like financiers the world over, when he made a loan he immediately added his profit to the capital sum. In the jargon, the loan became front-loaded. After all, what was the point of doing business if not for a profit? In borrowing twelve million, Todd was committed to repay nearly seventeen. To date he had paid two million, four hundred thousand. Outstanding was more than fourteen million. Pounds sterling, Moroni reminded himself. A great sum of money.

'Don't forget Sinclair,' Lapiere added helpfully. 'He introduced Todd to us, and he wouldn't want anything to go wrong in case we went after him. His involvement gives us further security.'

Security is the bedrock of banking the world over, and although Moroni had poured scorn on the concept in his meeting with Todd, he was as mindful of security as the chairman of Barclays. Sucking his teeth, he fixed his dark eyes on Lapiere and waited for the man to continue.

'I understand your concern,' Lapiere said smoothly. 'The loss of the Suntours business could create problems. On the other hand this man Todd seems resourceful. Sinclair is a wily old bird and he must be quite wealthy. So between them . . .' He paused in case his reassurances were sufficient, knowing in his heart he was wasting his time. He knew perfectly well that he would not reassure Moroni by his assessment of the individuals. Moroni would only be reassured by seeing his money made secure. 'The question is,' he continued. 'What do you want me to do in advance? I mean, in case Todd fails to pay in December?'

When Moroni remained silent, Lapiere steepled his fingers. 'Suppose we send an expert to value the site? I could arrange that quickly enough. Then if Todd does fail . . .' He permitted himself the ghost of a smile. 'We'll know what the place is worth if you force him to sell. I'm sure he'll want to meet his obligations.'

Moroni was equally sure. His lack of a formal charge on Todd's assets worried him not in the least. In his experience men were always ready to part with whatever was necessary when called upon to pay him.

'I'll send Philippe Roos,' Lapiere decided. 'I know he's expensive, but he's the best hotel man in Europe.'

Moroni thought it typical of Lapiere to hire someone expensive. 'Is'sa not your money,' he grumbled under his breath. But he gave the plan his approval. It made sense as far as it went. He intended to go further, but he had no intention of discussing that with Lapiere. Some matters were best not discussed with one's lawyer. Instead, he contented himself by asking one question about the insurance cover on Todd's life and, when that was answered to his satisfaction, he signalled the end of the meeting by raising his bulk from the chair. Declining Lapiere's offer to organize a taxi, he led the way to the outer office, where his man Jules Carbone was chatting to Isabella Vosges, Lapiere's blonde secretary who was also, Moroni suspected, his mistress. Carbone immediately collected Moroni's mohair overcoat from the cupboard and hurried forward to place it around his *pad-rone*'s shoulders. After which Moroni bade Lapiere *au revoir*, nodded courteously to Isabella Vosges and, with Carbone leading the way, descended the single flight of stairs which led out on to the streets of Montmartre.

When in Paris, Moroni rarely strayed from Montmartre. It was his patch and had been for thirty years. He felt safe in Montmartre. In Lyons or Marseilles, even in some parts of Paris, he would hesitate to walk the streets for fear he would be too tempting a target for his enemies, but he suffered no such fears in Montmartre, and although accompanied by Jules Carbone wherever he went, Carbone acted more as a messenger than a bodyguard. Men who had threatened Aldo Moroni had long since disappeared from the district. After so many years it was said that he was as much a landmark as the dome of Sacré-Coeur, and he was treated with equal respect. For the most part he shunned the opulent Paris of the Champs-Elysées, and the long, imposing vistas which fanned out from the Eiffel Tower. True, sometimes Nicole dragged him on expensive shopping expeditions to the fashion houses in rue du Faubourg St-Honoré. Occasionally they went to the Lido or the Crazy Horse, but such trips were rare and reserved for special occasions. If she wanted cabaret, where better than Moulin Rouge or the Folies-Bergère, both of which were close to the apartment? Or if they were too full of tourists, or had become too modern – and privately Moroni deplored the computerized light shows now featured at the Moulin Rouge – there was always the Lapin Agile where the raunchy shows were more to his taste. As for bars and restaurants, Montmartre was full of them, a dozen of which he partly owned, and when spending money he preferred to spend it where it did him some good.

It was to a restaurant that he was going, turning right from rue Norvins and strolling past the bars and tourist shops on his way to place du Tertre. Even in the cool days of October a handful of artists hung around in the square, ready to dash off a portrait for any tourist who fell for their patter.

Moroni pondered as he strolled, a knack learned on route marches in the Legion when he had used the time to think up schemes to win promotion. But today his pondering was less hopeful. Instinct told him that the Todd loan was turning bad, and he always trusted his instincts. Lapiere was right. Valuations were needed on Todd's assets, *all* of his assets, not just on Paloma Blanca, but also his assets in London. And if the total value failed to cover the loan, there was always the life cover to fall back on.

Not that the thought gave him much comfort. He would rather the arrangement was honoured. Killing is never as easy as shown in the movies. Killing is difficult, dangerous, expensive and time-consuming. Sometimes the police become involved and Moroni had a lifetime's aversion to policemen. Besides, insurance companies are not run by fools. Before parting with large sums of money they ask a vast number of questions. Such was his experience. Consequently he had developed a range of techniques which started right at the outset. Every new loan was put through a new company. When the transaction was completed, the company was wound up. As a result if a transaction went bad and an insurance claim became necessary, the insurers had no record of a previous claim. Neither had anyone else, for although Moroni used scores of different insurers in a dozen countries, they swapped information with a disregard for confidentiality which seemed shameless to him. So much so that, despite his elaborate precautions, even his record was less than a hundred per cent. Two claims had failed; one for two hundred million French francs and the other for twenty million US dollars. Expensive losses which had depressed him for months.

Of course he had learned from experience. Big bangs beat little ones every time. When an airliner explodes in mid-air, there are hundreds of victims. With dozens of insurers raking the ashes, rarely does the spotlight fall on a particular victim. The same if a bus goes over a cliff. Moroni had used big bangs five times, each one successfully, but the organization required was expensive. 'Is'sa lotta money,' he had sighed mournfully when adding up the costs. Consequently he preferred to rely upon another lesson – that most accidents occur in the home – which was why he was on his way to lunch with Vito Sartene.

Between them they had devised a dozen ways to make recalci-trant debtors drown in their baths, electrocute themselves with faulty appliances, fall from ladders while mending a roof, or break their necks while checking their cellars.

When Moroni arrived at the restaurant, Vito Sartene was at the door bidding farewell to two of the principal dancers at the Folies-Bergère. A big man with slicked-back black hair, he had the bruised features of a boxer which, although verging on ugli-ness were often considered attractive by women. A forty-seven-year-old Corsican, he was another of the ex-Legionnaires who owed allegiance to Aldo Moroni. Ten years before Moroni had given him the money to buy his restaurant; *given*, not loaned it, an action which had generated such loyalty that Moroni was able to call upon his services whenever he needed them. And he needed them now.

Dismissing the two women by kissing their hands with elabor-ate gallantry, Sartene turned to his benefactor with a broad smile of welcome. The two men embraced warmly; Sartene and Carbone slapped each other on the shoulder, then Sartene ushered Moroni into the restaurant. He took him through the room to an unoccupied booth against the back wall. Permanently reserved for Aldo Moroni as a sign of respect, the booth was roped off by a silken cord which Sartene unhooked with a flourish. Murmuring his thanks, Moroni slid his ample frame behind the table and settled himself into the corner. Carbone hesitated a moment, caught Moroni's eye, then turned away to find himself a table close to the door. It was then that Sartene knew that his benefactor had come on a matter of business. With a quick glance around the restaurant – which at two-thirty was beginning to thin out – Sartene beckoned the *sommelier* to the table.

Comfortable in each other's company, the two men settled down to an enjoyable meal. They talked as they ate – of family in Corsica, days in the Legion, politics in France – and by the time they had finished eating, the restaurant had virtually emptied. Two lovers lingered on the far side, their foreheads practically touching as they gazed at each other with mutual adoration. Carbone sat at his table near the door, discussing football with one of the waiters. Some of the staff gathered for their own meal at a table well beyond earshot.

Sartene knew it was time to talk business. After refilling their glasses, he raised his own in a toast. Then he said, 'You look troubled, my friend. You have a problem?'

And so Moroni told him about lending Todd the money for Paloma Blanca.

Sartene listened attentively, making no written notes, relying upon a memory which was infallible about matters of importance.

When he had finished his story, Moroni sipped his brandy, dabbed his mouth with his napkin, and admitted that his concern might be misplaced. Todd *might* meet the payment on time. 'Is'sa good if he does, eh? But . . .' he patted his ample stomach and pulled a face of displeasure. 'I gotta bad feeling, Vito. Is'sa best to be ready, eh? Specially when a lotta money involved.'

When Sartene volunteered to go to London to spy out the land, it was no more than Moroni had expected. Sartene had been on such missions before. When he returned he would know not only the value of Todd's assets in London; but having studied Todd's habits, his place of work and his home, he would know — should it prove necessary — where and how to stage a fatal accident. Sartene's own favourite was a gas explosion. It had two big advantages: conducting an autopsy on victims of blast is exceedingly difficult, and sometimes the insurer can obtain compensation from the public utility company, thereby making him more amenable to meeting a claim. Given the choice, Sartene opted for gas every time. He and Moroni had first used it in Amsterdam. They had rendered the victim unconscious by a blow to the head, fractured the gas supply pipe, set a time fuse and departed. The resultant explosion had destroyed the entire block, causing the deaths of eight other people, but the insurers had paid out seven months later, which given their tardiness, Moroni had said was almost a record.

Discussing their business in such matter-of-fact terms, they might have been tradesmen. Neither man considered himself a murderer. The recalcitrant debtors were at fault, not them. As far as Moroni was concerned, he had done his best to help

Todd, but some people were fools to themselves. They got their financial affairs into a mess, they showed no respect . . . if they failed to pay, they had to be dealt with . . . and if that meant killing them for the insurance Moroni would do so without a moment's compunction. After all, he had to recover his money. What choice did he have?

Business concluded, and having thanked his friend for lunch, he was easing his bulk out from the table, when he remembered Lapiere's comment about Leo Sinclair. Now that he thought about it, Sinclair's involvement could be doubly important. There was an angle which they had overlooked. Todd was Sinclair's son-in-law. Concerned for his daughter's safety, Sinclair might pay a great deal to keep her from harm . . .

Placing a hand on Sartene's arm, Moroni drew him back to the table.

Nine days after Sartene received instructions to go to London, Katrina arrived in Majorca, still blissfully ignorant of the extent of her husband's difficulties. Of course he had told her the bad news about Suntours, she knew he had problems and she was sorry, but he could hardly expect sympathy, could he? She had warned him enough at the outset. She had pleaded with him to abandon the idea.

As the cab wheezed past the flower market in the Rambla, she was tempted to ask the driver to stop. She usually did stop on the way in from the airport. When Todd was with her they would arrive at the villa clutching masses of flowers; she would spend the first hour filling vases while he went around unbolting shutters, opening windows, inspecting the pool and checking the bar . . .

But deterred by the prospect of coping alone, she allowed the cab to continue past flower stalls blazing with colour.

'Give me a buzz when you get there,' he had said on the phone.

Telephone conversations had been their only contact since that day in his office. The day she and Sophie went down to Broadlands. Ten days ago. Ten days which seemed more like twenty, though for reasons different from those she had expected. But then she had never expected to meet someone like Ossie.

He had been coming down the steps when Sophie pulled up at the front door. 'Hi!' he had grinned. 'New kids, eh? Welcome to summer camp. Want a hand with your bags?'

Sophie had said yes please and had shown a good deal of leg as she got out of the car. Katrina could have strangled her. She had even pointed to the porter at the front door, but Sophie had chosen to ignore her, and Ossie had taken charge by the time the porter arrived. 'Ladies,' he grinned with a slight bow. 'Pleasure to meet you. I'm Ossie Keller and you look like the cavalry.'

'Cavalry?' Sophie exclaimed in surprise.

'Don't you watch westerns? You know, just as the good guys are about to be annihilated the cavalry come to their rescue.'

Sophie's plucked eyebrows had risen an inch. 'You're about to be annihilated?'

'Suffocated by boredom,' Ossie said, pulling a face. 'I was losing the will to live when I saw you arrive, then I told myself, Ossie, you're saved.'

Sophie's pleasure at his flattery was marred by his suggestion that Broadlands was boring. 'You can't possibly be bored! This place is always full of interesting people.'

'Ah, yes,' he agreed. 'But few of them are beautiful.'

When Sophie came to her room half an hour later, Katrina exploded. 'How could you let yourself be picked up like that? Honestly, Sophie –'

'I think he's cute. As a matter of fact, he reminds me of Toddy.'

'Toddy! Toddy doesn't go around jumping on women!'

'He's jumping on someone.'

The memories were interrupted as the cab crested the hill and the harbour came into view. The sight of all the white boats on the brilliant blue water never failed to enchant her. She could still remember seeing the harbour for the first time, five years before, when Sam and Pamela had driven them over from Santa Ponsa. They had become her favourite people. Whereas Toddy came out to mix with the smart set at the Crow's Nest, she came to see Sam and Pamela. They were her ideal couple. With her passions for music and gardening, Pamela reminded her of her aunt, and old Sam had become almost a substitute father. Vaguely at the back of her mind, she had always hoped she and Toddy might be like them in twenty years' time; safe and secure, full of common sense, living for each other, enjoying their lives. Or at least, such had been her hopes until recent events.

The phone was ringing as she unlocked the front door. With brilliant sunshine streaming in over the threshold, she ran down the tiled hall and picked up the extension. 'Hello?'

'You were going to call me?'

'I've only just got in,' she protested breathlessly. 'The plane was delayed, we had headwinds or something. We were an hour late by the time we landed.'

'Oh. An hour? Wow, that's unusual. Everything okay at the villa?'

'Toddy, I just said! I've only this second come through the door. I'm still in the hall.'

'Oh.'

She punished him with her silence, deliberately making the conversation as difficult as when he had called her at Broadlands. Well, why not? He deserved it. He had still not said a word about his trip to the Midlands, if indeed he had been in the Midlands. He might have been in London for all she knew. He might have been anywhere!

'Ah, right,' he said with forced cheerfulness. 'What's the weather like?'

'Fine. It's not hot, but it's warm and sunny.'

'Good. So what's your programme today?'

'Pamela will be here any minute. We're having lunch in the square, then I expect we'll come back here afterwards.'

'That's nice, give her my best wishes. Er . . . I was talking to Hank earlier. He said he'd call round to make sure you're okay.'

She frowned, disliking the idea of Hank 'calling round'. It had been her intention to avoid him. She blamed him for all that had gone wrong in her life. He had been bad news from the day they met him. Without Hank there would be no Paloma Blanca, no worries, no problems, no big spending; and quite probably no other woman. It was all his influence . . .

Todd said, 'I expect he'll suggest dinner at the Crow's Nest.'

'He can suggest what he likes. I'm not spending that sort of money –'

'As his *guest*. To look after you. He is my partner, after all.'

'He got you into this mess, if that's what you mean.'

His long-suffering sigh caused her to relent a fraction but not enough to help with the conversation.

'Yes, well,' he said in a resigned voice. 'I'm glad you're there safely. Have a nice time with Pamela, and . . . er, I'll call you tomorrow, okay?'

'Okay.'

Returning to the porch to collect her overnight bag, she took it into their bedroom. With the outside shutters still closed, the room was dark enough for her to switch on the light. She opened the wardrobe and lifted a summery white cotton frock from a hanger. Her brow furrowed as she wondered if the weather was warm enough. Looking for alternatives in the wardrobe, her gaze strayed down the rail, passing Todd's denim jacket in the process. Her eyes went back to it. Casual but smart. She liked him in that; when she liked him at all . . .

Deciding on the white dress, she laid it out on the bed and turned her attention back to her overnight bag. Unzipping the top, she took out the presentation case of Barzini compact discs. She imagined Pamela's excitement when she gave it to her. Music, especially opera, and most especially Enrico Barzini were Pamela's passion in life. From morning to night the voice of the world's greatest living tenor reverberated around the villa at Santa Ponza; giving unceasing delight to Pamela and occasional irritation to Sam.

'Sure he's the greatest,' Ossie had smiled. 'Enrico's a genius. You don't think I'd devote my life to some second-rate bum, do you?'

She had been wary of him at first, suspicious of his constant geniality. It was only when he stopped smiling and started to grumble that she saw beyond the veneer of success and saw him as . . . she grinned as she remembered his own description . . . 'a warm human being, more vulnerable than the next guy and in constant need of love and affection.'

The grin remained on her face as she stripped off her clothes and went into the shower.

The first few days at Broadlands had been awful. *What am I doing here? I should be at home. What's Toddy up to? What's happening to us?* Questions had plagued her. They had been on her mind night and day – in the steam room, playing tennis, being massaged, even during what was laughingly called dinner. Nothing could divert her from her troubles. To add to her torment she had spent most of the time gasping for a cigarette and a large gin and tonic. In an atmosphere of unrelenting conviviality she was as morose as someone cold stone sober in a room full of drunks. 'Enjoy yourself!' Sophie had pleaded, on her way to play tennis with Steve.

She had never felt less like enjoying herself. During the day she had found herself waiting for Toddy's calls with the suppressed anxiety of a prisoner in the dock. He had phoned her most evenings. The absurd thing was that after spending the day looking forward to hearing from him, she had found fault with whatever he said. She had surpassed herself in bitchiness.

Ossie had rescued her on the fourth day. She knew who he was by then. Sophie had found out, in the way that she had discovered the business of everyone there. 'He's Barzini's manager. You know, the singer?'

Aware of his attention from the day they arrived, she had assumed his interest was in Sophie. She discovered her error on the Sunday afternoon. Having taken a book into the large Victorian conservatory, she was trying to concentrate when a shadow fell over the page. When she looked up, she found him grinning down on her, not from a great height for he was not much taller than Toddy, and he had a similar shape, even to his round face, flushed from exercise at that moment. Dressed in a blue track suit, he was carrying a tennis racket in one hand and holding a cup in the other.

'Hi. Mind if I join you? I was through there . . .' he pointed to the lounge beyond '. . . when I saw you out here by yourself, and I thought, this chance is too good to miss.' He grinned hugely, conveying the goodwill of a large dog wagging its tail. 'I've been wanting to talk to you ever since you arrived.'

She watched him put the cup on the table, drop the tennis racket and pull a wickerwork chair up to the table.

'Know something?' he sighed as he sat down. 'I lied when we met. This ain't a summer camp. This is Dante's Inferno, Devil's Island and Alcatraz rolled into one. Worse, it's a con. Who's kidding who? That's what I want to know? Half the inmates don't need diet or exercise or any of that crap. So why do they come here?'

She smiled politely, secretly amused by his schoolboyish earnestness.

'Don't you think it's crazy?' he asked, his brow crinkling. He looked at her intently, as if her answer were of the utmost importance.

'I suppose so. Why did you come here, Mr Keller?'

He pulled a face. 'Ossie, please. And you're Katrina, right?'

She nodded. 'So why did you come here?' she repeated, avoiding his name.

He answered with a short, ironic laugh. 'Call it a penance, if you like. For years of good living. See, I got this doctor. "Ossie," he says to me, "after two weeks you'll feel a new man." He was dead right. I tell you, Katrina, I can't take much more of this. It's killing me. Another couple of days and I'm ready for a lobotomy.' He rolled his eyes. 'Come to think of it, maybe I've had one already? Maybe they did it while I was asleep. My brain's gone phut, that's for sure. I gotta be crazy shelling out big bucks to be starved to death. If I went to India I could get this for nothing.'

She smiled at his anguish.

'Aren't you hungry?' he demanded.

'A bit,' she admitted.

'Wait till you've been here a week. Boy, I could murder a thick juicy steak. You know, black charcoal round the edges and red blood inside. Come to think of it, I could eat *anything* resembling proper food. And no matter how often they tell me, I'll never buy this crap about spring water. Give me a proper drink every time.' He looked at her with concern. 'Seriously, how you making out?'

'It's easier not to think about it.'

'Proves my point. That's why they hand out lobotomies.'

With a smile, she admitted, 'Right now I could down a whole bottle of gin without batting an eyelid. And I'd love a cigarette.'

'Smoker, eh?'

'Leper.'

He grinned. 'Ain't that the truth? It's getting that way, especially in the States. I used to go through two packs a day, but being around singers all the time . . .' lifting his chin, he touched the skin beneath his throat. 'Some of them get paranoid if there's a whiff of smoke in the air.' He shrugged. 'Not that I blame 'em. They ain't got a living without a voice. So I quit smoking, put on weight and end up in this place. I ask you, where's the justice? I'm still trying to figure out what I did to deserve it.'

She laughed for the first time since she had arrived.

The big grin returned to his face. 'Hey, that's nice. I like that.'

'Like what?'

'The way you laugh. You got a great laugh, you know that? It's warm and amused and . . .' his grin faded as he searched for the right words. 'Like it wraps itself around you. Like sinking into a bath. Lady, I could drown in your laugh.'

Unsure of how to respond, she smiled. *How many times has Toddy said that? About my laugh. Hundreds. But not for a long time.*

Collecting herself, she asked, 'Why don't you leave? Just check out?'

The look he gave her was searching enough to make her wonder if her hair was untidy, or if something was wrong with the way she was dressed. Her cream silk shirt and white linen slacks had looked perfectly presentable in the mirror in her room.

Finally he said, 'I almost did. In fact, I still might.'

'What's stopping you?'

As soon as she asked she knew his answer would confuse her. Something in his eyes told her that she was embarking upon a

213

conversation the like of which she'd not engaged in for a long time.

'You are,' he said.

Her heart pounded. Trying to sound surprised, she even managed a little laugh, but deep down she had known it was what he would say. She shook her head. 'That's very flattering, but –'

'It's the truth. Soon as I saw you, I said to myself – Ossie, here's someone you should get to know. Someone you can relate to. Someone who's *genuine*. See, Katrina, my problem is I work in a world full of rogues and charlatans. Maybe it's the insecurity of the life? You know, people who go from rags to riches are afraid the good life will be snatched away from them. They have nightmares about waking up and finding it gone. So they become paranoid. Or worse. You wouldn't believe how long I can go without meeting a genuine person.'

Lost for words, she simply stared at him.

'Take this place,' he said, waving his hand. 'You're no more one of this happy band of campers than I am. We don't belong. This place is full of posers. They'll drive us nuts, and that's not meant as a slur on your friend Sophie.'

Dragging her gaze from his face, she glanced towards the lounge as if expecting to find Sophie bearing down upon her. But the entrance was empty. There was no sign of Sophie or anyone else.

'I got an idea,' he said, making a sudden decision. 'I'm going over the wall tonight. How's about you coming with me?'

'Over the wall?' she repeated, amused by the way he sounded like a gangster.

Glancing back over his shoulder, he lowered his voice. 'Not a mass break-out, just you and me. There's a pub in the village. Okay, I'll admit, the Four Seasons it ain't, but the dining-room gets two stars in Michelin. I looked it up. In a couple of hours you could be in the bar, smoking like a chimney and knocking back all the gin you can handle. Then after that you've got a candle-lit supper with all the trimmings and me making eyes at you. What d'you say?'

Her throat ached for a cigarette and a proper drink. And the thought of appetizing food made her feel weak.

'Well?' he persisted.

'It's an intriguing idea, but I don't think I want you to make eyes at me.'

'So I'll wear a blindfold and tell you stories instead.'

She laughed. 'What sort of stories?'

'Anything to make you laugh. You got a laugh that makes my toes curl.'

It came as a shock to realize that her own toes had curled just a little. A warm tingle ran through her body.

The earnest expression of approval returned to his face. 'You've got to be a singer with a laugh like that. All the great singers are good laughers. I remember –'

'Of course I'm not a singer.'

'But you like music. I can tell. It's in your soul. I bet you're mad on opera?'

'I used to go to Covent Garden regularly,' she said truthfully.

'There you are,' he nodded happily. 'I knew it. I told you. I can tell. So this is what we'll do. Here's the plan. Over dinner I'll regale you with stories about all the great singers. All the backstage gossip. Okay? We'll drink some good wine and then afterwards you can smoke, and we'll talk long into the night about the meaning of life.' As he sat back in the wickerwork chair, he gave her a grin of pure mischief. 'What d'you say, Katrina?'

Hesitating, she began, 'It's very nice of you, but –'

'It would be nice of *you*. I'd be honoured. Seriously. And I'd be grateful. Come to think of it, even Barzini would be grateful. You'd be saving my life and he needs me around.'

'Nonsense,' she said, amazed at how much she was enjoying herself.

'You'd be giving me great pleasure,' he insisted.

'But . . .' Pleased and flattered, she was lost for words for a moment. 'What would I tell Sophie?'

'Why tell her anything? She your keeper or something? Tell her you're having an early night. Tell her you're washing your hair. Say you've had all the steamed fish you can handle. Tell her to mind her own business. Who cares?'

'But what about your bridge crowd?' she asked and then bit

215

her tongue, hoping that he had missed the admission that she had noticed him disappearing into the card room in the evenings.

He grinned. 'They can't come either. No one else is invited. Just you and me.'

Hesitating, she looked down at her hands, suddenly feeling awkward.

'We'll be back by lights out,' he promised in a hushed voice. 'The screws will never know.'

She repressed a giggle. The idea of a night out, with proper food and a drink, was hugely appealing. Smiling, she raised her eyes and then blushed at his look of undisguised admiration. Hurriedly she returned her gaze to her hands.

He said, 'Before you twist that wedding ring off your finger, there's something I ought to tell you.'

Surprised, she raised her face.

His expression was serious. 'In case you get the wrong impression,' he said, sounding apologetic. 'I mean, I don't want to get your hopes up.'

'About what?'

'Well . . .' he tried to keep the amusement from his eyes. 'I'd hate for you to be disappointed, but I've got a rule. Don't matter how attracted I am, I never go to bed on the first date.'

'And that's all that happened?' Pamela raised her eyebrows with unconcealed incredulity. 'He just took you to Gatwick?'

Katrina put down her glass and reached for her handbag. Glancing around the open-air café, her eyes brightened as Sally and Bobby Thomas took seats at a nearby table. Deep in conversation, they failed to see her, unlike the many others who had interrupted lunch with a stream of 'Hellos'. It was always the same in the harbour, especially in the autumn when the tourists thinned out. Most of the tables were occupied by friends or people she knew. After three years she felt more at home in the harbour than in Hampstead. 'Thank God to be back,' she said with satisfaction as she took out her cigarettes. 'Everyone still smokes out here.'

'Well, I do think it's a bit of a let down. What an anti-climax. How many times did you go over the wall with him?'

'Three, counting last night.'

'Three. And that was the best you could do? What time did you have to leave this morning?'

Katrina was interrupted by the waiter arriving at their table. Deftly he slid the bones of their grilled sardines on to one plate, picked up the salad bowls and glanced meaningfully at the nearly empty bottle of Rioja. Catching his glance, Pamela shook her head, 'I think coffee and a brandy? What about you, Katrina?'

'Please.'

'Si, señora.'

Thanking him with a smile, Pamela returned her attention to Katrina. 'So what time did you get away from Broadlands?'

'Oh, early. Just before seven. I had to be at Gatwick for eight.'

'So the poor man was up at the crack of dawn —'

'He didn't *have* to come. I could have got a taxi. Anyway, he was getting a flight himself later.' She glanced at her watch. 'He'll be in Rome by now. He's there for a month.'

'Goodness,' said Pamela. 'So you might never see him again?'

'No, I suppose not.'

'And now you're feeling sad?'

'Not sad, but . . . well, he was fun. He did make me laugh. And you wouldn't believe the life he leads. It's fantastic! Rome, Venice, New York, Paris . . .' she stopped in mid-sentence. 'What's that funny look for? Why are you shaking your head?'

'I was just thinking, what a wasted opportunity. You shouldn't have gone back to Broadlands last night. You could have found a nice country hotel near Gatwick and spent a night of unbridled passion. That's what I would have done.'

Katrina choked, spilling wine over her chin. Dabbing her mouth with a paper napkin, her eyes rounded with amazement. 'You would?' she croaked.

'At your age I would. Certainly. I'd have been flattered to death. You fancied him, didn't you? Heavens above, you've got this human dynamo panting after you, and what do you do?

Run away.' The look on Pamela's face was as reproving as her tone of voice. 'Really, Katrina, sometimes I wish you'd learn to enjoy life.'

Katrina gasped, 'But what about Sam?'

'Oh, Sam would get the benefit. The next night I'd be so good to him that he'd think it was his birthday and Christmas rolled into one.'

Katrina's surprised gurgle of laughter overcame her astonishment. Even so, she continued to shake her head in disbelief. 'Never,' she protested. 'Not you.'

'Why not?' A sparkle of enjoyment lit Pamela's blue eyes.

'But . . . because, I mean, you and Sam . . .' Lost for words, she started over again. 'You've always reminded me of my aunt. You're so like her that it's how I think of you. She sort of brought me up, I told you about her, remember? She was incredible; the most civilized person I've ever known, and you're the absolute image of her, with your passion for music and gardening –'

'If those were her only passions I'm not like her at all,' Pamela interrupted crisply. 'I know you meant it as a compliment, Katrina dear, and I know you thought the world of your aunt, but now and then I think . . . all very understandable I'm sure . . . but sometimes I think she must have been a very prudish old lady.'

A warm blush rose up Katrina's neck and into her face.

To soften the effect of her words, Pamela reached across the table. 'I'm only commenting upon what you've told me yourself,' she said, patting Katrina lightly on the arm. 'And what I know to be true. You've a highly developed sense of responsibility, and it's admirable, but my word, sometimes I wish you had less of it. I understand it, of course, it comes from the way you grew up. When you were a child you looked after your mother, you looked after your aunt's house when she left it to you, paying the bills, dealing with the upkeep; you looked after your friends Sophie and Gloria when they lived with you, then you looked after Toddy and his business – life has made you very responsible –'

'And turned me into a prude,' Katrina interrupted, hot-faced.

'All of this character assessment is simply because I didn't go to bed with Ossie.'

'Would it have done any harm? To be *irresponsible* for once? To let yourself go, have some fun?' Pamela's white hair bobbed up and down as she laughed. 'Even if all you did was lie back and enjoy it, at least you could have *pretended* you were being thoroughly wicked.'

Katrina would have been less surprised if Pamela had taken off her clothes. With or without clothes she was certainly seeing her in a new light. Her aunt would *never* have said that. 'Good heavens above,' she said softly and might have repeated herself but for catching sight of Sam on the far side of the square. And with him was Hank. 'Oh no,' she groaned. 'Hank's on his way over.'

Twisting around in her chair, Pamela raised a hand to shield her eyes from the sun. 'Oh good,' she said eagerly. 'I haven't seen him in ages. One of my favourite men. Of course he's got big troubles at the moment, poor man. Ah . . .' she paused as the waiter returned with their coffee and brandies. '*Dos beers, por favor. Si,*' she nodded before catching sight of Katrina's frown. 'Now what's up? I must say, Katrina, I can't work you out these days. Is that disapproving look because Hank has or hasn't tried to get into your knickers?'

'What? Oh, really. Why on earth should you think –'

'Why not? Most women adore him. If you don't, either he's made advances which you've rebuffed, like poor Ossie at Gatwick, or you're miffed because he hasn't.'

'Nonsense.'

'Then why take such a dead set against him? Suburban values never counted for much in this place, and even less in this day and age.'

'Prudish *and* suburban!' Katrina's amber eyes flashed with resentment. 'Besides, he's hardly likely to try anything with me, is he? He and Toddy are partners.'

'So you *are* miffed?'

She felt the colour flood back in her face. 'I wish I'd never set eyes on him,' she said bitterly. 'Toddy was content until he met him. Everything was going so well. Then Hank got him involved in this blasted Paloma Blanca nonsense, and nothing's gone right since then. I knew it wouldn't. I had a feeling. I begged Toddy to stay out of it. He used to listen to me but not about this. Oh no!' A scornful note came to her voice. 'He knew better. He was going to be the big international businessman. A tycoon. Damn fool. Now he's worried sick and God only knows what will happen.' She tried to stem the flow of frustration by biting her lip, but the effort defeated her. 'Why didn't he stick to cars? Like Sam. Sam would have had more sense. Sam wouldn't have involved himself in something he knew nothing about.'

'That's where you're wrong, my dear,' Pamela said firmly. 'Sam was green with envy. He thought it was absolutely brilliant.'

Katrina stared in surprise.

Turning in her chair, Pamela looked across the square to where her husband and Hank had stopped to chat with Paulo Torrella, the local doctor. 'Sam thought the tie-up with Suntours was wonderfully clever,' she said. 'In fact there wasn't a businessman on Majorca who didn't. They'd have given their right arms to get in on the act.'

'They'll have changed their tune now,' Katrina retorted gloomily.

'Yes,' Pamela agreed sadly. 'They wouldn't touch it with a barge pole now, but that doesn't mean anyone's gloating. Far from it. They're all crossing their fingers that Hank and Toddy can pull something off. Everyone on Majorca is affected by tourism, you know, even us expats. Facilities developed for tourists are ours to enjoy all through the year. We were looking forward to Paloma Blanca –'

'I wasn't.'

'No, and that's a pity,' said Pamela as she turned back to face her. 'It's a big thing on this little island you know. Important –'

'Don't you start. I've had enough of Toddy telling me how important he'd be.'

'And you didn't want that for him?' Surprised, Pamela gave her a quizzical look. 'Just now you said something about people changing their tune. Don't you think it's time you changed yours?'

The bluntness caused Katrina to blink in confusion. She could feel her head beginning to spin. Lunch had been quite different from what she had expected. She had imagined herself recounting Ossie's anecdotes about Barzini. She had made a particular point of remembering them. But this? Snide remarks from Sophie were one thing, to be expected from Gloria, but from *Pamela*!

'I should imagine Toddy's beside himself at the moment, so why aren't you with him?' asked Pamela. 'Seems to me, what's done is done. Whether you were for or against Paloma Blanca doesn't matter, does it? The point is he needs you –'

'That's a bit rich,' Katrina interrupted, her voice rising with indignation. 'Just now you were telling me to sleep with Ossie!'

'Sssh,' Pamela hushed, glancing at the adjoining tables.

'That's what you said! Now you want me to be the dutiful wife.'

'You *are* a dutiful wife. So am I, which is why it wouldn't have mattered to have a bit of fun with your Ossie. That's all it would have been. Unimportant, except it would have done my ego a power of good, and made me more fun to live with. But if Sam were in trouble, that *would* be important. If he was in trouble, I'd want to be with him. I couldn't live with myself unless I was working flat out to help him.'

Katrina could hardly believe her ears. The world was conspiring against her. 'Crazy,' she thought. None of this was her fault. Toddy had got himself into this mess. He had bitten off more than he could chew, he was playing around, keeping secrets, ignoring her advice . . .

'I *had* to come over this week,' she said insistently. 'There are things to do at the villa.'

'Nonsense. If you'd called me, I could have done –'

'Hello, Katrina!' boomed a deep voice as a shadow fell over the table.

With the sun behind him, Sam stood grinning down at her, making her squint as she looked up at him. His white, windswept hair stood out like a halo above his brown face. He kissed both of her cheeks and then stood back to allow Hank to do the same.

'Hello, Katrina.' Hank smiled with less than his usual confidence, sounding slightly doubtful, as if unsure of his welcome. 'Good to see you.'

'Hello,' she replied with a frostiness which was partly directed at him and partly at Pamela for the interrupted lecture.

'Well, now,' Sam grinned, pulling a chair out from the table. 'I must say you're looking well.' He regarded her with undisguised admiration. 'Pam tells me you've been off to some sort of posh health club. All by yourself.'

'No, I went with Sophie. You remember her? She was out here last summer.'

He nodded happily, his eyes shining with approval beneath white bushy eyebrows. 'Well, you're looking good on it, I must say. By God, if only I were twenty years younger —'

'Sam,' Pamela interrupted, pretending to scold.

'No, no,' he protested, grinning broadly. 'All I'm saying is Toddy'll have to watch his step. Letting her wander off by herself. Don't you think, Hank?'

'Sure do.' Hank grinned at her.

'Luckily,' Pamela said archly, 'I'm here to protect her.'

'Ah,' Sam countered with a wicked look. 'But you weren't at this health farm, were you? No telling what she got up to. Especially with that Sophie to lead her astray.'

To her horror Katrina felt the colour flooding back into her face. She couldn't stop herself. It was her day for blushing. She flashed a glance across the table, appealing for help, and Pamela was quick to come to her rescue. 'Oh stop it, Sam,' she said sharply. 'You'd embarrass anyone, you would. You've a one-track mind, that's your trouble. You judge everyone by your own standards. I've ordered you a beer by the way, and one for you too, Hank.' Giving him a quick look, her tone changed to one of enquiry. 'Someone was telling me you've been away.'

Hank nodded. 'I went over to London to see Toddy. I was sorry to miss you,' he said, looking at Katrina.

The speculative gleam in his eye gave her a moment of panic. *Sam's stupid teasing was bad enough, too near the mark, but . . . oh God!* 'Yes, well . . .' she muttered, shrugging her indifference and avoiding his eye, aware of her own boorishness, but not bothering to conceal it. Hank deserved her rudeness. Toddy had been happy until he met him . . .

Ignoring the snub, Hank turned to Pamela. 'Then I went to Berlin and to Jersey to drum up some business. The response was terrific. I was just telling Sam. Things might be tough at the moment, but everyone says the same about Paloma Blanca. It's going to be one of the best hotels in the world . . .'

'Liar,' Katrina thought as she listened to him boast. Looking at him, she could see his anxiety. Despite his bravado, worry was etched into every line of his face. 'Good,' she thought. 'Serves you right. You and your fancy ideas.' Casting her mind back, she remembered drinking coffee in this very café with Toddy, all that time ago, when he had first broached the idea of buying a villa in the harbour. 'I should have put my foot down then. None of this would have happened. We were quite happy as we were . . .' To escape Hank's sham optimism, she glanced at Pamela and tried to imagine her twenty years younger – having one-night stands, then going home to Sam and giving him his birthday and Christmas rolled into one. Had she? Would she really have gone to bed with Ossie? Am I prudish? And suburban! Sophie thinks so. But I didn't really fancy Ossie that way . . . well, not enough . . . I mean I did *like* him . . .

'Terrific,' Sam exclaimed. 'We'll have these . . .' he pointed to the beers which had just been delivered to the table. 'Then we'll go, okay, Katrina?'

'What? Sorry, I was day-dreaming.'

'To Paloma Blanca. Hank's going to show us round.'

She felt an immediate moment of panic. She began shaking her head. 'Oh no, thanks but I don't think so –'

'But you've never even seen it,' Hank said insistently, with a sideways look at Pamela and Sam.

Pamela's head jerked as if on a string. 'You mean you haven't been up there?' she exclaimed. 'To Paloma Blanca? Not even once? In all this time? I don't believe it.'

'Good God!' Sam sounded shocked as he reached for his beer.

They both stared at her, Pamela with reproach, Sam with astonishment.

223

Trying to avoid their eyes, she looked directly at Hank. *You bastard!* she thought, hating him. *You told them that deliberately.* Aloud she said, 'There's always such a lot to do at the villa –'

'Not today,' Pamela interrupted. 'You were planning a lazy afternoon, you said so over lunch.'

'But I ought to get a few things –'

'We'll get them on the way back.'

Sam said, 'You won't need food for tonight. Hank's invited us all to the Crow's Nest.'

She felt like a hunted animal with Hank as the hunter. They exchanged glances, hers defeated, his triumphant. She looked away and gazed out across the bay, searching for inspiration, desperately seeking an escape while knowing there was none. Angry and frustrated, the spiteful words were out before she could stop them. 'What's the point of going to gawp at a white elephant?' she sneered in a voice louder than she intended. 'The whole thing's a disaster, if you ask me. You'll have to find a new name for it now. Hank's Folly or something.'

'Katrina,' Sam exclaimed, sounding outraged.

She could have burst into tears. She prized Sam's good opinion. And Pamela's. It was Hank's fault! *Everything* was Hank's fault. *Damn and blast him!* Her hands clenched into fists and she wished the ground would open and swallow her.

'I'll get the jeep,' Hank muttered, rising quickly and hurrying off before the others could say a word, leaving them to exchange embarrassed looks, from which Pamela escaped by signalling for the bill. 'Mario,' she called, waving to the waiter.

Sam groaned with a sudden thought. 'Oh Lord. I've got that outboard motor all over the back seat. I was taking it into Paguera to get it fixed.'

'Not to worry,' Pamela said quickly. 'Hank can take Katrina. You won't mind riding in his jeep, will you, Katrina?'

What could she say? Still flinching with embarrassment, she dared not respond with another sour note. Managing a weak smile, she fumbled to find her purse in her bag. 'Here, let me –'

'No, no, my treat,' Pamela insisted as the waiter came to the table, while Sam pushed back his chair and stood up. 'I'll get the car,' he said at the moment that Hank's jeep screeched to a halt at the kerbside.

Overtaken by events, Katrina watched helplessly as Sam went over and said something to Hank. Then Pamela rose and was taking her arm. 'I've been aching to see over the site. There were pictures of it in the paper, you know, how it will all look when it's finished . . .'

Numb and trapped, Katrina rose from the table on leaden legs. She wanted to scream: *I don't want any part of it. You can go if you want – but for God's sake leave me out of it!*

Hank came forward to take her arm from Pamela, making her feel like a prisoner being escorted into custody. She shook herself free and climbed into the jeep, avoiding his eye, sliding on to the seat as he slammed the door. He shouted to Sam that he was going to the office and would meet them on the site. Next moment he leapt up behind the wheel, started the engine, crashed into gear and released the clutch so violently that she was thrown backwards in the seat. She looked at him with startled eyes – and saw the fury on his face.

'That was a cheap crack,' he shouted as the jeep shot forward.

Alarmed, she clutched the dashboard. 'Steady!'

'Hank's Folly! What sort of snide remark is that?' he asked furiously, wrenching the wheel and tilting the jeep almost onto two wheels. They lurched out of the square and on to the coast road, narrowly avoiding a bus full of school children. Thrown sideways, Katrina clung to the dashboard with both hands.

'Think I need that?' he demanded as he slammed the accelerator to the floor. 'Like we don't have enough problems? Poor ole Toddy might have to put up with your tantrums, but I don't. *Comprendo?*'

Her teeth rattled as the jeep hit a pothole then bucked into the air, jarring her spine. Ahead of them a truck loaded with fish packed in ice trundled along the crown of the road. Blasting his horn, Hank swerved out, alongside and then past it, causing two hikers with backpacks to leap despairingly for the side of the road. Katrina caught a fleeting glimpse of the fear on their faces. 'Slow down!' she gasped breathlessly, her voice rising to a scream as an oil tanker loomed around the bend in front of them. Wrenching the wheel, Hank pulled the jeep clear with inches to spare.

'You maniac!' she screamed. 'You'll get us both killed.'

'Yeah?' he shouted. 'Think someone will miss you?'

Clinging to the dashboard for dear life, she was jerked back and forth like a puppet. Her neck ached, her spine jarred, her vision blurred. She half-glimpsed the grove of almond trees, the white church, the petrol station, a horse-drawn cart loaded with vegetables – so many flickering images as they flashed past. 'For God's sake,' she pleaded, thrown backwards as the road climbed.

The jeep screamed up the hill, past the smart villas and into the pines.

The breath was knocked out of her as she bounced up and down on the seat.

'We need all the help we can get,' Hank shouted, half-turning towards her. 'Friends we need now, not –'

'Watch the road!' she screamed, closing her eyes as they rounded the bend. Thrown sideways, she clung to the door. Her stomach lurched. When she opened her eyes the road had disappeared. Vanished! One moment it was there, the next moment it had gone. She could see the sea lapping the rocks below. Loose chippings spat from the squealing tyres as the jeep screamed into the next hairpin. 'Please,' she begged, shaking with terror as the wheels lost traction. She could feel the skid, feel the sickening sliding loss of control and the start of the spin. Catching a fleeting glimpse of brilliant blue sky and the green spires of pine trees, she flinched at the thought of plunging over the side. Helplessly, tensing every muscle in her body, she braced herself against the impact. Then, suddenly, they were slewing away from the terrifying drop. The jeep was sliding away from the edge into a clearing. Crossing rough ground, they bumped and bounced and finally stopped.

Trembling all over, she sucked in her breath. Her ears buzzed. Marvelling at the sudden silence, she scarcely dared believe the cessation of motion. Slowly, fearfully, she raised her head. Through eyes blurred by tears, she saw her white knuckles gripping the dashboard. Beyond the fly-splattered windscreen the surrounding trees were mercifully motionless. The earth was still. Reassured, gulping a sob, she released her grip on the dashboard and rubbed her hands over her arms as if feeling for injuries. For a split second she whimpered with relief. Then anger welled up inside her. Turning, her hand flew out, her arm swung in an arc. 'You bastard!' she sobbed, smacking him hard across the face.

Temper blazed from his dark eyes. Her hand had left a vivid mark on his face. Fearing he would retaliate, she shrank back against the door. His hands bunched into fists, his whole body shook, then he flung himself out of the jeep. He kicked the wheel and slapped his hand down on the bonnet.

'Did that frighten you?' he roared, glaring at her. 'I damn well hope so, because you scare the shit out of me! I'm wiped out if we lose this. I've hocked the Crow's Nest, sold my boat, if this goes down I'm back where I was twenty years ago, skippering a boat for some fat-arsed —'

'That's not my —'

'We're fighting for our lives! Not just me, you don't give a fuck about me, fine, okay, but can't you get it into your thick head that we'll all go down. Toddy with me an' you along with him. You an' your big mouth. You wrote us off, for Chrissakes! In public! In the harbour, with half the fucking world looking on.'

Suddenly in her mind's eye she saw the tables at the café. Gossip spread like a bush fire in the harbour. Even so . . .

He continued to shout, 'Hanging on by our fingernails an' all you do is put the boot in.'

'I didn't mean —'

'That was Bob Newton at the table in the corner!' He kicked the tyre again and slapped his hand thunderously down on the bonnet. 'Bob Newton! He's the agent for Fanfare Travel. He could put a lot of business into Paloma Blanca. That's why I was giving out with all that bullshit.'

'Oh,' she said weakly with sudden understanding.

He swore and cursed for another minute, then started to cough. Leaning forward, he rested both hands on the windscreen. His chest heaved as he recovered his breath. After a long moment he looked up, his anger giving way to a look of bewildered frustration. 'What is it with you, anyway? Everyone else is trying to help. Every day someone calls me with the name of a contact. Toddy's working his butt off. Christ, even your old man is helping out with this money he's lending us. But that don't count, does it? Nothing counts with you, nothing!'

It was her turn to be bewildered. *My old man? What does he mean?* Confused and shaken, she opened her mouth but the words died on her lips. When she did find her voice it sounded faint and far off. 'What do you mean?'

But instead of answering he turned away and walked to the edge of the clearing, where he stood kicking the sparse grass and staring down at his feet.

Her hands had stopped shaking sufficiently for her to open her bag. Taking out her cigarettes, she fumbled with her lighter. Dragging smoke into her lungs, she exhaled, took another puff, cleared her throat and started again. This time her voice functioned so well that the words came out in a shout. 'What on earth are you talking about?'

He looked up and walked towards her. The anger had gone from his face. Now he looked strangely sheepish. His shoulders slumped and his expression was almost apologetic. But when he spoke there was no mistaking his frustration. 'You must learn to watch what you say when you're out here. This place is a village, right? People like Newton could be important.'

'That's not what I meant. Yes, I'm sorry about that, but just now you said my old man. D'you mean my father? Is he involved in this?'

He groaned and muttered under his breath.

He did mean her father. She could see it in his face. Somehow her father had inveigled himself into this business. 'Oh, my God!' she exclaimed, suddenly feeling weak. 'Now what?'

All the fury had gone out of him. With an air of defeat, he took out his own cigarettes and began to pat the pockets of his white linen jacket in search of his lighter. 'Here,' she said impatiently, thrusting her Dupont at him as her anxiety mounted to fever pitch.

'Thanks,' he said, lighting a cigarette.

'Look, I'm sorry about before,' she apologized, the words

coming in a rush. 'Honestly I am. I behaved badly. I shouldn't have said that to you.'

'Things are so darned sensitive at the moment. You never know who could be listening.'

'Yes, yes, I see that now, and I'm sorry. I swear it'll never happen again. Really, Hank. And I'm desperately sorry for slapping you. I just got so frightened –'

'Yeah, well.' He gave her a shamefaced grin and rubbed the side of his face. 'Reckon I deserved it. Sorry I scared you.'

'But what's this about my father?' she asked anxiously. 'You said something about him lending you money?'

He gave her a curious look. 'You still don't know about that?'

Her very silence answered his question.

Shuffling uncomfortably, he looked down at his feet. 'Yeah, well, he's helping us out. I wish you and Toddy –'

'I don't believe it! He's helping out? You don't *know* my father. You mean he's actually lent you some money?'

'Well . . . we ain't got it yet, but he's promised –'

'Oh, my God!' She groaned. 'You don't know what he's like. You can't rely on him. He's a liar. He's a cheat –'

'Steady on!'

'The things he promised my mother! He let her down every time. You won't get it. I'll tell you that now. I don't care what he said. You've more chance of borrowing money from the man in the moon!'

CHAPTER SEVEN

KATRINA'S SUDDEN RETURN from Majorca came as a life-saver for Todd. Trying to cope on his own, his very existence had been disrupted by her absence. The so-called joys of bachelorhood, in his opinion, were bloody nonexistent. Instead of extra freedoms there were extra chores. 'What sort of life is this, for God's sake?' he muttered to Mac. 'Coming home to you every night.' His thoughts were constantly of Katrina. He moaned to himself continuously. 'How can she do this to me?' he fumed. 'Just to walk out like that! What's all this crap about needing a break? Like she's the only one? Like my life's one long holiday, I suppose?'

The truth was, he missed her. He missed the order she created, the pleasures of good food, of things done when he liked, the way he liked. He missed her in bed. He missed her company. He missed just talking to her. They could talk for hours, some-times about nothing at all, or at least not of any importance, but between them they'd set the world to rights and then go happy to bed. They had never had a really serious disagreement about anything – except Leo and Paloma Blanca.

Her coolness on the telephone had troubled him. It was not their way to be cool with each other. In the past he would say, 'You got something to say? Fine, come out and say it – and she had. Now, these strained silences were getting him down.

But he had coped. In the evenings he stopped off on his way home to collect a take-away from the Chinese restaurant close to the office – 'Much more of this and I'll *look* like a bloody noodle,' he grumbled to Mac – and every day he persevered with his business calls and his meetings.

Hank also had coped. After leaving London he had flown to Germany. He had called from Berlin. 'I've been thinking,' he said. 'We didn't have time to finalize anything with Charlie the other night. You don't mind if I go and see her, do you?'

Todd had minded. He had minded a great deal. He was frustrated and lonely in London. But what could he say? It was on the tip of his tongue to suggest that he go, too. He nearly said it would be easy for him to fly out to Jersey, but he swallowed the words for fear of making a fool of himself. Hank was right. This was no time to screw around, even if the delicious Charlie was willing, and he was no longer sure that she was. Not that it mattered. His appetite for extra-marital sex had evaporated. Apart from the feelings of guilt, look at the problems it caused! So instead of complaining about being excluded, he discussed the terms they should offer Charlie, and left it to Hank. With characteristic tenacity he stuck to his task, working twelve hours a day, extolling the merits of Paloma Blanca to anyone willing to listen, but even so he would have been less than human not to feel irked when Hank called to say he had reached agreement with Charlie. Of course he was pleased. He liked Charlie. He liked her a lot. And she had impressed him from the moment they met, but he was still a bit rankled about Hank taking over.

'After all,' he complained truculently on the telephone, 'it was me who found her.'

Hank did his best to placate him. 'Listen, ole buddy, I'm confirming your judgement, that's all. You're right, we can't do everything ourselves. I'm busy on the site every day and you've enough on your plate. We need help. Charlie's bright, she's got personality and plenty of contacts. She's just right for us. And this guy Bob Levit has agreed to release her one day a week until the end of her contract . . .'

So what with the three of them pooling ideas, a new line of attack was devised. Todd continued to concentrate on the travel trade, although he dropped the idea of striking one big deal in favour of creating smaller packages, hoping that if he sold enough he would get the same volume of business.

Charlie set about developing the Paloma Blanca Gold Cup.

New brochures were commissioned.

Charlie wrote to the secretaries of yacht clubs all over the world.

Hank and Don Antonio talked about ways of extending the marina.

So a lot was happening when Katrina cut short her stay in Majorca . . .

As she flew back to London, Katrina reflected on her visit to Paloma Blanca. The scale and beauty of the place had overwhelmed her. Of course she had seen photographs; Toddy had strewn enough around the place to make them unavoidable, but space and area could be distorted in pictures and she had never been a good judge of distance. 'As big as the West End,' Toddy had once boasted, but her jumbled recollection of Regent Street and Piccadilly had merely confused her. It was the wrong thing to say. There was no comparison. The West End was full of buildings, most of them ugly, whereas even in their unfinished state, the buildings at Paloma Blanca conveyed a picture-book magic. Indeed, as Hank had said with unusual eloquence, 'It's the work of a great artist set in a place of rare beauty.'

Hank had also said, 'I've never met your old man, but anyone lending us three hundred grand is okay in my book. Toddy says he's a hell of a guy.'

A hell of a guy? The man who had ruined her mother's life. The father she had waited hours to see as a kid. *He* was a hell of a guy?

'People change,' Hank had insisted. 'Once a guy makes serious money and gains a bit of maturity . . .'

Katrina wondered. Had his gambling paid off? Was she really able to lend Toddy three hundred thousand? Did he have that kind of money? Alarmed and suspicious, she pondered his motives.

But what troubled her most was her conversation with Pamela. Pamela's criticism had cut to the quick. 'Disloyal?' she thought indignantly. 'Me. Of all people! It would have been disloyal to hop into bed with Ossie. That would have been disloyal. But I didn't. And supportive! I've *always* been support-

232

ive!' Her face burned at the slur on her character. It was so unfair. And untrue. Hadn't she gone to the office that day intent on reconciliation? And what had she found? Make-up all over his shirt! Sophie was right. And yet, although she had seethed about that at the time, talking to Pamela had diminished its importance. Now what plagued her was Pamela saying, 'If Sam were in trouble, I'd want to be with him. I couldn't live with myself unless I was working flat out to help him . . .'

So returning post haste, Katrina was in a vastly different mood from when she had stormed out of Todd's office. Pamela and Hank had done much to change her thinking. Even seeing Paloma Blanca had affected her, and it was no less than the truth when she confessed to Todd, 'I've never seen such a beautiful place.'

She said nothing about make-up on his shirt; nothing about his night in the Midlands. She delayed any mention of her father. Instead, taking a leaf from Pamela's book, she set out to make it his birthday and Christmas rolled into one.

Todd was like a drinking man whose favourite bar had reopened. The good life had returned. Hank was right to call him one of the world's great married men. Once again he hurried home to the scent of fine cooking mingled with French perfume, and to a wife whose sole concern was his happiness. It was like a second honeymoon. What was more, when they were not eating gourmet meals or enjoying themselves in the bedroom, they were talking again. And amazingly *Katrina* was talking about Paloma Blanca: 'Toddy, you should have *made* me visit the site, dragged me there if need be. It's idyllic. And everyone says you were dreadfully unlucky about Suntours. Sam said it was a marvellous deal . . .'

They talked and they talked. They ate and they drank. And they made love every night. They even made love in the bath and Todd couldn't remember when last they did that. 'Bloody hell!' he exclaimed with delight. 'You must have got all this energy from that fat farm.'

It was more than energy. Wanting a reconciliation, Katrina was doing her utmost to restore the magic to their marriage. And she was so pleased to be doing so with a clear conscience, so glad to have spurned Ossie's advances, so relieved not to have her actions tinged with guilt that for a week the house became a positive love nest. Over dinner every night they talked as they used to talk, full of plans for the future, and since she now accepted Paloma Blanca, it became a constant topic of conversation. Of course it was a pity that currently it was causing problems, but Todd was at his most confident best: 'There's no need to worry. Everything will come right in the end.'

She did try to share his enthusiasm. Determined to be supportive, she made every effort. Above all else she wanted to prolong the restored state of married bliss. And she had been genuinely impressed with Paloma Blanca – even if she did think the project was more suited to a multi-national corporation with millions to spare.

So she did try. The trouble was the more they talked, the more she discovered. And the more she learned, the more worried she became. Beneath her smiles and encouraging words, she grew deeply apprehensive. Not that she uttered a word of reproach. All her worries she kept to herself. But her bookkeeper's brain mulled over the figures. She was appalled by the way the motor businesses had been bled dry. She was shocked to learn that the bank no longer considered them a good risk. Her mind went back to the days when she had kept the books. The bank had *always* been keen to assist them. Always! 'Don't forget, Mrs Todd,' they used to say. 'Anything you want, we're here to help.'

Now the bank would *not* help. In fact they were now insisting on a separate wages account at the garage. 'That way,' explained Todd, 'they become preferred creditors if the worst comes to the worst.'

'What do you mean, if the worst comes to the worst?'

Her blood ran cold when he talked of liquidation.

Seeing her expression, he tried to reassure her with a confident laugh. ''Course it won't come to that. That's just the bank looking on the black side. You know what the gloomy buggers are like. We've just got to keep going, that's all.'

'I suppose so,' she agreed, while wondering *why*? If they were in a hole why not stop digging?

After about a week and a half she realized that financially they had passed the point of no return. The only hope of saving the motor business was to recover their investment in Paloma Blanca. She felt sick as she listened to Todd. And angry because where she would slash expenses, he continued to spend money. His plans were as grandiose as ever. He was even staging an international yacht race. The Paloma Blanca Gold Cup! And now someone else was involved. Someone called Charlie.

'Who's this Charlie you mentioned? When did he come on the scene?'

To her surprise, he went pink in the face. 'Ah, yes,' he said, looking guilty. 'Er . . . I was going to tell you. Er . . . as a matter of fact, he is a she.'

'Charlie's a woman?' New alarm bells rang in Katrina's mind. *My God! Now what?*

'Her proper name's Charlotte. Hank took her on. She's working part-time for us at the moment, but she's joining the board in the summer. She's going to be our entertainments director.'

'Joining the board?' Katrina exclaimed, struggling to hide her surprise. 'Is this Hank's idea?'

'Well, sort of, but I agreed. It was a joint decision.'

'Have you met her?'

'Er, yes . . . er . . . briefly. She's a qualified accountant. Very businesslike. Career type. You know the sort.'

Yes, I know the sort. Sophie's the career type, Sophie's a man-eater. And why has he gone red in the face?

'What sort of age is she, this . . . er . . . Charlie?'

'Oh, I dunno,' he shrugged airily. 'Not that old, I suppose, not that young either. Hank has more to do with her than I do. They're working on this idea I told you about, the Paloma Blanca Gold Cup.'

Katrina let it go, more preoccupied with the state of their finances than thoughts of Hank and his women.

'So you see,' Todd said in conclusion to that particular conversation. 'What with this Gold Cup and everything else, it will all come right in the end.'

She was not in the least reassured.

In the evenings she was encouragement personified, but during the day she worried as never before. Ignorant of the bank's charge on the house, she wondered about selling it in favour of something smaller. She wondered about selling the villa. She thought about going back to work in the office. She even considered sacking Mrs Bridges to save money. And with so much on her mind – worrying about this, and fretting about that – she was in no mood to entertain when Sophie dropped in for coffee.

'What are friends for, if not to confide in?' Sophie purred encouragingly.

Katrina did not *want* to confide.

'Have you heard from him?' Sophie asked about Ossie.

Katrina said she hadn't heard. She said she didn't expect to hear. She said there was no reason to hear. 'We sneaked out for a few meals together, that's all. Nothing happened. You can stop imagining –'

'Excuse me, I'm sure. I know what I saw, that's all. I just wondered what Toddy said when you told him?'

Bitch! Of course she had said nothing to Toddy. For heaven's sake, there was nothing to tell, although nobody would believe it from Sophie's expression. Impatient and short-tempered, Katrina invented a hairdressing appointment merely to get Sophie out of the house, which meant that she had to go out at the same time and spend an hour wandering aimlessly around the High Street like a girl playing truant from school. Being trapped by her own lie seemed symbolic of what was wrong with her life. She had lost control. When she kept the books, she had known to the penny the state of their finances. Even when she had given up working at the office, she had not worried. After all, Toddy was a sound, sensible businessman with his feet on the ground. Or he had been – until Paloma Blanca.

At the end of two weeks she was feeling the strain. Although the warmth had returned to their marriage there were times when she could have screamed at Todd, *How could you have landed us in this mess?* Not that she did scream, but she could stand it no longer. 'Be tactful,' she told herself as she prepared dinner that evening. 'And don't argue.' Tonight she would raise the subject of her father's offer to help pay these people in Paris . . .

'How on earth did you come across a firm in Paris?' she asked in a voice so warm with approval that she might have been saying, 'How clever of you.'

Dabbing his mouth with his napkin, Todd sat back in his chair. 'They're not one of the big banks or anything. It's a small outfit. Run by a lawyer.'

'Really? So how did you find them?'

'Leo put me in touch as a matter of fact.'

It was the worst possible explanation. Her blood froze. For the past hour she had chipped away, framing her questions obliquely when they touched on her father. Now she pressed harder. Not that Todd seemed to know a great deal about him; not even where he lived.

'He's got a chateau in the south of France. Some place between Marseilles and Nice. He told me the name of it once, but I've forgotten.'

A chateau? It was all she could do to hide her disbelief. *Oh, sure*, she thought sarcastically. *And I live in Buckingham Palace!* Aloud she said, 'He seems to have done very well for himself.'

Todd laughed with ready agreement. 'Bloody well if you ask me, to be able to lend me three hundred grand at the drop of a hat.'

Her heart thumped. Every muscle in her body tightened with tension. *Three hundred thousand! You'll be lucky to see three hundred pence. Oh, you blasted fool. How many times have I warned you?* She gnawed her lip in order to keep a still tongue in her head. When she trusted herself to speak, she said, 'It's very good of him, but I still can't understand why he's doing it?'

She could have screamed when he talked airily of such things as friendship and mutual faith in Paloma Blanca. Listening was like hearing the tick of a time bomb. *You fool. You can't rely*

237

on him. *He lets everyone down. Then where will you be? What happens then?*

'Oh well,' she said lightly, pretending to dismiss the matter with a wave of her fingers. 'It's not as if you're relying on him for the lot, is it? You said you'll have most of it. I expect this lawyer in Paris will be happy to wait for the rest.'

Watching his reaction, she read the dismay in his face. Hank had been the same on Majorca. When she had poured scorn on her father's promises, Hank had looked frightened. He had looked scared out of his wits, but the more she had pressed for an explanation, the more he had clammed up. 'Toddy knows all the details,' had been all he would say. 'You'd better ask him.'

Todd could not disguise his doubt when he answered, 'I don't know that he'll be very happy about it.'

'So what can he do, this lawyer?'

She watched him fidget in his chair. 'Well . . .' he said slowly. 'The important thing is to pay the interest. That's why Leo's lending me the money.'

His words confirmed her worst fears. Loath to admit it, she had suspected it for days. Hank had more or less told her in Majorca. For some reason paying the interest was vital. Despite which, they were relying on her father! *You daft pair of fools! Why take his word? Why not believe me? I grew up with him, remember?* She remembered the writs, the bailiffs, the knocks on the door, her mother's constant fear of losing the roof over their heads.

Biting her lip, she began to collect the dishes up from the table. Perhaps because she had already suspected the worst, she felt no shock. Even her anger was less fierce than she had imagined. She felt disappointed, let down, defeated. Paloma Blanca had won yet again. But she knew what had to be done. She had known for days. The villa would have to be sold. It would be a wrench, but she had steeled herself against this moment. She tried not to think of the hours spent improving the gardens, emptied her mind of memories of happy evenings on the terrace. They were gone, gone for ever. It was obvious that her father would renege on his promise. Selling the villa was the only way out. The only means left of raising the money.

238

'Don't criticize,' she reminded herself as she carried the plates out to the kitchen.

'Don't make a big deal of it,' she told herself as she brought in the coffee.

'Darling,' she said as she sat down. 'I've been thinking. We won't need the villa when Paloma Blanca is finished. So we could sell it, couldn't we?'

She saw the surprise in his face. Shaking his head, he protested, 'But you love the villa.'

'No,' she lied. 'Not really.'

'Rubbish! I know you do. You've always said buying it was the best thing we ever did.'

'Times change.'

'Nonsense. Look at all the work you've put into the garden.'

'It doesn't matter.'

'Of course it matters!'

'But we *need* the money!' The words came out more forcefully than she intended. Her voice was suddenly shrill, betraying her anxiety, surprising herself.

A flush came to his face. He looked indignant. 'Now hang about,' he said, sounding offended. 'Everything's under control. There's no need to worry. We don't *have* to sell the villa –'

'Of course we have to sell it!' she snapped, unable to contain her exasperation.

'No, thanks to Leo. That's the whole point.'

Mentally she was wringing her hands.

'It's all fixed,' he continued. 'And I'll tell you something. He knew you'd be upset if we sold the villa, that's another reason for him lending me the money.'

'You hope! Don't count your chickens.'

'What's that supposed to mean?'

'You won't get it,' she blurted out, so forcefully that the words came out as a shout. 'He lets everyone down –'

'Oh, Christ! Don't start that again.' Pushing his chair back, he stood up, his face flushed and angry. 'It's always the same. Whenever I mention Leo –'

'No! Please.' Shaking her head, she held up her hands in a gesture of surrender. 'Don't let's argue.' Drawing a breath, she made a last despairing effort to reason. 'All I'm saying is . . . what I mean is, wouldn't it be safer? You wouldn't need to rely on anyone if you sold the villa –'

'But Leo and I *agreed*. If I sell now he'd think I don't trust him. That's how it would look. It would be a slap in the face.'

Who cares? she thought, but bit her lip.

'Anyway,' he said as he turned for the door. 'I doubt there's time now. We need the money by December the first. And the market's lousy. Even if we could find a buyer, Hank reckons we'd drop thirty thousand.'

Defeated and miserable, she watched him leave the dining-room.

It was their least successful evening since her return from Majorca. In the hours remaining until bedtime they watched television, or rather he watched while she sat and stared uncomprehendingly at the screen, gripped more by her thoughts than the flickering images. *Nothing I say will convince him. He'll find out when it's too late. Then what will happen?*

The following weeks were the longest of Todd's life. Losing the air of contentment which had marked his features after Katrina's return, he began to look increasingly harassed. At home, now that the old wound was reopened, the love and laughter of the second honeymoon began to fade, and at the office the pressures were as relentless as ever. Not that his days were without some success. He had persuaded another holiday company to take an interest in Paloma Blanca and they were talking about committing themselves to ten per cent of the suites for eight months a year – well short of the Suntours deal, but any commitment was welcome in these hard times. It was something on which he could build. Meanwhile Charlie was more enthusiastic than ever about the Paloma Blanca Gold Cup and the builders were edging ahead of schedule, thanks to Hank almost living on the site, so there was a great deal about which he could be pleased. He still felt confident about the long term. It was the short term which worried him . . . and in particular the silence from Leo.

He told himself not to worry. He told himself that Katrina's absurd and unjustified hostility towards her father was fuelling his anxiety. He reminded himself that in seven years of knowing Leo the pattern of their meetings had always been irregular; he only ever heard when Leo was in London . . .

He filled his mind with reassuring thoughts. He told himself that Leo's offer was the most generous, the most unselfish act he had ever encountered. The act of a true friend who would never go back on his word.

On the other hand he cursed himself for not making a note of his address. One morning he had Sally try to trace Leo's telephone number through International Directory Enquiries, but without an address to work with, her efforts were fruitless. One evening he stopped off at the Ritz and after explaining that he was a close friend of Leo's, asked them to give him Leo's home address – a request which was refused with cool politeness and scarcely concealed looks of suspicion.

As the weeks slipped past – as October ended and November began – he regretted his decision not to sell the villa. He even called Hank about it. 'I *must* have the money by the first of next month,' he said. 'I can't wait much longer for Leo.'

'You've got no choice. This is Spain, remember? Nothing happens that fast out here. Besides, it's the wrong time of year. No one buys property a month before Christmas . . .'

Even though it was no more than the truth, Hank was equally worried, and it was Hank who volunteered to go to the local banks in the hope of raising a mortgage on the villa. It was all they could do. As it was, containing the shortfall at three hundred thousand would be a miracle. Todd had slashed margins at Todd Motors, put on special promotions, advertised extra discounts; but with his bank in London reducing his borrowing he was in the middle of an impossible squeeze . . .

Then – as if he hadn't enough to worry about – he began to suspect that the office was about to be burgled. One day, quite by chance, he glanced out of the window and saw a man on the other side of the street, staring back at him, gazing intently up at the window. Of course it was not unusual for passers-by to examine the windows – the expanse of plate glass and the display of shining motor cars was an invitation to stare – but the man was not looking at the showroom, he was looking at the offices above them, and it was the intensity of his gaze which caught Todd's attention. This was no casual glance. The examination was so searching that the man might have been an architect or a surveyor looking over a building in need of repair. Or a burglar planning a job.

Before leaving that night, he checked every door and window in the building. He even examined those in the workshops, and before going home he thoroughly tested the alarm system. The next day he dictated a memo reminding the staff of the need for security. Sally laughed as she pinned it up on the noticeboard. 'We never keep much cash on the premises. No burglar would get fat on his pickings from here.'

He managed a half-hearted grin of agreement. Even so he went to the window three times that day and peered down into the street, searching for the man he had seen the previous day. Not that he saw him, and after a couple of days, with so much on his mind, the incident lost its importance. Then he did see him – or he *thought* he did – not outside his office, but close to his home in Hampstead. That evening, as Herbert swung into the cul-de-sac, Todd noticed a car outside the Middletons'. Parked cars were unusual, especially in the evenings; residents put their own cars away in their garages, and every house was set so far back from the road that most visitors drove rather than trudged up the long drives. And it was raining heavily, so a caller would have been drenched by the time he reached the Middletons' front door. Not that the figure in the parked car showed signs of going anywhere. In fact the figure – a man, Todd realized as his own car swept past – was not even looking at the Middletons'. Instead he was staring straight ahead at the wall surrounding the Todd house at the end of the cul-de-sac.

It was a dark night and rivulets of rain ran down the windows, making identification impossible, but for a split second the cars were alongside and something about the blurred features reminded Todd of someone he had seen before. At the time he thought little about it, but later, when he was in bed on the verge of falling asleep, he realized that the black hair and bruised-looking features might have belonged to the man he had seen outside his office.

Of course he dismissed the idea. Not very imaginative at the best of times, he had enough on his mind without dwelling on facial similarities of people he saw in the street. Yet the fact that the thought occurred at all was proof of an increasing nervousness, which was further reflected in his irritability both at home and in the office.

Then everything changed.

'Mr Sinclair's on the line,' said Sally one morning.

Todd was unable to contain his relief. 'Leo!' he shouted into the telephone. 'My God, am I pleased to hear from you!'

'How are you, old boy?' Leo sounded as ebullient as ever.

'Where are you? In London?'

''Fraid not. I'm in Milan and will be for another day or two, but I thought I'd check on the state of the battle. Found a replacement for Suntours yet?'

So much had happened that it took a moment to realize that Leo knew nothing of their new plans. Quickly Todd plunged into a résumé of what had happened – their change of direction, the idea for the Paloma Blanca Gold Cup, and how Charlie had joined them. Painting the brightest picture he could, he tried to sound enthusiastic, but his relief was clear from his voice. He repeated himself continuously: 'God Almighty! Am I glad to hear from you! I can't tell you how glad.'

Leo laughed.

Todd laughed as well, but as well as being pleased he was unable to contain his nervousness about the loan, and a moment later he came out and said it. 'Er . . . Leo, the interest payment is due on the first of next month, and –'

'No problem, old boy. I can get over to London next week. That's partly why I called. How much do you need? Is it still three hundred thousand?'

Todd felt a weight lift from his shoulders. Then, when he had caught his breath and recovered, he explained sorrowfully that three hundred thousand might not be enough, for despite the special promotions and despite the two hundred thousand Hank had sent from the Crow's Nest, the most he could raise would be about eight hundred thousand. 'That leaves us four hundred short.'

'Don't worry,' Leo interrupted. 'I'll cover four hundred. I'll bring a bank draft with me when I come over to London.'

A more emotional man might have wept. Even Todd had a lump in his throat. For a moment he was literally speechless.

Leo chuckled. 'You didn't think I'd let you down, did you?'

In all fairness, Todd had always believed in Leo. True, he had sent Hank off to see a banker to find out about mortgaging the villa, but he told himself that had been simply a matter of prudence. 'No,' he croaked when finally he found his voice. 'No, I knew you'd come through with the money.'

And he was trying to find other words to express his gratitude when the idea came to him. It was such a simple idea, little more than a gesture really, but he knew it would mean a great deal to Leo. Besides which, he was overflowing with warm feelings and wanted to feel right with himself. He refused to take from Leo all the time and give nothing in return.

'Leo,' he said eagerly. 'When you're over in London, how about coming to dinner? I mean, to our place in Hampstead. Nothing fancy or formal. Just the three of us. You, me and Katrina.'

As she brushed her hair she realized how nervous she was. She tried to remember when she had last seen her father. There had been that brief glimpse when they were still living above the business, but that hardly counted; she had ended the encounter before anything could develop. From what she could recall he looked much as she remembered from . . . when she had last seen him. When was that? *I must have been about sixteen, or seventeen. My God, so long ago . . .*

She could have killed Toddy. Not just for inviting him home, though that was bad enough, but for the way he had boasted. He wouldn't stop crowing about the loan. All that stuff about being vindicated. Tempted to say the cheque would bounce, she was glad to have held her tongue when he had talked of a bank draft. *Four hundred thousand pounds!* Her father! So his gambling *had* paid off after all? In a way, when she thought about it rationally and calmly, she was not totally surprised. From what she had gleaned he had always been able to make money. 'Keeping it's something else,' her aunt used to say. 'He spends it as fast as he gets it. Too keen on having a good time, that's his trouble. Always was, always will be. Talk about the last of the big spenders. No sense of responsibility, that's his trouble. He's thoroughly selfish.'

Her thoughts were interrupted by the sound of water running into the bath. Raising her voice, she called, 'Don't be too long.'

'I'm only just getting in.'

'But you'll soak for hours if I let you.' With a final pat to her hair, she turned to the wardrobe. In bra and pants, she took a green silk dress from the rail and held it against herself. Turning to inspect the effect in the mirror, she examined herself with critical eyes. 'Blessed if I know what to wear,' she called. 'What about that green frock? The one I bought in Palma?'

'What green frock?'

Holding it in front of her, she took it to the open door of the bathroom. 'It's either this or the black and white one I wore at the golf club dinner. What do you think?'

Todd looked up from the bathtub, 'Turn round.'

She twirled without thinking.

'Great ass,' he grinned.

Laughing, she turned back to face him. 'Seriously. What d'you think?'

'That's fine.'

'Oh?' she exclaimed doubtfully. 'Do you think so?' Holding the dress away from her, she studied it carefully. 'I thought maybe the other one? It might be more suitable.'

He groaned and began to soap under his arms.

'This one's a bit . . . dressy. After all it's only dinner at home. We're not going out or anything.' Her brow crinkled. 'It's smart, of course, that's why I like it, but it's fairly low cut. A bit revealing –'

'Leo's seen tits before.'

'Not mine, he hasn't. And I wish you wouldn't use that word. Maybe the black and white would be better?'

Watching her go, he settled back with a grin of contentment.

Without being radiantly happy about Leo coming to dinner, at least she had stopped sulking. For two days she had scarcely spoken. Then for the past few days she had done nothing but make arrangements. She and Mrs Bridges seemed to have spring-cleaned the whole house . . .

Slipping the black and white dress over her head, Katrina contemplated the evening ahead. *This is my home,* she reminded herself as she stepped into her shoes and took a last look in the mirror. *He's on my territory. It's stupid to feel anxious. And even more stupid to feel guilty. You've no reason to reproach yourself.* Giving her hair a final pat, she turned away and went to the bathroom. 'I'm ready.'

He looked up. 'Fine, you look great.'

'I don't feel it. I feel downright awkward. This is a hundred times worse than meeting a stranger. You won't be long will you?' Her anxiety sounded in her voice. 'If he arrives early —'

'Stop worrying. He'll be so pleased to see you —'

'Hmm,' she murmured as she turned to go. 'Even so, the sooner you're downstairs the better.'

Accepting the inevitable, he heaved himself up from the bath and reached for a towel. Looking forward to the evening, his thoughts turned to Leo. He remembered their conversation when he had invited him to dinner. Leo's excitement had turned to emotion. He had choked up and sounded close to tears. Todd remembered that his own eyes had been moist.

As he dressed, he hummed under his breath. Everything was working out. He could feel it. He had survived bad times before. He would cope. *Just keep your head down, keep working, things always come right in the end. Something turns up. Look at what's happened with Charlie.* Plans for the Paloma Blanca Gold Cup were racing ahead. Charlie had been out to Majorca for a meeting with Hank, they had fixed upon the dates of different events . . .

'Toddy!' Katrina sang out from the foot of the stairs.

'On my way.'

'It's twenty to eight,' she called, giving the hall a final inspection.

In the study, she fluffed up the cushions. Going on into the drawing-room, she adjusted the lighting, rearranged photographs and twitched at the curtains.

In the dining-room she resisted the temptation to light the candles in the silver candelabra, and contented herself with moving one of the chairs three inches out from the table.

Wagging a finger at Mac in the snug, she warned, 'You behave or you'll be shut in the kitchen.' Which was where she went to check on the dinner, lifting lids from the pots, sniffing the steam, turning the gas down just a fraction. Returning to the study, she mixed a gin and tonic, carried it over to the sofa and glanced at her watch. Fifteen minutes to go. In fifteen minutes she would come face to face with her father . . .

'It's twenty past nine!' she exclaimed angrily, as she returned from the kitchen. 'Dinner's practically ruined. I'd planned for eight-thirty!'

'Give him another ten minutes.'

'You know how pheasant dries out. It can be tasteless if you're not careful. I've turned the gas down as far as it will go –'

He sighed and rose from his armchair. 'Let me fix your drink.'

She flung herself onto the sofa. Her face was flushed from the combined effects of gin, peering into a hot oven, and sheer exasperation. 'You're sure he had the address?'

'Of course he has. He already had it. He had the address *and* the time. Eight o'clock. We sorted it out on the phone. I should have insisted on Herbert picking him up.'

'Typical! My God, the dinners he ruined for my mother!'

'I can't understand it.' Shaking his head with disappointment, Todd was beginning to feel alarmed. 'Tonight means a lot to him. He was really excited.' With a puzzled frown, he handed her the glass. 'He was looking forward to it. You've no idea. Something must have happened.'

'It always does,' she retorted tartly, so agitated that she almost spilled her drink. Putting the glass on the table, she reached for her cigarettes. 'So what do we do now? If we wait much longer it won't be worth eating.'

247

He looked at his watch for the hundredth time. 'I could phone the Ritz? They might know what time he left.'

Her eyes were blank. She felt too confused to express herself. She had known tonight would be an ordeal. She had steeled herself. And now this! 'I told you,' she snapped shrewishly. 'He hasn't changed, he's just the same as he was, he's got no more consideration . . . the book's over there.' She pointed to the telephone directory in the bookcase.

'He's never missed an appointment with me,' Todd said defensively as he opened the directory on the desk.

'He's probably still in the bar,' she said spitefully.

Turning the pages, he found the number.

'He's met somebody and got talking. That was always his excuse.'

Todd dialled and waited.

'Some woman I expect!'

'Yes, hello. Um, I'm enquiring about one of your guests. Mr Sinclair. Leo Sinclair. That's right. No, I don't think he'll be in his suite . . . blast!' Covering the mouthpiece, he said, 'They're trying his room. He won't still be in his room.'

'He'll be in the bar.'

'Right,' Todd said into the telephone, nodding his head. 'No, I didn't think he would be in his room. Yes, thanks.' To Katrina, he said, 'They're putting me through to reception. Ah, yes, good evening . . .'

She studied his face as she waited. She had tried to tell him, she had warned him what her father was like . . .

'Oh,' said Todd. 'I see. Well, yes, if you could tell him I called. Todd. That's right. Yes, he's got the number. Yes please. Thanks.' His frown deepened as he returned the phone to the desk. 'They're expecting him. He's got a reservation, but he hasn't booked in. They said he usually arrives at midday. His flight must have been delayed or something.'

'Or something!'

'For God's sake!' he exclaimed angrily, watching her rise from her chair. 'Give him the benefit of the doubt for once, will you!'

But Katrina was already on her way to the kitchen.

*   *   *

248

Dinner was ruined. The pheasant was as dry as she had predicted, and their appetites had been blunted by too much to drink. Mac was the only beneficiary of Leo not coming to dinner. The domestic harmony re-established over five precious weeks was destroyed in an acrimonious three hours. The quarrel burst like a storm.

'This is your fault,' she exploded, red-faced and angry. 'We wouldn't be in this mess if you'd –'

'For Christ's sake! He's been delayed that's all.'

'Him and his promises. I grew up on them. They never come off.'

'Give him a break, will you?'

'Why? Did he ever give my mother a break?'

That was too much. Todd's head jerked upright. A fearsome scowl came to his face. 'Leo admits he behaved badly. He told me. Satisfied? But it was a long time ago, and if you ask me your mother wasn't so perfect!'

Flushed a moment before, Katrina's face emptied of colour. 'You never met my mother. Don't you *dare* –'

'Know something? Leo was in tears when I asked him to dinner. The poor sod couldn't talk for the lump in his throat. That's how much it meant to him! And I'll tell you something else. It made me feel a right shit for not insisting he come home before. Seven years I've known him, and not once has he let me down.'

'So where is he now?' she jeered nastily. 'And where's the money he promised?'

'Jesus!' Todd shouted as he jumped to his feet. 'I've had enough of this. I'm going to bed.'

He stopped on his way to the door. 'Out there,' he shouted, pointing vaguely to the front of the house. 'Is an old man, probably dossing down in some airport lounge because his flight's been delayed. That poor sod happens to be your father, but you don't give a damn.'

'I know him better than you do.'

'Bollocks! You don't know him at all.'

Tears stung her eyes as he left the room. She heard him crash the bolt home on the front door. She listened to him stamp up

249

the stairs. She winced as he slammed into the bedroom. Biting her lip, she stared at her empty glass and reached for the brandy decanter.

The reconciliation was over.

They were quarrelling again.

And always for the same reasons.

Conversation over breakfast was monosyllabic and strained. Of the two, Todd seemed slightly more relaxed. He was wearing his confident *business as usual* face which he donned every morning. The events of the day would determine what happened next – who would be proved right, who would be proved wrong, and who would apologize.

'That's Herbert,' he said, cocking his head. Swallowing his coffee, he rose to his feet. 'I'll call you when I hear from Leo.'

'*If* you hear from him,' she retorted waspishly. 'Which is highly unlikely.'

For the first time in weeks she let him go without at least pecking his cheek. One morning during the first week she had kissed him full on the mouth, he had kissed her back, and so fiercely had she clung to him that he had thrown off his jacket and kicked off his shoes. Next thing her housecoat was up round her waist and they were on the floor, with him thrusting into her . . .

'Be a long time before that happens again,' she sniffed as she carried the breakfast things to the sink.

Why bother? For weeks she had been as supportive as she knew how. But what was the point? In the old days he listened to her opinion. Her views used to count. But these days whatever she said was wrong. Even now he believed her father would come through with the money. *Even now! Such stupid blind faith!*

Upstairs she washed and dressed, made the bed, muttering under her breath as she went, and she had just returned to the kitchen when Mrs Bridges arrived, carrying half a dozen letters.

'I met the postman at the gate. "You're late," I said to him, an' d'you know what he said? "I overslept," he said. Just like that. Bold as brass. No apology. Up all night I expect, instead of getting to bed early. They don't care, people these days, do they?'

'No. Everyone lets you down,' Katrina agreed sadly.

Usually she spent ten minutes with Mrs Bridges, having coffee while discussing what had to be done, but she was not in the mood to gossip this morning. With a quick parody of a smile she hurried off to the study, shuffling the letters as she went. Most were bills, but one bore an unusual stamp, certainly not English. She stopped in the hall to examine it further. Italian. An Italian stamp, date-stamped Rome. Addressed to her, not to them both.

Sitting down at the desk, she opened the envelope and inside found a note.

> My dearest Katrina,
> How about coming over the wall again? I'll be back in London on the twentieth. What about dinner on the twenty-first? Or lunch? Or three days in the sack? Or a month in the Bahamas? Or a lifetime in paradise? Let me know which you choose when I call you.
>   Much love, Ossie.

Colour rushed to her face. She felt hot all over. Indignation bordered on outrage. He had no right to write such a thing. Three days in the sack! Suppose Toddy came across it? Snatching a furtive look over her shoulder, she crumpled the note before realizing what she was doing. For a moment she stared at the ball of paper in her hand as if afraid it might bite.

She remembered him asking for her address. 'I'll send you some tickets for a concert,' he had said with an innocent look.

Spreading the note on the desk, she used her hands to iron out the creases. Then, when she read it again, she forgot her embarrassment and was mildly amused. She was even amused at the thought of Todd reading it. *So what if he sees it? It might do him good. It would damn well serve him right if I left it on the mantelpiece and sat back to watch his reaction . . .*

Imagining his expression caused her to smile for the first time that morning. Sneaking a glance at the door, she read the note for a third time.

A month in the Bahamas.

He was mad; stark, staring mad.

A lifetime in paradise.

What was she supposed to make of that? What would she say when he called? *When* would he call?

What about dinner on the twenty-first? Or lunch?

That was today!

She caught her breath. *Today!* Her startled gaze went to the telephone as if expecting it to ring there and then. And even as she realized the absurdity of her action, she also reasoned that if he was inviting her to lunch he would have to call soon. He would have to call her this morning . . .

Her mind flew back to their dinners together. Quite apart from the flattering things he said about her, all of which were indelibly etched into her memory, he was an extremely interesting man. Organizing Barzini concerts all over the world he had met the Queen . . . the American President . . . countless foreign prime ministers whose names she had forgotten . . . all sorts of people.

A lifetime in paradise?

Returning the note to the envelope, she had no need to read it again. The words stayed in her mind. *Back in London on the twentieth . . . dinner on the twenty-first . . . or lunch . . .*

'You don't hang about, do you,' she thought, unexpectedly pleased and flattered by the priority he was giving to seeing her again.

Her fury with Todd was forgotten for a moment. For no clear reason that she could define, she went upstairs to her dressing-room where, in front of her wardrobe, she flicked through her clothes. Then she went to the mirror and checked on her hair, while all the time trying to decide what to do. Of course dinner was out of the question. But lunch? It would be a relief to escape from her troubles. She could go to lunch . . . if only to tell him not to write to her again, if only to tell him to stop behaving like a schoolboy. Glancing at her watch, she hurried into the bedroom to compare the time with the carriage clock at her bedside. They both said the same. Twenty past nine.

Downstairs again, she found Mrs Bridges still in the kitchen. 'I'm running a bath,' she said. 'I might be going out later.'

After taking the bedroom telephone into the bathroom, she hurried into her dressing-room, stripped off and stood naked in front of the closet. What to wear? Was there time to get to the hairdresser's?

As she sank into the bath, she practised what to say. And how to say it. She spoke the words out loud to test them, trying to sound casual, to sound offhand, coolly amused.

But when the telephone remained silent she began to feel foolish. And after twenty minutes she stopped tingling with nervous anticipation and started to feel as cool as the water. Getting out, she was towelling herself down, when the telephone rang.

'Hello,' she said eagerly.

'Katrina?'

Her heart pounded. It was him. Nobody else said *Katrina* like that. Making it sound Italian. Making it sound sexy.

'Oh hello. It's you.'

'You got my note?'

'Yes, it came this morning.'

'Did you like my choices?' He chuckled. 'I know which you chose.'

'You do?'

'But of course. What else but the star prize? A lifetime in paradise.'

She laughed. A silly schoolgirlish laugh. Not her normal laugh at all. 'I think . . . er . . . perhaps we should start off with something less ambitious.'

'A month in the Bahamas!'

'Um, could we settle for lunch?'

'Katrina.' His reproach was a flirtatious purr, full of teasing good humour. 'We've been apart a whole month, and you offer me lunch? I've been thinking about you all the time –'

'I'm sure that's not true.'

253

'Enrico says to me, "Get back to London and get this woman out of your system".'

'Ossie!' she laughed, scolding him gently.

'Oh well,' he sighed. 'Beggars can't be choosers, so I'll settle for lunch. Can you make it today?'

'I most certainly can.'

'You can!' He brightened so instantly that her heart leapt.

'I'm looking forward to it.'

'Bravo! Do you know the May Fair Hotel? I take a suite there when I'm in London.'

Her legs felt weak. Is that where they would have lunch? In his suite? 'Er . . . yes, I know the May Fair.'

'Good. Shall we say twelve-thirty in the bar? Or I could pick you up?'

'No, no, I'll meet you there.'

After telephoning her hairdresser, she rushed to her closet and flung dress after dress over the chaise-longue, finding fault with everything in her wardrobe. *Will we lunch in his suite? I hope not. Surely not? After all, he did say meet in the bar. But suppose . . . I mean, what will I do if it is in his suite? After-wards could be . . .*

Not that the thoughts deterred her. She felt a little shiver of anticipation as she told herself that she was old enough and wise enough to deal with any situation, that she would play things as they came . . . but most of her concentration was directed at her wardrobe.

It took forty minutes to dress, two minutes to undress, and fifteen minutes to dress all over again, so that it was almost eleven by the time she was ready. Allowing an hour at the hairdresser's, she would just be on time. She was just on the point of calling for a cab when the telephone rang.

For the slightest second she hesitated. It was bound to be Toddy relaying her father's latest pathetic excuses. As if she wanted to hear them? As if she hadn't heard them a hundred times before? Her hand hovered over the receiver in an agony of uncertainty.

Suppose Ossie was calling with a change of plan?

Suppose . . .

She picked up the telephone. 'Hello?'

'Er, *oui*. Er, Madame Katrina Todd?'

Her heart pounded. It was not Toddy. Or Ossie.

Frowning at being addressed as *Madame*, she said, 'Yes . . . er . . . Katrina Todd speaking.'

'*Ah, bon.* Er, I am through to Madame Katrina Marion Ann Todd? Formerly Mademoiselle Sinclair?'

Why was he saying *Madame* and *Mademoiselle*?

'Yes,' she answered impatiently.

'Ah, er . . . Madame Todd, we have not met. My name is Rochère. Gérard Rochère. I am er . . . how you say in English . . . an attorney? *Oui*? I am calling from France.'

Glancing at her watch, she restrained her impatience and listened in mystified silence.

'Madame Todd, you are the daughter of Monsieur Leo Sinclair?'

'Yes, I am.'

'Ah. Madame Todd, I . . . er I don't know if you are sitting down, but if not –'

'Has something happened?'

'*Oui*. I am afraid an accident has befallen your father. A serious accident. You must be prepared for the worst.'

'Oh?'

'There has been a fire at his chateau. A bad fire. A terrible accident. You understand?'

'A fire? No. I mean yes, I hear what you say –'

'I . . . er . . . am sorry to . . . to bring such bad news, but I have to tell you your father is dead. He was killed in the fire.'

'Oh?' she said so softly that the sound remained on her lips.

'Madame Todd?'

'Yes. Sorry. I . . .' she tried to collect herself. 'What happened? I mean when –'

'Two nights ago. Yesterday was . . . er, chaotic. That's how you say it, *oui*? Chaotic?'

'Chaotic, yes, that's right. Yes, it must have been,' she said without knowing what she was saying. 'Er . . . how did you know about me?'

'But you are his daughter, *n'est ce pas?*'

'I mean how did you know to call me? It's very good of you, but –'

'From my files. You are his next of kin. You are . . . er, how do you say . . . the sole beneficiary in his will . . .'

Her hand was trembling so badly that she could scarcely write down his number.

Afterwards, when she did sit down, she felt suddenly cold and had to hug herself to stop shaking. Toddy's voice came back to her from the night before: *Seven years I've known that guy, and not once has he let me down.*

She felt nothing for herself. No grief, nothing. Her father was dead and her only emotion was a curious numbness. But Toddy would be devastated.

She smoked a cigarette before she telephoned the office, collecting herself, composing what she would say.

Todd snapped at her when she got through. 'Before you ask,' he snarled. 'No, I haven't heard from him yet, but I will, so I don't want you crowing about it.'

'I wasn't going to.' She swallowed, deciding that she couldn't break the news on the phone. 'I was wondering if you were free for an early lunch? A drink would do, a drink and a sandwich perhaps? I could pick you up at the office.'

Before she left the house she cancelled her hairdressing appointment and called the May Fair Hotel.

Mr Keller's extension was engaged, so she left a message at the switchboard. 'That's right,' she said. 'Katrina Todd. Could you convey my apologies and say I couldn't make it.'

CHAPTER EIGHT

AT LEAST LEO'S DEATH brought them together. Returning home from a lunch at which they both drank more than they ate, they sat in the drawing-room like the survivors of an accident, exchanging dazed looks and talking in the hushed tones people adopt when confronted by death. Still shaken, Todd was more upset than he would have thought possible, and Katrina was more shocked than she realized. She had arrived at the office white-faced and trembling. Sitting next to each other on the sofa, fresh drinks in their hands, each drew comfort from the other, yet their conversation was oddly disjointed, interrupted by long silences as they grappled with the news in their different ways.

Suddenly Katrina blurted out, 'I feel so bloody guilty.'

'There's no need. He never blamed you for not wanting to see him. He reckoned you had plenty to forgive him about. He said that to me twice, on separate occasions, so you shouldn't feel guilty.'

She knew she had other reasons to feel guilty. When the telephone had interrupted her she had been on her way to meet Ossie. After lunch they would have gone up to his suite and made love. *Why pretend? Why lie to yourself? You were going to make love all afternoon, then come home, cook dinner and not say a word . . .*

'It's the shock,' said Todd.

She looked at him, feeling unworthy but grateful. *Thank God I didn't go. Suppose Rochère had called while I was out and Mrs Bridges had given him Toddy's number . . . he might have come home and not found me here, and then . . . suppose, somehow, he'd found out?* The thought so frightened her that she reached out and squeezed his arm as if to reassure herself that they were still together with their marriage intact.

When he responded with a look of surprise, she managed a wan smile. 'I felt a fraud on the phone. I didn't know what to say to this Rochère man. I mean —'

'You were shocked.'

'A bit, I suppose, but let's be honest, you're more upset than I am. I should feel *something*! But I can't mourn for him. I just can't. He's dead and I don't feel a thing. Just sort of numb. God knows what I'll do at the funeral. I shall feel a complete hypocrite.'

'Shock,' Todd repeated, patting her hand. 'If I'm more upset it's because I knew him better. He was a good friend.'

She shook her head as if still mystified that he should have made a friend of her father. 'I keep trying to imagine him. That's what I've been doing ever since I heard. Trying to understand him. I know it's too late now, but . . .' she searched for the right words. 'For instance, he never married again did he? Or did he?'

'Not that I know of. I don't think so.'

'Rochère said he lived alone. There was a housekeeper, apparently, but she lived out. Lucky for her, I suppose, otherwise she'd have died in the fire. The strange thing is, I can't see him living without women. From what I heard they all liked him. I think that's what started my mother drinking. He was out spending money on women while she was having to make do and mend —'

He sighed. 'Don't start criticizing.'

'I didn't mean to,' she interrupted quickly. 'Quite the opposite. I was thinking of what you said last night. It takes two to make a marriage. Perhaps if she'd been more supportive? I don't know, I suppose I only heard her side of the story. By the time I was old enough to understand things, he'd gone off to Africa.'

'The Congo.'

She looked at him.

'He went to the Congo.'

'See? You even know that.' As she looked at him she felt an overwhelming urge to confess about the note from Ossie and her assignation and what might have come of it. Instead, in an effort to assuage her feelings of disloyalty, she said, 'I could have been more supportive at times, couldn't I? Something like this makes you look at yourself. Ask yourself questions. It makes you think.'

'I keep thinking about Leo. What a way to go. For someone like him.'

'Rochère thinks he was suffocated while he slept, by the fumes I suppose. He died in his sleep. He probably didn't know a thing.'

'Let's hope not.'

When she fell silent, he sighed and looked down at his feet. After a moment, he asked, 'What time did you say the funeral was on Thursday?'

'Two-thirty. Apparently we can get a direct flight from Heathrow to Marseilles. It gets us there at noon their time. Rochère's making all the arrangements. He said he'll meet us at the airport and drive us to Le Ciotat –'

'That's it!' Todd gave a start of recognition. 'Le Ciotat. I remember now. Leo talked about it. It's along the coast towards Nice. I'd forgotten.'

Watching his expression, and trying to imagine him with her father prompted her to ask, 'Did you know he'd left everything to me?'

'No. We never talked about it.'

'I suppose that's why I feel guilty. I don't deserve anything from him. I couldn't believe it when this man Rochère told me.'

Todd made understanding noises, although in all truth at that moment he was contending with guilt of his own. *Seven years! Leo waited seven years for a reconciliation. And I let him down. I should have invited him home before. God, I wish ... I wish ...*

But he had greater reasons to feel guilty, and he knew it. His first reaction had been shock and a deep sense of loss. After which had come shame for not bringing father and daughter together, and then selfishly he had thought of the four hundred thousand needed for Moroni. Only ten days were left until the end of the month! *Oh Leo! Why now?*

259

Katrina cleared her throat. 'Rochère said he'll book us into a hotel for the night. We're to have dinner with him after the funeral. I suppose that's when he'll tell us about the estate and everything.'

Todd sipped his whisky in silence.

She made a brave attempt to lift his mood. 'He was quite a character, wasn't he? From Wembley Park to a chateau in France via the Congo.'

'Yes,' he managed to say sadly. 'A hell of a character. I'm going to miss him.'

Nervously she smoothed her dress over her thighs and tried to put into words what she was thinking. 'I wish he'd left his money to you. You were his friend, not me. You're the one who deserves it. I know I'm his daughter, but I feel such a fraud.'

'There's nothing fraudulent –'

'I *feel* a fraud,' she insisted vehemently. 'It's how you feel that matters. When you came home and talked about this money he was lending you, I was about to say his cheque would bounce until you said he was bringing a bank draft. Then you talked of a chateau and I didn't believe that either. I didn't believe a word of it. Any of it. I never once gave him the benefit of the doubt. And it was all true, all along . . .' she gulped, shaking her head and biting her lip. 'And now he's left me this money and I feel ashamed.'

'Steady on,' he said gently, realizing she was close to tears. He put an arm around her shoulders. 'It's what Leo wanted.'

'But it must be a lot, mustn't it? He was lending you four hundred thousand. Then there's the chateau. And *you* said he was well-off. You told me that yourself.' Turning in his arms, she looked him full in the face. 'The only way I'll ever feel right about this is if we treat it as *our* money. I'm sure he'd have wanted that.' Looking at him intently, she hurried on before he had a chance to respond. 'Can we use it to sort out Paloma Blanca? You know, pay everything off? So that we can get back to the way we were –'

'Sssh,' he hushed.

But she was determined to make him understand. 'It's all we

argue about, Toddy. We quarrel over it all the time. I try not to get into a state, but I can't live with this constant worry. It's like living under a cloud.' Tears came into her eyes. 'Don't you see? This is his way of putting things right. He's saving our marriage . . .'

Then she wept, not as Todd imagined from remorse or grief, but as a way of easing her guilt.

It was not until the following morning that the full implications sank in. Looking strained and tired, Todd went into the office and called Hank in Majorca. Holding the telephone between his chin and his shoulder, he reached for a cigar. 'We're talking serious money here. I mean, God knows I didn't want this to happen, who would for Chrissakes, but think about it. Leo was lending me four hundred grand. Stands to reason he wouldn't leave himself short. So on top of that there's all of his business interests, which must be considerable, then this chateau in France and God knows what else. Katrina inherits everything. The whole lot goes to her.'

Hank whistled softly at the other end of the line.

'I feel a shit talking like this, especially when we only heard yesterday, but Leo would understand better than anyone. His whole life was spent wheeling and dealing . . .'

Talking helped ease his conscience and made him feel better. He and Katrina had sat up half the night discussing the news and examining their feelings. But of course she was right. Leo's estate must be substantial, and he'd have wanted them to use it to save Paloma Blanca.

'So how about you?' Hank interrupted, concern in his voice. 'Are you okay?'

'You mean am I in shock?' Todd puffed out his cheeks and blew out a long breath. 'I was yesterday. I was gutted. I was like a zombie all afternoon. I went home. I couldn't work, couldn't take it all in. And last night . . .' he groaned. 'I don't even want to talk about it. What a night I had with Katrina. Guilt, tears, remorse, the whole bit. And I still can't get over it. Leo, for God's sake! Gone. Just like that. I always pictured the four of us at Paloma Blanca together; Leo and Katrina, you and me. I figured I'd have got them together by then and we'd be having this great big celebration.'

'He's made a celebration possible. You can always look at it that way.'

'Yeah, right. You're *exactly* right.' Todd nodded vigorously. 'That's how I *am* looking at it. To tell the truth, I woke up this morning and first of all I'm feeling gutted and sad and upset and hung over, and then . . .' his voice lightened with surprise. 'Suddenly I feel this great weight lift off my shoulders. I mean, God knows, like I said I wouldn't have had it this way, who would, but it means we're out of the woods, Hank. We're talking millions here, right? There's this chateau for a start. Okay, the whole place is gutted according to this lawyer, but it must have been insured.'

'Have you spoken to the lawyer?'

'Katrina did yesterday. I'm calling him in a minute. I thought I'd update you first. He sounds an on the ball guy from what Katrina said. He's arranging the funeral and everything. Then we're seeing him after to talk about Leo's affairs.'

'And that's on Thursday?'

'Yes.'

Hank hesitated. 'Four days before payment is due to this Moroni. You've only got until the following Monday.'

'Time enough. It can't be complicated, can it? Everything goes to Katrina. Simple as that.'

'I suppose so,' Hank agreed with a nervous laugh. 'Shit, I don't know about these things. No one ever left me a dime.'

'Me neither,' Todd laughed dryly. 'Now my wife's an heiress. It's still sinking in.'

'All thanks to good ole Leo.'

'Yeah, well,' Todd sighed. 'I wish you'd met him, he was something else, but what you just said – you know, about him making a celebration possible, that's *exactly* what he'd want. He'd kick my arse if he thought I was moping. Seriously, he was that kind of bloke. "Here's the money, Toddy," he would say. "Now get on and finish the job." That's the only way I can thank him, Hank. Thanks to him our troubles are over.'

They fell silent for a moment, absorbing the implications in their different ways. And when Hank finally spoke, he sounded relieved. 'It makes giving you the bad news a hell of a lot easier,' he said. 'Because I have to tell you I'm getting nowhere mortgaging the villa. The best offer I've had is for about eighty thousand sterling.'

'It's worth half a million!' Todd exploded with a quick rush of temper.

'You know what these locals are like,' said Hank, sounding defeated. 'Anything big has to be sent to Madrid for approval. And that takes for ever. But I can pursue –'

'Don't bother. Fuck 'em! Bankers! They're all the same.' Todd snorted with disgust. 'Thanks to Leo we don't need the tight-fisted bastards. They can keep their money from now on.'

After he had finished speaking to Hank, he gathered himself for his call to Leo's lawyer in Le Ciotat. Somewhat to his surprise and impatience, it took him the rest of the morning to get through. The first time he tried the number was engaged, then he dialled a wrong number, then came a whole series of incoming calls to which he had to attend, so that what with one thing and another it was almost lunch time before finally he got through to Rochère.

'*Monsieur Todd? Ah, oui. Bonjour.*'

'*Bonjour, Monsieur Rochère.*' Rather than trust his fractured French, he reverted to English. 'You called my wife yesterday with the terrible news.'

'*Ah, oui,*' Rochère agreed, sounding grave. 'I have just finished making arrangements for Thursday. I am sorry we shall meet under such sad circumstances. *Tragique, n'est ce pas?*'

'Very,' Todd agreed. 'Yes, tragic. I'd like to thank you for arranging the funeral.'

'*Non, non.* I am the executor? Do you say that in English?'

'Yes, that's what we say.'

'So it is part of my sad duties, though in this case there is not much to arrange . . .'

While listening to how Leo's remains would be taken from the hospital mortuary to the cemetery, Todd rehearsed what he would say. His genuine feelings for Leo would in any case ensure that he sounded respectful, and he desperately wanted to be tactful, he would hate to sound grasping, but he was determined to start as he meant to continue. Lawyers were known to procrastinate and he was in no position to countenance a delay. Waiting until Rochère had finished, he cleared his throat and edged into his speech. 'Monsieur Rochère, naturally we are devastated, especially as we were expecting Leo in London two nights ago.'

'Uh huh. The day after the fire.'

'Yes. Well, the point is . . . I really hate to mention it at a time like this, but we . . . er, that is Leo and myself . . . were about to conclude some business arrangements. He was bringing a bank draft with him. For four hundred thousand pounds sterling. I feel awkward about mentioning it. It's just that . . . well, it is rather important. Otherwise, naturally I'd have waited . . .'

Thankfully, Rochère seemed to understand. 'And your wife was aware of this arrangement?'

'Oh, sure. Absolutely. She knows all about it.'

'Then you have no reason to worry. After all, your wife inherits everything. The whole of his estate goes to her.'

'Right.'

'But you will appreciate, monsieur, things are confused at the moment. There is much to sort out. I will have more answers next week. *Oui?* You would like me to meet you at Marseilles as I arranged with Madame Todd?'

'That would be very kind of you. Thank you.'

'*Bon.* I must go now. *Au revoir* until then, Monsieur Todd.'

'Okay, thanks. Thanks a lot. Goodbye.'

Afterwards, he told Sally to hold his calls for a while. He sat quietly at his desk thinking about what had happened. What he had said to Hank was true. Last night he had been desperately upset, and this morning he had woken feeling heavy and mournful. Then had come this huge wave of relief; this wonderful realization that their troubles were over. The burden of worry had lifted, making him feel ten years younger. Now, after speaking to Rochère and having the money confirmed, he felt almost lightheaded. Most of all he felt safe. He was no longer living on the edge of his nerves about having enough money to pay

Moroni. Peace of mind was his for the first time since he had embarked on Paloma Blanca. All thanks to Leo.

It rained all day. It was raining when they left Heathrow and rain followed them across the Channel to France, cloaking the countryside of Provence with clouds so low that they brushed the tops of the trees. In the seaport of Marseilles, pedestrians scurried along rain-slicked pavements, their collars turned up against a wind bitter enough to cut through to the bone. Outside the city, in the open fields, cattle shivered in hedgerows and huddled together for warmth. Sodden earth squelched underfoot . . . and no earth was more sodden than that of the grave-yard.

Katrina lay back in the bath. 'I've never been so cold. My teeth are still chattering.'

In the bedroom, Todd stopped towelling his hair and peered out of the window. 'It's still lashing down. Rochère said there's flooding along the coast.'

'It's the cold, not the wet. This is the south of France! It's not supposed to be cold,' Katrina complained, as she slid deeper into the water. What a relief to reach the hotel. The hot bath was saving her life. 'Why didn't they hold the service in the church? Why does it have to be at the graveside? Those umbrellas were useless.'

'Tradition, I suppose. And their weather's not normally like this. You heard what Rochère said, "An English day for an English gentleman." He thinks God's doing this especially for Leo.' In his underwear he rummaged through the contents of their single suitcase, wishing he had brought another suit. 'I hope they can dry my trousers. The jacket wasn't so bad, my coat took the brunt of it, but the trousers were soaked.' Transfer-ring underwear, shirt, tie and socks to the bed, he stood back and shook his head wearily. 'God, what a day. I'm bloody glad it's over.'

But only the funeral was over – an overlong service for an understrength congregation – which Rochère had arranged with the thoroughness of a man expecting hundreds instead of Todd and Katrina and the half-dozen strangers they had met in the churchyard.

'I didn't know who else to inform,' Rochère had confessed, when he met them at the airport. 'Naturally I knew one or two of his friends, but I thought you'd be in touch with other people . . .'

He was not what Todd had expected. He had imagined Leo's lawyer as someone like Lapiere, if not in appearance at least in manner. But where Lapiere was short and thin, with sharp watchful eyes and a quick business mind, Rochère was a large, clumsy-looking man whose manner did little to suggest a fast-moving brain. He spoke with the deliberation of an elderly schoolmaster addressing a reluctant pupil, partly because he was speaking a foreign tongue, but mostly because it was his nature. He was slow and cautious in all that he did. Yet there was an appealing sincerity about him, especially when he talked of Leo, which suggested he had been a good friend. Todd liked him for that.

'What were those people called?' Katrina queried from the bath. 'Those people from Lyons?'

'Bielenberg, I think. Apparently they used to stay with Leo in the summer. Rochère was saying that sometimes as many as twenty people stayed at the chateau in August.'

'What did you think of him?'

'Rochère? He seems all right. A bit slow and bumbling, but genuinely cut up about Leo. The Bielenbergs contacted him, apparently, not the other way about. So did the others. There was a bit in the French papers about the fire. Poor old Rochère said he met a lot of people at Leo's, but he's no idea where they live. He said more would have come if he'd known how to contact them. By the way, he suggested we look over the chateau in the morning. Or what's left of it. Do you want to go?'

'Do we have to?'

'Only if you want to.'

Sometimes she wondered what she did want. It was a familiar question lately. Not this upheaval in her life. Not rushing off to Broadlands with Sophie. Not hopping into bed with Ossie. Not living with this constant worry about Paloma Blanca.

'You might want to live there.'

'No thanks,' she said firmly, at least sure about that. Reluctant to leave the warmth of the bath, her thoughts turned to her father. It had been easy to think of him before – he was the blight of her childhood, the cause of her mother's drinking and subsequent death – but ever since the news of his death she had thought about him afresh. More so than ever today, standing shivering at the graveside. There was a side of him that she had never known. Even her aunt, in a charitable moment, had once said, 'He means well, but you can't rely on him. That's where your mother went wrong. She relied on what he told her. She always *believed* his promises. I dare say when he makes them he means them himself, but something always happens and he lets people down.'

Would he let them down? Even now? It had been easy in London to imagine her inheritance, as Toddy insisted upon calling it. All too easy, making her feel ghoulish at times. She had been ashamed. Then she had told herself she wasn't being selfish and callous; she didn't want the money for herself, she wanted it for Toddy, to free him of this awful worry, to get Paloma Blanca off his back. But it had been a mistake to tell him her thoughts. He had built it up in his mind. Every day for the past week he had come home with a new figure, a bigger figure, until anyone listening would think he was describing a latter-day Barbara Hutton inheriting the multi-millions from Woolworth.

'You okay?' he asked, coming in from the bedroom.

'A bit frightened.'

Surprised, he sat on the edge of the bath and slid a comforting arm around her wet shoulders. 'What about?'

'About finding out from Rochère. You know, about the money.'

He laughed. 'You're frightened of money?'

She was unable to answer for a moment, afraid to tempt fate by voicing misgivings.

'Funerals are depressing,' he said gently. 'And travelling is tiring. Then there's this bloody weather on top of everything. You're a bit down, that's all.'

She nodded miserably. Yes, she was down. She had woken that morning feeling depressed.

But most of all she had woken feeling frightened. And her fears had grown during the day. She felt crushed by a premonition of impending disaster. Clearing her throat, she said, 'Suppose it's not as much as we think? Suppose –'

'Hey!' he interrupted. 'Why suppose anything? Rochère will tell us in an hour's time.'

'But just suppose?'

'What's to suppose? There isn't a chateau? We know there's a chateau. Leo wasn't going to lend me four hundred thousand? We know he was. That he didn't stay at the Ritz and jet all over the world? I know he did. That he wasn't very well off?'

'But you must have this money by Monday. It's so urgent!'

'So? Rochère said there was no problem.' Todd laughed with a mixture of relief and excitement. 'Mind you, Rochère's a typical lawyer, he was quick to point out it's your money. You're an heiress, remember? Leo's left you a fortune.'

She managed a smile. 'So I'm being stupid?'

'Absolutely.' After kissing the top of her head, he got up and went back to the bedroom. 'How about making room for me in that tub?' he called to her as he stripped off his clothes. 'And you'd better get used to the idea. From now on we're rich. Filthy, stinking rich!'

His buoyant confidence reassured her as she pulled herself up from the bath. She told herself he was right, that her worries were groundless.

But later, as she dressed for dinner, she realized that the hot bath had merely taken the chill from her body. Cold tentacles of fear still clutched at her mind. Her premonition of disaster was stronger than ever.

'It's this place,' she told herself, shuddering at the sound of the rain beating on the windows.

But she knew she was wrong. The place had nothing to do with it. Her father would let her down wherever the place or whatever the circumstances. Dead or alive he would let her down. And Toddy needed this money on Monday . . .

* * *

Although less torrential than in Provence, the rain was exceptionally heavy in Paris. Gutters and gulleys overflowed, and the cobbled streets of Montmartre were so full of puddles that every passing car threw a shower of dirty water over pedestrians as they scurried along the pavements. Not that many pedestrians were about. Such filthy weather kept them indoors, either in their own homes, or in the bars and cafés where they lingered over drinks and meals while waiting for the cloudburst to pass.

In Vito Sartene's restaurant customers and waiters vied with each other to remember when last it had rained so hard or for so long. 'Not since Noah,' someone joked.

But jokes and talk of the weather were ignored in the booth in the corner. In the booth in the corner it was business as usual.

Sartene summed up the results of his visit to London. 'There's the two businesses,' he said. 'Todd Motors and Owen's, both in hock. Even if he sold them his bank would take all the money. He's bled them both dry.'

Moroni sighed and pushed the remains of his *coq au vin* to the side of his plate. Such news did nothing to encourage his appetite. Dabbing his mouth with his napkin, he sipped his wine to give himself strength.

'Also,' Sartene concluded gloomily. 'His house is charged to the bank. To be honest, I can't see how he'd raise a centime in London.'

Disgusted that a man should get his affairs in such a mess, Moroni shook his head and sucked on his teeth. He glanced out from the booth to where Jules Carbone sat by the door, eating with gusto. Watching him consume the expensive food, Moroni reflected that even such meals had to be paid for. Everything cost, one way or another. Nothing was free. A man had expenses, obligations; but for a man to pay out, money had first to come in.

Unhappy about conveying bad news, Sartene fidgeted as he searched for a silver lining in his gloomy report. 'The wife would be easy,' he said. 'Give me the word and we could lift her tomorrow.'

Moroni shook his head sadly. The thought had crossed his

mind that Leo Sinclair might pay handsomely to keep his daughter from harm. Now it was in the papers that Sinclair had died in a fire. So even that solution was denied him. Everything that could go wrong with this wretched deal was going wrong. There had been such deals before, not a lot, thankfully, but even one was too many. When they happened, he had learned from experience to cut his losses as soon as he could.

'So what will you do?' Sartene asked, guessing the answer.

Moroni had the look of a man who hoped for the best while expecting the worst. He smiled wearily. 'Is'sa not due to be pay until the first of the month. Maybe he pay? Eh? Is'sa possible? Okay if he does. No problem.'

'And if he doesn't?' Sartene asked hesitantly. 'You want me to go to London again?' He put the question reluctantly. December was a good month for business. Takings were high. The restaurant was booked solid from the tenth of the month until Christmas. 'I only ask,' he explained hastily, 'because I'll need to make arrangements.'

Moroni nodded his understanding. Similar thoughts had occurred to him. With advancing years he had become a creature of habit, and he liked to share early December with Nicole in Montmartre. After which, in common with married men all over the world, he spent Christmas and New Year with his wife. To be deprived of the nubile twenty-one-year-old Nicole for even twenty-four hours was upsetting, for him and for her, since she had planned a number of outings. A visit to London was the last thing he wanted.

A scowl settled on his face as he considered his options. Tomorrow he and Lapiere would see this property expert Roos and hear his valuation of Paloma Blanca. Maybe Roos would say it was worth a fortune? Maybe Roos would even know of a buyer?

Knowing better than to interrupt when Moroni was thinking, Sartene waited in patient silence.

Finally Moroni reached his decision. 'If he pay, we gotta no problem. Huh? We find out next week. If he don', we go to London. If this place in Majorca covers our money . . .' He shrugged. 'We persuade him is'sa our place. Huh?'

Sartene nodded. He had been a party to such persuasions before. Most debtors paid quickly enough. Only a few stubborn ones held out. A tough Swede in Oslo had resisted for eighteen hours, but that was a record, and he had been beaten so badly that he had subsequently died.

Moroni looked across the table from beneath his shaggy eyebrows. 'But if it don' cover our money, we gotta no choice.'

Sartene agreed. They would go for the insurance.

Todd would not have believed the conversation in Paris. He would have laughed. He might even have jeered. There he was with Katrina about to inherit Leo's millions, and Moroni was worrying about the current payment! It was absurd. There was no need. Eight hundred thousand was already in the bank and Rochère had confirmed they could count on the rest. In fact all week long Todd had been speculating about the *size* of Katrina's inheritance. How many millions were there? Maybe enough to pay off Moroni's *entire* loan, all of it, down to the last penny.

So it was a supremely confident Todd who entertained Rochère to dinner. His only concern was Katrina. Pale and wan-looking, she picked at her food with obvious lack of interest. He knew that inwardly she was quaking. She was so *sure* that Leo would let her down. But what could he say? Nothing in front of the lawyer. Besides, Rochère would shortly prove Leo's worth once and for all. Todd smiled to himself. After championing Leo's cause for seven years, it would be a moment to savour.

Not that Rochère came at once to the point. He even *ate* slowly. He chewed every mouthful twice over, and thought long and hard before answering questions. Content to talk in generalities, he seemed determined to leave the main business until later.

Todd had no choice but to go at his pace. Recognizing that the proprieties had to be observed, he did his best to lighten Katrina's mood while coaxing what answers he could from

271

Rochère. He guessed him to be in his late sixties, not as old as poor old Leo, but getting on. He had wispy grey hair, a countryman's weathered face and a large, bony nose. His English was good, but he spoke painfully slowly, forming words in his mind before translating them. It transpired that he was the local lawyer whom Leo had used when he had purchased the chateau ten years before. Since then Leo had consulted him on several minor matters, all local to Le Ciotat, and the two had become friends. He was perfectly happy to talk about Leo. During the meal he recounted tales of house parties at the chateau, and of long, lingering Sunday luncheons in the summer. Socially he seemed to have known Leo reasonably well, but he had little knowledge of Leo's business affairs.

'He was away so much of the time,' Rochère apologized, looking up from his plate. 'In the summer he was here more often, but . . .' he gave a little shrug. 'Even then, usually he was preparing to go on a trip somewhere.'

'He was always like that,' Katrina said drily.

Rochère gave her a curious look. 'I think you did not visit your father?'

She flushed. She had already decided that any questions would best be answered by being completely straightforward. 'No, I never visited him,' she admitted. 'We were estranged, as you probably know. I expect it was my fault more than his. It's not something I'm very proud about, especially now, but –'

'I saw him whenever he came to London,' Todd interrupted to save her further embarrassment.

Rochère's gaze remained on Katrina.

'We became very good friends,' Todd added.

Rochère nodded. 'A pity,' he said to Katrina. 'You missed some good times.' His wistful expression suggested that he doubted he would see their like again.

At one point Todd managed to steer the conversation to the chateau and how the fire had started. Rochère had already explained during the drive from Marseilles that it had been caused by badly insulated electrical cables in the roof, but at least, Todd thought, discussing the accident might stop him 'rambling on'.

Not that it did. Rochère rambled even about that. He was an old man who liked to take his time by dwelling on every detail. He explained that the local fire chief was his nephew, the local police chief was a personal friend, and that both had carried out the fullest possible investigations. 'But old timbers are old timbers,' he shrugged. 'And old wiring is old wiring . . .'

'And old bores are old bores,' Todd sighed to himself, while signalling to the waiter that they had finished at the table.

Finally, after thanking Todd for the excellent dinner, Rochère rose and led the way to a small room which, as he explained in some detail, was occasionally used in summer as an additional residents' lounge. Naturally he knew the hotel well. He knew the owner, the owner's wife, the owner's son-in-law – and he stopped to talk to them all – but eventually he ushered Katrina and Todd into the room and closed the doors behind him. A fire burned in the grate, wing chairs had been drawn up to the hearth, and coffee and three large glasses of Armagnac had been set on a low table.

Todd looked around with approval. Although lacking the subdued luxury of Leo's suite at the Ritz, the room possessed a certain faded grandeur. Paintings in heavy gilt frames decorated the walls. The sideboard boasted some good pieces of silver. He could see Leo in this room.

As they took their seats at the fireside, Todd tingled with excitement. At last! After lighting his cigar, he reached for his brandy. 'To Leo,' he said, raising his glass, a toast in which the others joined, Rochère willingly, Katrina hesitantly, with a frightened look in her eyes.

'So, monsieur,' Todd said expectantly as he sat back in his seat. 'The floor is yours.'

Rochère smiled politely and nodded. '*Merci, monsieur*,' he said with a look of enquiry. 'Er . . . just exactly where would you like me to begin?'

It seemed obvious to Todd. With a startled look, he glanced at Katrina who was looking equally lost. Gathering his wits, he turned back to Rochère. 'Sorry,' he said with surprise. 'I'm not used to these things, but isn't this where you read us the will or something?'

Rochère flushed, slightly embarrassed. '*Oui*,' he agreed hastily. 'When there are many different bequests, *certainement*. But in this case?' He looked at Katrina in bewilderment. 'You are the sole beneficiary. I have already told you. I have the will in my office. You may examine it tomorrow if you wish, but . . .' He shook his head. 'I have told you. Your father left you everything.'

Seeing his embarrassment, Katrina scolded Todd with a look. 'I'm sure reading the will is unnecessary,' she said diplomatically, smoothing Rochère's ruffled feathers. 'It's just that we didn't know what to expect –'

'For instance,' Todd interrupted rudely. 'What does "everything" mean?'

Rochère looked at him.

'You said "everything". Leo left everything to Katrina. What does it mean?'

'"Everything",' Rochère said slowly, translating to himself as he went, 'means the entire estate.'

Having endured a long, tiring and stressful day, and a dinner which seemed to have lasted for ever, Todd could restrain himself no longer. He ran a hand through his hair and sucked in a breath. 'This might be indelicate,' he sighed with impatience. 'And I wouldn't say it, except Leo would forgive me, but perhaps you could give us an idea of what the estate is worth? You know, a ballpark figure, something to work on?'

Frowning, Rochère asked, 'What is this ballpark?'

'A round figure.' Todd demonstrated with his hands. 'Approximate. You know. A rough idea.'

'Ah.' The frown lifted and Rochère indicated understanding with a smile. Then he said, 'I do not know.'

'You don't *know*?' Todd stared in disbelief. 'How can you not know?' His voice rose incredulously. 'Surely Leo went through everything when you drew up the will?'

'There was no need. Leo's entire estate was to go to his daughter. Perhaps some day he intended to tell me more of what was involved, but . . .' Rochère sighed and shook his head. 'Sadly this terrible accident . . .' He let the words tail off, hoping to have made himself clear.

The palms of Todd's hands felt suddenly clammy. He moistened his lips. 'Wait a minute,' he said, clearing his throat as he sought clarification. Perhaps he had misunderstood? 'Katrina inherits everything, but you don't know what everything's worth? Is that what you're saying?'

Rochère nodded with a smile of agreement.

Todd's heart sank. He had not misunderstood. Thinking quickly, he searched for a solution. After a moment, he said, 'Okay, I see what's worrying you. You're a lawyer and the executor of Leo's will, and so you're accountable and all that. You have to be cautious.' He forced himself to smile. 'So nobody's expecting you to be precise. Okay? I won't hold you to an exact figure, but you must have some idea.'

Rochère frowned and for a moment sat in silence. Then he held up a finger. '*Un point*,' he said. 'I knew nothing of Leo's . . . er . . . business affairs, so first I have to investigate. But an investigation will be *très difficile*.' He tapped his forehead. 'Leo kept his business up here. All in his head. There was a room at the chateau which he used as an office, but I told you, everything was destroyed by the fire.' He looked accusingly at Katrina. 'Did I not say this on the telephone? I am sure I explained –'

'Everything was destroyed?' Todd interrupted incredulously.

'*Oui*. The whole place was gutted. I did tell you –'

'You don't have any records?'

Rochère turned to Katrina. 'Your papa . . .' he frowned '. . . was a dealer? *Oui*? He made deals all over the world. I know this from what he told me. But he employed no one. Madam Ferrier and her daughter went in to clean, old Alphonse Chamoix looked after the grounds, but of course they know nothing of his business affairs.'

'What about a secretary?' Katrina interrupted.

Rochère shook his head. 'Sometimes he brings things to my office to have typed, but only . . .' his brow crinkled '. . . maybe six, seven times in ten years. And the last time –'

'What about his accountant?' Todd said abruptly.

'Did he have one?' Rochère asked. 'I know of no one. Perhaps he employed one in Paris? Or London? As I said, he was away a great deal of the time. He used the chateau almost as a holiday home.'

'His bank,' Todd interrupted triumphantly. 'His bank would know about his finances.'

But again Rochère shook his head. 'The local manager is a friend of mine.' He smiled modestly. 'You understand this is a small community, we all know each other. So I can tell you there is enough in Leo's account for a few local expenses, but not a great sum of money.' Reaching into his inside jacket pocket, he brought out a small notebook. 'To be exact . . .' he permitted himself a small smile. 'Not a figure from the ballpark, eh? To be exact twenty-eight hundred francs.'

Todd heard Katrina catch her breath. His own breathing seemed to have stopped. His heart thumped and he felt dizzy and a moment passed before he could speak. Finally he cleared his throat. 'Monsieur Rochère,' he said, his voice falling to an urgent whisper. 'You remember when we spoke on the phone? I told you Leo was bringing me a bank draft for four hundred thousand pounds. Remember that?'

Rochère nodded.

'You said there was no problem.'

Rochère frowned. 'Pardon, monsieur, I said if Leo was bringing this money, and if Madame Todd was in agreement, then you had nothing to worry about. Eh? Is that not what I said?' He smiled. 'But first we have to sort everything out. Obviously this local bank account was used merely for local expenses. So there are other bank accounts.'

'Other accounts?'

'*Naturellement.* This one had nothing to do with his business, so there must be another account somewhere. A business account. Perhaps more than one? It is logical, *oui,* you agree? And he was bringing you a bank draft for a great sum of money?'

'Yes.'

'Drawn on which bank?'

'How the hell would I know?'

Rochère's face fell. 'You don't know?'

'Of course I don't.'

'Ah, *quel dommage*. A pity. It would give me somewhere to start.'

Horrified, Todd listened to Rochère recite a whole string of difficulties. There were no cheque books, no bank statements, no share certificates, no receipts, no account books. Nothing! The fire had destroyed everything. Rochère's friend the local banker had asked his head office in Paris to search the records to try to trace the source of previous funds. The local tax office had confirmed that Monsieur Sinclair did not have a business registered in Provence, but they were making enquiries further afield . . .

Todd could scarcely take it all in. Earlier he had been impatient, even contemptuous, seeing Rochère as a bumbling old fool. Now he realized he was wrong. Rochère had already been busy. Even so, trying to define what was wrong, accusations sprang from Todd's lips. 'But you said not to worry about the four hundred grand. I told you it was urgent. I *told* you!'

'*Non*. You said important, and I agree,' Rochère nodded, his face stern. 'Such a lot of money *is* important. But monsieur, you needn't worry. We will sort everything out. I have already set enquiries in motion.'

Todd was in motion himself; crossing and uncrossing his legs in a fever of anxiety. 'I need answers now. I need that money on Monday.'

Rochère's bushy eyebrows rose. '*C'est impossible!*' Shaking his head, he reverted to English. 'Impossible, monsieur. Quite impossible. There is a great deal to do . . .'

Todd was no longer listening. Finishing his brandy, he leapt up from the chair and began to circle the room. Leo's words came back to him. *Moroni won't hang about . . . he won't take excuses . . . he'll want his money . . . the whole loan will become repayable . . . he'll use his insurance . . .*

'Insurance!' The word exploded in his head. 'What about insurance? You said the chateau was insured.'

Interrupted in his list of the jobs to be done, Rochère looked faintly pleased. '*Oui.*' He nodded. 'I arranged the insurance myself. The policies were held at my office. They are in good order.'

'Thank God for that! So how much was the chateau insured for?'

Rochère consulted his little book. 'Fifty eight million francs.'

As he converted French francs into sterling, Todd sighed with relief. 'That's more than half a million!' He threw a triumphant look at Katrina. 'Thank God for that! That sorts us out.' Returning to the fireside, he slumped into his chair. 'If we get on to the insurance and lodge a claim –'

'I have done that already.'

'You have!' Todd could have hugged him. 'Well done,' he sighed with a huge feeling of relief. A grin came to his face. 'By God, you had me worried.' Suddenly he felt warm with gratitude. 'So there's no problem.'

'*Naturellement* they have their formalities, but the local representative is a friend of mine and –'

'So we get them together – the insurance guy and the bank manager. When the insurance company complete their formalities they can pay the bank, meanwhile the bank advance me the money. Okay? Can we do that first thing in the morning?'

'*Oh, non. C'est impossible.*'

Once again Todd was rocked back on his heels. 'What d'you mean, impossible?'

'*Oh, non. Non. non.*' Shaking his head, Rochère looked shocked, horrified, even offended. 'Monsieur . . . er, Toddy, you must understand. Nothing can be paid until I produce a statement of affairs. It is the law. In England it would be the same.'

The goodwill Todd had felt moments before began to evaporate.

'I have to trace bank accounts,' Rochère continued. 'Advertise for creditors –'

'Advertise! Bloody hell! I got enough creditors without advertising for them.'

'I must find out what other claims there are. Even then, death duties and taxes have to be paid before I can hand over any assets. Surely you understand? You must be patient. These matters take time. Even a straightforward estate would take months.'

'Months?' Todd echoed in horror. 'I can't wait months!'

Rochère looked severe; the face of an official who knew his duty and intended to carry it out. 'You have no choice,' he said firmly. 'And I should warn you. There are so many complications that in this case it might be a year before you see any money.'

A year. A month. They were equally useless to Todd. He had to pay Moroni on Monday.

CHAPTER NINE

THE NEXT DAY, while Todd was flying back to London, empty-handed and feeling utterly desperate, his fate was sealed.

Aldo Moroni and Claude Lapiere were listening to Philippe Roos deliver his verdict on Paloma Blanca.

During his career Roos had given hundreds of valuations, but none before had amounted to a sentence of death.

Without being well-liked, Roos was well-known in the hotel world. A large, heavily built man in his mid-fifties, with a round, bland face, he had grown up in New York and London. The only son of a Dutch cigar salesman and an English character actress, he had moved to Paris when his father retired there at the end of the Fifties. It was a friend of his father's who had helped him start in real estate. Once started he had never looked back. He first made his mark in the Spanish hotel boom of the Sixties. It was said that Roos had sold every hotel in Torremolinos at least once and possibly twice, and what with his partners busy with office developments, the firm of Arlsruher, Wormack and Roos had never stopped growing. They now boasted offices in almost every capital city in Europe, and Roos spent his life flying from one to another. So much so that it was rare for him to visit a client – usually they called upon him; but, as he joked to his partners, he would be happy to call on the Devil in Hell and give him a valuation, if the Devil paid his fee and expenses.

Large fees and expenses were what Roos's life was about, and even without being told the reason for his valuation, he already saw himself earning a great deal of money from Paloma Blanca. In his experience people only asked for a valuation when they intended to sell, so having earned one fee for a valuation, he was already working out how to earn a lot more. In fact he had spent the cab journey to Montmartre trying to decide which of his hotelier customers to call first, and that inevitably meant the one who would pay him the most money. A finder's fee of three per cent was not to be sniffed at, especially when he saw himself earning a fee for selling the place. Of course it was against all the rules. Agents should act for one party or the other, not both. But who would know? Roos could be the soul of discretion.

He was full of praise for Paloma Blanca. It was, he said 'easily the best resort being developed in Europe at the present time'. Talking of the site, he used the words 'a place of rare beauty'. Highly complimentary about the architect, he forecast that Paloma Blanca would win at least one architectural award. And while he talked, he observed their reactions. Lapiere beamed, but his client, this big granite-eyed man Moroni, merely nodded. Philippe Roos assessed him as a hard man to please.

'And I like this Paloma Blanca Gold Cup idea,' he continued smoothly, his gaze fixed firmly on Moroni. 'I think it will attract great prestige in the future.'

Moroni's expression remained as impassive as ever.

Roos watched him carefully. Clients were always delighted when he sold a place for more than his valuation, and always upset when he got less. He would be a fool to cripple himself with a high price, even though he intended to ask a fee of three per cent for selling Paloma Blanca. On the way to Montmartre, he had done his sums carefully. He would give them a valuation of between twelve and fourteen million sterling. He would then tell the buyer to expect to pay twenty. Then he would conclude a deal at seventeen and a half. Both parties would be pleased, Roos would enhance his reputation, and earn over a million pounds in the process. It was an admirable arrangement.

But Moroni's manner was intimidating. Something about this brooding hulk of a man, with his hard-eyed stare, filled Roos with unease. Moroni was the sort who would demand any sum quoted in full, so although it would make no difference to the final outcome, Roos cautioned himself to be careful at the start. So he said, 'At the present time, my valuation would be between eight and nine million sterling.'

Lapiere was shocked to the core. 'It must have cost twice that to build,' he exclaimed in horror.

'It's still being finished,' Roos pointed out, transferring his gaze to Moroni. 'My valuation is based on the present state of the site.'

'Even so,' Lapiere protested, with a frightened glance at Moroni.

'And don't forget,' Roos added. 'Tourism is depressed at the moment. This world recession –'

Lapiere groaned. 'Such a low figure,' he muttered, the picture of misery. 'Surely it's worth more?'

'Well . . .' Roos considered with the air of a man who was ready to look at every possibility. 'It could be. Once it opens and people get to know about it. The ingredients are there for a successful operation, but it will take time for the place to become known.'

'You said this Gold Cup would do that.'

'I think it will in time. Say in five or six years . . .'

'Not sooner?' Lapiere asked weakly. He sat with his hand inside his jacket, massaging his chest to ease the pain around his heart.

'It takes time to build a reputation,' Roos said in his most reasonable voice. Ignoring Lapiere, he was still searching for a reaction from Moroni. He sensed that the man was equally shocked, though his face was a mask and he had not uttered a word. But a mean man, Roos decided, a cautious man who dislikes spending money. To test his theory, he said airily, 'Of course, it would be different if you spent a lot of money on advertising. The key to success is to get the place known. With enough exposure, and I mean *mega* exposure with the way tourism is at the moment, you'd be booked out. Then you'd achieve the profit potential.'

'What would it be worth then?' Lapiere asked eagerly.

Still watching Moroni, Roos was convinced that he had detected a reaction; a twitch of the mouth, a faint movement of the broad shoulders – the body language of a man shuddering at the suggestion of spending a vast sum on advertising. Feeling on safer ground, Roos delivered an honest verdict. 'I suppose if the place were booked out . . .' his face creased into a look of concentration. 'You could multiply the current valuation by three, even by four. Like I said, it would be achieving its full profit potential.'

But Moroni had ceased to listen. Heaving his bulk up from his chair and after a brief nod which told Lapiere to finish the meeting without him, he ignored Roos and went out to the other office.

Five minutes later, with the faithful Jules Carbone at his side, he was on his way to see Vito Sartene.

And twenty minutes later, Philippe Roos was on the way back to his office intent on making the first of the several calls needed to put Paloma Blanca on the market.

By the Wednesday, Todd was feeling better. He was not feeling well, but less panic-stricken than at any time since the shock of seeing Rochère the previous Thursday evening. 'Fucking French moron!' was his oft repeated assessment of Leo's lawyer. 'I pleaded with the guy. Give me a piece of paper, I said, something I can take to a bank so they'll lend me four hundred grand!'

But Rochère had pointed out that such a document would be too vague to have any value until his investigations were complete.

Todd had stewed all weekend. At one point he had almost blurted out the whole story to Katrina – almost told her Leo's theory about the insurance money and the threat to his life. He had stopped himself in time and managed to confine his fears to a telephone discussion with Hank, and when Hank failed to come up with any fresh ideas, he had called Manny in for a meeting first thing on Monday. As soon as Manny sat down, he recounted every word of his talks with Rochère.

'Look at the bottom line,' he said, his voice hoarse with desperation. 'The insurance on the chateau is half a million. Then there's the site itself, we can sell that. Rochère reckons it would fetch the same again. And don't forget Leo was lending me four hundred grand. A lot of bread's stashed away somewhere. Who knows what it all comes to? But it's gotta be a million, maybe two, maybe *three* . . .'

Unexpectedly, Manny had sided with Rochère. 'Yeah, yeah,' he had said, with a dismissive wave of the hand. 'Then there's French taxes and death duties and –'

'They won't take *everything*!'

'What's with this everything? You keep on about everything. Maybe everything's nothing? You ever think of that? Maybe your friend Leo was hocked up to the eyebrows. So he lived in a chateau. Big deal. You live in a big house. You die, what happens? The bank takes the lot.'

With his own painful experience of owing money, even Todd had to agree it was possible.

'Everyone's got creditors,' Manny had rammed the point home. 'Stands to reason they got to be paid before this whasisname Rochfort can settle the estate. He's doing his job, that's all . . .'

Todd had wanted to tell him Leo's theory about Moroni and the insurance, but he feared that Manny would laugh at him. After all, Manny had never met Moroni. He wouldn't understand.

But at least he was helping. He had made an appointment with a new bank. Now, at ten o'clock on Wednesday morning, as Todd loaded his briefcase with papers in preparation for the meeting, Manny warned him, 'Let me do the talking when we get there. You know something? You foam at the mouth once you start describing Paloma Blanca.'

'You think there's a chance?'

'A new bank's got to take chances. How else do they get customers? Maybe they'll fancy a long shot.'

'We need a banker like Larkins. Remember him? We need someone with faith.'

Manny scowled. 'A rabbi he ain't. He's a moneylender. Talking of which, have those people in Paris called back yet?'

'Not a word,' said Todd.

The silence from Lapiere was his reason for feeling less panic-stricken. After he had paid the eight hundred thousand on Monday, he had telephoned Lapiere to explain about the shortfall.

He had told him all about Leo's death, he had played on Katrina's inheritance for all it was worth, he had talked about the Paloma Blanca Gold Cup and progress on the site; he had talked solidly for thirty minutes. Finally Lapiere had said he would report to his client.

'No news is good news,' Todd concluded cheerfully as he closed his briefcase.

Every hour that passed without word increased his confidence. Why not? He had a good track record. He wasn't trying to renege on the deal. 'They had their other payments on time,' he said. 'They know I'm not trying to cheat them . . .' he paused, interrupted by the telephone ringing. Picking it up, he covered the mouthpiece. 'It's Hank.'

Manny sighed and glanced at his watch, before sitting down to wait. Sometimes he marvelled at the way Todd kept going. Although at times infuriated, secretly he admired his buoyant optimism, his conviction that everything would come right in the end. He liked Todd. And he adored Katrina. In his opinion Katrina should never have stopped working at the office. With Katrina keeping the books, none of this would have happened.

Todd whistled into the telephone. 'I don't believe it!' he exclaimed, his face lighting up with excitement. 'That proves we're on the right track. Fantastic. That's great, Hank!'

Manny rolled his eyes as he listened. *Fantastic. Great. Creditors are knocking the door down and you'd think it's his birthday.* With a deep sigh, he pushed his sleeve back from his wrist and pointed meaningly at his watch.

Todd nodded. 'Hank, I've got to go, but that's great news. Exciting, eh? Okay, I'll call you tonight.' Putting the phone down, he beamed at Manny. 'Listen to this! This will cheer you up. A few days ago some guy was sniffing around the site, asking questions. The builders thought Hank sent him over, but Hank didn't know anything about it. Anyway, it seems this guy's in the property business, specializing in hotels all over the world. Dutch name, Roos or something. Anyway, he's one of the top men. So you see what I mean? The experts *know* we're on to a gold mine.'

'Is that what he said? This Dutchman?'

'Hang on. It gets better.' Todd was breathless with excitement. 'Majorca's a village. Everyone knows everyone. So this guy's back at the airport, waiting for his flight when he bumps into José Carrier who owns the Bella Vista, the big hotel in Palma. Carrier knows him. Apparently this Dutch guy sold him the Bella Vista eight years ago, so they get talking and Carrier asks a few questions and puts two and two together, and figures we're getting ready to put Paloma Blanca on the market. So today he calls in to the Crow's Nest and says *he* wants to buy it.'

Manny's whistle mingled surprise with relief. 'You're kidding! This is serious? He made a firm offer?'

Todd nodded.

Manny made as if to sink to his knees. He cast a look upwards, 'There is a God!' He looked at Todd. 'So tell me? How much will he pay?'

'He offered us nine million the day it gets finished.'

The excitement in Manny's face died. Anticipation turned to surprise and surprise changed to a look of pain. 'Nine million?' He even sounded in pain. 'This is good news? You borrowed twelve. You owe more than fourteen. You've hocked everything you own –'

'It's only his opening offer,' Todd protested. 'No one starts high, do they? And what about this Dutchman sniffing around? I tell you, Manny, people are waking up to what we've got.'

'Vultures! The vultures are waking up and getting ready to tear you to pieces. So what did Hank say to this . . . er, this man with the offer?'

'What do you think?' Todd grinned. 'He told him to stuff it. Hank's like me. He's got faith in what we're doing. All we've got to do is get through this bad patch. Everything will come right in the end.'

Katrina felt like beating her head against the wall. On the telephone in the kitchen, she tried to remain patient. 'No,' she said firmly. 'Ossie, of course I can't come to dinner. It's out of the question. Yes, I'm sorry too.'

Not that she was. In truth she was sorry to have promised to meet him in the first place. Since Monday he had telephoned twice and sent her a bouquet of red roses.

He continued persuasively. 'Katrina,' he purred. 'You're still depressed about the death of your father. I can understand that, but come to dinner and let me take your mind off your troubles.'

How could she say what she was thinking? How could she admit that her reaction to his first note had been out of character? That it had arrived when she was furious with Toddy, that she had been flattered out of her mind, but contrary to what he so obviously thought, she was a married woman who did not indulge in affairs.

'I'd be awful company,' she said. 'You're right, I *am* depressed at the moment.'

But it was less the death of her father which depressed her than the mess they were in. Toddy had been impossible since the funeral. He had been grey with worry at the weekend. She felt sure he was keeping something from her . . .

'Then how about lunch tomorrow?' Ossie persisted. 'I've only got two more days in London. Then I go to New York for six weeks.'

'What a relief,' she thought as she listened. Ossie leaving London would be a complication less in her life.

'Just lunch, then,' she said severely. 'But don't go getting any ideas.'

'Katrina!' he exclaimed sounding excited. 'I'm already full of ideas. We'll have a *wonderful* lunch.'

As she hung up she couldn't help smiling. At least he was a diversion. Even so, tomorrow she would tell him; no more roses, no more letters, no more plans of seduction. 'But let him down gently,' she warned herself. 'After all, be honest, you must have encouraged him. How were you to know things would get out of hand?'

After which she went back to tidying the kitchen. Mrs Bridges did not come in on Tuesday, the one weekday when Katrina coped on her own. Not that she minded. Some mornings she preferred the house to herself, alone with her thoughts instead of being obliged to listen to gossip. In fact she had almost decided to let Mrs Bridges go at the end of the month. Something had to be done to reduce expenses.

She had insisted on putting the villa up for sale. It was the one decision which they had taken since their meeting with Rochère. Rather than trust Toddy to do it, she had called the real estate firm in the harbour herself. 'You've enough to do,' she had told Todd, taking the matter out of his hands. Not that a sale sounded imminent, but at least she was doing something . . .

The ring on the doorbell came as she was preparing her lunch. Shutting the kitchen door on Mac, she went out to the hall, drying her hands on a tea towel. When she opened the front door all she could see was a huge bouquet; lilies and roses and carnations under a great cloud of gypsophila.

'Flowers for Mrs Todd,' said a voice from a man scarcely visible.

'Oh no,' she groaned. 'Not more!'

Suddenly the flowers were thrust into her face. She staggered backwards and turned her head, but not in time to avoid the hand slapped over her mouth. Her scream was muffled as she was pushed down the hall. She glimpsed other men before her head was forced upright and then all she could see was the ceiling. Stifled, she could scarcely breathe. She heard the front door slam, heavy feet running up the stairs, bedroom doors opening and slamming, a commotion as someone entered and retreated from the kitchen, Mac barking furiously. Then she was pulled into the drawing-room and flung down onto a sofa . . .

Rape! The terrifying fear exploded like a bomb in her head. Her eyes bulged. Her ears rang as she screamed. She clawed at the hand over her mouth. Twisting and turning, she tried to scream, to bite, but the man forced her away and pushed her face into the upholstery. A knee thumped into her spine. Her head was jerked back, a cloth was stuffed into her mouth. She screamed through the tea towel as it was fastened around her face. Her lungs were bursting. Her arms were pulled behind her as she was jerked upright into a sitting position.

Retching, her heart pounding, she looked up at the two men standing above her. Amazingly, she felt almost gratitude as she saw not lust but callous indifference in their faces. Another man appeared in the doorway, carrying a suitcase. His gaze went beyond her to the French windows. He nodded. She flinched as she sensed someone behind her. Then a fourth man came into view; a powerfully built man with a weathered face, older than the others, who strolled across the room and sat down in an armchair.

Where were their masks? Stockings? They wore gloves, but she could see their faces. The big man had dark eyes and a gaze which went right through her. Her mouth opened and she screamed. She heard a roaring in her ears, felt veins knot in her throat, but the towel stifled her sounds. All she could hear was Mac barking in the kitchen. And the clock chimed in the hall. Once. One o'clock. *Dear God, please don't let them hurt me. Please don't let them hurt me. Please . . .*

The two men moved away; one to sit on the stool at the piano, the other on the opposite sofa. The man in the doorway put down his suitcase, came and sat next to her. She flinched when his arm brushed against her.

'Mis' Todd,' said the big man, looking at her.

Her heart pounded. His gravelly voice had a strange accent. Foreign. And his skin was too dark to be English. But his tone was not threatening. Mac continued to make such a noise in the kitchen that she had to strain to catch what the man was saying.

'Is'sa your husband we wan'a see. He'sa at his office? Huh?'

For a moment she remained silent, confused, frightened. The man repeated the question. 'Yes,' she said, dry-mouthed through the towel, forgetting that speech was ineffective. Nodding her head, she flinched as the man next to her touched her thigh. Looking down she saw something metallic in his hand. Then a blade sprang out with such force that she jumped. She screamed silently, her gaze going back to the big man, pleading for help: *Don't let him hurt me. Please don't let him touch me.*

The big man was talking to her. She needed all of her concentration to interpret his accent. Finally she understood that if she promised not to scream they would remove the towel from her mouth. They wanted her to call Toddy and ask him to come home. Just that, nothing more, no explanation. There were conditions. If she screamed the man next to her would cut her throat. She froze in terror. Pushing her hair aside, the man rested the blade on her neck. Just rested it on her skin. She sat rigid with fear, not daring to breathe, feeling the razor-thin blade, imagining a slight pressure . . .

'Is'sa understood? You nod your head.'

She dared not nod because of the knife.

Frowning, the big man flicked his dark eyes sideways and the knife was withdrawn.

Swallowing hard, she nodded.

The man at the piano rose and came to stand behind her. He unknotted the tea towel and let it fall. A great shuddering sigh escaped her. They were all watching. Their stares stopped her from bursting into tears. The look in their eyes warned her against screaming. Not that the warning was necessary. *I'm too frightened to scream. I won't scream.* When she opened her mouth, she gulped, cleared her throat and sucked in a breath. The knife glinted at the corner of her eye. Opening her mouth, she tried again. 'Please,' she begged in a whisper. 'Make him take that thing away.'

The big man nodded. The blade disappeared with a click, but the hand remained on her shoulder. The knife was still there, inches away. Every muscle in her body was shaking. Terrified that the blade would spring out again, she whispered, 'Please, I . . . don't understand . . .'

The big man repeated his instructions.

Her body refused to respond. Her limbs were rigid with fear. Her throat felt constricted, her mouth was dry.

They brought her a drink – a brandy poured from the decanter on the sideboard – and she asked for a cigarette. They had to light it for her. Her hands were shaking too much to hold it against a flame. And some of the brandy dribbled over her chin.

The man repeated his instructions all over again.

The idea of telephoning Toddy appalled her. Who were they? What did they want? She sensed they would hurt him. *Dear God, what can I do?*

'He might be out,' she whispered when they brought her the telephone. 'He might not be there.'

'You try,' said the big man as he rose from the chair. Then he spoke to the man at the piano in Italian. She was *sure* it was Italian. Ossie came and went from her mind. Closing her eyes, she could see Toddy in the office, but for the strangest reason he was much younger. She saw herself across the desk from him, dressed in a grey tailored suit she had thrown out years ago. Toddy was asking why she didn't want to go to Scotland with the people she worked for . . .

'You be very careful,' someone said and she opened her eyes to see the man from the piano crouched in front of her. He was speaking English with an accent which sounded more French than Italian. He said, 'We'll be on the extension in the other room. One wrong word, and —'

The blade clicked out at her throat.

She felt sick.

Mac had fallen silent in the kitchen.

She could hear the hall clock ticking.

Her hands shook when she tried to dial. Her whole body trembled as if she were shivering from cold.

'What's the number?' asked the man in front of her.

She told him and he dialled it for her. She realized that the big man had left the room. Perhaps he had gone to the study to listen?

'It's ringing,' said the man, giving her the receiver.

She put it to her left ear. The knife was close to her right. *God, what shall I say? What shall I do?*

'Owen's. Good morning . . .' A laugh. 'Sorry, I mean good afternoon.'

'Sally?'

'Katrina? How are you?'

A pause while she moistened her lips. 'Is he in?'

'Putting you through.'

'Hello.'

'Toddy?'

'Yes?'

Words burst from her lips. 'Thank God. Can you come home? Now? Right this minute?'

'What's up? What's the matter?'

'Please. *Please!*'

Then she screamed, 'Toddy, don't come. Don't come –'

The telephone was snatched from her hand. She was knocked sideways. The coppery taste of blood filled her mouth, she expected to feel the knife . . .

But there was no knife.

Just the big man coming into the room with a smile on his face.

'Please!' Her voice rose in panic. '*Please –*'

'Katrina?'

She had hung up. Puzzled, Todd stared at the telephone. Quickly he dialled his home number. Engaged. He dialled again. Still engaged. Or was the receiver off the hook? Unsure what to do, he sat there, listening, his frown deepening. He dialled again, trying to imagine what was wrong, re-playing her voice in his mind. When the line remained engaged his concern became alarm. Pictures of accidents raced through his mind – Katrina with her arm scalded from an overturned saucepan, the kitchen telephone dangling loose from the wall . . .

Shrugging into his jacket, he was out into Sally's office with a couple of strides. 'I think Katrina's had some sort of accident.'

'What?'

'Where's Herbert?'

'You sent him to the printers when you came back with Manny. He won't be back for an hour. What sort of accident? Is she all right?'

'I can't get through on the phone. Look, keep trying, will you? If you get an answer, tell her I'm on my way.'

'Davis can run you there.'

'No, I don't want the showroom left empty. I'll get a cab.'

He had never known Katrina panic. He had known her upset, angry, furious, hurt. *She sounded frightened!*

The cab on the corner started up as soon as he raised his arm. Breathlessly he clambered in and gave his home address. 'As fast as you can,' he said urgently.

Why did she hang up?

Why not answer the phone?

And her voice: *Can you come home? Now? Right this minute? Please!*

Vaguely he realized the cab driver had turned off the main road and was taking a route through the back doubles. 'It's murder at Golders Green,' the man said over his shoulder. 'They've got the road up again.'

'Right. Thanks.' Sitting back in his seat, he took out his cigar case, looked at it, and put it back into his pocket.

Ten minutes later the cab swung through the pillars at the end of the road.

'The end house,' he said, edging forward and reaching for the door. 'Set me down at the gate.'

As he hurried across the drive he could hear Mac barking inside the house. A blue Ford Granada was parked at the front door. Not a car he knew, not one owned by a friend – he was familiar with the cars of his friends. Taking out his keys, he bounded up the two steps to the door. To his surprise it swung open and his impetus carried him over the threshold.

'Katrina!'

The door slammed revealing a man, a stranger, although despite his surprise Todd vaguely recognized the face without being able to place it. 'Who are you? Where's my wife?' Even as he asked, he was turning away, not waiting for an answer, striding down the hall to the open drawing-room door. 'Katrina!'

And there she was, her face empty of colour, her amber eyes wide . . . sitting on the sofa next to Aldo Moroni.

Never in a million years would Todd have imagined Moroni invading his home. An Englishman's home is his castle. For men to seize a house in broad daylight was a thought so alien that it never entered his head. Whereas it was second nature to Moroni. It had been part of his training. There had been at least twelve occasions in French Algeria when he had invaded men's houses. Twelve men dead with their families alongside them. In a land whipped to a frenzy by nationalist agitators, it had been his duty to enforce the rule of France. And he had, with an effectiveness which won him a chestful of medals before he swapped the Legion for a more lucrative living.

Katrina leapt up and flung herself into his arms, shaking violently, sobbing, 'Thank God you're here! Oh thank God! They . . . just burst in . . . I couldn't stop them . . .'

Too outraged to be frightened, Todd could not imagine what was to come. He could not even *conceive* of what was to happen. Muttering reassurances to Katrina, he sat her down in a chair, then bristling with anger rounded on Moroni. 'What the bloody hell's going on here?' Extending a finger, he stepped forward, but Sartene rose from his place at the piano. Todd felt himself grabbed by the shoulder and then an explosion of pain as the man kneed him in the testicles. With a cry of agony, he doubled up and sank to the floor.

Katrina screamed and threw herself from the chair to cover his body.

Mac barked and whined and scratched the kitchen door, making even more noise than Todd's groans.

With chilling casualness Sartene returned to the piano. He stooped over the suitcase carried in earlier. Flicking the catches, he lifted the lid. He had already seen the gas cooker before the dog had driven him out of the kitchen. Taking a wrench and two heavy spanners from the case he set them on the floor in readiness.

'It's all right,' Todd gasped to Katrina. 'I'm okay, it's okay.'

'Oh, Toddy,' she cried, her hands shaking as she tried to help him.

A moment passed before he rose to his knees, and a moment more before he reached a chair, with Katrina supporting his weight. Wheezing and gasping, he stared at Moroni's impassive face. 'Get out of here,' he hissed breathlessly. 'Get out before I call the police.'

No other words could more clearly show their inability to understand each other. A meeting of minds was impossible – for if Todd was outraged, so was Moroni. None of this was his fault. It was Todd who had begged him for money. It was Todd who had breached the agreement. It was Todd who had shown no respect. Even now, the man showed scant signs of contrition.

And to threaten the police suggested he had taken leave of his senses.

'Mist' Todd,' Moroni said, trying to preserve his usual icy calm. 'You don' honour our agreement. What I do now?'

'For Chrissakes! I explained everything to Lapiere. I gave him chapter and verse. You'll get the rest of the money –'

'Is'sa not what was'sa 'greed.'

'I'm four hundred grand short. That's all. You'll have it in a month if I can sell the villa.'

'An' in six'a month? What'a you do then? You ain't gotta no money from Suntours.'

Even then Todd failed to see the immediate danger. Even with his testicles aching, his neck throbbing, his home invaded, Katrina trembling at his side – even feeling outraged and violated, even after being clubbed to his knees – he *still* failed to recognize where Moroni was leading. Such was his faith in Paloma Blanca. He could *see* the light at the end of the tunnel.

'I don't know what you're so worried about. You'll get paid. So much is happening,' he said as he launched into his vision of the future. He itemized points on his fingers – one, two, three, four reasons why the project *had* to succeed. His belief reached out to the man at the window, who turned to stare at him with unconcealed interest. Even the man near the piano stopped unpacking the suitcase and listened. Even Katrina stopped trembling and turned her head to watch her husband's face until finally he ran out of breath.

'So you see?' he concluded. 'It'll come right in the end.'

But Moroni was unmoved. 'Is'sa not what we agreed. Is'sa too bigga risk.'

Todd slapped a hand to his forehead as if to stop his skull from exploding. 'How can you say that? We're winning, for Chrissakes! Even without Suntours. You wouldn't even be four hundred grand short if Leo had lived.'

'Ah! Is'sa 'nother thin'. Huh? If'a he still alive maybe 'e help, but now –'

'That's just it!' Todd interrupted, shaking his head, his voice rising with excitement. 'That's the point. Didn't Lapiere tell you? Leo's left everything to Katrina.' Turning to Katrina, he hugged her as if to demonstrate what a united couple they were. 'You see, we'll even have Leo's money. I mean, God knows how much it'll be, but . . .'

A glimmer showed in Moroni's dark eyes, but when he heard about the complications of probate, his interest faded and died. 'We dunno is'sa lotta or'a nothin'. Is'sa today or tomorrow you get pay? We dunno. Huh? What'sa point? Our agreement is'sa finished. You pay me. I wanna fourteen million, eight hundred an' –'

'How can I pay fourteen million? If I had any money you'd have the four hundred grand.'

Moroni's look was so chilling that – *at last* – Todd realized what was to happen.

Confirmation came from Moroni. 'Is'sa the agreement,' he said. 'Is'sa why I take'a out'a insurance.'

'Oh Christ! Hang on a minute,' Todd objected, sweat bursting from every pore in his body. 'I'm not trying to welsh on the deal. I'm doing everything I can to get you the money. Maybe I can refinance the whole deal? We're talking to new bankers. We saw them this morning. There's always a chance. I'll try that if you want –'

'Mist' Todd. Is'sa today or never.'

'How d'you mean?' asked Todd, his mouth going dry.

He gaped when Moroni explained about the gas explosion in Amsterdam. His stomach heaved. Vaguely he heard Katrina's stifled whimper of terror, but mainly he was concentrating on what Moroni was saying. The man was a monster! A mass murderer. Eight people dead!

Moroni shrugged an apology. 'Is'sa all I can do.'

'You want me to *understand*?' Todd had a great longing to go berserk, to throw himself at Moroni. It took all his willpower to remain in his chair. 'You want me to condone this? You want me to say okay, go ahead, blow us to pieces –'

'Is'sa not my fault you don' honour our agreement.'

The physical discomfort of sitting still while erupting inside became unbearable. Todd jumped up. 'I'll *honour* the fucking agreement if you give me time!' he shouted, so forcefully that

Mac heard him in the kitchen and started barking again, this time louder than ever. And Katrina shrieked and burst into tears, so that suddenly the whole house erupted with noise.

As Moroni covered his ears, Sartene rushed into the hall with Carbone behind him. The air was full of Mac snarling and snapping, and the men cursing and bellowing to each other. Then came such a bloodcurdling sound that Todd stopped shouting and Katrina stopped shrieking. They froze in horror. The squeal of pain went right through them. A second squeal made them shudder. As the third squeal turned to a whimper, Todd was on his feet, evading the outstretched hands of the man by the door, running into the hall with the man on his heels, throwing himself into the kitchen, fists bunched as he leapt at Mac's attackers.

But he was too late. Mac's strength was already draining from him along with his blood. His sad brown eyes were glazing over. Seeing Todd he tried to raise his head, but the feeble movement was reduced to a gesture by the gash in his throat. Falling to his knees, Todd attempted to cradle him. His efforts were rewarded by the flicker of his tail and a gurgling whimper. Then Mac died in his arms.

Overcome, Todd was stunned. It had happened so quickly. Mac was part of the family. He had come into their lives when they bought the house. Todd remembered carrying him up the stairs at the garage, a birthday present for Katrina . . .

But even as he lowered Mac's head to the floor, rough hands were pulling him upright. Anger came then, a great red blinding rush of outrage that set blood pounding in his ears. Pushing one assailant aside, he kicked another and lashed out at the third. But they were three to one, bigger and fitter, who responded with punches and kicks of their own, delivered with deadly precision. He was dragged from the kitchen, gasping with pain, doubled up, one arm twisted behind him, soiled by Mac's blood and some of his own.

Katrina needed no telling. She had heard. Confirmation was in his bleak face as he was pushed into the chair. Throwing her arms around him, she clung to him, sobbing piteously as he embraced her, his hands patting her, squeezing her, providing

297

what little comfort he could. Over her shuddering shoulders, he spat at Moroni, 'Bastard! You bastard!'

Moroni was amazed. Truly the man was insane! About to be blown to pieces, he was upset by the death of a dog? The English were mad. Something was wrong with their brains. Even their instinct for self-preservation was defunct. God had been kind to give them their own little island. In a bigger world they would be extinct.

'Jesus Christ,' Todd muttered emptily, while he tried to comfort Katrina.

But the complication of the dog had brought a frown to Moroni's face. They would have to dispose of it. Injuries from explosion are not clean-cut. Bodies are torn apart like pieces of bread. Even a superficial investigation would show that the animal was killed by the slash of a razor. And a superficial investigation would become thorough with an insurance claim for millions involved. Not that Moroni moved a muscle to help. His men were well-trained. Through the open door he saw Carbone return from upstairs, clutching a blanket. He heard movement in the kitchen, and a moment later Carbone appeared in the hall with his cousin Marcosi at the opposite end of the blanket, puffing slightly from the weight of their burden. Moroni checked his watch. One thirty-five. Thirty-five minutes since their arrival.

'For Chrissakes!' Todd exclaimed over the sound of Katrina's sobs. 'What more do you *want*? I'm selling the villa. We'll have that money through soon —'

'Is'sa too late.'

'I'll sign it over to you.' Casting looks to either side, Todd searched for pen and paper. 'I'll sign anything!'

Moroni tightened his lips to demonstrate the futility of discussion. From experience he knew when the time for talking was over.

'You name it and you've got it!' Todd cried, trying to forget his blood-stained clothes, stifling horror and revulsion as he tried to think of a deal. He could always do a deal. It was what he was good at. 'We can work something out. It just needs talking about, that's all . . .'

Interrupted by a sound from the front door, he flinched as the other two men entered the room. They nodded to Moroni, signalling that the dog was in the car, to be disposed of later.

Moroni checked his watch as he did every minute.

Shutting his knife with a click, Sartene returned it to his pocket and crossed the room to pick up the wrench. Wordlessly, he turned and went out to the kitchen, with Carbone behind him, leaving Marcosi to stand guard on the victims.

The hastening pace galvanized Todd. 'Hang about!' he protested, throwing Moroni a look of appeal. 'We can talk about this, can't we?'

Moroni raised his open palms in a gesture of futility.

'I'll give you a charge on Paloma Blanca! Take a charge on *everything*, for God's sake!' Todd laughed, trying to release his tension, trying to win some sort of response from Moroni. 'It's only for a few months. Then there's Leo's money. You can call this guy Rochère if you like. He'll tell you. I explained all this to Lapiere. I told him everything. I'm not like that guy in Belgium that time. I'm not trying to welsh on the deal! For Chrissakes, you've *got* to believe me!'

The sound of metal scraping on floor tiles came from the kitchen.

'She's got money,' Todd exclaimed suddenly, pointing to Katrina. 'Tell you what. If she goes to the bank . . . I mean, she's got money of her own.' Seizing on the lie, words flew from his lips. 'She's wealthy, even without Leo's money. She could pay you. Now. Today. One of you could go with her if you like, collect the money and bring it back here.'

Katrina's tear-stained look of surprise was enough for Moroni to dismiss the stupid lie without comment.

'But she's got nothing to *do* with it!' Todd howled. 'She wasn't part of the deal. She didn't even know about it. Let her go, for God's sake!' He started to his feet, only for Marcosi to push him back into the chair. 'Get off,' he shouted, thrusting him away. 'There must be *something* –'

Sounds of metal hitting metal came from the kitchen.

Moroni sighed at the unpleasantness of life. All so unnecessary. If only people would keep their word. He vowed never again to deal with the English. Maybe he was getting old? Time to retire? He could spend more time with Nicole in Paris . . .

'I'll *get* the money,' Todd shouted despairingly. 'I promise. Just give me time. Let me *call* someone. If you let me make a few calls . . .'

Moroni remembered other men making such promises. Such words had no meaning.

Faces flashed through Todd's mind. Who could he call? Who would help? Hank, Manny, Smithson at the bank, old Carruthers at the golf club . . . old Carruthers had come into money recently, a lot of money, he was boasting about it, maybe he would . . . Charlie . . . Charlie! *Charlie!* He could hear her confident voice: 'Sure I can go up to six million without refer-ence to anyone . . . but it's boring . . .'

'Six million,' he croaked. The words were out before he was aware of opening his mouth. 'Suppose I get six million?'

A gleam of interest came into Moroni's dark eyes. 'Today?'

Todd nodded, more to himself than Moroni. *Could she? Would she? She might if I explained? Don't be bloody stupid, Moroni won't let you explain. What if I lie to her? I can explain afterwards . . . we can go to the police . . .*

Skilled at reading facial expressions, Moroni's interest quick-ened. Clearly the Englishman had thought of something. It had happened before. The prospect of death concentrated men's minds like no power on earth.

Rubbing the creases in his forehead, Todd infused his voice with all the confidence he could muster. 'There's a chance. There is. A *real* chance. Maybe I could get six million today? Suppose I do that? They could wire it to your bank. How about that?'

Six million? Today? Without complications. Moroni had never forgotten the insurance claims which had failed. He was haunted by memories of expensive losses; painful reminders of how even the best-laid plans can go wrong. And even when they went right, insurers took all the time in the world. Months could pass before he was paid his money. 'Is'sa less than half,' he said. 'How you pay the rest?'

'I'll sell Paloma Blanca,' Todd blurted out. 'We've had an offer. There's a guy in Majorca who's offered nine million.'

Moroni was so startled that even his granite features betrayed a flicker of interest.

Salesmen as well as murderers can read facial expressions, and Todd seized upon the reaction. 'See,' he shouted triumphantly. 'You'll get your money. All of it. I told you we'd come up with something . . .'

Moroni's interest was so intense that he allowed Todd to remain on his feet. With a flick of his head, Moroni motioned Carbone to the seat in the window and Marcosi to the piano. Sartene appeared in the open doorway, signalling all was ready in the kitchen, but at a glance from Moroni he remained where he was while Todd paced up and down, pummelling one hand into the other, like a lawyer seeking to convince a jury. 'I can clinch the deal tomorrow. All I've got to do is fly out to Majorca. This guy Carrier's already made us an offer. He's the biggest hotelier on the island. Nine million, right? Payable the day we get finished.'

'Finished?' Moroni queried, scowling with disappointment, feeling his excitement recede.

'In April,' Todd said quickly. 'Christ, it's only a few months away! You'll make your full profit! You'd get six million today and nine when I sell. Fifteen million! You've already had over two. Seventeen million! You only lent me twelve. For God's sake what more do you want?'

In April? Moroni frowned, but as he stifled his disappointment about the delay, he realized that even April was earlier than when he might expect the insurance. The last insurance claim had taken a year to settle. *A year!* Merely to recover the capital. No profit. He sucked his teeth as he sat back on the sofa.

'It's a hell of a deal,' Todd said insistently.

'Is'sa only a good deal when I get pay,' said Moroni, thinking of Roos's valuation. Nine million sounded about right. He looked at Todd. 'How I know you tellin' the truth? Huh? You gotta letter? You gotta somethin' in writin'?'

Todd almost blurted out their reaction to Carrier. Only a fool would sell for nine million. Or someone with a gun at his head. *Anyway why bother? Charlie won't lend me the six million.*

This is crazy! Resisting an insane urge to laugh, he managed to say, 'I can get it in writing if I go and see him.'

Moroni considered. Six now and a written undertaking of nine from someone of substance. Not a man of straw like Todd. It was a huge step forward. Fifteen million instead of twelve. By April he could be out of this mess with his full profit. Reaching a decision, he nodded. 'Okay. You get this in writin' an' give it to Lapiere. Understan'?'

Todd's heart leapt. 'I'll have to fly out to Majorca.'

'Sure. You go tomorrow, an' you got . . .' Moroni scowled as he calculated dates, remembering that he was due to go home to Corsica on the eighteenth. 'Okay, is'sa deal. But Lapiere must have it on the seventeenth. Huh?'

Todd was lightheaded with relief. 'I know,' he retorted. 'Don't tell me. If he doesn't you'll come back and kill me.' And he laughed. It was a stupid, hysterical laugh, but it caused Moroni to laugh too, and Sartene to smile, and Carbone to roll his eyes as he glanced at Marcosi.

Only Katrina remained unmoved, her hands at her mouth, her white face frozen in horror.

'Now you getta the six million,' said Moroni.

Sartene stood behind Katrina, with one hand holding her shoulder, the other hand holding the knife, while in the study, Moroni listened on the extension, ready to break the connection.

Todd dared not look at Katrina. Her terror would render him speechless. Instead he sat hunched in the chair, his body twisted awkwardly as if to ward off a blow, his eyes fixed on his pocket book and the number of Charlie's direct line at her office.

She answered briskly on the third ring. 'Hello.'

'Charlie? It's Toddy.'

'Hi!' Her voice warmed immediately. 'How you doing? This is a rare honour. I'm the one who calls you, remember?'

He laughed. He actually laughed! Katrina had a knife at her throat and he was laughing like a fool. *Dear God, you're out of your mind!*

'What's so hysterical?'

'No, no, it's just . . . er . . . I'm so pleased you're there. I've got some . . . er . . . what I mean is . . . have you got a minute?'

Suppose she says no? Suppose she's in a meeting? Suppose . . .

'You have to ask?' Her voice lowered as it did when she teased him. 'After what we've been to each other.'

Jesus! Clasping the telephone tight to his ear, he twisted himself deeper into the chair. 'I . . . er . . . just wondered. Are you alone in your office?'

'Why? You want to talk dirty?'

'Charlie!'

'Oh come on, you know what being here does to my hormones. Just for a little while —'

'Charlie, please!'

'Okay, okay. As a matter of fact you just caught me. I'm on my way to the big city.'

'London?'

'On the four o'clock flight. Hence my carefree abandon. Twenty-four hours away from this smug little island. I've an appointment first thing in the morning, but I can make dinner tonight if you ask me.'

'Yes,' he said at once. 'Yes, terrific, yes, let's have dinner. I'd love that.' *Please God I'll still be alive . . .*

'Great,' she said, sounding surprised.

'I'll get Herbert to pick you up at the airport. Give me your flight details.'

His hand shook as he wrote down the flight number. *Will they let me call Herbert? Could Herbert get to the police? Can . . .*

'. . . fine,' Charlie was saying. 'I'll see you later.'

'No! Charlie!' He shouted in panic. 'Don't go. I'm calling about something important.'

'You *do* want to talk dirty?'

Hunched forward, elbows on his knees, the telephone between his legs, he spoke at the floor in an effort to achieve total concentration. He knew a simple loan was out of the question, but he wished he'd had more time to prepare his story, longer to polish his lies, but time was denied him . . .

'I've . . . er, got a chance to refinance Paloma Blanca,' he

303

began, trying to sound pleased and excited. 'In fact I've set up a great deal. It saves us a bundle on interest. It cuts our costs by half a million a year –'

'Wow! Oh, well done!' The teasing note vanished, leaving her voice glowing with approval. 'That's some going, especially these days!'

'Yeah, well, the point is . . . er . . . this is the deal. We pay off the old loan today and get the new money tomorrow. Right?'

'Sure.'

'But . . . I mean, we must pay six million today to show we own clear title to Paloma Blanca. Understand? Before close of business. So I've just been on to our bank and . . . I mean, you won't believe this . . .' he forced a laugh which again made him sound too close to hysteria. 'It's totally ridiculous . . . but they've got to get sanction from head office.'

There was no answering laugh from Charlie, not even surprise. 'Six million *is* six million,' she pointed out. 'You're talking big money.'

'It's only overnight. We can pay it back tomorrow. But unless I have it today I lose the deal. Charlie, I'm frantic,' he admitted, at last being truthful.

'What's the rush? Surely your new people understand –'

'Look, the guy we're dealing with goes to . . . er . . . he flies to Japan tomorrow and I want it all signed before he goes, and . . . er . . . the point is, will you help out?'

'Me?' Charlie yelped, shocked and surprised. 'You're kidding? Where do I get six million?'

'I meant your outfit, your people there.'

'I can't involve the firm in that sort of deal. We only deal on the overnight money market.'

'This is overnight!'

'Toddy! We don't back properties, you know that. I told you. We're not allowed to. We can only invest client's funds in securities.'

'I'll pay more than the overnight market –'

'It's not that. It's simply I can't do it. We're not allowed to.'

The finality in her voice sent a shiver down his spine, driving him to new desperation.

304

'Charlie, *please*! You can't say no. For God's sake, I'll wire the money to your office tomorrow. Before noon. Listen, your future's with us. Right? You're coming on the board . . .'

Faltering slightly, he almost gave up. In his heart he sensed it was futile. No matter how many lies he told, Charlie would say no . . . and afterwards they would refuse to let him make other calls . . . Moroni would kill them . . .

'. . . Charlie, I'm asking a favour, that's all. It won't cost your investors a penny. You're doing them a favour, earning extra interest . . .'

He went on non-stop; pleading, cajoling, laying his tongue to every lie he could invent. Beads of sweat stood out all over his forehead. Twisting and turning in the chair, he averted his eyes for fear of drying up on sight of Katrina.

Then, miraculously, a slight hesitancy crept into Charlie's voice. She sounded less adamant, more helpful than before. 'Can't your new people pay the existing mortgage off direct? That would be the usual procedure.'

'Spain,' he lied quickly. 'Spanish law. We pay double stamp duty if we do it that way. I dunno, it's complicated, the lawyers explained it. But believe me, we went into that option . . .'

On he went, fearful that Moroni would break the connection, not daring to look at Katrina.

'I hate bending the rules,' Charlie said doubtfully.

'Everyone bends them now and then.'

'I don't. I wouldn't even *think* of doing this for anyone else. Toddy, I really don't want to do this.'

His heart thumped. 'We can't let this chance slip through our fingers. Charlie, you must understand. Our whole futures are on the line here, your future, my —'

'I don't know —'

'Please, Charlie. It's only overnight. You'll have the money tomorrow.'

'I'd have to be absolutely sure of that. You can't let me down.'

'I won't.'

'You promise?'

'Of course I promise.'

'Can you give me a bank draft while I'm in London?'

Inspiration came in a blinding flash. 'Charlie, come to the meeting with me.' His voice rose with excitement. 'Why didn't I think of that before? You'll be in London. Come to the meeting with me. You *should* be there! You're joining the board, for God's sake! I can introduce you to this guy. You can meet the man for yourself –'

'I've an appointment first thing –'

'I'll delay our meeting. When can you be free?'

'Ten, ten-thirty –'

'Ten-thirty. I'll fix it for ten-thirty. How's that? Charlie, you'll actually *be there* when we get the funds –'

'And you'll give me a bank draft? For me to bring back with me?'

'Sure,' he lied, as sweat streamed down his face. 'No problem.'

'You won't let me down?'

'Charlie! How can you even *ask* a question like that? This is me, remember? I'll tell you more over dinner, but this is a tremendous breakthrough –'

'Well, yes,' she sighed, sounding unhappy. 'I can see that, but –'

'*Please*, Charlie!'

Another sigh, then she said, 'Okay. So where do I wire the money?'

He was sweating so badly that the telephone slipped in his hand. His voice was hoarse. 'The First Bank of Berne. Hang on, I've got the code and the account number.' He read it out. 'Charlie, and this is important. The money goes to the Paloma Blanca loan account. Can you include that in the documentation?'

'Sure, that's easy.'

'And Charlie, one last favour, can you do it right now? Our people want to call their bank for confirmation of receipt in ten minutes.'

CHAPTER TEN

EVEN INCLUDING THE NAIL-BITING wait while Moroni called the bank in Berne, the men were in the house for only an hour and ten minutes. It had seemed a lifetime. It had literally almost amounted to Todd's and Katrina's lifetimes, yet bewildered and terrified though they were, they were flabbergasted at Moroni's reaction after he spoke to his bank.

'Is'sa good we sort'a everythin' out, eh?' he beamed, looking well pleased with events. He even wanted to shake Todd's hand.

Too frightened and exhausted to refuse, Todd came closer to understanding him at that moment than at any time since they had met.

'Is'sa not personal, is'sa business, huh?'

And it was – Moroni was simply protecting his interests, and as far as he was concerned the outcome was far better than trying to collect the insurance. Three million pounds better.

But after the moment of warmth, came the chilling reminder. 'Is'sa two week from today,' Moroni said, jabbing a finger into Todd's chest. 'Okay? Two week. Else I be back.'

Mute and white-faced, Katrina watched them prepare to leave. Sounds from the kitchen suggested that two of the men were clearing up, like decorators at the end of a job. Then they returned to the room, signalling to the big man. She flinched as he patted her shoulder. 'Is'sa okay. No problem no more,' he said on his way into the hall. She heard the front door open and close, and a moment later the sound of a car turning in the drive. For a moment she held her breath, then she burst into tears.

Todd was at her side in an instant, cradling her in his arms, rocking back and forth on the chair.

She pressed into his jacket to smother the sound of her sobbing, as if afraid the men would hear and come back. Choked by emotion, he could only hold her tight in an effort to provide comfort. Minutes passed before either of them could speak. Then she choked, 'Mac. I must –'

'No.' He held her in the chair to restrain her. 'It's no good, he's not there. They . . . er . . . took him out to the car.'

She stared, her eyes vacant for a moment before lighting with painful understanding. 'But . . . they . . .' She swallowed, her face contorted with misery. 'Did they . . .'

Clearing his throat, trying to find his voice, finally when he could talk he tried to say the right things – that Mac's death had been mercifully quick, that the dog hadn't suffered – he did *try* to find the right words, even lies, anything to alleviate her pain, but Katrina seemed inconsolable. Eventually he dropped to his knees and took her hand, squeezing it tight. 'It's all right, darling, they've gone, it's all right . . .' He whispered the words over and over; trying to comfort her, to reassure her, while all the time telling himself that remorse could come later, now he had to take charge, to act, to think. A voice in his head said *Do something!* But his brain failed to respond. *Do what?* Shock and terror had left him traumatized. He had lost the power to reason. All he could do was repeat, 'It's all right, it's all right.' Minutes passed before he rose to his feet. Leaving her on the sofa, he went to the sideboard. With shaking hands, he poured a whisky for himself and a brandy for her.

'Here,' he said, kneeling before her. 'Drink this.'

He found her a cigarette, fetched her some tissues from across the room, and sat down beside her. It was only after insisting that she finish her drink, and after he had gulped down his whisky, that he stirred into action. 'Hang on, I won't be a minute.'

'No!' She clutched his hand in alarm. 'Don't leave me –'

'It's okay. They've gone. Let me just check the house. Stay there, I'll be as quick as I can.'

After refilling their glasses, he carried his own with him, taking sips as he went. He was still confused – thankful to be alive, full of wonder to have survived, but outraged by what had happened. His thoughts were everywhere and nowhere at once. His brain was still trying to absorb events before deciding on what to do next.

Without particular purpose, he went first to the kitchen, expecting to find chaos. When he got there he stared in amazement. It was as if nothing had happened. The gas cooker was in place, looking no different. The floor was clean, without a trace of a bloodstain. Everything looked incredibly and totally normal – except that the floor tiles still glistened with water, the telephone dangled from the wall bracket, and the only reminder of Mac was his empty basket.

Shaken, feeling the need to sit down, he sat on a stool and gazed about him, rubbing his eyes as if awakening from a nightmare. Everything looked as it usually did. It could have been a dream. Or a hoax. Or some kind of bluff.

Realization dawned slowly. Only one thing had mattered when he was talking to Charlie. Getting the money. Fear had stifled thoughts of what happened next. If he had thought at all it was that he could put things right later, he would explain, they would go to the police and tell them what had happened. But the truth was that he *hadn't* thought, not clearly, he had been too scared, terrified by the knife at Katrina's throat . . .

Now, sitting on the stool, trying to think, he remembered other things. His spine tingled as he recalled the look in Moroni's eyes afterwards, a gleam of triumph, a sneer on his lips.

Almost reluctantly he began to piece things together. Lighting a cigar, he willed himself not to panic. He concentrated on seeing things as Moroni would see them. 'We can't prove anything,' he thought desperately. 'We can't even prove they were *here*!'

The realization sent a further chill up his spine. 'What happens if I involve the police? Moroni's bankers might confirm that the loan for Paloma Blanca was reduced by six million. So what? As far as they're concerned it was a legitimate receipt. They won't return the money without Moroni's authority. And Moroni will say everything's in order. He's done nothing wrong. He's in the clear. He *knows* I can't go to the police, not without Charlie being arrested for fraud, and me along with her.'

Charlie's number rang for twelve rings before it was answered.

'Hello.'

'Charlie?'

'No, this is her secretary. May I take a message?'

'Is she there?'

'I'm afraid not. She's left for London. She'll be back tomorrow afternoon. Would you like her to ring you?'

He went all over the house, going from room to room without quite knowing why or even what he was checking. Blankets had been stripped from the bed in the guest suite, but nothing else looked even slightly unusual.

'Everything looks so bloody normal,' he muttered as he hurried back into the drawing-room. 'You'd never know they were here.'

Katrina dabbed her tear-stained face. 'What did the police say?'

He shook his head. 'I didn't call them.'

'But . . . I thought I heard you –'

'I tried to get Charlie,' he interrupted, feverish with agitation. 'But she'd left.'

'So call the police.'

To give himself time to think, he said, 'There's nothing wrong with the cooker in the kitchen. I don't think it was even pulled out from the wall.'

She frowned, shaking her head slowly from side to side, not understanding.

'I think they were bluffing,' he said, waving a hand at the room. 'I mean, just look at this place. There's no sign of anything. You'd never know they were here.'

'But . . . Mac –'

'He's missing, that's all the police would say. Dogs go missing all the time. They wander off and –'

'They threatened to kill us,' she protested, her voice rising with disbelief.

'We can't prove it.'

'You've got blood on your jacket.'

'So what? What does it *prove?*'

'But . . .' swallowing hard, she shook her head and repeated, 'they were going to kill us!'

'We can't prove it!' he exclaimed, his voice rising. 'We can't even prove they were *here!*'

Hunched in her chair, she watched him with frightened eyes. Still shaken by her ordeal, heartbroken about Mac, she struggled to understand what he was saying. 'You mean, you're *not* going to the police?' she asked in bewilderment.

'Jesus!' Fear and frustration were making him angry. 'I just said so, didn't I? I just explained. We can't prove anything! We can't even prove we were threatened. Charlie certainly can't. She wasn't threatened. She wasn't even in danger, yet she used six million in part payment of one of my debts. The money had nothing to do with her firm –'

'But . . . they'll understand. Surely . . . I mean, it was extortion –'

'How was it? I just said. Charlie wasn't threatened. Yet she committed fraud, embezzlement, theft. That's what they'll say. Unless she gets the money back she'll be arrested. She'll go to jail. So will I. We *stole* that money. We stole six million pounds!'

'No . . .' Katrina's voice was a whisper. 'It wasn't like that.' She raised her fingers to her throat, remembering the knife. 'They threatened to kill us –'

Whisky slopped from Todd's glass as his arm swung in an arc. 'Look at this room. The whole house is the same. Nothing's out of place. There's no proof! We *can't* go to the police without getting Charlie into trouble. And me. Will you get that into your thick head!'

Hurt, Katrina's eyes glistened with tears.

Blinded by worry, Todd paced the room. 'I daren't do a thing until I get hold of Charlie –'

'I don't know where I am any more,' Katrina interrupted, more bewildered than ever. 'I feel totally lost.' An accusing note came to her voice. 'I don't know what's true and what's not true any longer. You said you were dealing with a lawyer in Paris. That's what you said . . .'

Then, amazingly, they were quarrelling. An hour before they would have died for each other, yet fuelled by alcohol and worry, grief and guilt, they were at each other's throats. Old grievances were quick to resurface.

'I warned you,' Katrina exclaimed. 'I told you the sort of men my father mixed with. But you wouldn't listen, would you? Oh, no! You went sneaking off behind my back –'

'No one was sneaking –'

'Not much! And what about this Charlie woman? A friend of Hank's,' she sneered. 'That's what you said. And I believed you. I didn't know you were such an accomplished liar.'

'What's that supposed to mean?'

Suddenly she was mimicking his voice. 'Oh, Charlie, I'd *love* to have dinner with you. I'll send Herbert to collect you from Gatwick! Oh, Charlie, this is *me*, remember? How can you even *think* I'd let you down!'

He avoided her eye by turning his back.

'How long's this been going on? That's what I want to know! You lied to me! You lied about that . . . that thug, that gangster . . . and you lied about this woman. That's why you won't call the police. You're protecting her!'

'We *stole* six million pounds!' Todd roared at her. 'Don't you understand? We'll end up in prison.'

But as she dissolved into tears, Katrina saw prison as a just reward for his deception. 'Damn well serves you right,' she bawled helplessly.

The telephone saved them. There was no telling what abuse they would have hurled at each other. Slumped in opposite chairs, Todd was glowering and Katrina was sobbing her heart out when, providentially, the telephone rang.

It was Todd who answered.

'Ah! You're back on,' exclaimed Sally, sounding triumphant. 'I tried earlier, but there must have been a fault on the line. Is Katrina okay? What was wrong?'

He was too dazed to invent an excuse. It seemed an age since he had left the office. 'What? Oh, yes, nothing much. Er, look

'. . . er, Sally, I need Herbert to go to Gatwick to meet a flight from Jersey.'

Talking to Sally brought him to his senses. Immediately full of remorse, he regretted his harsh words. So did Katrina. Fleeing from the room, she hurried to the downstairs bathroom, where once again she burst into tears, this time from frustration and anger with herself. *How can you fight at a time like this?* Dazed and weak-kneed, she sat on the linen basket, trapped in an unending nightmare. What did he mean about going to prison? She saw herself talking to him through the grille of prison bars . . . she tried to imagine . . .

In the kitchen, making coffee, Todd dressed himself down. *To endure an ordeal like that, then have me shouting at her instead of helping her get over it . . .*

Moments later they were in each other's arms, reconciled, each determined to comfort the other.

It was Todd who took charge. After sitting her down, he brought her some coffee and topped her cup up with brandy. He fetched another pack of cigarettes from the kitchen cupboard. And he never stopped talking, for effect to begin with, wanting to steady her nerves and to bring the colour back to her cheeks. 'They were bluffing,' he said. 'I can see that now . . . nothing would have happened . . . they were just trying to scare us . . .'

Not that she believed him. She listened with a bemused look on her face, feeling numb, caring about only one thing, that they were together and safe – at least for the moment.

'But you do understand about not calling the police?' he asked anxiously. 'Moroni will be on his way out of the country by now. Even if the British police get on to the French police, so what? Moroni will deny he was here, and his bank received some money I owed him, that's all. Where I got it was up to me, not up to him. Meanwhile Charlie's committed fraud . . .'

They talked for a long time.

Katrina struggled to explain her misgivings. That thug was the one who deserved to be in prison, not him or Charlie. Yes, they had broken the law – she shied away from using words such as embezzlement and fraud – but they had done wrong for the right reasons. Hadn't they? Surely the police would understand? Wouldn't they? But eventually, when he repeated his arguments, she saw that it might be unwise to involve the police, even though excluding them left her equally frightened. She made him explain about the offer for Paloma Blanca.

'Sure there's an offer. It only cropped up this morning. Hank's had this guy Carrier in to see him. He owns the Bella Vista, you know, that big hotel in Palma.'

'And he's really offered nine million?'

'When it's finished. The clever bastard. He won't believe his luck when we accept. We've had all the blood, the sweat and the tears, now he'll get it for peanuts.' His voice rasped with bitterness. 'Christ knows what Hank will say. I don't even know how I'll tell him . . .'

Manny Shiner would not have recognized him at that moment. Slumped on the sofa, his natural ebullience had evaporated. Strain showed as dark patches beneath his eyes. The trauma of dealing with Moroni, of negotiating at knife-point, had left him exhausted. His spirits were lower than at any time in his life. There would be no bouncing back this time.

'You warned me,' he said softly. 'I've been a bloody fool.'

The truth was that his stupid dream to become *someone* had almost cost them their lives.

She tried to encourage him. 'You've been desperately unlucky,' she said, squeezing his hand. 'Everyone says that. Sam and Pamela were saying it the last time I saw them . . .'

She bathed him with her words, doing her utmost to lift his spirits. And although grateful, most of his concentration was directed elsewhere. 'What a mess,' he muttered under his breath. He was trapped. His heart sank at the size of his debts. He needed nine million for Moroni to stay alive . . . six million for Charlie to stay out of prison . . .

'Do you think this man will put his offer in writing?' Katrina asked fearfully. 'What was his name . . . Carrier?'

Todd snorted with disgust. 'Too bloody right. For nine million. He won't be able to get his pen out fast enough.'

And then, remembering his conversation with Hank prompted a thought. His brow crinkled. 'Maybe he'll pay more?'

he said thoughtfully. 'It's an opening offer, that's all. He *should* pay more. It's worth at least twice what he's offered and he knows it. Nobody bids high to start with, do they?'

Katrina frowned as she looked at him.

A flicker of Todd's old determination returned. 'If I can get him up in price . . . if I can get him to fifteen I can pay Moroni *and* Charlie. Even then Carrier's getting a bargain. Fifteen's less than it's cost us . . .'

The more he talked, the more it made sense. And the more he encouraged himself. Except that even fifteen million would leave nothing for the motor businesses. And unless money was restored to them they would collapse. In which case the bank would seize the house. Everything would go . . .

'Everything will go,' thought Katrina, not caring as long as they were safe from that thug and Toddy stayed out of prison. Her heart went out to him. In talking about selling Paloma Blanca he was describing the end of his dream. How she had yearned to be rid of this jinx, this albatross, this constant source of friction between them. But she felt no joy now it was happening.

'We can start again,' she encouraged. 'We're still young enough. If we found a small garage somewhere you could build it up. I could run the office . . .'

They sat on the sofa, hands clasped, sharing their strength. From time to time they unlinked their fingers and Todd went to the sideboard to refill their glasses — which was what he was doing when Katrina glanced at the clock. 'What time is this woman arriving?'

'What?' He stared at the clock on the mantelpiece. 'My God! Six already? She'll be here any minute.'

'Then I'm going up to change,' said Katrina with a fearful glance out to the hall.

Seeing the look on her face, Todd reacted at once. 'Hang on, I'll come with you.'

But he finished his drink first: not to give himself Dutch courage for what he might find in the hall — he was bracing himself for his meeting with Charlie. He wondered what he would say to this amusing, clever, good-looking woman, who had been lover and friend, who had done nothing but help him from the day they first met.

Jumping up from her chair, Charlie crossed the room and slumped into the seat by the window. Then she leapt up and went to the stool at the piano. No sooner had she sat down than she was up again, in a fever of agitation, circling the room like a caged animal. 'I don't believe it!' she cried. 'You mean there's not a meeting tomorrow?'

'There's no one to meet.'

'No bank draft?'

He wrung his hands. 'No,' he admitted, swallowing hard.

'You won't have the money?' Her voice was a whisper.

'Charlie, they'd have *killed* us!' He was almost on his knees. 'All the time I was on the phone, they had a knife at Katrina's throat. Can you imagine –'

'You lied to me. How could you do this? I trusted you.'

'If only you'd listen a minute.'

'Listen?' She echoed angrily. 'I listened before. Look where it got me. Don't you understand? I *stole* six million pounds. I committed fraud. I did it for you!'

'Hang on a minute, please!'

But Charlie ignored him. Circling the room, hands over her ears, she was visualizing what would happen. She imagined the shame it would bring to her widowed mother in Bournemouth. She remembered being voted 'The student most likely to succeed'. She recalled her time at university, her elation at qualifying as an accountant, the rapid advancement in her career, the trust placed in her by Bob Levit, her Technicolor plans for the future. Her entire life flashed through her mind. Gone. All gone. Finished. No one would ever trust her again. 'Oh, my God,' she whispered. 'Oh, my God,' she repeated as she collapsed into the chair by the window.

She had known something was in the wind when Herbert met her at Gatwick. 'Are you sure?' she had asked when he said he was taking her to Hampstead.

'Yes, miss.'

'Not to my place in Baker Street?'

'Oh no, miss. Sally said the Guv'nor was quite definite.'

'It's a party,' she had thought. 'To celebrate this refinancing deal. I bet Hank's flown over . . .'

She would have liked to change into something more glamorous. Surprises were all very well, but a party's a party and she wished Toddy had told her. Especially when she would be meeting his wife. Her lips had puckered into a smile. She had grown ever more fond of him without falling in love. Meeting him had changed the course of her life, set her off in a new direction. Paloma Blanca now consumed her thoughts night and day. Their plans were already yielding results. The response from yacht clubs was encouraging, and no one was querying price. 'More expensive is better,' she continued to insist to Hank, who was only too willing to listen. And Toddy. They both listened. Not that they were without ideas of their own. This refinancing deal sounded brilliant. 'Great guys to work with,' she had thought happily as Herbert drove past the Middletons'.

Her happiness had ended with the look on his face. She had known something was wrong when he opened the door. *He looks like death and smells like a distillery.* And Katrina's flushed face had confirmed her worst fears. *My God, he's told her about our night together. The bloody fool! Why can't men keep their mouths shut?*

'If I explain to Bob Levit,' Todd began, crouching in front of her. 'I'll tell him what happened –'

She jumped up and flew to the telephone. 'Don't even *think* of speaking to Bob!' Her hands hovered as if to rip the phone from the wall.

'But I'll take the blame. He won't want to involve the police either, will he? Think of the publicity. Charlie, I'm sure he'll understand –'

'Understand!' Her voice rose to a scream. 'He'll understand, all right. Clients' funds have been stolen. He'll understand that only too well.'

Retreating to the sideboard, Todd made another despairing effort to placate her. 'I'll get the first flight out to Majorca in the morning,' he promised. 'If I see Carrier in the afternoon, you could be laughing about this by this time tomorrow.'

'I'll never laugh again!'

'Believe me –'

'Believe you!'

Charlie's shriek cut through Katrina's head, making her flinch. She had scarcely spoken since Charlie's arrival. She had been stunned to see this woman – this *young* woman – tilt her face for Todd to kiss, while gaily exclaiming, 'Toddy! You might have warned me, springing this on me when I'm looking a wreck.' Anyone less like a wreck Katrina could not have imagined. But it was not the beautifully tailored grey suit which had held her attention. It was the glossy red hair. Even fuddled by brandy and worry and shock, her memory had been quick to recall her phone conversation with Sally that night. 'Very dolly,' Sally had said. 'Jim Davis was green with envy. Redhead. Good figure, green eyes, smartly dressed. Quite a looker.'

So this is the one!

Katrina had gritted her teeth. 'Hello,' she had said.

'Cow!' she had thought as she studied the long shapely legs.

'Bitch,' she had thought as she examined the flawless complexion.

The flawless complexion was glowing at that moment. 'If Bob as much as gets a sniff of this,' Charlie said hotly, 'he'll be off to the police. Like a shot. That's why everyone trusts him. That's how he built his reputation. Mr Squeaky Clean. That's what they call him. Unlike some of the little shits in this business, he does everything by the book . . .'

Sipping coffee and brandy, Katrina chain-smoked and watched with rapt attention. Part of her derived a sadistic pleasure from Charlie's dismay. When Charlie wailed, 'I'll go to prison,' Katrina inwardly exulted, 'Serves you right! It's what you deserve.' But part of her agonized over her husband. Poor Toddy! Having to humble himself before this woman. 'His mistress,' she reminded herself, sipping her brandy to remove the sour taste from her mouth.

'You've ruined me!' cried Charlie.

'It was life or death!' Todd repeated, wringing his hands, red in the face from his efforts to explain.

Katrina consoled herself with the thought that whatever had happened between them could never happen again.

'Listen,' said Todd as he carried another pink gin over to Charlie. 'You're safe if you get the money back.'

'And how will you do that? You said this man's only offered nine million.'

'That's just his opening bid. I'll get him up. I'll get us out of this mess. Trust me!'

'Trust? *You?* You have the effrontery to ask me to trust you?'

Todd groaned. 'The point is,' he persisted with his head in his hands. 'If I get the money, can you replace it without Bob Levit knowing?'

A look of incredulity came to Charlie's face. 'Keep quiet about it? Become your accomplice? Is that what you're suggesting?'

Resisting an urge to beat his head on the wall, he explained everything all over again. This time he went right back to the start. He explained every detail. The entire history. How Hank had first shown him the site. How he had tramped around London, going from one bank to another. How he had negotiated with Suntours. How he had come to meet Moroni. How the recession had started. How everything had gone wrong . . .

A lump rose in Katrina's throat as she listened. He had struggled so valiantly, fought so hard. 'And what help have you been?' she reproached herself bitterly.

Todd was exhausted by the end of his speech, but it seemed vitally important to tell Charlie every detail. A hope lingered that he might salvage some self-respect if he could make her believe him. 'I know it's a terrible shock,' he admitted. 'But I've had a chance to think. We can't go to the police. Apart from anything else, a scandal destroys everyone. We'll go to jail, Bob Levit will be ruined by the publicity, what good will it do? He's better off not knowing. So all I'm asking is for some time to recover the money.'

Charlie shuddered. Frightened by the thought of prison, goose bumps rose all over her skin. 'I'll be crucified if they find out –'

'They *won't* if you don't tell them,' Todd interrupted, his heart thumping with hope. 'The question is can you keep quiet about it until I sort something out?'

Technically she could, Charlie knew she could. Bob Levit trusted her totally. The auditors would discover the truth eventually, but the auditors were not due until next summer. 'Perhaps for a while,' she admitted doubtfully, before changing her mind. 'But I don't think my nerves could stand it.' Turning away from him, she agonized over her dilemma. No, she didn't dare tell Bob Levit. But no, she couldn't remain quiet until Paloma Blanca was sold.

'I thought it was just overnight,' she complained bitterly. 'That's what you told me.'

The recriminations surfaced all over again. It was like swimming through treacle, testing Todd's endurance as well as his powers of persuasion. He repeated that at the time he had thought they could go to the police, that it was only when Moroni had left that he realized he had compromised her position. Hurt and shaken by her rejection, he talked himself hoarse. Then he braced himself for the next hurdle. 'I must call Hank,' he said, glancing at his watch, amazed to see it was nine o'clock. 'I can't sell Paloma Blanca at all unless Hank agrees.'

'He doesn't *know*?' Charlie went white.

Seizing an excuse to escape, Todd turned on his heel. 'It might take a while. He'll be in the restaurant. I'll call him from the study.'

'No,' Katrina began but she stifled her protest. One glance at his face was enough for her to realize that he wanted to break the news to Hank in private, not in front of an audience. He looked so drained that she prayed he would receive more understanding than from this wretched woman . . .

Blind to Katrina's seething indignation, Charlie fell silent as Todd left the room. She was still coming to terms with the news. She had trusted Todd. Believed in him. Now, to be landed in this mess – by him of all people! 'My God!' she muttered, unaware that she was speaking aloud. 'Never trust a man! How did I get involved with this?'

The criticism was too much for Katrina. 'In bed,' she said tartly, surprising herself. 'That's how you got involved.'

Charlie's green eyes widened. She stared as if seeing Katrina

320

for the first time. Then she exploded. 'I don't believe this!' she cried, springing up from her chair. 'Men hold you at knife point, they threaten to blow you to pieces, they involve you in fraud, and all you worry about is me bonking your husband?'

Katrina went red in the face. 'I answered your question, that's all!'

'I'll ask for an answer when I want one.'

'Then you shouldn't have said it.'

'It was a rhetorical question!'

'You were blaming him! You were happy enough to go to bed with him —'

'Now see here,' Charlie protested, her voice rising. 'It wasn't a world-shaking affair or anything.'

'You don't have to make excuses.'

'I am *not* making excuses!' Charlie's voice rose even higher. 'I'm not the one on trial here. It's not my virtue we're talking about.' Snatching up her glass, she peered into it only to find it was empty. 'Oh boy! Have you got a weird sense of priorities? You're losing all this . . .' she waved a hand at the room. 'You'll end up in a cardboard box, and all you can think about —'

'Is defending my husband,' Katrina interrupted with chilling dignity. 'Exactly!'

Taken aback, Charlie puffed out her cheeks. 'Excuse me! I stand corrected, but I'm involved in this too, you know. I could get ten years thanks to your husband.'

'Would you rather he'd let them cut my throat?'

Charlie opened her mouth and closed it again. For the first time she tried to imagine herself in that situation. She had always had a terror of knives. In her kitchen knives were invariably put away, rarely left out. Sometimes, dependent upon her mood, even the sight of a simple kitchen knife could cause her to shudder. The thought of a sharp blade being held any-where near her face petrified her. 'Oh, my word,' she said softly as the realization sank home. 'That must have been terrifying. Absolutely terrifying.'

Katrina stared down at her lap.

Watching her, Charlie felt a tinge of guilt. *To have gone through all that, then to have me to deal with!* She managed to clear her throat. 'Er . . . look . . . about Toddy and me. It was –'

'Just one of those things? Yes, well, I'd rather not discuss it, thank you.' Katrina said crisply, compressing her lips to make clear she had said all there was to say on the subject.

Charlie carried her glass to the sideboard. 'Oh boy,' she said wearily, feeling a hundred years old. 'Do you mind if I have another drink? If we're going to have a row on top of everything else –'

'Help yourself. And we're not having a row. I merely remarked –'

'I heard what you said,' interrupted Charlie, who had no wish to hear it again. But as she reached for the bottle the thought of what Katrina had endured made her shudder. 'I . . . er . . . yes, well, it must have been awful. I didn't think just now. You've been to hell and back and there's me only thinking of me. Right? And I was pretty damn bitchy to poor old Toddy. I . . . er, I'm sorry. I lost my nerve, that's all.'

The prospect of her *recovering* her nerve worried Katrina. She had already credited Charlie with nerves of steel. But the apology took her by surprise. Wondering whether it was genuine, she was eyeing the red hair when Charlie turned round to face her. For a moment they regarded each other with unsmiling faces. Then Charlie said, 'And about that other business –'

'I don't want to discuss it.'

'We can't just ignore it. I don't want you suspecting . . .' Charlie's words faded as she turned to go back to her chair. 'Seems to me we're in this together, whether we like it or not. It's best if we clear the air.'

She sat down before her legs gave way. Inwardly she was quaking. *What have I let myself in for? This is her house and her husband.* Her hand trembled as she raised her drink. She watched Katrina across the rim of her glass. *If looks could kill, you'd be dead. She hates you!* Taking a deep breath, she cleared her throat.

'Look . . . er, yes, I admit I was attracted. We went to bed once, that's all, and if you want the truth I was the one who made all the running. He didn't have a chance. But it won't

322

happen again because I don't make a habit of sleeping with married men, and they don't come more married than he does. You should know that better than anyone.'

Subconsciously Katrina supposed she did, but at that moment her attention was riveted on Charlie's shaking hands.

Blushing furiously, Charlie blurted the rest out in one breath. 'He's a nice guy, okay? That's why I was so knocked over about this . . . I mean until I understood what happened . . . so anyway after that one and only time we became friends instead of lovers, especially when I met Hank and got involved in Paloma Blanca.' Catching her breath, she emptied her glass at a gulp, stood up and returned to the sideboard. 'End of speech. That's the truth, the whole truth, nothing but the truth, so help me God, and I don't want the subject referred to again. Ever! Agreed?'

Taken by surprise Katrina was even more surprised to feel grudging approval. She had no doubt that she had heard the truth. She wondered how she would have coped if the situation was reversed. Not that it ever could be, of course, but . . .

'Agreed?' Charlie repeated insistently.

'What?' Katrina stammered as Todd returned to the room.

'Hank's number's engaged,' he said wearily. 'I'll try again in a minute.' Catching sight of Charlie's red face, he asked in surprise, 'You all right?'

'What?' Charlie's face was now as red as her hair. Collecting her thoughts, she threw Katrina a warning glance, and stuttered into speech. 'Er . . . we were just talking. I was just saying, I haven't been much help, have I? Um, sorry, okay? I shouldn't have blown my top like that.'

And she managed to smile, a bit shaky perhaps, but a smile for all that.

Looking at her, Todd saw again the vivacious woman he had first met at the Ritz.

Katrina saw her as well. 'No wonder he strayed,' she thought drily. Not that she had chance for further thought because Charlie was apologizing to Todd and Todd was apologizing to Charlie so volubly and effusively that it was as if their earlier exchanges had never happened. But this time there was a difference. Earlier Katrina had been so excluded that she might not even have been there. Now she was involved every time Charlie opened her mouth.

'I was just saying to Katrina,' said Charlie, sitting down next to her on the sofa. 'Okay, if we're forced to, we'll *have* to sell Paloma Blanca. But where does this jerk get off with his nine million?'

Sometimes luck turns for the oddest of reasons. Todd's had been abysmal, but it could have become worse. He might have returned to find Katrina and Charlie at each other's throats. Katrina had every reason to dislike Charlie, and Charlie owed Katrina nothing except perhaps the apology she had already given. But they were all in shock, and shock does strange things to people. They were also in danger and people in fear draw together in a search for survival.

Not that Katrina and Charlie fell into each other's arms. Katrina was behaving with dignity and Charlie with courage, but an understandable tension remained between them. Having established eye contact they took every opportunity to look at each other, but the warmth in their glances was more apparent than real. It took the accident of circumstances to create a thaw. As Todd returned to the study for another attempt to reach Hank, he said, 'I'm hungry. Any chance of some food?'

It was ten o'clock. All three of them needed something. Charlie, who had long since abandoned expectations of a lavish dinner, was none the less feeling vague stirrings of hunger. Todd had not eaten since breakfast, and although unable to contemplate a proper meal Katrina needed something to soak up the brandy.

'I'll fix something,' she said on her way to the kitchen.

'Can I help?' asked Charlie.

'No, it's all right.'

But it was far from all right. Katrina's mind was on the conversation when she went into the kitchen. Her thoughts were of food until she switched on the light. Then the sight of Mac's empty basket hit her with the force of a blow. With a cry of pain, she stopped in her tracks. Her eyes brimmed with tears. The next moment her head was in her hands and she was sobbing uncontrollably.

Hearing the cry, Charlie rushed into the kitchen and reacted instinctively. 'Hey!' she cried, embracing her, hugging her tight. 'It's all right, it's all right.'

Katrina was sobbing so violently that her words were unintelligible.

'It's all right,' crooned Charlie repeatedly, imagining some sort of delayed reaction. It was only when Katrina wailed, 'They killed my dog' that Charlie understood why she was weeping.

Those words, perhaps more than any other, brought home the full horror of what had happened. Trying to ease Katrina's torment, Charlie led her back to the drawing-room. She fetched tissues and cigarettes. She poured another brandy and went back to the kitchen for more coffee. And when she returned she sat with her arm around her, nursing her until the worst moments were passed. Then gently she said, 'Now you sit there a while, I won't be a minute.' Hurrying back to the kitchen, she put Mac's plate and his water bowl into his basket. Casting around for a hiding-place, she opened the kitchen door and carried them out to the step. She had no idea where else to put them, or what to do with them, but at least when she closed the door they were hidden from sight.

'Now,' she said brightly as she returned to the drawing-room. 'I bet you're a hell of a cook.'

Katrina looked up with smudged eyes.

'Toddy said he was hungry, remember?'

Sighing with resigned acceptance, Katrina made to rise from her chair.

'I'm a lousy cook,' Charlie said cheerfully, turning the admission into a joke. 'But I'll get supper if you promise not to shout at me. Okay? I'll go on strike unless you bear with me.'

They bore with each other that night.

Charlie insisted on Spanish omelettes. 'They're about all I can do, but you sit there and supervise,' she pointed to a stool as they returned to the kitchen. 'I could fix us a salad to go with them. What do you think? I'm pretty good at salads . . .'

Warmed by such consideration, especially by the way Mac's things had been hidden away, Katrina said not a word for fear that gratitude would start her weeping again, but that was the moment when they took the first tentative steps towards friendship.

Even Todd sensed a changed atmosphere when he came into the kitchen. Charlie was at the stove and Katrina's expression as she watched was almost whimsical, an odd mixture of bemusement and the faintest of smiles.

Charlie looked up. 'Hi. You got a bottle of wine to go with this? Nothing too delicate. Something strong enough to deaden the taste buds.'

For the next twenty minutes they were too busy to dwell on their problems. Todd was instructed to open the wine, Katrina was set to work mixing a French dressing, and while Charlie finished her omelette she chattered incessantly, lifting their spirits in the process in a way that was quite amazing. Of course Todd had seen her do it before – Charlie in full spate was irresistible – but it was all new to Katrina, who responded with dazed little smiles which formed with a will of their own.

That was the moment when Todd's luck took a turn for the better. True, a whiff of hysteria lingered in the air. True, nobody's nerves could have withstood more recriminations. And booze played a part. Todd and Katrina had been drinking steadily all afternoon, and Charlie had been hitting the gin almost from the moment she came through the door. It was as well they sat down to supper, for all of them would have trouble walking a straight line. But instead of arguing, Charlie and Katrina were laughing together, and the tension of that traumatic day lifted a little.

Cutting her omelette, Charlie savoured a mouthful. 'Guaranteed heartburn for a week,' she pronounced with approval. 'So, okay,' she said, looking up from her plate. 'How did Hank take the news?'

Hank had not been given the news. Busy in his restaurant, Hank had been able to spare only a moment and Todd had lost his nerve to explain.

'I couldn't blurt it all out on the phone,' he confessed. But he had booked his flight for the morning; an early one via Barcelona, which meant leaving at dawn and not reaching Majorca until noon. 'The trouble is, I won't be with Hank until after midday, then I'll need to explain everything, so we might not get to Carrier tomorrow . . .'

But the urgency had diminished for Charlie. Marshalling her courage, she had taken the big decision. 'I'm dead if I tell Bob,' she admitted. 'And I could be dead if I don't, but somehow I'll bury this until you sort out a deal.'

Todd gave her a look of thanks and was about to express his gratitude, when something clicked in his mind. For a moment, he stared across the table. Then a look of excitement came to his face. 'The Dutchman!' he exclaimed. 'I forgot about this bloody Dutchman!'

'Dutchman?' Charlie frowned.

Katrina set down her knife and stared.

Pushing his plate away, Todd jumped up from the table. 'There's some Dutchman been sniffing around at the site,' he said, after which he repeated, word for word to the best of his memory, his conversation with Hank. 'This bloke's supposed to be one of the top hotel men in Europe. He sold Carrier the Bella Vista. He's *got* to be interested. Stands to reason. He flew out to Majorca just to *look* at Paloma Blanca.'

Taking his cigar case from his pocket, he began to pace up and down. 'That means we've got Carrier *and* this Dutch guy wanting to buy. Maybe I can get an auction going.'

'An auction?' Katrina and Charlie chorused together.

'Why not? Get them bidding against each other!' Lighting his cigar, Todd was wreathed in smoke. Nodding emphatically, he paced from one end of the kitchen to the other. 'If I can start an auction, who can say what could happen? We could get *more* than fifteen million. Charlie and Moroni get their money and I end up with enough to save the motor businesses. Then there's Hank, of course. Hank's got to get his money back . . .'

And he was away again, surfing up onto the crest of a wave. Once he had seized the idea he clung to it and embellished it and polished it until it shone like a star shining in the firmament. Once more the abundance of optimism shone through. 'We just need one lucky break, that's all. It's like selling a house. One buyer paying the right price and our troubles are over . . .'

Manny Shiner would have recognized him then, Manny would have been proud of him. Katrina might have been proud of him too except for her fear of Moroni.

'But . . .' she interrupted, collecting her thoughts. 'That man will only wait if you get a written offer by the seventeenth –'

'No problem. Carrier can put his offer in writing and make a floor for the auction. Moroni won't care, will he? He still gets his nine million.'

CHAPTER ELEVEN

OF COURSE THEIR MOODS were different in the morning. Gone were the alcohol-induced hopes, the overwhelming sense of relief, the need to draw together for common protection. Gone was the reckless euphoria and whiff of hysteria.

Charlie woke first. At five o'clock. In the guest suite, she was roused by an urgent need to visit the bathroom. Disoriented, waking in a strange bed in a strange house, she would have remained where she was except for the demands of her bladder. With fumbling hands she switched on the light, crawled from under the covers, went to the bathroom – and by the time she returned sleep was impossible.

Further along the landing, Katrina woke to the faintest of sounds. She flinched as yesterday's terrors leapt from the darkness. Her heart thumped. Her hands clenched instinctively, and it was only when she recognized the noise as a cistern flushing that she stopped holding her breath. But once awake there was no hope of sleep. She had woken to a different world, a place so frightening that she turned to snuggle into Todd for comfort, only to stop herself for fear of disturbing him. Knowing he would need all the rest he could get, she slipped from the bed and went into the bathroom.

The alarm clock roused Todd at five-forty. Groaning into consciousness, his first thoughts were at least as depressing as Katrina's. After the blackest day of his life, he had to confront Hank with the news about selling Paloma Blanca. Dreading the prospect, he got out of bed, went into the shower, closed the glass door, sat on the tiled floor and let the water hammer down on his scalp. *Maybe I'll drown*, he thought hopefully.

Downstairs Charlie and Katrina were already in the kitchen,

having their first cup of coffee and trying hard not to panic. Last night it had been easy to believe that Todd would solve all their problems. How different things looked in the chill darkness of a December morning.

'I don't know,' said Charlie doubtfully. 'I've been thinking. This Carrier's only offered nine million. Nine to fifteen is a hell of a jump.'

Katrina agreed. Before going to bed she had allowed herself to hope for more than fifteen. Carried away by Todd's heady talk of an auction, she had dreamt of eighteen, nineteen, even twenty million – enough to save the motor businesses, the house and their whole way of life. And although her heart ached for Mac, she did wonder what would have happened? Charlie's dire warning about living in a cardboard box preyed on her mind. If they lost the house, there was no telling where they would be forced to live. At least Mac had spent his life in a lovely garden . . .

'Paloma Blanca's certainly *worth* fifteen million,' said Charlie, trying to sound determined. 'A lot more than fifteen, if you ask me.'

It had all seemed so different last night, with Todd pacing up and down, glass in hand, cigar billowing smoke, talking of auctions and millions and millions.

'The first thing is to get this written offer,' Katrina said, with fear in her eyes. 'We only have until the seventeenth. That man will be back. I *know* he'll come back.'

Such was the conversation when Todd came down the stairs. Ready to go, he had already telephoned for a cab to take him to the airport. He paused, eavesdropping, listening to voices of mutual despair. His own spirits sank. For a second he wanted to turn tail and flee, but as he braced himself something clicked in his brain. Anger was part of it. He *was* angry, angry with himself for creating this havoc. And ashamed for letting them down. Katrina, Charlie, Hank, even Leo in an odd kind of way. Leo would have expected more of him, Leo would have looked for solutions. He could hear Leo saying, *It's a setback, old boy, not a disaster*. The memory prompted a wry smile. *Bloody hell, Leo. I've had so many setbacks I'll eat a disaster*. But it fuelled his determination. He told himself that he'd got them into the mess, it was up to him to get them out. And he would. Somehow. So marshalling his courage, he took a deep breath and advanced into the kitchen. He kissed Katrina, squeezed Charlie's shoulder, bade them good morning, and sat down at the table.

It was his smile which took them by surprise. Charlie was feeling desperate, Katrina was verging on tearful – and there he was with a smile on his face. But he had been selling all his life and he knew when a smile was important. 'We're living, ain't we?' he said cheerfully. 'So why the long faces? Once I get hold of Carrier our troubles are over.'

Casting an encouraging look at Katrina, he patted her shoulder. 'You know me, I can always do a deal. I'll sell it to Carrier, no problem.' And when she looked doubtful, he laughed with bravado. 'Be honest. Was there ever a time I couldn't put a deal together?'

Remembering the pianos and the furniture and *objets d'art* taken in part exchange for used cars, her lips twitched with a faint smile. 'No,' she admitted huskily. 'Not even yesterday when I had a knife at my throat.'

'Forget yesterday. Carrier *wants* to buy, so he won't be a problem. It's this auction I'm concentrating on. I need to get hold of this Dutchman and tell him to chase up his contacts. Then we set a date for the auction. My preference is April. What do you think?'

It was the oldest trick in the world. Avoid objections by changing the subject. It worked every time.

Cocking his head, he regarded them quizzically. 'Paloma Blanca will be finished by April. Everything will be looking good. And it gives us time to talk it up . . .'

Gradually he lifted their spirits. They began to think more positively. As Katrina went to and fro with the coffee pot, her gaze remained glued to his face. Charlie was the same as she buttered her toast. Then she groaned as his words caused her to remember. 'The Gold Cup! We planned the first race to coincide with the opening!'

There was genuine pain in her face. She *felt* pain. Thanks to her efforts, yachting magazines the world over had carried news of the Gold Cup. She had a file of press clippings ten inches thick. Paloma Blanca had become her dream. Last night, overwhelmed by shock, fear, and then hope, there had been no room for a sense of loss. But now she felt the loss so keenly it was all she could do to hold back her tears.

Todd coaxed her through the bitterness of disappointment. 'I know,' he soothed repeatedly. 'I know how you feel. I feel the same way, but we have to let go, Charlie, we must let go . . .'

Later he would face the same ordeal with Hank. Only it would be a hundred times worse. *Hank will go mad! Oh, Jesus . . .*

Somehow he kept his nerve. He even encouraged Charlie to think about the future. 'Keep sending stuff out on the Gold Cup. The more people who know about Paloma Blanca, the higher the price we'll get at the auction. Think about it, Charlie. What will fetch the most money? An international hotel everyone knows about, or something no one's heard of? The Gold Cup will give us publicity and publicity will get us our price.'

He could have been talking to old Larkins all those years ago. *Think about it, Mr Larkins, if you were buying a used car, where would you go? Somewhere like this with a big stock . . .* He had always been able to enthuse people.

'. . . and we need some special publicity, Charlie. Something a bit different.'

That was too much. 'Like what?' she protested. 'All the yachting magazines know about the Gold Cup, they've promised to cover it, but that's not until –'

'So we need something else. Something to get the name known before the auction.'

'We can't bring the Gold Cup forward.'

'So create something, another angle. Something that grabs media coverage. You can do it, Charlie. You've a flair for these things.'

Despite everything, she felt a flutter of pride. Even bemused and bewildered, she couldn't help thinking, *Yes, he's right, I do have a flair for these things.*

And leaving Charlie with her brow crinkled in thought, Todd turned his attention to Katrina. He began by stressing how much Sally would value her help at the office. '. . . I don't mean all day, but if you could look in this afternoon, just to give her a pat on the back for keeping things going . . .'

He was keeping her busy. Occupying her mind. He even persuaded her to chase up her inheritance. 'It's no good me talking to Rochère, I'll lose my temper, but he took a shine to you. That was obvious. I bet you can sweet talk him into moving a lot faster.'

Throughout it all he drank two cups of coffee, ate one slice of toast and set fire to the first cigar of the morning. He was only in the kitchen twenty-five minutes. Then the cabby was ringing the doorbell and it was time to leave for the airport.

Katrina was smiling as she kissed him goodbye. So was Charlie as she waved from the doorstep.

Todd was smiling as well. Until the cab was out of the gate. Then he scowled as they passed the Middletons'. 'Arseholes,' he muttered. 'Dickheads.'

But that was a reflex action. His mind was not on the Middletons. It was on his meeting with Hank and the impossibility of talking Carrier up from nine million . . .

Think about it. What will fetch the most money? An international hotel everyone knows about, or something no one's ever heard of? The words went round and round in Charlie's mind and brought a sigh from her lips. Of course she saw his point. It made sense. But it was easy for Toddy to say think about it.

'Thanks,' she said gratefully, when Katrina poured her more coffee.

She had tried to imagine Todd's wife, and Katrina had come close to her expectations. Perhaps more determined, even better-looking, with a good figure and a fashionable haircut, but as conventionally domesticated as Charlie had expected. She liked her without being able to imagine herself leading a similar life. The man hadn't been born who was worth her career. *If I still have one*, she thought fearfully, which reminded her of her appointment that morning, a routine matter which could have been dealt with by phone except it had offered an escape from

333

Jersey for twenty-four hours. Thinking of it prompted her to check the time. She shuddered. 'It's not seven yet! What a time to be up.'

You look rested, thought Katrina across the table. *Oh to be that young again.* Not that she was feeling too bad herself. Amazingly, considering her ordeal, she had slept solidly for five hours. *I think I was so exhausted that I forgot to be frightened.*

But her fear was still there. Moments later a noise at the front door drained the colour from her face. She held her breath, and it was only when some letters fell through the box that she sighed with relief. 'It's the postman,' she said with a look of embarrassment. 'Sorry. I suppose I'm still a bit jumpy. It's a good job you're here.'

Charlie gave her an anxious look. 'Will you be all right by yourself?'

'Oh, I think so, thanks. My cleaning lady comes in this morning. She's due at nine.'

'What about tonight? With Toddy away?'

Katrina thought for a moment. 'I could ask a girlfriend to stay. I'll ask Sophie, though I don't know what I'll tell her. It's bad enough trying to work out what to say to my cleaning lady. I can't tell her the truth about Mac.'

'I could hang on if you like. Until your cleaner arrives. I'll tell her Mac had an accident and you're too upset to talk about it. She'll understand, won't she? Then you can call your friend . . .'

So they edged into the day, not friends but at least sisters in adversity, tentatively making their plans, drinking coffee, trying to behave normally when their situation was anything but normal. Inevitably their conversation veered back to their fears. Lighting her third cigarette of the morning, Katrina said, 'Poor Toddy. He'll have a terrible time with Hank, then he's got to get this letter, this . . . er, offer in writing.'

'He'll get it,' said Charlie with a display of false confidence. 'Don't worry.'

Katrina managed a wan smile. 'Don't waste time thinking about it. Isn't that what he said? Concentrate on this auction.'

'Don't think I'm not,' Charlie groaned, shaking her head.

'Though I really don't see how I can help. I can see his point about needing publicity, I agree, but what more can I do?'

Without meaning to boast, she knew she had done well in promoting the Gold Cup. Working one day a week and evenings and weekends, she had mailed letters to yacht clubs and sailing magazines in every country in Europe, as well as to parts of the United States, and even to Australia and New Zealand. 'I've followed up on the phone. The time difference makes it easy to work in the evenings. It's been a slog, but the response has been incredible.'

Impressed, Katrina realized that her own ambitions had never included a career. She had enjoyed keeping the books, it had been part of their lives; but she had never felt much inclination to take initiatives, to make things happen. Had she been asked she might have said her career was helping her husband, a thought which made her feel guilty when she listened to Charlie. Charlie was so *committed.* Just like Toddy and Hank. They had spent months pushing and shoving, working and working, doing all they could think of to make Paloma Blanca succeed. *And what have I done except sit on the sidelines?* Even now Charlie was racking her brains . . .

Charlie was saying, 'I can see the need to get the name known, but it's all very well for him to say create other angles. I mean what other angles?'

Katrina felt diffident about making suggestions. 'Does it have to be a yacht race?'

'The Gold Cup *is* a yacht race.'

'Yes, I know, but can't you do something else?'

Charlie looked at her. 'Not with yachts.'

'Isn't that the point? Shouldn't we forget yachts? Isn't that what he meant?'

'And do what?' Charlie retorted. 'What do we have? An unfinished hotel, a marina, some tree-covered hillsides and a long golden beach. Where's the story? How do you interest the media in that?'

'It is difficult . . .'

Charlie snorted scornfully. 'Put Paloma Blanca on the map, he says. Create media coverage. How? Just tell me how?'

Her increasing exasperation shrivelled Katrina's fragile confidence. She fell silent, thinking, racking her brains for an idea, more with hope than conviction.

'Well?' Charlie demanded, giving way to frustration.

'Oh, I agree. I did say it was difficult —'

'Impossible would be more accurate,' Charlie said bitterly.

Katrina flinched. There was an explosiveness about Charlie which was unnerving and which in a different mood she would have resented, but at that moment she was trying to concentrate. 'Yes, impossible,' she agreed vaguely without really listening. Searching for ideas, she was picturing Paloma Blanca and, prompted by Charlie's remark, she could see the hillsides. She remembered standing with her back to the sea and looking up at the layers of terracing and having an extraordinary feeling of being in a theatre. She had remarked about it to Hank, something about the fall of the land creating an amphitheatre, but he had been so anxious to show her the yacht club that he had been too busy to listen. Now it came back to her.

'You know,' she said vaguely. 'When you think about it, Paloma Blanca is a natural auditorium. The way the hillsides are formed and everything. If you built a stage over the swimming pools and decorated the hillsides with lanterns and things, you'd create a wonderful setting.'

'For what?'

'Er . . . well . . . for anything. A concert, for example?'

Charlie looked baffled. 'A concert?'

'It's just a thought,' Katrina admitted, ready to retreat, but even as she spoke a thought was taking substance in her mind.

Charlie could be impatient with others. And impatience led to sarcasm. 'Oh, great,' she said. 'Spanish guitars and flamenco dancers. I can see the press falling over themselves to write about that.'

'No, I didn't mean —'

'That would really put Paloma Blanca on the map.'

Katrina flushed. 'Look,' she said. 'I admit I haven't thought this out properly, and I know it's just an idea, but what about staging a sort of Glyndebourne?' She glanced hopefully at Charlie, and when the suggestion failed to draw a response, she

336

elaborated, 'A sort of Glyndebourne in the Mediterranean?'

'Opera?'

'Or a concert of classical music. In the open air. In the evening.'

Charlie was completely bewildered. 'But why? We're trying to sell a resort, not open a concert hall!'

The dismissiveness was too intimidating for Katrina. She picked up her cup, set it down again and toyed with her butter knife. Tentatively, she suggested, 'To create publicity . . .'

'With whom?' Charlie's voice was sharp with impatience. 'The people of Majorca? It's not them we're after. We want rich international businessmen.'

'Businessmen go to Glyndebourne. They're the only ones who can afford it.'

The reply was so unexpected that Charlie fell momentarily silent. She was surprised, even a bit contemptuous. *I thought she was bright. You'd think she'd have more common sense.* Making an effort to curb her impatience, she set out to explain.

'Without wishing to be rude,' she began heavily, 'it's hard to see a benefit. For a start, imagine the cost. You'd have to hire artists and an orchestra, fly them out there, then there's the cost of turning everything upside down at Paloma Blanca.' She laughed shortly. 'Hank would love that. No, sorry, I can't see it. Not in terms of cost, or even for its publicity value. Certainly not international publicity, which is what we need. Okay, it might get a few headlines in Majorca, but I just said, that's not what we want, is it?'

Deflated, Katrina fell silent. After a moment, she admitted, 'I suppose not. It was only an idea. It was just that I thought if someone like Enrico Barzini –'

'Barzini!' Charlie interrupted. Rolling her eyes, she tried not to laugh. 'You must be joking!'

'That would make it international, wouldn't it?'

'Oh, sure. So would the Pope singing Ave Maria, until you ask what's Barzini doing at Paloma Blanca? He'll be at La Scala or the Met in New York or Covent Garden. He's a mega star, not some beach entertainer.'

'He does do open-air concerts,' Katrina retorted sulkily.

337

'Several in Italy. And he did that big one in Hyde Park. Thousands of people went to that. It was on television. All of it. Two and a half hours. That's what made me think of it. It would be publicity. A Barzini concert always gets plenty of coverage.'

Tired of idle talk, Charlie sighed. 'Yes, well,' she said dismissively. 'It's an idea, but I don't suppose you'd book the greatest tenor in the world just like that, would you?'

'No,' Katrina agreed, red-faced and embarrassed. 'I expect you're right. And if it's a bad idea there's no point in asking.'

Coffee cup half-way to her mouth, Charlie paused. She frowned. 'How do you mean, asking? Do you know him?'

'Well, no, not personally.'

Charlie swallowed some coffee.

'But I know his manager. He seems to make the decisions,' said Katrina. She had taken her own decision at seven o'clock to cancel her lunch date with Ossie, but it had been remembering it which had led to thoughts of Barzini.

Charlie lowered her cup slowly. 'You know him well enough to ask about this?'

Katrina's flush deepened. 'I think so. I think I could ask him a favour.'

Charlie wondered why she was blushing. *Now what's up with her? But Enrico Barzini! My God!* For the first time she began to consider the idea.

'I just thought,' Katrina said hastily to cover her confusion. 'If it made the papers, and maybe there was a bit of coverage on television, you know the sort of thing, it would help get Paloma Blanca noticed. That's the idea, isn't it? That's what we want.'

'Sure, that's what we want.'

'If I were buying Paloma Blanca it would influence me. A big international concert with lots of media coverage. It would get the name known.'

Charlie looked at her.

Gaining confidence, Katrina continued, 'It's just that Paloma Blanca would make the most wonderful venue. After all, everyone agrees it's an exceptionally beautiful place. An international concert there would be something unique. There's this picture in my mind – lanterns flickering over the hillsides, a blaze of lights on stage, that fabulous voice soaring up into the trees, with the orchestra and everyone in evening dress. You know, a sort of gala performance. I mean, can't you just see it?'

Charlie realized that she *could* see it, exactly as Katrina had described. Paloma Blanca would make the most romantic, atmospheric venue.

'Visually it would be terrific,' she admitted. 'Better than a film set.'

'That's what I mean.'

An unexpected shiver ran up Charlie's spine. Hairs tingled at the back of her neck. A vague idea began to form in her mind. She looked at Katrina. 'This is on the level, right?' she asked, surprised by her own excitement. 'You have access to this manager? I mean, what is he, someone who bought a car from Toddy? An acquaintance? A friend? How well do you know him?'

'Er . . . quite well, I suppose.'

Again the blush, Charlie noted. *Why is she blushing?* But the question was pushed aside by her half-formed idea. 'A gala performance,' she said softly, more to herself than Katrina. 'I wonder?' Famous faces raced through her mind. She saw cameras flashing like starbursts in the trees, television cameras closer at hand. *Television cameras.* Mike Thompson was there. She could see him! 'Wait a minute,' she held up a hand like a policeman. 'What you said just now? About coverage on television. We want more than just coverage.' Her eyes stared into space. Then she blinked. 'Tell me a Spanish opera? You know something that goes with Paloma Blanca? To give us a link, some sort of hook?'

Frowning, Katrina thought for a moment. 'There's *Carmen.*'

'*Carmen!*' Charlie whooped. 'Fantastic! Listen, there's a guy I know, lives on Jersey. Mike Thompson. The film director? You must have heard of him. He's big, independent, respected, got all the right contacts. I was on to him last week, asking if he'd do something on the Gold Cup when it got going. You know, a TV documentary or something. I think it's a no no, but he's got a soft spot for me so he said he'd think about it.

But if I could offer him this? Barzini in *Carmen*! On Spanish soil.' Her face lit up. 'That would be different!'

'It would?'

'Barzini? Do you know how big he is?'

'Oh, yes,' said Katrina, pleased to have won a favourable reaction at last.

Suddenly Charlie groaned. 'Oh, my God!' she moaned, as if in sexual ecstasy. Pushing her chair back, she stood up and raised her gaze to the ceiling. The glazed look returned to her eyes. 'Forget *Carmen*,' she whispered in awe. With her arms outstretched she splayed her hands and peered through them as if through a view finder. 'Do you know what we've got here? We've got a TV spectacular. Say an hour long, maybe even two hours. Mike would kill for the TV rights on something like that. The world rights. He'd sell it all over the place. So he makes a fortune, but in return we get lots of footage of Paloma Blanca. And we call it . . .' she paused for effect. 'Listen to this. We call it *Barzini at Paloma Blanca*! Just that. *Barzini at Paloma Blanca*!' she repeated reverently.

Lost for a response, Katrina sat in stunned silence.

'Well?' Charlie demanded, oozing excitement. 'What do you think?' She began to pace the kitchen, taking long strides which stretched her wool skirt across her thighs.

'It . . . it was only a thought,' said Katrina, feeling nervous. Her skin was beginning to itch with a heat rash.

'But don't you see? A concert's not enough, not by itself. Television's the key. World television. Imagine the exposure. And we get the name in the title. That's the trick. *Barzini at Paloma Blanca*. Screw *Carmen*,' Charlie laughed joyously.

'Screw *Carmen*?'

'Absolutely. Bizet eat your heart out.'

Shaking her head, Katrina was having severe second thoughts. 'It was just an idea,' she began but broke off in alarm. 'Now what's the matter?'

Charlie had turned to the sink and was gripping the taps so tightly that Katrina could see the whites of her knuckles. One foot was stamping up and down.

'Are you all right?'

340

'Oh, my God!' Charlie groaned. Releasing the taps, she turned from the sink. 'Oh, my God! What's the first thing Mike will say? The *first* thing!'

Katrina took a step backwards.

'Video!'

Katrina blinked.

'The cassette market. It's enormous.'

'Cassettes?'

'Absolutely. And I bet there's a CD in this. Your man would know about that. And we'll get our name on everything. *Barzini at Paloma Blanca.*' Throwing her arms open, she hugged Katrina and began to dance on the spot. 'My God, Katrina! It blows your mind! I mean, the spin-offs from this are monumental . . .'

Thoroughly alarmed, Katrina disengaged herself and sat down. Reaching for Charlie's hand, she tried to draw her into the chair beside her. 'Steady on,' she said and then repeated herself. 'Steady on. Sit down a minute.'

But Charlie was up again and circling the kitchen, so that Katrina was reminded of Toddy, especially when Charlie stooped over the table. 'We're talking huge money. Millions –'

'Oh, no!' Katrina exclaimed, getting her breath and suddenly determined to put an end to this nonsense. 'It was talking millions that got us into this mess. You're as bad as Toddy!'

Charlie stopped in her tracks. Pulling a chair from the table, she sat down. 'Excuse me?' A crease appeared in her forehead. 'Did I just miss something? We were discussing your idea here?'

'I wasn't envisaging anything on this scale. Not spectaculars and videos and CDs and –'

'International stars don't play village halls,' Charlie retorted crisply. 'You have to create the right platform. And look at what we get out of this. What a promotion! Imagine what this exposure would cost in advertising. Millions!'

'Stop talking millions!' Katrina shrieked. 'Why does it have to be millions? Toddy's the same. And look where it's got us!' As Charlie opened her mouth to protest, Katrina went rattling on. 'You've gone right over the top,' she scolded. 'It was just an idea, that's all. Besides, I expect you're right. Barzini wouldn't do it, why should he?'

'You said you could ask?'

Katrina no longer wanted to ask. She wished the thought had never entered her head. Beginning to squirm, she tried to explain. 'It wasn't even a proper idea. Idea's too strong a word. It was more thinking aloud.'

'Oh, was it?' said Charlie, her voice becoming hard, even harsh. 'So let me do some thinking aloud. How's this for example? Everyone's heard of Paloma Blanca, so it's a hot property and Toddy sells it for mega bucks. Result happiness. Or nobody's heard of it and it goes for peanuts. He goes to jail, I go to jail, and this guy Moroni chops you in half.' With a snort of disgust, she pushed her chair back from the table. 'It's up to you, Katrina.'

Fear mingled with the confusion in Katrina's amber eyes.

'Well?' Charlie demanded.

Katrina swallowed hard.

'I'm asking you a question, Katrina.'

For a moment she could find no response. Eventually clearing her throat, she asked nervously, 'Do you really think this could make all the difference?'

'God give me patience!' Charlie drummed her fingers on the table, then hugged herself to try to contain herself. 'It'll make all the difference if Mike sells it all over the world. Millions of people could see it. *Barzini at Paloma Blanca*! Imagine what that would do to the price?'

Reaching for a cigarette, Katrina imagined in silence.

Charlie threw her arms in the air in frustrated disgust. Dismissing Katrina with a look of contempt, she stared at the clock. 'Five to nine. I wonder if Mike's in his office this morning? Getting hold of him is . . .' pausing in mid-sentence, she looked at Katrina. 'What about your guy? How do we reach him?'

'Er . . . he does come to London occasionally.'

Charlie's eyes widened. 'We could get to him? Could we make an appointment?'

'Couldn't we just phone him –'

'Oh no! Not likely. Not something this big. We need a meeting.'

'Um . . . ah, well, as a matter of fact, I was supposed to have lunch with him.'

Charlie sat bolt upright. 'Lunch?'

Katrina nodded.

'Lunch when?'

'Today –'

'You're having lunch with him *today*!'

'But I'm not going,' Katrina said hastily. 'Not after yesterday. My nerves need a month to recover.'

'Oh, really? You don't have a month. Remember what I said about being chopped into dog meat. Don't you see?' Charlie pleaded, waving her arms. 'This is a chance in a million. Fate, karma, whatever you call it!' Glowing with excitement, she began to calculate how long it would take her to finish her meeting in Fenchurch Street. Then she decided to make a phone call instead. 'What time is lunch?'

'What? Oh, er . . . twelve-thirty, at the May Fair Hotel.'

'Terrific! Mike might be back in his office by then. If I can get him on the phone . . .' Charlie's voice tailed off as she rehearsed her approach. 'Okay, I know how to sell this to Mike,' she concluded, shooting a look at Katrina. 'So what about your guy? Tell me about him. We need to work out the best way to present it. Ask yourself the question. What turns him on?'

Two hours later, Katrina was trying not to panic. Events had overwhelmed her. She had tried to be evasive when explaining about Ossie, but Charlie had been relentless. One question had led to another. Once the bare bones of the situation had been grasped, Charlie had added flesh faster than a farmer fattening a turkey for Christmas. The resentment could still be heard in Katrina's voice. 'I still think you should come. You said you would.'

'That was before you explained the situation.'

'There's not a *situation* as you call it. And I think you should be there. You're more businesslike than I am.'

'He doesn't want businesslike.'

343

'There's no need to smirk. He's an interesting man, that's all.'

'Oh sure, you're just good friends,' Charlie said drily. 'That's why you told Toddy all about him. Come on, you already admitted the guy's drooling over you –'

'I never said drooling.'

Katrina had been routed in the battle of wills. She had even been sent upstairs to bathe while Charlie talked to Mrs Bridges. Then Charlie had telephoned Mike Thompson's office in Jersey, spoken to his assistant, and rushed upstairs to report progress. 'He's in Brussels,' she had announced breathlessly. 'But he'll be back around lunchtime. Josephine, that's his PA, wet herself. She bought the whole concept. I've given her this number in case Mike gets back early. I also called my office and I killed my meeting in Fenchurch Street. This is more important.'

Since when Katrina had been in constant retreat. She was still suffering from reaction to the previous day – even she realized that – just as she realized that beneath Charlie's confidence raged an urgent desperation. 'You heard Toddy!' Charlie had said when they argued. 'Get him media coverage. So here's something you can do and you won't even *try*!'

They had been in her dressing-room half an hour and she was still wrapped in her kimono. 'Anyway,' she said resentfully. 'I don't see why you're so worried about how I look. I thought you were the modern woman. Surely the whole point of business school is to learn –'

'How to cut a deal. Exactly. Swap what you want for what the other guy wants, and any idiot can figure out what your friend Ossie wants.'

Katrina opened her mouth to protest, but Charlie held up a hand. 'And presentation always helps. If you're talking a million dollars, look a million dollars.' Taking Katrina's green silk dress down from the rail, her eyes lit with approval. 'Hey, this I like. What about this? I bet you look terrific in it.'

'I can't wear that for lunch,' Katrina sounded horrified. 'It's far too dressy.'

'Only women know dressy. Men know what turns them on.'

'Well, I'm not wearing that!'

'Okay. So what's it to be?'

Determined to make at least one decision herself, Katrina said, 'I know exactly.' Taking her navy blue suit down from the rail, she spread it across the chaise longue before opening the drawer of the tallboy. 'And I'll wear this top to go with it.'

'Hmm,' mused Charlie, with only partial approval. 'It looks smart –'

'It *is* smart.'

Charlie slipped the skirt from the hanger and held it against Katrina. 'Nice,' she agreed, squinting as she judged the effect. 'But I wonder if the skirt could be shorter? Just a fraction. I'm good with a needle –'

Katrina snorted with indignation.

'Okay, okay!' Charlie held up her hands in surrender.

Placing the white top alongside the suit, Katrina glowered as if they had displeased her. But only part of her mind was on what she should wear. Confused and indecisive, she said, 'I still think we're going about this the wrong way. Suppose I ask him to do this as a favour –'

'We've been through that. It's not his favour to give, not if he's professional –'

'He's very professional –'

'Then he won't risk Barzini's reputation for a favour.'

Katrina retreated into a sulky silence.

Taking a deep breath, Charlie plunged into her argument all over again. 'Favours are for amateurs. You don't win respect by asking for favours. You must enthuse him. Make him want this for business reasons. Barzini gets terrific exposure. Okay? Plus they'll make a bundle.'

'I'm not a salesman,' Katrina interrupted miserably. 'I don't even know if we should be doing this. I wish I could talk to Toddy –'

'To say what? There's this man he doesn't know about –'

'But suppose he hates the idea?'

'How will he hate it? This is our salvation. The more people who know about Paloma Blanca, the higher price he can get. Isn't that what he said as he went out of the door? He needs publicity. Just think, Katrina. A TV spectacular. Shown all over the world! I can't understand your reluctance about this. It was *your* idea! And Ossie's *your* contact. We'll never have a better chance. He's Barzini's manager, for God's sake!' Charlie broke off as the telephone rang. 'I'll get it.' Turning on her heel, she was already hurrying into the bedroom. 'I've given a dozen people this number already. You finish dressing.'

'Yes, ma'am,' Katrina said wearily. Resigned to the situation, she sank defeated down at her dressing table. While she checked her hair in the mirror, she listened to Charlie.

'. . . Josephine. Hi! He called before he left Brussels? I should think he was interested! Oh? Now before you go any further, stop right there. Don't do me any favours here. We're talking Enrico Barzini. Exactly. No, no, I'm not going off the deep end, but with a deal like this I'm buying not selling. With anyone, I don't care who he is. Quite . . .'

Katrina groaned under her breath. Taking off the kimono, she reached for her skirt.

'. . . absolutely. Right. Uh huh, Majorca. No, no, it's a lot more than a hotel. My God, yes! It's new, that's why. Very exclusive. Once it gets known you'll have to book years in advance. It's the most beautiful spot on God's earth. Visually Mike will love it. I promise. That's the whole point. A classic combination. The world's greatest performer singing the world's most beautiful music in this magical Garden of Eden . . .'

Katrina resisted an urge to rush into the bedroom and snatch the phone from Charlie's hand. She wanted to tell this Josephine woman it was all a mistake. Hurriedly she slipped into her blouse.

'. . . sure, of course, Enrico's crazy for the idea. We're tying up the details now. Sure, dates and timings, that sort of thing. Absolutely. But Josephine, I've got to tell you. We're already way down the road on this. Seeing a lot of people. It's just that with Mike on Jersey, and me being a big fan of his work . . . exactly . . . but speed is the essence here . . .'

Katrina felt faint as she stepped into her shoes. *Tying up the details!*

'. . . back over in Jersey tonight, but Mike can reach me here when he gets in. Right. Good. 'Bye for now.'

346

When she hurried back into the dressing-room, looking flushed and triumphant, she was pounced upon by an angry Katrina.

'How could you *say* those things? Enrico's crazy for the idea! Giving the impression that we know him. That's the most irresponsible –'

'Sssh,' hushed Charlie, patting the air with her hands. 'Don't get uptight. All I was doing –' she broke off with a look of approval. 'Now that *is* smart. Oh yes. Now that is very elegant.'

Diverted from what she was saying, Katrina automatically looked down at herself.

'*Très chic.*'

Feeling pleased, Katrina turned to look in the mirror. 'You think so?'

'Definitely.'

Her irritation forgotten, Katrina said, 'I do think it suits me.'

'It does. And it fits like a glove. Ossie will be bowled over.'

Katrina was amazed to hear herself giggle. 'Hark at me? Laughing! But if I don't laugh I shall cry.'

'You can't cry, you've done your face,' Charlie said sternly. 'I'll get us some coffee while you finish off. Okay?'

'I could come down. I'm nearly finished.'

Charlie hesitated. A frown clouded her face. Taking a step backwards, her gaze raked Katrina. Then her frown deepened. 'You know,' she said doubtfully. 'I do wonder a tiny bit about that top? I know it's beautiful and all that, but does it live up to the suit? That's the real question. I'm not sure of the answer. What do you think?'

Katrina had bought the blouse to go with the suit. On the four times she had worn the outfit, she had worn them together. Until that moment she had been sure they complemented each other. 'Well . . .' she mused, regarding herself in the mirror. 'Failing this, I've got a powder blue shirt that might go. Oh, and there's a blouse I bought in Majorca . . .'

Minutes later, Charlie was back with the coffee, and as Katrina changed one top for another she was reminded of her years with Sophie and Gloria in Harrow. 'We used to spend hours doing

347

this,' she remembered aloud. 'We used to swap everything we owned. Sophie was a model and she'd come home with the most incredible things. Designer originals and all sorts of stuff that we couldn't possibly afford.'

Talking about her past helped steady her nerves and leant an air of normality to the situation.

Charlie rejected the powder blue shirt.

She rejected the blouse bought in Majorca.

She rejected the top which Katrina had bought specially.

'They detract from the suit,' was her opinion.

'There isn't time to go shopping,' Katrina said sharply.

Charlie walked around in a circle. 'Mmm,' she mused thoughtfully. 'It's so *nearly* there . . . but it's just a little bit provincial.'

'Provincial! I bought it at Harrods.'

'As if something's missing,' said Charlie. Suddenly her eyes widened. 'I know. You're overdressed. You don't need a top.'

'No top?'

'Exactly. It will give you that international look.'

'You'll see my bra.'

'So don't wear one,' said Charlie, laughing at Katrina's horrified expression. 'Go on. Try it.'

Reluctantly Katrina did as she was told. Then she lowered her chin and stared down her cleavage. 'I can't go like this,' she gasped. 'You can see my navel!'

'I can't. And the effect is stunning. You look marvellous.'

'Really?'

'Fantastic!'

'I feel naked!' Katrina caught her breath as she stared into the mirror. 'You'll get me arrested if I go out like this.' Then she groaned as the silk lining brushed her nipples. 'Besides . . . er . . . well, you know, it feels –'

'Wonderful! It'll put you in exactly the right mood. Looking gorgeous and feeling sexy. After all, you're dealing with a sophisticated man of the world.'

Katrina groaned again.

'Now what?'

'That's half the trouble. He's not behaving like a sophisticated man of the world.'

'Oh?'

Having blurted out more than she intended, Katrina had no choice but to continue. 'If you must know, he's acting like an adolescent. True, I was going to lunch today, but only to put an end to this nonsense. You should see the letters he writes! Toddy would have a blue fit. The trouble is now . . . I mean now we've had this idea, I've got to be nice and do my best to persuade him and . . .' she shook her head. 'I just know I'll get further out of my depth.'

Charlie's green eyes were alive with amusement. 'Oh,' she repeated softly.

'It's all right for you! You're not even coming. What happens if he's got plans for afterwards? It would have been all right before, he'd have got the message over lunch, but suppose I *can* get him interested in Paloma Blanca –'

'Great! That's what we want. And you do *like* him –'

'Oh, shut up!' Katrina began to unbutton her jacket. 'I'll wear that blue shirt.'

'Suppose I change my mind and come with you?'

'Oh, will you?'

Charlie considered. 'Not to muscle in on you and Ossie. We can't arrive together. That would put him in quite the wrong mood. We need his interest in you to interest him in the proposition.'

'I don't like doing this,' said Katrina.

Charlie ignored her. The thought of being unable to influence events made her itch. It was contrary to her nature. Waiting for Katrina to return would drive her frantic. On the other hand, if she was there, in the background.

'Suppose I call Mike from the May Fair,' she said suddenly. 'If I call him at one o'clock we could be comparing notes by quarter past. We could meet in the loo or somewhere.'

'But why? Why not join us at lunch?'

'I just told you. Besides, it will help to update each other in private, me on Mike's reaction and you on Ossie. What do you think?'

Katrina hesitated.

'You're the bait, Katrina. You hook him and I'll help reel in the catch. But no top. You wear a top and I'm not coming.'

Having opted for orange juice with his in-flight breakfast, Todd was drinking more of the same in the bar at Barcelona airport. Not that he enjoyed it, but he had put himself on the wagon until meeting Hank. He would need alcohol then. They both would. By the end of the evening they'd be paralytic, but he was determined to start with a clear head.

He had spent the flight cursing himself for not telling Hank last night. True, Hank had been busy, true it was a bad time, but when was a good one? When was a good time to explain they were broke, that Hank would be lucky to hang on to the Crow's Nest, that Charlie could wind up in jail and Todd with his throat cut?

The flight was the worst three hours of his life. Last night's burst of optimism had evaporated. Just thinking of Hank's reaction made him shudder. Hank still believed in the dream. Hank would fight the idea of selling. Todd flinched at the thought of their forthcoming argument. Enveloped in a black cloud of depression, he knew he had let them all down – Katrina, Hank, Charlie. *Manny warned me. So did Katrina, my God, she never stopped telling me . . . but I was so bloody sure it would come right.*

Nursing his drink, he imagined Katrina at home by herself, worrying herself sick, still recovering from the trauma of yesterday, and moments later he hurried off in search of a phone, telling himself that it was time to forget his own depression and fire up the troops.

Twenty minutes later he was through to his home number.
'Hello.'

'Ah, Mrs Bridges. Get Katrina quickly, will you. I'm calling from Spain.'

'Oh, I can't do that. She's gone out. You just missed her.'
'Gone out?'

'With the lady with the red hair. They went out together.'

Surprised, he looked at his watch. 'Did they say where they were going?'

'Not to me they didn't,' Mrs Bridges sniffed huffily. 'They went out like a couple of schoolgirls. They've been the same all morning. Chattering away upstairs like a pair of daft kids. I'm surprised at Mrs Todd, really I am. I thought she was more sensitive. You'd have thought she'd still be upset about Mac being run over . . .'

'But Ossie,' Katrina persisted. 'You do *like* the idea?'

He responded by reaching across the table to place his hand over hers. 'Katrina,' he said wistfully in that dark brown voice which made her name sound Italian and sexy. 'I didn't come here to talk business. I came to see a beautiful woman whom I missed very much.'

Like a diver on a springboard, his body seemed poised to follow his gaze down her cleavage.

She let him hold her hand. Mrs Katrina Todd, wife of the local Jaguar dealer, would have been embarrassed and nervous about such a public and indiscreet display of affection. But she no longer felt like Mrs Katrina Todd. She was sick to death of Mrs Katrina Todd. Mrs Todd was responsible, careful, cautious and boring. And provincial! All she did was worry. And what did she get for her trouble? Some brute breathing garlic into her face while he held a knife at her throat. This other Katrina, this *new* Katrina, feeling Italian and sexy was having a much better time, lunching in this smart restaurant with this international high roller in his beautifully cut suit and silvery silk tie.

Turning her hand until her palm fitted his, she teased him with a smile. 'Ah,' she said. 'But you know that's not true. Admit it. You had to come to London on business.'

Amazingly, she was quite enjoying herself. She was enjoying the way he looked at her. She had once read of a man who was born on February the twenty-ninth and could only celebrate his birthday every leap year. Ossie looked just like him.

She had enjoyed turning men's heads when she had walked

into the restaurant. Never again, she had vowed, would she wear a top with this suit. *All these years and I didn't know how to dress myself.*

She was even enjoying the attention of the boggle-eyed waiters.

'An excuse to see you, that's all,' Ossie protested. 'I've set the whole day aside. Now all you want to talk about is a concert.'

She felt daring and reckless and wicked. But most of all she felt in control.

'That's not true, either,' she rebuked with a smile.

Nor was it. During her Parma ham and melon she had not said a word about Majorca. While eating her sole Véronique she had plied him with questions about his forthcoming trip to New York. Over strawberries and cream she had quizzed him about Barzini's season in Milan which, she noted slyly, was now at an end. All of which she had enjoyed, for she was genuinely interested and his answers were as entertaining as ever.

She had said nothing of what she had intended the day before. How could she? Indeed when he had implied she might go on a trip to Paris with him, she merely laughed.

'Ah,' he said. 'How I missed the sound of your laughter.'

'Then I'll laugh again in a minute,' she said and was so pleased with her little joke that she laughed there and then.

And Ossie laughed too, but he also began to pick the photographs up from the table. 'Now,' he said. 'If we've finished here, let's go to my suite. We can have another brandy up –'

'No, no,' she interrupted, her hands reaching for his. 'We were still discussing this idea.'

'We can talk upstairs.' Leaning back in his chair, he extricated his hands and wrote his signature in the air for the benefit of the waiter.

Nodding his understanding, the waiter hurried off in search of the bill.

'Ossie,' Katrina purred reproachfully. 'This is all a game with you, isn't it?'

'A game?' He pretended surprise.

'You play it all over the world. I bet you left one woman in

Rome and there's another waiting for you in New York. Or if there isn't, you'll soon find her.' She encouraged him with a laugh. 'Come on, admit it.'

A gleam came to his eyes. His mouth lifted at the corners.

'You look like a little boy who's been caught scrumping.'

'Scrumping?' He frowned.

'Stealing apples.'

'Ah,' he smiled. 'Forbidden fruits.'

'You know I'm flattered. You're interesting, charming and very attractive, but I'm *very* married.'

'I forgive you.'

'But I wouldn't, you see. That's the point. I know it's stupid, but I wouldn't.' Her eyes pleaded with him. 'Can't we be just friends?'

His gaze moved from her face down her cleavage and back up again. Reading her serious expression, he gave a deep sigh of acceptance. 'What a waste –'

'Nothing's wasted. We'll do lots of lovely business together and remain friends for the rest of our lives.'

In response to her laugh, he managed a wry smile of his own. Reluctantly he turned his attention to the photographs. 'Maybe we'll stay friends,' he said doubtfully. 'But I don't know about doing business. Like I said just now. The scenery's wonderful. It looks like a beautiful place and I hear what you say about it all, but this idea –'

'This one's taken from out at sea,' she interrupted, inwardly sighing with relief as she picked up a photograph. 'See what I mean about a natural auditorium. Now if you can imagine . . .' she broke off to smile at the waiter who had returned with the bill. 'I think we might have some more coffee,' she said, allowing him to peep down her jacket.

Sending him away happy, she embarked upon a description of her idea all over again.

The time had turned two o'clock. From the corner of her eye she caught a glimpse of Charlie's red hair in the bar. Charlie had been once and gone away again, no doubt to rendezvous in the powder-room. But with nothing to report Katrina had remained in her chair, though after all the wine and brandy and coffee, shortly she would have genuine reason to leave in a hurry.

'Katrina,' said Ossie, shooting his cuffs to put both elbows on the table and cup his chin in his hands. 'I must tell you something. Being Enrico's manager is like a sacred trust to me. Seriously. This is one of the great talents of the world and looking after it is something I cherish. My job is to watch out for his reputation, all the time. Understand? You wouldn't believe the places he's asked to perform. Okay, now and then . . .' he shrugged. 'But Katrina, I have to tell you, I couldn't commit him to this. Majorca's a backwater. We play an international circuit. I can't risk the loss of exposure.'

'That's the whole point,' she exclaimed. 'We use the visual qualities of Paloma Blanca as a backdrop, as a magical setting, something truly unique, and television gives us the exposure.'

Reluctantly he lifted his gaze from her cleavage. 'Spanish television?' he asked doubtfully.

'More than just Spain. We're thinking of screening this round the world. A two-hour spectacular.'

This time his gaze remained on her face and his surprise turned to a look of amusement. 'My dear Katrina,' he laughed. 'You think it's that easy?' He rolled his eyes. 'That would be a hell of a package to put together. It might even be a hell of an idea, but you want a big producer for something like that. You're talking important. So where's your credentials? You wouldn't believe what's involved –'

'Does Mike Thompson have the credentials?'

His smile faded as his eyes widened. 'You know Mike Thompson?'

A sixth sense came to her rescue. *He likes my laugh, so laugh.* Waving her hands, she made as if to draw the whole restaurant to her bosom. 'Don't be so silly,' she giggled. '*Everyone* knows Mike Thompson.'

He sat staring into her eyes, her cleavage momentarily forgotten. 'Yeah, well,' he nodded, rubbing his chin thoughtfully. 'He's got a big reputation. He's done some excellent work.'

'Wouldn't he make a wonderful job of it?'

He turned away from her, as if an examination of the

restaurant would be less of a distraction. 'Certainly his involvement makes a big difference.'

Katrina felt a tingle start in her toes and run right up into her body.

His gaze strayed back to the photographs. 'Naturally, if we did anything we'd insist on artistic approval of the entire programme.'

'Oh, naturally,' she nodded eagerly, prepared to make any concession. 'That goes without saying.'

Picking up the top photograph, he looked at it, set it aside and examined the one underneath. 'What about the video market?'

'It's enormous,' Katrina said quickly. 'It's huge. You wouldn't believe how big it is these days.'

He smiled. 'I don't think you need tell me. I know how big it is. What I meant was do you have a figure pencilled in for our participation?'

'Er . . . yes, absolutely!' Nodding wildly, she tried not to flounder. 'Everything's pencilled in. Er . . . including the title. We . . . er . . . we've been giving serious thought to the title.'

'And?'

Pausing for effect, she tried to emulate Charlie. Swivelling in her chair, she stretched out her arms and spread her hands to peer through her fingers. She cleared her throat as if about to make an important announcement.

The man at the next table set down his knife and fork and stared at her.

A waiter paused, coffee jug tilted at an angle.

Taking a deep breath, she whispered, '*Barzini at Paloma Blanca.*' Turning, she tracked her arms around the room. '*Barzini at Paloma Blanca,*' she whispered huskily up to the ceiling.

Ossie beamed. 'I like it,' he said approvingly, nodding his head. 'Name at the top of the bill. Strong sound. International appeal.' He paused to think, then nodded again. 'Yes,' he said. 'That's a title we could live with.'

She had never felt so proud in her life. Or so excited. She could hardly believe what she was doing. A housewife from Hampstead, signing up the most famous singer in the world.

I'm doing it. Me. Not Toddy. ME! But sudden panic marred her excitement. Suppose Mike Thompson had said no to Charlie? Oh no, surely not, not now, not with us coming so far . . .

Ossie mused thoughtfully. 'You want an idea?' he asked, stroking his chin. 'There's a big CD in this. You know, simultaneous release with the video. We could set everything up to follow on from the screening dates in individual markets. Maybe get Enrico to go on the road and do some promotion?'

'That's a *wonderful* idea, Ossie,' Katrina enthused, giddy from the combined effects of excitement and panic. *Please God, let Thompson have said yes!*

He looked pleased. 'You like it?'

'It's absolutely brilliant!' she exclaimed, knowing she could go no further without an update from Charlie, longing for a moment alone to re-group her thoughts . . .

Nodding approvingly, he made as if to rise from his chair. 'Now I think we deserve a little celebration. A reward for working so hard. Leave the details –'

'No, I love details. Details can make all the difference. We shouldn't skimp details.'

'Katrina,' he scolded gently.

She smiled at him. 'You never stop trying, do you?'

'Would you even deny me the thrill of the chase?' he asked, good-humouredly.

'Would we cease to be friends if you fail to catch me?'

A reproachful look came into his eyes. 'Is that what you think?'

She shook her head. 'Not for a minute. You're too big a man to be petty.'

He laughed and raised his coffee cup in a toast. 'To your good opinion of me.'

She could have kissed him. Instead, she rose from the table. 'Give me a minute,' she smiled. 'Finish your coffee, and study the photographs.' As she crossed the restaurant she turned her head to Charlie in the bar. Without betraying a flicker of recognition, she hurried out to the lobby. Turning left, she fled down the corridor and into the powder-room. Scarcely had the door

356

closed when it opened again and Charlie burst in. 'Well?' she demanded breathlessly. 'How's it going?'

'Did you speak to Mike Thompson?'

'Mike loves it.' Charlie was jumping on the spot with excitement. 'Especially the bonus of the video market. He says it's huge!'

'Huge?'

'Vast!'

'Yes, well,' Katrina said airily, flushed with success. 'We covered the video market. I've already pencilled in Ossie's participation.'

'Pencilled in . . .' Unable to contain her astonishment, Charlie's eyes widened and she burst into laughter. 'Participation? Hark at you! So I take it lunch has gone well.'

'The next hour could be tricky.'

'So he wants to do it?'

Seeing herself in the mirror, Katrina blanched. 'You send me in there like this and ask a question like that?'

Hugging herself, Charlie went back to jumping on the spot. 'We've cracked it!' Grabbing Katrina's arm, she said, 'I'm seeing Mike for dinner, but we've already covered most of the points. I was on to him for half an hour. He's crazy hot for the idea.'

Katrina glowed with the most wonderful sense of achievement. For the first time in her life, she understood her father. She remembered being at home as a child, with her mother in tears after fending off the bailiffs. Her father had just arrived, full of excitement. 'Don't worry. Everything will be all right,' he cried. 'I've just pulled off this marvellous deal.' Now, as her heart pounded and her mouth went dry and she tingled all over, she understood his excitement.

Charlie said, 'I suppose the next step is to get him and Ossie together. He's dead keen for a meeting. When can we set one up, do you think?'

Suddenly everything fell into place. Katrina knew exactly what she would be doing during the next hour. Packing. Her voice rose in excitement. 'Suppose we come with you? To Jersey. Ossie and me. Then we could all have dinner tonight. Maybe we could tie everything up?'

357

CHAPTER TWELVE

THE BARMAN POLISHED A GLASS and watched from the corner of his eye. The chubby little Englishman was still there. He had been there an hour, drinking San Miguels at the far end of the bar. Every now and then he muttered under his breath, as if arguing with himself. He looked harmless enough, certainly not menacing or dangerous, but after three years of working at the airport the barman knew better than to rely on appearances. Ten months before a deranged woman had managed to get herself on to the flight deck of a 707. How she got there nobody knew, but there had been hell to pay when she was discovered. It transpired that she too had been drinking in the bar beforehand, and she had looked harmless enough.

Pursuing his own thoughts, Todd was unaware of the attention he was attracting. Just for once he was not on parade – he had no need to exude confidence, no need to bestow courage upon Katrina or Charlie or Hank. In private he could wallow in his own doubts and misgivings. Which is what he was in danger of doing. In particular he was seething with frustration as he wondered whether to stay in Majorca, or go back to London, or fly to Paris.

He was meeting Katrina. Not that he knew why. Yesterday when he had arrived in Majorca, Hank had said, 'Katrina called. She won't be home tonight. She said not to worry.'

And he hadn't; he was too busy worrying about Hank. He assumed Katrina had made arrangements to stay with Gloria or Sophie. It was Hank he had been worrying about.

Lifting his empty glass, Todd rapped the counter.

The barman came over. '*Señor?*'

'Same again.'

Even when he had gone to bed, he had been worrying about Hank. *What a night. I'd have killed him if it had been the other way round. If he'd come to me with news like that . . .* It had been Hank who had dominated his thoughts, not Katrina. Charlie's call this morning had come as a bolt from the blue. He had been in the shower when the phone rang; dripping water all over the place when he answered. 'What?' he had cried in alarm. 'She's in Jersey with you? Why?'

Not that she had told him. Apparently she was in a racing hurry herself, and Katrina had already left for Jersey airport, en route for Gatwick airport, en route for Heathrow airport, en route for Palma airport.

His heart had missed a beat. 'You haven't told Bob anything –'

'No, no, nothing like that. Katrina will explain. She's connecting with a flight that gets her there at six this evening. I can't stop, I'm late as it is, but it's good news. Don't worry.'

Good news. There was no such thing. Carrier was away. Not even on the island. He was in Madrid or Seville, his staff seemed unsure, but he was uncontactable until Wednesday wherever he was.

Already two days had gone. Two of the fourteen to Moroni's deadline. Two days without obtaining a piece of paper. Not that he had expected a written offer today. He'd not even intended to ask for one. Today he had envisaged a leisurely lunch, a sounding out, a talking up of the price, an assessment of intentions. He had imagined himself saying this . . . he had anticipated Carrier saying that . . . the one thing he had not expected was that Carrier would be away from Majorca.

As he opened his wallet to pay for the beer, his glance fell on the business card. It was still there, safe and sound. Philippe Roos. Partner. Arlsruher, Wormack and Roos. Roos had left it with the site foreman who had given it to Hank who had passed it on to him. As he looked at it he scored a line down the card with his thumbnail. *What I want to know, Mr Philippe bloody Roos, is what were you doing on our site? Why were you there? You must have a buyer . . .*

More frustrations. Roos seemed to have an office in every

country in Europe. On telephoning the office in Paris, he had been assured that Roos was in London. On calling the office in London, he was told Roos had left for the day, but would be in the Paris office on Monday. Eventually, in a bad temper, he had called Paris again and spoken to Roos's secretary, and given her his own numbers in Majorca and London.

Now he was unsure whether to stay until Wednesday to see Carrier, or return to London and try Roos from there. He ought to go back to London. There were things he should be doing at Todd Motors. Urgent things. Business was awful. Even worse were his suspicions that some of the staff were ripping him off, doing their own deals on his site with his cars. He needed to appoint a new manager, someone he could trust. He needed to . . .

'What I *don't* need,' he told himself angrily, 'is Katrina not being where she should be!'

The sudden chattering of the indicator boards above his head interrupted his thoughts. Looking up he saw the announcement that the Heathrow flight had landed. About time! He returned the card to his wallet and began to think about what he would say to Katrina. What was she *doing* with Charlie? Surely she could have stayed with Gloria or Sophie? He could understand that she might be nervous in the house by herself, but why trek all the way over to Jersey?

He had been relieved at the way she and Charlie had taken to each other. That was fine. It was good they had got on, he was glad, but for them to become friends . . . *Women talk. Yap, yap, yap. Next thing she'll find out about that night in Rugby and there'll be hell to pay. That's all I need.*

As if I don't have enough to worry about . . .

'What I don't understand,' he grumbled as he drove Hank's jeep out of the airport car park, 'is what were you doing in Jersey?'

'Didn't Charlie tell you?'

He snorted derisively. 'She said you'd explain when you got here. Like thanks very much!'

Shifting sideways, she studied him. The late afternoon sun

lit every line in his face, making obvious his worried expression. 'You don't seem very pleased to see me.'

'Of course I'm pleased. It's just that –'

'Ouch!' she winced as the jeep hit a bump. 'I wish Hank would get a decent car.'

'He'll be bloody lucky to keep this.'

She shot him a glance. 'How did it go last night?'

He groaned at the memory. 'Don't ask,' he said bitterly. 'Know the worst thing? I unloaded all this bad news, told him we've lost our shirts, that we won't have a pot left to piss in –'

'But you explained about Moroni?'

'Of course I did.'

'And?'

'That was the worst bit. His first thoughts were about us being safe. You and me. Then he was concerned about Charlie. He was just so bloody decent about everything . . .' swallowing hard, Todd shook his head. 'I'd have gone berserk in his place, but not Hank. No wonder he was a sea captain. He stays calm in a storm, I'll vouch for that. He didn't even blame me. Not really. He was shocked of course. You can imagine. Shocked rigid. And upset. Bloody upset.'

Although he kept his gaze fixed resolutely ahead, she could see the pain in his face.

Taking a deep breath, he said, 'I promised him that if by some miracle we get anything over fifteen million it's his. You know, before me, before us.' As if fearful that she would complain, he threw her a sideways glance of apology. 'I'm sorry, but I had to do it. It was only fair.'

'It's all right, I understand.'

He breathed a sigh of relief. 'Hank's agreed about selling. We've no bloody choice.' Concentrating on weaving through the early evening traffic, he fell silent for a moment. Then he said bitterly, 'Okay, I know I've made a lot of mistakes, but I was right about Hank. I couldn't have asked for a better partner.'

'And I got him wrong,' she thought, grateful for Hank's understanding. Aloud she said, 'You didn't make mistakes. You took a chance raising the money, that's all.'

He was heartened by her attitude and grateful to her for being

361

so supportive, yet he was more than a little puzzled. He was feeling desperate, on the verge of despair, but she was showing no signs of strain. On the contrary. Mystified, he threw her another glance. Dressed in shirt and jeans, with a sweater knotted around her shoulders, she was looking good. Very attractive. She had come through the airport laughing and chatting with a young man of about twenty. Almost flirting . . .

'Oh, look,' she said suddenly, pointing across at the Club Nautico. 'Isn't that Tommy Gosling's boat?'

Slowing for the traffic lights, he followed her arm. It was Gosling's yacht, but something else caught his attention. 'Bloody hell. You've not got a bra on.'

'It's too hot.'

Stopping for the lights, he gave her his undivided attention. 'What's happened?' he frowned. 'You're acting . . . you're different. Peculiar.'

She laughed, sounding almost carefree. 'Because I'm not wearing a bra? You are funny at times. Anyway, I don't think I'll bother in future. After all, Charlie doesn't wear one, does she?'

To avoid her eye, he swivelled his head and stared at the traffic lights. In a sulky voice, defensive enough to be a complaint, he said, 'You don't have to do everything Charlie does.'

'I don't know what she does, do I?'

He willed the traffic lights to change colour. There was a sweet reasonableness in her voice which disturbed him. He was reminded of how easily she could lull him into a false sense of security. From experience he knew her tone could alter abruptly. His ears twitched with suspicion. Searching his mind for a change of subject, he kept his eyes fixed firmly ahead. 'I think these lights have failed,' he said irritably. 'Typical!' Feeling her watching him was making him nervous. Anxious. *What the hell has she been talking to Charlie about?* He felt the heat rise in his face. 'Bloody lights along this stretch of road are always packing up. It's always along this bit, every time! You can bet your life – ah!' he grunted as the lights turned to green. Taking his foot from the clutch, he slammed the gear lever forward and stalled the engine. 'Oh, fuck!'

The driver behind tooted a horn.

He swung round and stuck two fingers into the air. 'And you can shut up!' he shouted angrily, ready to leap from the jeep to do battle. Instead, seeing a diminutive figure at the wheel of a small white-painted van, he turned back to the dashboard and re-started the engine. 'Did you see that? It's a bloody nun! What's her hurry?' As the engine burst into life, he slammed the gear lever into place and lurched forward. 'Got an appointment with God or something?'

'You are in a foul mood.'

'Of course I'm in a foul mood! What do you expect? My whole life is fucked up! Moroni's breathing down my neck. I'm about to go bust. My wife buggers off God knows where –'

'I didn't bugger off. I went to Jersey.'

'But why?' he shouted, throwing her a sideways glance and swerving dangerously. 'That's what I want to know. Why?'

They say that a man's whole life flashes through his mind as he is about to die. Much the same had happened to Todd. In the two days since Moroni invaded his home, he had spent a good deal of time thinking – the journey crammed into an aircraft, the hours at Barcelona airport, kicking his heels, waiting for the overdue connection to Palma – and although not alone in the true sense of the word, people around him might not have existed. He had been alone with his thoughts. He had thought and thought . . . and mostly he had thought about Aldo Moroni.

Of course a hundred lurid scenarios had passed through his mind. He saw himself laying a trap, he imagined himself with a gun, threatening Moroni instead of the other way round. He even saw himself working with the police to have Moroni arrested. But such ideas were the stuff of fiction, not of real life and least of all of his life. Where would he get a gun? He had never as much as fired a gun, not even in a fairground. He wasn't James Bond, he was a fat little car dealer from London. And even going to the police was out of the question unless he was ready to send Charlie to prison. And ready to face prison himself.

For two days he had sweated through one hopeless scenario after another.

Other thoughts had come to mind, bringing memories – such as Katrina's opposition to Paloma Blanca from day one and the endless arguments with Manny. Of course they had been right and he had been wrong. He saw that now, only too clearly. He'd been greedy. *You ran Todd Motors seven years before Sam gave you the chance to buy Owen's. Seven years of hard work. Plus all the years afterwards. Building up all the time. Good steady growth. Then you chanced everything for this. Crazy!*

He blamed himself for the mess he was in – not the recession or Suntours going bust, or his own bad luck or the miserable state of the market. Not even – when he was being searingly honest with himself – did he blame Aldo Moroni. He had known from the start what Moroni was like. *Leo warned me. Besides, I knew at that first meeting in Rome . . . in my heart I always knew.*

The only thing he really hated Moroni for was for involving Katrina. *Never again. I'll make sure she's safe next time. Next time will be different.*

And there would be a next time. There was no doubting that.

He almost drove himself mad with his thinking; searching for a way out, like an animal trying to free itself from a trap. But gradually along with the agonizing came a kind of acceptance. A letting go of false hope. The thought of selling Paloma Blanca no longer tore him apart. After two days he found he could accept the idea. His pain had been numbed.

His only remaining ambition about Paloma Blanca concerned the price. It was all very well to be contemptuous of Carrier's offer of nine million, he *was* contemptuous, but how much higher would Carrier go? How much higher would this man Roos go? As Charlie had said, *Nine to fifteen is a hell of a jump.* Even fifteen wasn't enough. Fifteen would pay Moroni and save him and Charlie from jail, but fifteen would still leave him and Hank on the breadline.

364

And now only twelve days remained until Moroni returned . . .

Such were his thoughts. Ill-formed, inconclusive, hesitant and
frightened, edging towards conclusions instead of attacking them
boldly.

Then Katrina arrived with her news.

'I can't believe it,' he kept saying. 'Let's go through it again.'

She had told him as soon as they arrived at the villa. She had
led the way out on to the terrace, looked out at her much loved
view of the harbour, taken a deep breath, and then plunged into
her story. That was at seven o'clock. An hour later they were
still on the terrace; and he was still dazed, still trying to take
everything in. He was not an opera lover, or even a music lover.
Tone deaf, he had an abysmal singing voice. Unusually for
someone so plump he had no sense of rhythm. The truth was
that he could scarcely carry a tune in his head. Yet even he had
heard of Enrico Barzini. And of course he was quick to understand the power of television. 'How many countries?' he kept
asking, knowing her answer already but wanting her to let him
say it himself, as if hearing it in his own voice would help him
believe it. 'Nine, ten, maybe more, including the States *and*
Japan!' He felt lightheaded with hope and excitement. Questions
poured from his lips. 'How big did you say the video market
is? What did this Australian guy say about compact discs?'

The last question stumped her for a moment. 'What
Australian guy?'

'This Aussie.'

Her face cleared. 'It's Ossie with an O. He's not Australian.'

'Funny bloody name.'

Her eyes glimmered as she recognized another similarity
between the men in her life. 'I expect it's short for Oswald or
something,' she said lightly. 'Perhaps he doesn't like the name
he was given?'

The gentle humour escaped him. He scarcely bothered to
listen to her answer, preferring instead to insist that she
describe, yet again, her vision of the concert itself – with the

stage built over the swimming pools, lanterns flickering on the hillsides, spotlights on the performers and Barzini's voice soaring up into the night sky.

'Bloody marvellous,' he kept saying. 'Absolutely bloody marvellous!'

Which was what he was saying when the bell rang at the front gate.

Katrina held up a hand. 'Sssh! Listen.'

'That'll be Hank!' he said, leaping up from his chair. 'Wait until he hears this!'

He had dreaded Hank's arrival earlier. He had imagined another gloomy post mortem. Then Katrina's news had given him a new lease of life and driven all other thoughts from his head. Now he rushed down the path, flung open the gate and grabbed Hank by the arm. 'Hank! You won't believe –' he stopped, taken aback, rendered momentarily speechless.

Caught in the lamplight Hank looked shabby and crumpled – due less to his clothes than his air of defeat. He was dressed in his sailing gear, sweater, blazer and cotton twill trousers, but it was the anxiety in his face which made him look crumpled and worn. He looked grey with worry. Todd was shocked. He realized that last night Hank had reacted with the courage of a professional skipper handling a yacht in a storm. Now he looked like a man who had spent the day grieving over the wreckage.

Todd dragged him up the path. Gripping his arm tightly, he steered him on to the terrace, almost shouting, 'Come and see Katrina.' And once they reached the terrace they all started talking at once – Hank with concern about Katrina's ordeal, taking her hands into his, telling her how relieved he was to see her safe and sound – Katrina trying to assure him that she *was* safe and sound – while Todd hopped from one foot to the other, wanting to get the greetings over and done with. 'Sit yourself down,' he kept saying. 'Sit down, Hank. Let me get you a drink. Katrina's got some staggering news.'

Finally he hurried over to the bar and returned to push Hank down into a chair. 'Here,' he said, thrusting a beer into his hand. 'Listen to Katrina for a minute.'

After which he made her explain everything all over again,

366

and while she talked, he paced up and down, so excited that he peppered her explanation with his own observations.

'Oh, Toddy, stop interrupting!' she cried. 'Who's telling this, anyway?'

Bewildered by the excitement, Hank turned his head from one to the other, trying to follow a garbled story which was coming to him from two directions at once. 'Hey, slow down,' he pleaded. 'One at a time.'

Katrina plunged on breathlessly. 'We're talking of a world-wide viewing audience of millions. And the video and CD will carry the same title as the show. *Barzini at Paloma Blanca*. That's the trick. Gettting the name in the title. Don't you see?'

Hank was completely bemused. 'Wait a minute,' he protested. 'Where did these guys spring from all of a sudden?'

Katrina began to pull her sweater on against the cool of the evening. She had been so busy talking that she was still in her travelling clothes. She smiled happily. Having answered that question already, she was well prepared with her answer. 'Charlie's known Mike for some time, they met out in Jersey,' she said as her head disappeared into the sweater. Emerging again, she continued, 'And Sophie met Ossie at Broadlands. I met him too, of course . . .' she waved a hand airily before putting her arm into a sleeve '. . . but you know how easily Sophie makes friends.'

'Don't I just,' Todd thought drily, but having been rebuked for his interruptions, he remained silent, caught between enjoying Hank's astonishment and watching Katrina's excitement. He had to remind himself that this was his wife. Of course, he knew she was bright. He had never thought her stupid. She was methodical with paperwork, faultless at remembering birth-days and anniversaries, reliable in taking messages, marvellous at creating a comfortable life . . . but to listen to her now was to hear someone else; someone not exactly a stranger, yet at the same time not quite Katrina.

'. . . Mike says he'll include some introductory footage of Enrico walking on the beach, to show off the hillsides and Don Antonio's architecture, shot in daylight of course, and I was thinking we could include some shots of the marina . . .'

367

A sudden tingle ran up his spine. He knew exactly who she reminded him of; the resemblance was there in the tilt of her head and the emphatic use of her hands. 'All these years,' he thought, stunned with surprise. 'And it's the first time I've seen it. She's her father's daughter after all. Leo would be proud of her. I wonder what she would say if I told her?'

'. . . Mike's sure he can sell it as a live broadcast in Europe,' Katrina continued. 'He's certain they'd take it in the UK, and Italy of course, and in Spain. Oh and France, I nearly forgot.'

Todd thought, 'She sounds so . . .' he searched for the right word '. . . so authoritative.' There was an excitement about her, a vibrancy which commanded attention.

Hank was shaking his head as he listened. Some of the anxiety had gone from his face, but he continued to look puzzled. 'So where do we come in?' he asked, unsure where it was leading. 'Do we earn on this? The television and the video –'

'Oh, Hank!' Katrina scolded, with a reproving look. 'No, of course we don't. That's their end of it. Obviously they hope to make a big profit, but they take their own risk. Some of their costs are enormous. Apart from the orchestra and the supporting artists, Ossie's talking about a huge chorus and goodness knows what. We get the gate money which should cover our expenses, but the most important thing is our massive exposure.'

'Massive,' Todd agreed with a nod of his head. 'That's the point, Hank. Paloma Blanca will get tremendous coverage. We thought the Gold Cup would create exposure, but this swamps –'

'Oh, totally,' Katrina interrupted. 'This swamps everything. This will make Paloma Blanca the best-known resort hotel in the world.'

For a moment they fell silent, as if suddenly and simultaneously they had run out of breath. Each as excited as the other, they exchanged glances and then looked at Hank, waiting for his reaction, but for at least a minute there was no reaction at all. Hank nursed his beer and scratched his chin. He avoided looking at them by staring into the swimming pool. On his face was the look of a condemned man who was afraid that the news of a reprieve might be a rumour.

Todd went to the bar to collect some more beers. As he straightened up he turned slightly and caught sight of the lights of the harbour below. Out at sea blinked the navigation lights of a yachtsman on his way into port. He grinned to himself. *Maybe my boat's coming in after all?*

Hank raised his gaze from the pool and watched him come back from the bar with beers in his hands. 'Quite something, eh?' he mused softly. 'To have created the best-known resort hotel in the world. I mean, even if it's an exaggeration to say the world, it must rank with the best.'

There was awe in his voice.

Todd guessed what he was thinking. It was hard to let go of a dream which had become real. He had felt a pang or two himself earlier. Aware of the irony, he was no less determined. He pulled up a chair. 'This gives me cards to play, Hank,' he said as he sat down. 'Big cards. Imagine what I can make of this with Carrier and this other guy. And come to think of it, with anyone else. I'm selling world-wide recognition. A universally known brand name. A guaranteed success! Hotels work thirty or forty years to get this sort of recognition. We'll do it in one night!'

'But when's all this meant to happen?'

'February.'

'February?'

'The end of February,' Katrina said hastily. 'It's the only time Barzini can do it. You should see his engagements. Ossie showed me his schedule. Some months are booked years in advance –'

'But what about Moroni?' Hank exclaimed, looking at Todd. 'You've only got until the seventeenth –'

'To get an offer,' Todd grinned. 'That's all he wants. He'll wait until the spring for his money. We need an offer from Carrier, but we don't have to accept it, do we? Nobody accepts the first offer they get, and imagine the interest this will generate. Screened all over the world! Everyone who sees Paloma Blanca falls in love with it. We know that, don't we? That's our trump card. So *millions* will see it. Paloma Blanca will be booked solid before it even opens.'

Hank responded with a dazed smile, 'I get it. And *then* we sell it?'

'Right. In March. We'll set up an auction. What d'you think?'

'Colossal.' His smile broadened into a grin. 'I think it's phenomenal. Breathtaking.'

Todd fairly beamed. Leaning sideways in his chair, he kissed Katrina on the cheek, then jumped up and went through the open doors into the sitting-room, returning within a moment with a cigar in his hand.

'Wait a minute,' said Hank, frowning and cocking his head. 'You going to tell Carrier about this auction?'

'Why not?' asked Todd, lighting up.

'Suppose he won't go along with it? That fouls you up. Moroni wants a written offer –'

'We'll give Carrier an inducement. I'm not asking for something for nothing,' Todd said cheerfully from the middle of a cloud of blue smoke. 'We'll tell him straight out about the auction, but we'll give him topping-up rights. He gives us a written offer now and in return he gets the right to top any bid at the auction. It puts him in the driving seat. He can just sit at the auction knowing that whatever the price goes to, he can top it by five per cent and he gets Paloma Blanca. It makes him totally safe.'

Hank poured a fresh beer into his glass and set the bottle down at his feet.

Sensing disagreement, Todd looked at him. 'What's wrong with that?'

'Nothing on the face of it. It's a fair enough way of doing things, I suppose, but Carrier won't like it. He'll be scared stiff of an auction.'

'So? If the greedy bastard makes us a decent offer now, we won't have an auction. He can buy it now at the right price. Or he can stick to his offer for nine million and grab pole position at the auction. It's his choice. I think he's getting a hell of a deal.' Todd grinned. 'Besides there's always this other guy. Roos. He's got access to all the big boys. Imagine their reaction to this television thing?' He spread his arms wide as if to embrace the whole world. 'This is enormous, Hank. I thought we'd lost our shirts on this. Now we could even come out with a profit.'

Hank stared up into the night sky as if searching for God. He even put his hands together in a gesture of prayer.

Relieved that the worry had gone from Hank's face, Todd was still feeling guilty for causing it in the first place. Fidgeting in his chair, he began anxiously, 'I know what this means to you, Hank. Being forced to sell like this. Let's face it, Paloma Blanca is your creation. You found the site, you even *bought* it for God's sake before taking me on as a partner. Then you found the right architect and sweated your guts out with the builders. Christ, there's not a decision made on site without your approval.'

'That was my end of the deal. My responsibility –'

'And you did it. In spades. Paloma Blanca is *your* creation. So I can understand –'

'Hey!' Hank held up his hands. 'Did I ever say I wanted to run a hotel the rest of my life? We were always going to sell it, weren't we? Build it up and sell it. Wasn't that the idea? So now we'll do it in one hit.'

Todd looked at him in surprise. They had spent hours talking about getting Paloma Blanca built and opened and launched and financed, but as far as he could remember they had never discussed how long they would keep it.

'I'll tell you something,' Hank grinned, not a proper Hank grin, but at least a grin. 'I've had fun organizing this site. I've really enjoyed it. But I don't want to be a hotelier. If I'm bored running a restaurant, I'd get bored running a hotel. I want to be a developer. There was a guy in the bar the other night, talking about a site in the Seychelles that might be going cheap –'

'Jesus! You'd go through this again?' Todd sat back with a look of amazement. 'You *like* doing this?'

Instead of answering, Hank got up and walked over to the bar where he fidgeted for a moment, putting his glass down, pulling a stool back from the bar, patting his blazer pocket for cigarettes, taking them out and lighting one. Then he sat on a stool and turned round to face them. Something in his expression filled Todd with foreboding. The grin had gone, replaced by the same worried look he had worn when he arrived, and when he looked at Todd he looked away again as if unwilling to meet his eye. 'There's something I should tell you,' he began. 'I was going to tell you as soon as I got here, but you didn't give me a chance.'

Instinctively Todd feared what was coming. He wanted to remind Hank of their good news, to retain the mood of hope and optimism, but he remained silent, flinching at the prospect of some new disaster. 'Now what?' he asked himself fearfully.

'. . . the truth is,' Hank was saying, 'I've been feeling guilty all day.'

'*You've* been feeling guilty?'

Hank nodded. 'See, I always reckoned I could do this. You know, find a site, hire an architect, work with builders and create a development that was a bit special. It was something I always thought I'd be good at —'

'You are,' Todd interrupted. 'You've proved that.'

'But what you don't know is that I discussed it with a few other guys before I took you up to the site.' To avoid Todd's eye, he looked for an ashtray and seeing one at the end of the bar, got up and carried it back to where he was sitting. When he sat down again, he said, 'The best I could expect from any deal with them was about fifteen per cent, and I thought fuck it, I deserve more, I deserve fifty per cent out of this. After all, like you said, I set the deal up, commissioned the architect and everything. I deserve half. That's what I told myself. The truth is I got greedy.' He looked directly at Todd for the first time. 'Raising the money was always the shit end of the deal. I knew that before we started, but I sort of bounced you into it. I always expected you'd come back and say the only way you could raise it was by forming a consortium and sharing the cake. But you got the bit between your teeth about raising the money and then, well . . .' he shrugged. 'When you said you'd cracked it with these people in Paris, I kept quiet.' He looked at Katrina with a plea for understanding, even forgiveness. 'If anyone's to blame for this mess it's me for being so bloody greedy. If I hadn't insisted on fifty per cent things would have been different.'

Todd was too surprised to speak for a moment. In a different mood, in other circumstances, he might have felt let down, even betrayed, but his immediate reaction was more relief than anger. 'We bit off more than we could chew, that's all,' he said. 'We were both greedy. I didn't complain about getting fifty per cent, did I? Anyway, what about when money began to get tight? You sold *The American Dream.* That wasn't part of the original deal. Neither was throwing in the profits from the Crow's Nest —'

'I'm not a complete shit,' Hank exclaimed sharply, looking offended. 'I saw what you were going through. Of course I sold *The American Dream.* Every cent I've got is tied up in this —'

'There you are, then,' Todd interrupted with a shrug. 'Fifty-fifty.' He shot a sideways glance at Katrina, fearful that Hank's revelation would open old wounds.

But Katrina smiled. 'The point is we're selling it. That's all that matters.'

'Exactly,' he said, nodding agreement before looking at Hank. 'Thanks for telling me. It makes me feel less guilty.'

'But that's it. You shouldn't feel guilty. And no more talk about me getting money before you. We went into this as partners and that's the way we'll come out,' said Hank with a show of his old enthusiasm, as if having unburdened himself he felt able to be as optimistic as they were.

And they were optimistic. In fact the more they talked the more convinced they became that *Barzini at Paloma Blanca* would solve all their problems. With one marvellous idea, Katrina and Charlie had pulled them back from the brink, and what Todd found almost as exciting was that they were all talking with the same voice; they all agreed on the way forward. And it was true what he said, Hank's revelations had lifted his sense of guilt, at least about Hank. Charlie was another matter. He felt desperate pangs of guilt about Charlie, but all he could do was what he was doing and try to get the money back as fast as he could.

'So what's the next step?' Hank was asking eagerly. 'When do we sit down with these guys?'

'Tomorrow,' Katrina said eagerly. 'Not Ossie, he's gone to the States, but Mike Thompson gets here tomorrow. If he likes what he sees, they'll sign contracts. Convince him and we're in business.'

In his race against time to get a written offer for Moroni, Todd felt confident of success. He was sure Carrier would put his miserable offer in writing, and if Carrier proved difficult there was always this man Roos to fall back on. He felt certain that *one* of them would put an offer in writing. What he misjudged was that other deadlines would become even more pressing.

Time was always destined to defeat him. No one could have tried harder, or been more inventive, but the odds were always against him.

For a start Paloma Blanca would not be finished by February. They knew that, but as Hank said, 'This guy Thompson won't film everything, will he? If he gives us his priorities, we can work round the rest. The marina's almost finished. The yacht club will be finished by Christmas. The main hotel's a long way from ready, but it looks finished from the outside –'

'Like a film set!' cried Katrina. 'Of course. Mike will be in his element. He won't have any problems with that.'

And she was right because Paloma Blanca as good as sold itself the next day. Mike Thompson loved it. His flying visit – he arrived at mid-morning and was away again on the six o'clock flight – could not have gone better. A tall, loose-limbed, athletic man, full of nervous energy, he charged around the site, taking pictures and dictating notes into a tape-recorder, with Todd huffing and puffing behind him, trailing Katrina and Hank in their wake, all making lists of jobs to be done.

'What about this?' asked Thompson.

'No problem,' Todd assured him.

'What about that?'

'We'll fix it,' Hank promised.

Truly it was a triumph of positive thinking. And Katrina became ever more deeply involved, for after spending hours talking about camera platforms and angles, Thompson said he would need to liaise with someone on a daily basis, and they all looked at Katrina and the job became hers. Who else? Todd would be busy chasing Carrier and this other man Roos, Hank had more than enough on his plate, Charlie was still working four days a week for Bob Levit . . .

That summed it up, really. There weren't enough of them. There never had been. The project had suffered from inadequate manpower and money from the day it was born. Now the lack of another resource began to haunt them.

'Time's the problem,' Todd confessed to Thompson on the way back to the airport. 'But we'll manage, don't worry.'

He crossed his fingers as he thought of the enormous amount of work Hank had to do – and of his own problems awaiting him in London – and his need to get this written offer for Moroni.

To his surprise, Thompson was equally worried about time. 'The end of February's only three months away,' he pointed out. 'Believe me, three months is nothing when it comes to selling something like this.'

And so Todd listened to a recital of another man's problems. Like most people he had little idea of how television programmes are made, let alone sold. He listened fascinated as Thompson talked of slots in programming schedules and the long lead time between the commissioning of a show and its reaching the screen. 'They'll make an exception for this,' Thompson said confidently. 'It's a unique one-off with a lot of international appeal. Something like this might never be repeated. But I'll need to sell it hard. I'll have to beat the drum like crazy and that means starting tomorrow.'

'Tomorrow's Sunday,' Todd pointed out.

It was when Thompson laughed that he recognized a kindred spirit. Thompson listed television executives in half a dozen countries whom he could call at their homes, even on a Sunday. 'But I'm going ahead with this on our handshake,' he said with a hard look at Todd. 'And to be honest, that always makes me a bit anxious. I want firm contracts drawn up pretty damn fast.'

Todd agreed. He wanted proper contracts as well. The faster the better. So he accepted the suggestion of a meeting in London on Monday, despite his many other commitments.

It had been his intention to sort out the problems at Todd Motors on Monday.

On top of which there was a full day's work at Owen's.

Not forgetting his need to speak to Roos and if necessary fly over to Paris to meet him.

But when Thompson suggested a meeting, he said, 'Yes, okay, I can make it on Monday.'

The way he saw it, he had no choice. *Barzini at Paloma Blanca* was his salvation. He *had* to give it priority. But by ten o'clock on the Monday morning, back at his desk in London, he was already in trouble. Having left another message for Philippe Roos, he was delighted when Roos called back an hour later, even though it proved to be a strange conversation. Roos sounded cautious at first, almost evasive. After admitting that he had visited Paloma Blanca, he refused to say if he was acting for a potential buyer. He claimed he had been in Majorca on holiday and had called at the site only out of curiosity.

Oh yeah? thought Todd. *You weren't on holiday. That was a business trip if ever there was one.*

'Pity you weren't wearing your business hat,' he said. 'One of your clients could miss a big opportunity.'

Even when Roos learned that Paloma Blanca was for sale, he continued to sound reticent.

Throwing caution overboard, Todd embarked on a description of the Barzini concert and the media coverage it would attract, and then – at last – Roos began to respond. His attitude changed after that. Unable to disguise his interest, he began to ask questions.

Todd talked it up for all he was worth. 'Sure, half the world will see this on television . . . right, that's what it's called, *Barzini at Paloma Blanca*, great title, eh? Absolutely . . . screened in February, exactly at the start of the holiday season, just before Paloma Blanca is ready to open . . .'

His enthusiasm must have had some effect because ten minutes later Roos said he might be in his London office on Wednesday.

'I can't promise,' he said carefully. 'But if I do come over, maybe we could get together?'

Todd squirmed. He had planned to fly back to Majorca to see Carrier on Wednesday. But he told himself that Carrier was one hotelier, whereas Roos acted for hundreds. Roos was big league. So he asked, 'Can you let me know in the morning?'

'I think so.'

'Okay, I look forward to hearing from you.'

He was already in a cleft stick, wanting to be in two places at once. The next call, fifteen minutes later, aggravated the situation. It was from Mike Thompson, convening a two o'clock meeting at the Lincoln's Inn offices of Carling, Lewis and Woods, Ossie Keller's lawyers in London. 'I'll bring my lawyer,' he said. 'You bring your man and we'll try to sort this in double quick time. If Ossie's people hit any problems, they'll have to call him in New York.'

What could Todd say?

'Okay, fine,' he said. 'I'll be there.' Then he called his own solicitor, Bernard Francis in Hampstead. 'Bernie, I need you to drop everything . . .'

By that time, Katrina was already on her way into the office, having spent the first hour of the morning establishing a new routine with Mrs Bridges. 'It's very simple, Mrs Bridges, in future I shan't be here in the mornings because I'll be at my husband's office, so you'll have to let yourself in . . .'

He could have sent Katrina to the meeting with the lawyers. He could have delegated, but when a meeting promises to be that important, few men would be ready to leave it to anyone, even their wives. Besides, Bernard Francis knew next to nothing about Paloma Blanca. He couldn't even answer a question, let alone make a decision. And even Katrina's knowledge was fragmentary. And she lacked experience. And . . .

He *had* to go. So instead of dealing with his urgent troubles at Kilburn he cleared the most pressing matters on his desk, signed a few letters and half a dozen cheques – and went to Lincoln's Inn with Katrina.

'Delay always breeds danger,' cautioned Cervantes in *Don Quixote*, yet Todd wasn't delaying anything intentionally, he was running as fast as he could, but everything took *time*! Like

377

the meeting in Lincoln's Inn. It went well. Progress was made in a harmonious atmosphere, no one round the table had cause for complaint, but inevitably with three sets of lawyers representing three different interests, at six o'clock that evening their work was unfinished. 'But we've made excellent progress,' said either Carling or Lewis. 'I suggest we reconvene at ten in the morning.'

Todd groaned under his breath. He had no alternative except to agree, but as he nodded that old advice of Sam's came to mind. 'A business is like a vegetable patch,' Sam had said. 'Tend it every day and you'll live like a king. Neglect it and you'll end up a pauper.'

His neglect of his motor businesses was not deliberate. The way he saw it he had no choice. Staying alive and out of prison ranked top of his priorities, and to do that he had to sell Paloma Blanca for the best price he could get. He was working flat out to that end, but the problems piling up in Owen's and Todd Motors were to prove his undoing.

What made it so galling was that he was winning. Progress was remarkable. After leaving the lawyers, they went for a drink with Mike Thompson at a pub in Chancery Lane. Mike was in ebullient mood. Confident that work on the contracts would be completed in the morning, he was more anxious to talk about his Sunday telephone calls. 'I had a fantastic response,' he said, grinning from ear to ear. 'With a bit of luck I'll have at least the BBC and RAI signed up by next week!'

In all truth they were moving faster than any of them had a right to expect.

Thompson was now so confident that he had leaked the news to two newspaper columnists. 'Chums of mine,' he said. 'We'll get a good story in the papers tomorrow. The truth is I need to generate some publicity. In fact I meant to say to you, as soon as contracts are signed, we ought to call a press conference to make a formal announcement. Can you set one up?'

Todd raised his eyebrows. Press conferences were not things which happened at his end of the motor trade.

'Naturally I'll help,' said Thompson. 'But you should host

it. After all, you represent Paloma Blanca in this.' A slight hesitancy came into his voice. 'I don't wish to be rude, so don't take offence,' he said. 'But are you any good at banging a drum? You know, at creating publicity?'

Todd's eyes gleamed. 'What do you have in mind?'

It all sounded easy when Thompson explained, and of course Todd, being Todd, wanted the biggest, most lavish press conference money could buy. He wanted Barzini to fly in from New York. He wanted to invite every music editor and music correspondent in London. 'Is London enough?' he asked as he carried another round of drinks back from the bar. 'What about the overseas media? How do we get them? Do they have representatives in London?' He wanted all the travel press invited. 'You bet. They'll be writing articles for publication in the New Year. Early New Year is a big time for booking holidays.'

So he involved himself in yet another commitment, depriving the motor businesses of even more time, but of course it made sense – after all the motor businesses were doomed unless he recovered his investment in Paloma Blanca. So he took that decision without thinking. It was the next one which stopped him.

'How about a week on Wednesday?' Thompson suggested, his pocket diary open in front of him. 'December the seventeenth. We can't hold it before because there's too much to do, and we can't hold it any later because Christmas is looming.' He groaned at the thought, 'God, how I hate Christmas. Everything stops. You can't reach anyone . . .'

Katrina felt numb as she listened. Never in her whole life had it seemed less like Christmas. Even though the pub was decorated with sprigs of holly and streamers of tinsel, she'd not given Christmas a thought. Past Christmases had been spent baking mince pies, decorating the house and dressing the tree. Sophie and Gloria came to dinner with their men of the moment, and Toddy dressed up as Santa Claus for the West Hampstead Hospital.

'The seventeenth,' she murmured, looking at Todd. Earlier, during the journey to Lincoln's Inn, he had told her about Roos and his decision not to go to Majorca on Wednesday.

379

Instinctively she had flinched, hating the delay, despite his promise to go on Thursday or Friday. 'It will probably suit Carrier better,' he had said optimistically. 'Give him time to get over his trip. We'll still have time to spare. We've got until the seventeenth.'

'The seventeenth,' Todd repeated, returning her worried look, encouraging her with a little grin. 'It's okay with me if it's all right with Katrina. She'll have to do most of the work.'

After which they concentrated on matters like booking a suitable venue, sending invitations to a list of people Thompson would provide, arranging for photographs of Paloma Blanca to be mounted on display stands, organizing food and drink and everything else.

As she wrote down the list of jobs to be done, Katrina wished she could have involved Charlie, even though it was out of the question. She had spoken to her twice, once from Majorca after Thompson's flying visit, and again last night when they returned to London. Charlie had sounded . . . Katrina frowned and tried to define exactly how Charlie had sounded. Excited, pleased, envious to have missed out on the triumph of Mike Thompson's trip, but also a bit worried . . .

'I'll ask Gloria and Sophie to help,' she said. 'I'll call them in the morning.' She smiled at Thompson and explained, 'Friends of mine. It's all hands to the pump, isn't it?'

And so the day edged towards a close. Monday the eighth of December, leaving Todd little more than a week before his next meeting with Moroni.

Without a hint of the troubles to come, Tuesday could not have started better. When Herbert arrived at the house, Todd and Katrina were both ready and waiting, intent on snatching an hour at the office before going to Lincoln's Inn. The surprise came when Todd opened the front door. Herbert stood on the step, flourishing his newspaper. 'Bloody hell, Boss! You're a dark horse you are. I didn't know about this.'

And there, on page seven, was a photograph of Paloma Blanca, alongside a picture of Enrico Barzini.

INTERNATIONAL CONCERT AT
NEW LUXURY RESORT
Paloma Blanca in Majorca, planned as the Mediterranean's
most luxurious holiday retreat, will start life in February
by staging one of the most glittering concerts of the year.

The story continued for a third of the page. Todd read it aloud all the way into the office. He read it twice, some of it three times. He hugged Katrina. 'Holy Christ! You're an impresario!' And she hugged him, and then hugged herself, and for a few moments they forgot Moroni and their desperate race against time. 'Wait until I see Roos tomorrow,' Todd grinned triumphantly. 'And I'll take it out to Majorca to show Carrier. Can you imagine his reaction? This'll put the price up for sure. It's just what we needed.'

It seemed such a good omen that they arrived at the office in high spirits. Katrina settled herself in the general office and began to call one banqueting manager after another in her search to find a venue for the press conference, while Todd sat at his desk and went through the post with Sally.

Sally was angry about events in Kilburn. 'You must do something,' she said, anxious and flushed. 'They're fiddling their expenses, I know that for a fact, so there's no telling what else they're getting up to.'

'I'll go across this afternoon,' he promised. 'After I finish with the lawyers.'

Among the pile of post, Sally had left one envelope unopened. It was from Paris, marked 'Private and Confidential'. Inside was a letter from Lapiere, requesting a copy of a written offer for Paloma Blanca no later than the seventeenth.

As agreed, the letter said, as if the agreement had been made over a convivial drink instead of under threat of death. The needless reminder brought Todd out in a sweat. And made him angry. He felt like getting on the phone and shouting, *For fuck's sake! Get off my back! I'm doing all I can.*

But after a cup of coffee he was calm enough for other thoughts. It would do no harm to tell Lapiere about *Barzini at Paloma Blanca*. It might provide some reassurance. And Lapiere *might* be a tempering influence with Moroni. It was a long shot, not one which filled him with confidence, but even long shots were worth playing, so he played it, and to his surprise had a not unreasonable conversation with Lapiere.

The little Frenchman was hugely impressed about Barzini. He was a fan. Todd was so surprised that on impulse he suggested, 'Come over to the press conference next Wednesday. There's a chance he'll be there.'

For a moment Lapiere fell silent. Then he queried the date and fell silent again.

Todd knew what he was thinking. 'I'll have the offer in writing by then,' he said confidently. 'Don't worry. I'm working flat out to sell Paloma Blanca.'

Which evoked a curious response. 'I know,' said Lapiere. Not 'That's good' or 'Good luck'. Just 'I know.'

Todd thought nothing of it at the time. It was only later, rushing to Lincoln's Inn with Katrina, when he was playing the conversation back in his mind, marvelling that someone who worked for Moroni could be a music lover, that it occurred to him that Lapiere's 'I know' had sounded odd. Not that he had time to dwell on the thought because something else occurred to him at the same time. 'Blast! Roos promised to call me.' He glanced at his watch. 'Oh well, not to worry, I'll phone him from Kilburn.'

But even that was not to be. He never got to Kilburn. First everyone at the meeting wanted to talk about the story in the papers, so it was half an hour before they settled down to their work, and after that the discussions dragged on and on, through a working lunch of sandwiches brought in from the pub across the road, until at three o'clock, impatient with progress, Todd took Francis aside. 'Jesus, Bernie, can't you hurry things up? Is all this nit-picking really necessary? How much longer will it take?'

Francis was offended. 'We're making bloody good progress,' he protested. 'At this rate we'll have the contracts sewn up by tonight.'

And he was right. At eight o'clock, after six different drafts had been typed up and found wanting, version number seven met universal acceptance. Pens were extracted from pockets, flourished in the air, held poised over paper, and the contracts were signed. *Barzini at Paloma Blanca* had officially come into being!

The lawyers marvelled at what they had accomplished in so little time. Carling sighed with satisfaction: 'Thank goodness we don't often have to work under that sort of pressure.'

'Pressure!' Todd snorted on the way home. 'They don't know the meaning of pressure. Lawyers make mountains out of molehills. This deal was agreed with Thompson in Majorca.'

'Oh, thanks very much,' Katrina said with feigned indignation. 'Forgive me, but I thought I agreed it in Jersey.'

He laughed, and she laughed, and once again for a brief moment it was possible to forget their worries. For a moment they were simply a husband and wife, like any other married couple. 'Going home to our house,' Katrina said softly as the car crunched up the drive. When they walked up the steps, she reached for his hand. 'I remember our first year here,' she said. 'Before that holiday in Majorca. It seemed to be just us in those days, just you and me.' She stopped short of saying, *Not thugs like Moroni*. Instead she looked at him and said, 'That was a good year, wasn't it?'

He paused, the key still in the lock, the door half-open. 'Don't worry,' he said, drawing her into his arms. 'We'll have lots of other good years.'

But it seemed less likely ten minutes later.

'He sounded ever so angry,' Sally said on the phone. 'He called three times. The last time he said if he couldn't speak to you he wanted to speak to our accountant. So I gave him Manny's number. I hope that was all right.'

'Yeah, that was okay.'

'Manny phoned back to say he's fixed an appointment for eleven in the morning. He said he'll come with you.'

Katrina watched his face as he put down the telephone. 'Problems?'

Todd shrugged. 'It's Smithson at the bank. He wants a meeting tomorrow. It's nothing to worry about.'

But he was wrong. Smithson was going to give him a great deal to worry about.

'This is absolutely the last straw!' Smithson pointed at the newspaper. He had been reading it when they arrived, or rather re-reading it, since he seemed to know every word of the article about *Barzini at Paloma Blanca*. At the moment the paper was on the desk, but he had picked it up several times, only to slap it down again with a mixture of fury and disgust.

Wearily, Todd ran a hand through his hair. 'I just told you, the concert won't cost us a penny. It's not a question of me spending more money. And it's not a speculative venture. Besides, I thought you'd be pleased about us selling Paloma Blanca.'

Half an hour of Smithson was as much as he could take. He had never liked him. In his opinion Smithson was a smug, tight-arsed, self-righteous bastard. They bristled across the desk at each other, scarcely able to conceal their mutual hostility. Todd felt the loss of old Harry Larkins more keenly than ever.

'This hotel venture's nothing to do with the bank,' Smithson snorted. 'We made our views clear at the outset. We wanted no part of it. But you've used funds from your motor business to support it and you show no sign of stopping. Now you're wasting even more money staging a concert!'

Todd could have hit him. 'I'm not staging it,' he said through gritted teeth. 'Mike Thompson's organization is staging it. Read those!' He pointed to the contracts which he had brought along with him. 'They were only signed yesterday, but everything's there in black and white.'

Smithson pushed them away with the tips of his fingers.

Todd tried again. 'Anyone would think it was bad news in the paper. It's not. It's good news and that's only the start. We'll have this press conference next week, and keep building up the excitement until the concert in February, then we'll hold the auction. By that time every hotelier in the world will have heard of Paloma Blanca –'

'I'm not waiting until then. I want action now.'

Husbanding his patience, Todd stuck at his task. 'Fine,' he said, as agreeably as he could. 'I've already started the ball rolling. I'm setting up meetings with all sorts of people. If you hadn't wanted me here this morning I'd probably be sitting down with Arlsruher, Wormack and Roos right now. And I'm flying out to Majorca on Friday to see —'

'And who's paying for that?'

'For what?'

'Your air fare? All these extra expenses. On top of everything else, we've now got a press conference to pay for. Spend, spend, spend! That's all you do, Mr Todd, and it's nothing to do with Todd Motors or Owen's. You're obsessed with this place in Majorca —'

'I'm *selling* it, for God's sake!' Todd retorted, as the heat rose in his face.

'You *hope* to sell it. After this concert. That's what you said. Meanwhile you expect the bank to continue to fund you. Well it's not on, Mr Todd. It's not on! Forget about this concert in February —'

'How can I forget it?' Todd's voice rose in a howl. 'We'll have bookings coming out of our ears after this television exposure. Big hoteliers will fall over themselves to make us an offer. We'll sell out at a profit and our problems are over!'

'And how much will it cost us in the meantime?' Smithson demanded. He held up a hand. 'No, let me tell you. The answer's nothing, because I'm cutting our lending to you with effect from today.'

Todd rocked back in his chair, as if struck by a blow. He cast a sideways look of alarm at Manny.

Smithson said, 'I've asked you to cut back time and again —'

'I'll clear the whole bloody lot after this auction!'

'But I want it cleared now!'

'Don't be so bloody daft!' Todd retorted. 'I *can't* clear it now!'

Manny leaned forward in his chair. 'Mr Smithson,' he said, in a soft and reasonable voice. 'Mr Todd needs time, that's all. Apart from his other plans, his wife is about to inherit a very large sum from her father's estate.'

'Right,' Todd exclaimed hotly. 'And that'll be a fortune when it comes.'

'It needs to be,' Smithson said sharply. 'You owe us two million, which is a lot more than we ever agreed to lend you.'

There could be no meeting of minds. Smithson was not open to persuasion. He had made his decision before they arrived, and he remained adamant. 'The only cheques we'll meet in future are those for your motor businesses, and even for those I'll want to see invoices. Cheques for anything else we shall bounce.'

Todd was taken aback. It took him a moment to find his voice. 'But that's crazy,' he protested. 'The more we get at the auction, the more goes back into the motor business. That's obvious isn't it?' Without waiting for an answer, he hurried on, 'If I get eighteen million I can pay everyone off, including the two million I owe you. And I'll get a lot *more* than eighteen million at an auction. So I've just got to keep going until then –'

'That's your problem. I'm only interested in what happens now. If you had a firm offer now it might be different –'

Todd spluttered. 'For God's sake! We've already had one offer.'

'Oh?' Smithson exclaimed sharply. 'You didn't tell me. What have you been offered?'

Cursing under his breath, Todd put his head in his hands. Then he tried to explain that Carrier's bid was only an opening shot: 'No one starts high, do they? That's why I'm going to see him –'

But any chance to salvage the situation was lost.

'Nine million!' Smithson's voice rose to a screech. 'You just admitted you need twice that. Dear God, this is even worse than I thought!'

Nothing could have retrieved the situation after that. Smithson pounded on his desk, Todd protested, but a meeting which had started badly concluded in disaster when Smithson said to Manny, 'I want immediate proposals on how this debt will be discharged. Immediate proposals, do you understand? In writing. I'm sick and tired of this account.'

He addressed Manny, not Todd, making the proposals Manny's responsibility, a responsibility which Manny accepted simply as a means of ending the meeting.

They left the bank in an atmosphere of silent hostility. Todd didn't even bother to shake hands.

Afterwards they adjourned to a coffee shop across the road. Their spirits could not have been lower. Finding a free table in one corner, Todd collapsed into a seat while Manny went to the counter for two cups of coffee.

Todd smouldered. He was grinding his teeth when Manny set a cup down in front of him.

'What does he expect?' asked Manny as he pulled a chair back from the table. 'I should make up some figures? You need time and time he won't give you.'

Time! Todd laughed bitterly. He'd be dead in a week unless Carrier or Roos came up with a piece of paper. And now this! Everything was happening at once! He still hadn't had a chance to go to Kilburn. His head ached with conflicting priorities. 'Pompous bastard,' he muttered as he reached for the sugar. 'If he starts bouncing cheques –'

'He will. You heard him. You daren't spend another penny on Paloma Blanca. Even this press conference –'

'How can I stop now?' Todd groaned. 'Katrina's already booked the Park Lane Hilton. Besides what could I say to Mike Thompson? How could I explain it? Anyway, we *need* this press conference. We've got to keep going. The auction's my only way out.'

'But Smithson won't wait. We need a new banker fast.'

'So find one. We went to see that guy Drury but he said no.'

Manny sighed and peered out of the window which was steamy with condensation. 'We weren't so far off with Drury. So he said no, but there's a no and a no. I got the feeling he wants to be coaxed. You know what worried him? Paloma Blanca.'

'You and him both,' Todd scowled. 'You've never believed in it.'

'Who said I did? You're right. You running Paloma Blanca I've never believed in, but this television thing I believe in. You I believe in. And you *selling* Paloma Blanca?' Manny's eyes gleamed. 'That's different. That I believe in. I want a suit, I go to a tailor, I want a good meal, I go to a restaurant, I want something sold . . .' His face creased into a look of approval. 'You're the best salesman I know. So if I go back to Drury and say you're selling Paloma Blanca, then maybe he'll refinance you and pay Smithson off.'

Todd looked at him. 'D'you think there's a chance?'

'If I can take him some good news there's a chance.'

'You mean like an offer?'

'What else? But not from this schmuck in Majorca who wants to buy at half-price.'

To avoid Manny's eye, Todd looked down at his coffee. He felt his hopes fade. He was tempted to tell him about Moroni and the threat to his life, but he stopped, knowing that to explain about Moroni would mean explaining about Charlie. The whole wretched story would come out. Charlie deserved better. She was depending on his silence. He had even felt bad about telling Hank. The fewer people who knew the safer she was. So instead he explained about his plan to offer Carrier topping-up rights. 'I wanted to get the ball rolling, that's all.'

'At nine million?' said Manny with obvious contempt. 'You're starting too low.'

Todd stared with dull eyes. *Nine million keeps me alive.*

Manny jerked his head in the direction of the bank across the road. 'He'll pull the plug, Toddy. You must come back with a better offer from Carrier. Something nearer the real value. Get me that and I'll get you a new banker.'

Todd sat in silence. The stakes were being raised every day.

'Without that,' said Manny. 'I don't think you can survive. Smithson will go for you. To get his money he'll try to snatch everything, Todd Motors, Owen's, your house, he'll take the whole lot.'

'It went fine,' he lied to Katrina when he returned to the office. 'Nothing to worry about. Manny's going to deal with Smithson from now on, to leave us free to get on with other things.'

Luckily there were plenty of other things to keep Katrina

388

busy. And to keep Gloria busy since she had come into the office to help. By mid-afternoon, they had addressed 130 invitations to the press conference. They were working as fast as they could, but Mike Thompson's list contained over 300 names.

'We'll have to go faster to catch the post,' said Katrina, reaching for another envelope.

Without a word, Sally joined in, taking a batch of cards to her desk.

Everyone was working flat out, and Todd was *thinking* flat out. Could he get a written offer from Carrier for more than nine million? And where was Roos? There had been no word from him. Todd called the London office of Arlsruher, Wormack and Roos, but Roos was not there. He called the Paris office who said Roos was away on business. 'So let me speak to someone else,' he demanded. And he did speak to other people, both in London and Paris, but nobody seemed capable of making a decision. He gave them copious details of Paloma Blanca, he urged them to discuss the matter with their clients, now, today, without delay, he warned them they would miss a wonderful opportunity – but all to no avail, for they all said the same thing: that the matter would be passed to Mr Roos immediately on his return. *When* he would return, and from *where* were questions which went unanswered.

And as if to underline that time was running out, Hank called to say that the earliest Carrier could see them was Saturday morning.

'Saturday?' Todd echoed in dismay. 'I've only got until Wednesday.'

But Hank had pushed as hard as he dared.

By Thursday, Todd was calling every major real estate firm in London. None were as big as Arlsruher, Wormack and Roos in the hotel market, but he talked them through the project, told them about the Barzini concert, invited them to the press conference and promised to put details in the post.

He made another unsuccessful attempt to contact Roos on Friday morning before leaving for the airport to catch a plane to Majorca. Katrina was still ignorant of what had happened with Smithson. She was so worried about getting a written offer for Moroni that Todd was afraid to tell her that Manny needed a higher offer almost as quickly. So he concentrated on making light of his task: 'Sure, Carrier's anxious to see us. There won't be a problem. I'll be back tomorrow evening with everything in writing, don't worry.'

Luckily she was too busy to dwell on the subject, and after kissing him goodbye let Herbert take him off to the airport while she turned back to what she was doing – which was telephoning everyone on the guest list for the press conference. Gloria was doing the same, urging and coaxing journalists and travel agents alike to come and hear all about *Barzini at Paloma Blanca*.

In fact on that Friday afternoon, everyone was working flat out. In Jersey, during a break from discussing the project with television companies all over the world, Mike Thompson was talking to Ossie Keller in New York. 'No, no, no!' Ossie shouted when it was suggested that Barzini fly to London for the press conference. 'I don't *care* about Concorde. It would be too exhausting. Enrico needs his strength for his performance.'

With the skill of a diplomat Thompson backed off. Instead he suggested that Barzini film a five-minute interview which could be shown at the press conference. Mollified, Ossie agreed. 'Okay, we could do that on Sunday. And I'll issue a statement from here for the papers next Wednesday, the same day you announce it in London.'

On the site in Majorca, Hank was explaining the list of priorities to Don Antonio and the builders. Everyone marvelled at what was to happen. *Barzini at Paloma Blanca*! Don Antonio's eyes gleamed at the prospect of his buildings being seen all over the world. 'But only,' Hank warned as he picked up the schedule of work to be done, 'if we can give Mike Thompson what he wants.'

In Paris, Vito Sartene was putting the telephone down after a frustrating conversation with Aldo Moroni. He shrugged at his cousin Pietro Carlioni on the other side of the bar counter. 'Maybe we go to London next Wednesday, maybe we don't. He don't know yet.'

At a bank in Threadneedle Street, Manny was discussing Todd's business with Drury. 'Sure, he overreached himself. You saying I don't know? You think *he* doesn't? But who do you want for a client, some schmuck dead from the neck up or someone with balls? He's still a young man. The experience will be good for him, he'll be more cautious in future . . .'

And one other person was working flat out. Philippe Roos. His meeting with Lapiere at the beginning of the month had given him a head start on selling Paloma Blanca. He had set wheels in motion immediately after his meeting in Montmartre. Having decided to sell Paloma Blanca for seventeen and a half million, he had done his usual trick of talking the price down with the vendor and up with the purchaser. 'A snip at twenty million,' he had told his friends at Hilton and others at Sheraton and yet more at Hyatt. 'Give me the word and I'll steal it for you. The price will double when this place becomes known.'

Now, to his horror, it was about to become known. Worse, it was about to become famous. The headlines about *Barzini at Paloma Blanca* had come as a shock. And an even bigger shock had been this guy Todd on the phone demanding an arm and a leg for 'one of the most famous hotels in the world'.

Of course, he had checked with Lapiere. 'I thought you were the vendor,' he complained. 'I thought I'd be dealing with you.'

But Lapiere had pretended a misunderstanding. He had no objections to what Todd was doing. He even knew about this concert with Enrico Barzini. He couldn't stop talking about it. He was hoping to be invited.

Roos had been compelled to get back to his clients and to explain what was happening. He had told them all about *Barzini at Paloma Blanca.* He put the blame on them. 'I knew something like this would happen,' he shouted down the telephone. 'You had a chance to move in on this before this hoopla. Isn't my judgement vindicated as always? What's the point of me consulting my crystal ball if you guys don't act when I tell you?'

And while he scolded, he prepared his next move. 'They're talking about screening this Barzini concert in eleven countries. Eleven, for Chrissakes! Including the States and Japan. Plus the video! Plus the CD. You can't *buy* that kind of publicity. You bet your sweet ass the price will go up. I'll *still* steal it for you, but I want your authority to talk real money when I sit down with these people. Okay, talk it over at your end and call me back . . .'

Which was why, after similar conversations with his six biggest clients, Philippe Roos was avoiding speaking to Todd. 'Let him sweat,' he told his secretary when she reported Todd's repeated phone calls. 'I should have an offer in my back pocket by Monday. I'll be ready to talk to him then.'

Not once did he doubt the deal would be his. The price would go up, but so what? He had warned his buyers. They wouldn't blame him. He abandoned his earlier private estimate of seventeen and a half million. With all this publicity, Paloma Blanca would be booked out from the day it opened its doors. And if that happened it would be worth at least another eight million. From Roos's point of view, the deal got better and better. In his mind, he settled on a new price. Twenty-five million. So he called his clients yet again. 'I reckon you should be prepared to go up to thirty million for this.' And when they demurred, he said, 'Don't say I didn't warn you. That's right, you think about it some more, but I need your instructions real fast.' Meanwhile he calculated his cut. If he took three per cent from the buyers and three per cent from this man Todd, he would make a very satisfactory one and a half million himself.

He was unworried that Todd might contact other agents. Already ahead of the game, he was in any case better connected than most of his competitors. He had so often beaten them that he was contemptuous. But he did overlook one possibility – that José Carrier would enter the fray. The thought never entered his head. José Carrier was small beer. Carrier had struggled to raise the money for the Bella Vista, and that had gone for a great deal less than Paloma Blanca would fetch. Carrier was an independent operator, not one of the big corporations. In fact so dismissive of Carrier was Roos that he had forgotten their chance meeting in Palma airport.

But Carrier had not forgotten. Carrier blessed that meeting whenever he thought of it, and he thought of it often as he looked out across the manicured grounds of the Bella Vista. It was a fine hotel. It boasted a championship golf course, twelve tennis courts, four squash courts, three swimming pools, a superb restaurant, a beauty parlour, six shops which sold expensive clothes and souvenirs, a sauna, a gymnasium and a coffee shop which stayed open all hours. The Bella Vista boasted every facility. Except one. Set inland, it lacked access to the sea. 'Who wants a beach?' Carrier would scoff dismissively when the subject arose. 'Don't you know the Mediterranean's the most polluted sea in the world? The water's filthy! And diseases you don't catch in the sea, you'll catch on the beach. I'm telling you, even for money you wouldn't mix with those people.'

But it wasn't the lack of a beach which upset his guests. It was the lack of a marina. Many of the regular guests had boats of their own. Gin palaces mostly, but a few yachts among them. And of those who lacked boats quite a number liked playing in boats. What they disliked was having to park their boat at the end of the day, get into a car with guests whom they were trying to impress, and drive half an hour to the Bella Vista's superb restaurant for dinner. That was a bore. They disliked that very much. They disliked it so much that if an equally fine restaurant were to open as part of a marina, they would desert in droves at the drop of an anchor.

The development at Paloma Blanca had come as a bombshell to Carrier. He'd not even known the site was for sale. He had cursed his advisers. 'We're Majorcans!' he had shouted at his lawyer, which was not quite true since Carrier's father had come from South Africa and his mother from Ibiza. 'It's our island. You'd think we'd know what was going on better than some American beach bum! Now he's gone into partnership with that fat little car dealer from London . . .'

For over a year mere mention of Paloma Blanca had been enough to send Carrier into a rage. Then various events occurred almost on top of each other. First a rumour had reached him that the American and his English partner were in financial difficulties. It was obvious – the American had sold his big yacht, the Englishman had sold his small one – their money was running out. Then Carrier bumped into Roos at the airport. True, Roos was tight-lipped about what he was doing in Majorca, but Carrier knew that if Roos was on the island someone was selling. And that very same evening a banker friend of his dined at the Bella Vista and mentioned that the fat little Englishman was trying to raise a mortgage on his villa. Carrier had persuaded his banker friend to invent difficulties, to stall, to pretend that such a decision had to be taken in Madrid. And after that Carrier believed it was simply a matter of time . . .

Undismayed to have his first offer rejected, he had settled back to wait. After all he was the premier hotelier on the island. 'They'll come to me,' he told himself.

And now they were coming.

CHAPTER THIRTEEN

THE MEETING WENT BADLY for all of them. It went badly for Carrier even before it started. The local papers and broadcasting station had picked up on the Barzini concert. 'Majorca TV show to be seen all over the world,' ran one headline. In his bath on that Saturday morning, Carrier actually heard a reporter say, 'Paloma Blanca is set to become the most luxurious and fashionable hotel on the island.' Carrier shivered in his bath water. He was a proud man. Some said he was a pompous man. Certainly he liked people to know he was the leading hotelier in Majorca. In fact he never stopped telling them. Now his status was threatened as well as his pocket.

Naturally he had sent his spies to Paloma Blanca, but until that morning he had never set foot there himself. After touring the site for two hours, his heart was in his boots. Paloma Blanca was everything he had been told – and then some.

But while Carrier struggled to hide his dismay, Todd and Hank were having to work hard to conceal their own anxiety. Todd had told Hank all about Smithson. Arriving the previous evening, he had recounted word for word his conversation with Manny. 'I must get a better offer. Manny can't keep me in business without one.' Hank had been appalled. 'Carrier will hate this idea of an auction. Now we're asking him to swallow that *and* come in at a much higher offer. He ain't going to like it.'

And Hank was right. Carrier disliked it intensely.

By now they were in the third hour of a meeting which had started in the yacht club at ten-thirty. Then had followed a tour of the marina, so near completion that leases on some of the berths had been sold. Carrier was visibly startled to see fifty boats at the quayside.

'Oh sure,' Hank had said breezily. 'The yacht club will be ready for a grand opening on New Year's Eve. We're having a big party. You must come.'

'Thank you,' Carrier declined stiffly. 'We shall be having our own celebrations.'

But his smug superiority changed to concern when they toured the main hotel. Huge arc lamps had been erected to extend the working day beyond dusk, and he saw a hive of activity wherever he looked. 'All the public rooms will be finished in time for the concert,' said Hank, who had provided a non-stop commentary every step of the way. 'But I want to show you one of the suites.' It was the only one finished; the rest were concrete shells, as Hank freely admitted. 'But all the furnishings and fittings are in storage. Don Antonio organized that months ago.'

Todd remembered the heart-searching decision. Designed by Don Antonio, the unique furnishings and fittings had been hand made by specialist craftsmen who had wanted payment up front. It was the decision which had cost Hank *The American Dream* and Todd *The Sea Princess*, plus a lot more money besides – but as he followed Hank into the suite and saw the look on Carrier's face, Todd counted the money well spent. The Bella Vista's days as Majorca's most luxurious hotel were numbered – and Carrier knew it.

So they returned to the yacht club which was smelling faintly of paint and resin and polish, and where Max was waiting to take their order for luncheon.

'You'll be in the driving seat at the auction,' said Todd as they took their seats at the table. 'You won't have a thing to worry about.'

'No, no,' Carrier protested. 'I don't like the idea of this auction. That's not the way I do business.'

'So pay us the right price now and we'll scrap the auction.'

Carrier looked offended. 'I've already increased my offer,' he said frostily.

And he had. After three hours of talking, he had increased

his offer to twelve million. It was a substantial increase, but far from enough.

Todd talked of the Barzini concert and what it would do for them. Paloma Blanca would be fully booked out. He talked of the value of the video market as a continuing source of fame. 'Not to forget the CD audience,' he said, waving his arms to suggest that soon the whole world would be listening to *Barzini at Paloma Blanca*.

But Carrier stuck at his offer of twelve million.

Half-way through the meal, Todd was so desperate that he said, 'Come on, José, Paloma Blanca's worth twice that and you know it. You're not even giving us a chance to get our money back.'

It was the wrong thing to say. It betrayed his anxiety, and he kicked himself, but what was said was said and could not be taken back.

Carrier had to concentrate to hide his excitement. His heart pounded. The rumours were true. These two weren't just in difficulties, they were on the verge of going broke. He sensed a wonderful opportunity. Ownership of Paloma Blanca would make him Majorca's premier hotelier for the rest of his life. With the Bella Vista *and* Paloma Blanca, no one could catch him. But twelve million was his absolute limit. It was all the money he had and all he could borrow. The idea of an auction terrified him. He had no doubt the price would go up. He would lose out to one of the big international hotel groups . . .

When lunch ended Todd was no further forward than when he sat down. 'So okay,' he said with feigned indifference. 'We can't do business. Pity, you'll just have to take your chance at the auction with everyone else.'

Which brought Carrier out in a sweat. He *had* to buy Paloma Blanca before it went to auction.

Of that he was certain, but how? They would not accept twelve million, but he sensed the prize was within reach. If he could just go a little higher. A vague idea began to form in his mind. He would take in a partner. It was not what he wanted, but it was the best he could do. It was *all* he could do. His only hope. 'Tell you what,' he said slowly to keep the tension out of his voice. 'Juan Gonzales is coming out from Seville tomorrow. You've heard of him, of course?'

Hank frowned. 'The Gonzales on the bottles?'

Carrier smiled. The biggest wine grower in Spain, Juan Gonzales was an extremely wealthy man. He *might* be interested in becoming a sleeping partner. After all, Carrier was already a good customer and Paloma Blanca would be another outlet for the Gonzales wines. The idea gave Carrier enough hope to say, 'Juan's a good friend of mine. I'd like to discuss this with him. Why don't we meet again on Monday?'

Monday! Todd hesitated, anxious about what had to be done in London, but above all worried about having a written offer by Wednesday. He had given up on Roos. What sickened him was that by the end of their one and only conversation Roos had sounded interested, really keen on the project, but ever since then . . .

'I'm only asking for another couple of days,' Carrier said pleasantly.

You don't know what you're asking, Todd thought gloomily. *Every day counts.* He glanced at Hank, who responded with a barely perceptible shrug. Trying to gain an advantage, he said, 'Okay, José, I'll stay over until Monday, but on one condition.'

Carrier looked at him.

'When we meet you put your offer in writing.'

Yet again it was the wrong thing to say.

Carrier's eyes gleamed. His suspicions were confirmed. Rising from his chair, he held out his hand. 'How can I accept conditions before we agree on a price? Let's see how we get on, eh?' He smiled, 'Why not come up to the Bella Vista for lunch? Say about one?'

Afterwards Todd cursed himself for his clumsiness. 'A rookie salesman would have done better,' he confessed to Hank. 'I pushed him too hard. I blew it.'

And later when he called Katrina he tried to avoid telling her. But she insisted upon knowing. He put the best gloss he could on events. 'He's up to twelve million now and he's gone off to raise some more money. So don't worry. I'll get the written offer on Monday.'

Luckily she was so busy that she accepted his confidence at face value. 'Great,' she said, impressed by the fact that Carrier's offer had increased at the rate of a million pounds an hour. 'There's no telling what you'll have him up to by Monday.' Meanwhile, having discovered that many journalists were available at weekends, she and Gloria were continuing their telephone campaign. 'We've a hundred and four acceptances so far,' she reported triumphantly. 'And we'll keep phoning all day tomorrow.'

At least it gave her something to do. Todd had nothing to do on the Sunday, except worry. At around lunchtime he called Jersey, hoping that a chat with Charlie would revive his spirits. But that hope was dashed when he spoke to her. Yes, she was excited about the press conference. She had already arranged with Katrina to be there to help. 'Bob's being very good about giving me time off,' she said, and then unexpectedly burst into tears.

Tears would have unsettled him at any time, more than ever on the end of the telephone, and worst of all when the tears were Charlie's. Charlie of all people! Not that she wept for long. Within a few moments she had pulled herself together, but it was clear that the strain of keeping her guilty secret was becoming too big a burden for her conscience to bear. 'It's just that Bob trusts me so implicitly,' she said. 'You know? He's such a straight guy. It makes me feel an absolute cow.'

Then Todd heard the worst words of all.

'I'm not blaming you, Toddy, honestly. Don't think that for a moment. It was my decision as much as yours, but . . . well . . . I don't think I can live with this on my conscience until the auction. Not until March. I'll just have to tell him.'

Todd's heart almost gave out. Hunched over the telephone, he talked and coaxed and persuaded, but he sensed he was hearing the truth. He doubted that Charlie could last until March. She'd have a nervous breakdown before then. He remembered Katrina expressing concern after talking to her. He had dismissed her worries as groundless. 'Nonsense,' he had said. 'Charlie's all right.' But once again Katrina was right and he had been wrong.

Finally he said, 'Charlie, let's talk about it after the press conference. We'll all be there. Hank's coming over, and we'll put our heads together. What do you say? We'll come up with something. Don't worry.'

Afterwards he was struck by the irony of telling Charlie not to worry and Katrina not to worry and Hank not to worry, while he was so worried himself that he could hardly think straight. As for going out to dinner on Wednesday – *I'll be dead on Wednesday unless I get this offer in writing.*

He called Manny, hoping progress might have been made with Drury. Manny replied with a question: 'You want the good news or the bad news?'

The good news was that Drury had accepted an invitation to the press conference. The bad was that he was still undecided about Manny's refinancing proposals. Even after hearing about Carrier increasing his offer, Manny remained doubtful. 'Twelve million's not enough, Toddy. Another no is something I can't risk at this stage. Drury's tempted, but you need a bigger figure than that.' He laughed and tried to sound encouraging. 'I've still got faith. You'll do it tomorrow.'

But Monday brought more bad news.

Carrier called first thing to say that Gonzales had been delayed in Madrid. 'He didn't get here yesterday, but I'm expecting him later today. This afternoon as a matter of fact.'

Todd was furious. 'You're jerking me off! I can't hang about here. I'm going back to London this evening.' But even as his temper exploded he knew he would stay. He had no alternative. His only chance of a written offer rested with Carrier, and as he listened to Carrier apologize and ask for 'just another twenty-four hours' he sensed that Carrier was as desperate as he was himself. 'Give me a chance to discuss this with Juan,' Carrier said with such urgency that he was almost pleading. 'I'm sure it will be to our mutual advantage.'

'Not at twelve million,' Todd retorted.

And Carrier said slyly, 'Perhaps I can go a shade higher with Juan in my corner? Come up for lunch tomorrow and I feel sure we'll do business.'

Todd was a fish on a hook. *If only I'd been able to get to Roos. If only I had an alternative! Someone! Anyone!*

Afterwards he telephoned Katrina. This time she shared his alarm. 'You're staying until tomorrow! But tomorrow's Tuesday. Oh, Toddy!'

Hearing the fear in her voice, he did his best to placate her. 'Gonzales is major league,' he said, encouraging himself at the same time. 'And Carrier's panting for a deal. You should have heard him on the phone just now.'

In the end they encouraged each other. They rationalized the situation. They told each other that *of course* Carrier was the obvious buyer, *of course* someone like Gonzales would be interested, and *of course* Todd should stay over until the Tuesday. Meanwhile Katrina could report good news from London. The number of acceptances to the press conference had grown to 320. 'And Mike's invited even more, and then there's all the travel trade people, and these real estate agents you've spoken to. I think we could have as many as five hundred.'

Todd shuddered at the cost. A picture of Smithson leapt into his mind.

Then Katrina said, 'Oh, and that man Roos called from his office in Paris. He said could you call him? Hang on a minute, I'll give you the number.'

Todd knew the number by heart, he had called it so many times. Which is what he told Roos ten minutes later. 'Where have you been?' he demanded. 'I thought we'd have got together by now.' Not that Roos even apologized. He said, 'I had a client in trouble, Mr Todd, which means I drop everything. It's the way I work, my clients always come first.' And he went on about how he had rushed to the rescue of some unfortunate client who was now ten times richer as a result of his efforts. Few stories would have made a bigger impact on Todd. *He* was in trouble. *He* needed to be ten times richer. *He* needed Roos on his side. So although angry about the lost time and disliking Roos's superior tone, he was very amenable to Roos's suggestion of a meeting. The question was when?

'How about in London on Wednesday?' Roos asked. 'Your

people have invited me to this press reception at lunchtime. Perhaps we could meet in the morning beforehand?'

And so it was settled.

'Better late than never,' Todd thought as he hung up.

He had done all that he could do. No one could have done more. Now he would have to wait until tomorrow . . .

'But I'm not stalling,' Carrier protested. 'That's why I called and asked you to come early. Stay and have lunch as my guests. It's just that I'll have to go because my flight leaves in . . .' he broke off and glanced at his watch. 'Fifty-five minutes.'

They were in the cocktail lounge at the Bella Vista, a vast room with an elaborately decorated ceiling and pale marble floors on two levels. Todd needed a drink to recover from the shock of learning that Gonzales had not arrived the previous afternoon.

'But that's why I'm going to him,' Carrier said insistently. 'I'll have dinner with him in Madrid tonight and see you at your press conference in London tomorrow. I can't see why you're making a fuss. I wouldn't go to all this trouble for nothing, would I?'

Todd and Hank exchanged worried glances. The excuse sounded plausible. They had arrived just as a porter was taking Carrier's bags out to the car.

Scowling, Todd complained, 'But you promised your written offer today. That's why I stayed. I'd have gone back to –' He stopped, aware of saying too much, hoping it was better to sound petulant than frightened.

Carrier beckoned a waiter and flourished his hand to indicate another round of drinks for his guests. He waited while the man collected up the empty glasses and returned to the bar. 'I made no such promise, Mr Todd. I hoped we could take our talks further, but unfortunately Juan was detained on business.' His face softened into a smile. 'So I called him, we talked, we'll talk some more tonight and I'll see you in London tomorrow.'

'With an offer,' Todd said, grimly suspicious.

'But of course.' Carrier smiled. He had spoken the truth –

Gonzales had been delayed, they had spoken on the telephone and agreed to have dinner together. He had even outlined what was in his mind, and Gonzales had sounded at least interested. Meanwhile Carrier had made up his mind about the written offer. He would let them stew for another day. They were obviously desperate for a deal. He would give them one. But on his terms and without an auction.

Which was how things were left. No matter what Todd said, Carrier refused to give them a written offer, but held out the promise of bringing one tomorrow. After which he left for the airport.

They stayed there for lunch. They had nothing else to do. Booked on the evening flight to London, they had the entire afternoon to kill, but Todd had expected to be in a far different mood.

Hank provided what comfort he could. 'He's bluffing, making us sweat, that's all. He'll bring an offer, don't worry.'

Except that Todd did worry. He worried about telling Katrina.

'She'll be okay,' said Hank, trying to provide reassurance. 'Once she knows Carrier's bringing the offer with him.'

Even so, Todd worried about Moroni.

'You don't even know if he's coming,' said Hank. 'Besides, he won't try anything in front of five hundred people will he? And anyway, didn't you say his lawyer is coming? We can explain everything to him. We *are* selling Paloma Blanca. That's what they wanted, isn't it?'

Todd nodded dejectedly.

'And anyway you're worrying unnecessarily, Carrier will come up with an offer . . .'

Hank said everything he could think of, over lunch and all afternoon, but it was not until later, when they were on the Boeing over London, that he succeeded in restoring Todd's hopes. They were talking about the next morning, and Todd was saying that while Katrina and Hank went directly to the Hilton, he could get an hour's work done at the office before his meeting with Roos.

'That's it!' Hank exclaimed suddenly. 'Roos!'

Todd looked at him.

'That will shake Carrier rigid. When you walk in with Roos! That's what we're forgetting. They know each other, remember?'

Todd stared.

'Carrier thinks he's got this to himself, but he'll be so frightened when he sees Roos that he'll sign anything we put in front of him.'

Todd's face cleared. 'Bloody hell!'

'I'll warm him up before you get there.' Hank grinned. 'I'll tell him that you've gone to collect Roos personally. That'll make him sweat.'

And they both laughed as they imagined the expression on Carrier's face. It gave them something to cling on to, a reason for hope . . .

'Big day today, Boss.'

'You can say that again.'

'Read all about it, eh?'

'Not half. The papers should be full of it tomorrow.'

Herbert squinted in the mirror. 'So what's the programme this morning?'

Todd told him about the meeting at Arlsruher, Wormack and Roos in Grosvenor Square. 'Then on to the Hilton.'

'Righto. How you feeling? Nervous?'

'A bit,' he admitted, talking at cross purposes, not nervous about the press conference, Mike Thompson and Katrina had that well in hand, but nervous about Carrier and this wretched offer. He was nervous about Moroni turning up . . . he was nervous about his meeting with Roos . . .

And his nervousness increased when they arrived at the office. Sally was waiting down in the showroom, hovering by the front doors as if she had been there for some time; and instead of greeting him with her usual smile, she looked shaken, even frightened.

'Morning, Sally. What's up?'

With a glance over her shoulder, she gripped his arm. 'There's a man in your office,' she whispered, casting another worried

404

look behind her. 'He just walked in. I couldn't stop him. He says he's come to take over. He says – '

'Steady on. What's this about?'

'There's two of them. The other one went down to the workshops.'

His heart thumped. His first reaction was disbelief. Then outrage that Moroni should do this to him. *There's no need for this. I told Lapiere what was happening, I explained! I even invited him to the press conference.* He stared at Sally, sharing her alarm. Then he found his voice. 'Just two of them? Not four of them? Big men?'

She looked at him in surprise. 'I've only seen two. Why, were you expecting them?'

Whatever he had expected, it was not this. 'Not for them to come here,' he admitted in dazed confusion. 'Not now, not like this.' He realized that reporting to Lapiere was useless. Last time had been the same, he had explained everything to Lapiere but it had made no difference, Moroni had still arrived with his thugs. Taking a deep breath, he tried to collect himself.

Sally said, 'He told me to carry on with what I was doing until he'd spoken to you.'

Then anger overwhelmed his fear. He was doing everything possible. No one could do more.

'Oh, did he!' he snorted as his temper took over. 'They can't just burst in like this. They'll just have to wait until Carrier gets here.' With which he brushed past her, ran up the stairs and wrenched open the door to the general office. Ahead of him the door to his own office was closed. Charging across the room, he was in such a blind hurry that he caught his thigh painfully on the corner of Sally's desk. Flinging open the door, he rushed in to confront Moroni. Then he stopped in his tracks. The man sitting at his desk was a stranger.

'Ah, Mr Todd?'

Todd stared, taking in the well-cut business suit, absorbing the English accent, noticing horn-rimmed spectacles set in a middle-aged face.

'My name's Atkinson,' said the man, rising to his feet.

'Yes?' Todd said blankly. The name meant nothing to him.

Neither did he recognize the man; he was sure he'd never seen him before. Too surprised to say more he stood stock still on one side of his desk.

'Bad news, I'm afraid. I . . . er,' the man coughed in a deprecating way. 'I represent your bankers. I've been appointed receiver of Owen's and Todd Motors.'

The unexpected words failed to make sense. Then the shock registered and Todd swayed and supported himself by putting a hand on the desk.

'Naturally I have the necessary court order,' said the man, indicating some buff-coloured papers set out on the desk.

Todd sucked in a breath. 'A receiver!' Taking two paces around the desk, he slumped into his chair before his legs gave way. 'Jesus Christ,' he said softly, staring up at the man. He realized that Sally had followed him in. She stood in the open doorway, her hands raised to her mouth, a look of alarm on her face. Beyond her, he could see Herbert entering the general office.

'Always a shock, I appreciate that,' said the man.

Todd had already forgotten his name. His brain had not cleared enough to absorb details. 'You mean that bastard Smithson appointed you?'

'Actually the court appoints me. The procedure is that the bank apply to the court, and then –'

'You just arrive? Out of the blue? Without warning?'

'That's the whole point. Advance warning would allow time for assets to be removed.'

Todd stared blankly.

'You see, I take over the assets. The whole business really. To protect the bank's interests. Hopefully to recover their money.'

Todd's heart pumped. He understood the role of receiver, but his thoughts were so all over the place that he scarcely listened to the man's explanation. With one damp and sweaty hand he fumbled through the official forms on his desk, while his other hand reached for the telephone. Looking up, he saw Sally still in the doorway. 'Get me Manny Shiner will you? And don't be fobbed off by his office. I don't care who he's with, or if he's in conference –'

'Who's Manny Shiner?' the man interrupted.

With his gaze still on Sally, Todd answered, 'My accountant.'

As Sally turned and fled, the man said, 'Strictly speaking, you need my authorization before you can make any calls. Not even a phone call can be made without my approval.'

Todd's neck bulged inside his collar. Colour rose in his face. His voice was hoarse with outrage. 'This is my bloody office –'

'Not any longer,' the man interrupted sharply. 'Not once a receiver has been appointed. I'm in charge until I recover the bank's money or put the businesses into liquidation. There's nothing you can do about it.'

To stop his hands from bunching Todd pressed his palms down on to the desk top. A red haze seized his brain. 'We'll see about that!' he snarled as he levered himself up from his chair.

Sally shouted, 'It's ringing!'

'That attitude won't help you,' Atkinson retorted crisply. 'You'll find co-operation is in your best interests.'

Todd dropped back into the chair. He snatched up the phone. 'Manny!' he shouted, only to find himself talking to a telephonist. A moment later, Manny himself came on the line. Through gritted teeth, Todd explained what had happened. Manny made a moaning noise that was incomprehensible. Then he swore and fell silent, as if thinking. After which, he said, 'I'm on my way over, but you I want out of there. You'll only make things worse. Don't start an argument. Just get up and leave.'

Nothing was further from Todd's thoughts. Leave? They'd have to carry him out feet first. He looked around his office, *his* office from which he ran *his* business. Through the open door he saw Herbert standing by Sally's desk. *His* people. Manny was still saying that he'd do more harm than good, but only half of what Manny was saying penetrated Todd's shock and sense of loss.

'What were your plans for this morning?' Manny was asking.

Plans? What was the point of plans now?

'Get round to the Hilton,' Manny was saying. 'Give Katrina a hand.'

Imagining standing up before 500 people and confessing that a receiver had been appointed to his businesses brought a groan from Todd's lips. 'Manny, I can't go there, I have to stay here —'

Manny exploded. Todd had never heard him so angry. He was shouting with temper. Holding the telephone away from his ear, Todd heard expressions like 'pull yourself together' and a lot more besides. Atkinson heard as well because a smug smile showed on his face as he went over to close the door. Next moment the door almost burst from its hinges as Sally marched into the room. With a few strides she was at Todd's side, where she swung round to face Atkinson. Placing a hand on Todd's shoulder, she stood next to him as if ready to defy receivers, the bank, the courts or anyone else.

Atkinson's face betrayed his surprise. Then with the slightest of shrugs he hitched up his trousers and sat down.

Manny continued to talk with such urgency that he was calming himself and Todd at the same time, making them concentrate on what had to be done instead of what they were feeling.

As Todd listened, he reached up to pat Sally's hand on his shoulder.

Across the room, Atkinson glanced at his watch.

Manny was saying, 'Get round to the Hilton and get this offer from Carrier. Drury *might* just step in. If he pays Smithson you can say goodbye to the receiver. It can be done real fast. But *only* if you get the offer today. Without that, Toddy, it's all over. You're finished.'

Staring at the picture of Paloma Blanca, Todd cursed the day he had set eyes on the place.

'. . . now get out of there,' Manny was saying. 'I'm on my way over to see this . . . what's his name, you didn't tell me? Did he give you a card? I might know him.'

Todd looked across the room. 'I didn't catch your name.'

'Atkinson. And the firm is Manley and Chambers. I'm sure your accountant will have heard of us.' He stood up and advanced to the desk, his hand outstretched for the phone. 'Shall I speak to him?'

Todd left them talking. He went out to the general office, closed the door, and sat on the edge of Sally's desk for a moment, trying to collect his thoughts. Sally was full of concern, wanting to make him some coffee, while Herbert shuffled his feet and looked as desperate and upset as Todd himself. But he knew Manny was right. If he stayed, he would lose his temper and make things a hundred times worse.

'No, it's best if I go, Sally,' he said, patting her hand. 'Manny's on his way over. He'll know what to do. Take your lead from him.' He walked to the door and turned to look at her. 'I'll be back,' he said.

Then he went down the stairs, with Herbert on his heels, and out through the main doors at the front of the showroom.

'I'll be back,' he repeated as he got into the car.

Herbert drove out of the forecourt without waiting for instructions. He stopped at the traffic lights at the crossroads and then continued in the general direction of the West End, cocking an eye at Todd in his mirror.

Todd looked ill. He felt ill. He needed a drink. It was only nine-thirty, but he needed a drink, and he said so to Herbert. Five minutes later they pulled up outside a wine merchants. Herbert returned clutching a tissue-wrapped bottle which he passed over the back of the seat. Then he took his thermos flask from the glove compartment and handed it to Todd.

For a moment he was reminded of Leo up in the suite at the Ritz, talking about his potent mixture. 'Half and half's the best mixture for shocks, old boy.' *Bloody hell, Leo! I can't keep taking these setbacks!*

Not that there would be any more. This was the last one. He was finished. Within a couple of days everyone would know about the receiver. *You can't keep something like that secret. I'm bust. It's all over.*

'Where to, Boss?'

'I dunno,' he said emptily, sounding totally defeated. His only thought was to share his grief with Katrina, but it would be pointless to go home. She would have left for the Hilton, and his despair deepened as he thought of her busy and excited.

Herbert looked at him. 'You still want to be at Grosvenor Square at half-ten?'

Todd stared back at him, incapable of making a decision, still trying to come to terms with what had happened. He felt humiliated and angry and sick all at the same time.

'You have a drink,' said Herbert in an encouraging voice. 'And I'll drive round Hyde Park for a bit.'

The Scotch and hot coffee helped. The second one helped even more than the first. Then he had a third which was mostly neat Scotch, after which he rolled down the window and sucked in the damp air.

But at least he started to think. His brain came alive again, even if his thoughts roamed all over the place, even if they were full of if onlys – *If only I could have kept going long enough to set up this auction. If only I'd had another three months.*

He shuddered at the prospect of being on display at a press conference on the worst day of his life. The ultimate humiliation. He imagined going up on to the stage. He saw himself looking down from the lectern; faces staring up at him – Katrina, Hank, Charlie, Manny. Manny was supposed to be bringing Drury. Fat chance now. He saw other faces. Carrier. Lapiere. MORONI!

He flinched.

'You all right, Boss?'

'What?'

'Do you want to stop? Stretch your legs? We've got time.'

They were crossing the bridge over the Serpentine.

'All right. Why not?'

Leaving Herbert with the car he turned his collar up against the chill of the day and walked down the towpath. The smell of rain was in the air, making the breeze more damp than cold. The Serpentine was as grey as the sky. The park benches were empty. Not that he noticed. Blind to his surroundings, he thrust his hands into his pockets and walked with his head down.

He muttered under his breath as he walked, and laughed bitterly at the thought of his pathetic insistence on an auction in March. There was no point now. By March, Todd Motors and Owen's would have gone out of existence. Sold off under the hammer to pay that bastard Smithson! He might as well let Carrier have Paloma Blanca today. Better in a way, to be finished with the whole bloody lot. At least Charlie would get her

410

money. She'd be off the hook. 'And Carrier will be pleased,' he told himself drily. 'He's terrified of an auction.'

He stopped and turned to look back in the general direction of the car, gazing more into space than at objects, and as he did so the desperate idea of an immediate sale took shape in his mind, prompted by the thought of Carrier's opposition to an auction. *Suppose I go to Carrier and say, 'Okay, fuck the auction. You can have it today if you pay another . . .'*

Standing at the edge of the path, he kicked a pebble and heard it plop into the water. Vaguely he registered ripples widening across the surface, but his concentration was on his idea. His only chance to save himself was an immediate sale. Today. It was the last option. He worked out how much he would need. Two million would clear Smithson, nine for Moroni, six for Charlie . . .

Without being aware of it, he had started to walk back towards the car. He imagined taking Carrier aside at the press conference. *Okay, José, you can have it today for eighteen million. Outright sale. Forget the auction . . .*

But even then Carrier would haggle.

There was no time to haggle.

Once again, he stopped walking. Even in the damp air he was sweating at the realization of how little time he had left. His hands felt clammy. His fingers bunched into fists as he thought of Carrier arguing.

Roos! He remembered his conversation with Hank. Roos was the perfect decoy. If Carrier thought Roos was there with a bid, there was just a chance he could be bounced up on the price. Just a chance!

He glanced at his watch. It had turned ten-thirty.

He started to run back towards the car . . .

Roos picked up one of the photographs which Todd had sent him. 'My instinct tells me to go with this on the cover of the brochure. It makes a solid statement. Says what we're selling. Class. Seclusion. Exclusivity. Then on the inside pages . . .'

Todd let the words wash over him. Carrier didn't need a

brochure. It was irrelevant. There wasn't time. But he listened in silence, afraid to say anything which might deter Roos from coming to the press conference. And it was obvious that Roos liked the sound of his own voice. Todd had scarcely uttered a word since he had arrived. Roos had not given him a chance.

He would have disliked Roos even without the man's discourtesy in avoiding his calls. Now he disliked him for being so bloody successful. Everything about the Arlsruher, Wormack and Roos building smacked of wealth and prosperity. The reception hall downstairs reeked of big money. The atrium housed London's largest collection of exotic plants outside Kew Gardens. Hessian covered walls were decorated with photographs of some of the most prestigious buildings in Europe. The leather couches were flanked by low tables upon which rested scale models of developments in Copenhagen and Corfu, Berlin and Birmingham, Lisbon and Lille.

It was even more opulent upstairs. Todd had been shown into a conference room panelled with rosewood, he had walked across carpet which felt ten inches thick, and been ushered to a table long enough to seat half the United Nations. And there was Roos, standing up with his hand outstretched in greeting. 'Mr Todd! We meet at last!'

Todd had wanted to say, 'It's not my bloody fault. I'd have met you before.' Instead he had smiled and shaken Roos's hand while assessing the sleek Armani silk suit and matching silk tie . . . and the tan . . . and the fake smile . . . and the way Roos himself had poured the coffee from a tall silver pot into Dresden china cups.

Then had come an insufferable lecture on why Arlsruher, Wormack and Roos were the most successful real estate agents in Europe. Todd fidgeted with worry and impatience. He wondered how Manny was coping? Time was ticking past. He should be waiting for Carrier at the Hilton. He only needed Roos to say he was coming – but Roos seemed intent on saying everything but.

'So we produce a really classy document,' he was saying. 'Printed on vellum weight paper and enclosed in a hand-stitched leather folder.' He paused, sensing that his visitor's attention was wandering. 'Is something wrong, Mr Todd?'

'No, no, it sounds fine, but . . .' Todd glanced at his watch. 'I must be getting to the Hilton very soon.' He shot Roos an anxious look. 'You are coming, aren't you? It's only round the corner.'

'I'll try to look in later,' said Roos, with an encouraging smile. 'I must say I'm intrigued. As a matter of fact I've already given a great deal of thought to your little project.'

Todd flinched, offended to hear the biggest mistake of his life described as a 'little project'.

'Of course, it's this little concert which gives your place such a plus.'

Two 'littles' inside a minute! Todd churned inside. *You smug bastard. If I didn't need you to be there so badly . . .* He managed to smile. 'Hardly a little concert, Mr Roos. We estimate an audience around the world of about fifty million people.'

'Absolutely.' Roos nodded genially. 'I take my hat off to you. It gives me something to sell. You wouldn't believe the difference it makes. Especially these days. I've never known the market so bad.' Leaning back in his chair, he waved a hand at a coloured photograph on the wall. 'See that?' he asked, and then made a point of squinting at it. 'Oh, no, that's the wrong one. I thought it was a shot of the Beach Hotel in Rimini. Ever heard of it?'

When Todd shook his head Roos was not surprised. He had only just invented the name. 'Sold it last month,' he lied. 'Great hotel. Fine location. About the same size as yours. Two years ago it would have fetched thirty million. Last month it went for eleven, and that was only because we handled it. The owners had it with another agent before asking us to handle it and he only got an offer of seven.'

Having scored two points with one lie, he sat back to watch the effect.

Todd forgot his indignation. His heart sank. *So the market's that bad! I wonder if Carrier knows? Dear God, I hope not.*

Pleased with such obvious alarm, Roos continued, 'Don't look so gloomy, Mr Todd. I'll make sure you do better. For a start you've come directly to us. That puts you ahead of the game, and second you've got this TV coverage coming up, and we must take advantage of that. So there's a great deal to do.' With a sigh, he turned in his chair and reached for a document on the cabinet behind him. 'So the sooner we get the paperwork dealt with, the sooner the machine starts to roll.'

'Paperwork?'

'Just the standard agreement.' Roos pushed the printed contract across the table. 'Once that's signed I'll slam the whole machine into gear. There'll be a team of people working on this by the end of today.' Stretching across the table, he offered his pen. 'I thought we'd agree the brochure this morning,' he said breezily. 'You sent us so many good pictures that we can use more on the inside, so I thought . . .'

And away he went, designing the brochure all over again. He had seen clients show more pride over photographs of their properties than of their families. It was a lesson he drummed into his assistants: 'Hook them on the brochure and they'll sign the contract without thinking.'

But clearly this fat little man was thinking about something! 'You have a problem, Mr Todd?'

With Roos's pen in his hand, Todd looked up from the contract. 'This gives you three per cent of the sale price, is that right?'

'That's all, I'm afraid,' Roos sighed. His shoulders rose in a shrug. 'Truth is, I'd like more. We deserve more. It galls me at times, but the most valuable part of our work is the part the client never sees. All the work backstage. Believe me it's a hell of a sweat, but it's what makes all the difference. That's why our clients always get top dollar. I'll be talking this project up solidly for the next couple of months. So will the rest of my team. Writing letters, making calls, holding meetings, pushing our top contacts, warming the bed for this Barzini concert. Then we get all this TV exposure and after that . . .' he grinned '. . . we hit them with an auction. What d'you think, Mr Todd? Could your nerves stand an auction?'

The question could not have come at a worse moment. Todd had tried to shut his mind to what he was losing by doing a deal in a hurry. He had to sell Paloma Blanca today. It was his only chance, and now Roos was reminding him of missed opportunities.

Roos laughed. 'I can see you're surprised, but that's the way I want to play this.'

Todd wasn't surprised. He was hurting inside. Hearing his own plans was like having a knife turned in his wound. He set Roos's pen down on the table. He wanted to say, 'That's *exactly* what *I* wanted to do.' Instead he looked at Roos in pained silence.

'Yes, sir, I'd plan on having an auction in March, about three or four weeks after all this television exposure. But I'll tell you what happens, Mr Todd. We talk this up and up and up.' Roos cocked his head. 'You follow, we keep building the pressure, and then a few days before the auction someone makes us *exactly* the offer we're looking for, so we can cancel the auction and avoid the expense.' He sat back in his chair and beamed. 'And that, Mr Todd, is why our clients always get top dollar. Because we never stop pushing.'

Todd felt so miserable that he could no longer sit still. What Roos was describing was obvious. He didn't need to be told. He knew! Pushing his chair back from the table, he stood up and went to the window to stare down into Grosvenor Square.

Taken by surprise, Roos stared at the back of Todd's head, then at the unsigned contract. More than a million pounds profit rested on Todd's signature. And the man hadn't signed!

Feeling a flutter of alarm, Roos gathered his wits for his final push. 'Ah,' he said, trying to sound jovial. 'I know what you're thinking. You're asking the big question. You're saying to yourself, "What *is* top dollar for Paloma Blanca?"'

Todd turned from the window and managed to nod miserably. 'I suppose so,' he said gloomily on his way back to the table.

Roos allowed a twinkle to come to his eye. 'Okay, what I'm going to do now,' he said portentously, 'is forecast what I'll get for you. Eventually. Eh? The actual sum.' He held up a warning hand. 'Remember the important word. Eventually – after we've done the brochures and sent out all the letters, made all the phone calls, held all the meetings, after all our hard work and your TV exposure. In other words, when we put the squeeze on in March. Okay?'

Todd nodded, beyond caring.

'And don't forget what I said about the state of the market. People are giving hotels away as we sit here.'

Todd shuddered as he slumped into his chair.

'On the other hand, faith can move mountains.' Roos laughed happily. 'So I'm setting my sights high.' He gathered himself for his big moment. 'Okay then, here we go.' Allowing his eyes to stray from Todd, he glanced down at the papers in front of him. 'How'd you want this, Mr Todd? Spanish pesetas, US dollars, Deutschmarks, sterling –'

'Sterling will do,' Todd mumbled.

Pulling a pocket calculator towards him, Roos tapped in some figures. 'At today's rate of exchange,' he said, looking up with a smile, 'I'd be disappointed not to see twenty-three million British pounds.'

A blow between the eyes would have stunned Todd less. For a long moment he just stared at Roos in mute amazement. Then in a dull-sounding voice he repeated the figure to make sure he had heard properly. 'Twenty-three million?'

'That's my estimate,' Roos nodded with a good-natured smile.

Part of Todd wanted to weep. He wanted to tear his hair and gnash his teeth. But another part of him wished Katrina could hear Roos. And he wanted Manny to hear. He wanted that bastard Smithson to hear. He had *told* them. Time and time again he had told them. Hadn't he? God, how he'd told them! He had been right all along, but they'd *never* believed in Paloma Blanca.

'I take it we're talking about something very acceptable, eh?' asked Roos, rising from his seat to reach across the table. 'So if you'll just sign the agreement, we'll set the wheels in motion. As I said, if we can sort out the brochure today . . .'

Sickened by the cruel injustice of life, Todd cast a beseeching look upwards. 'Twenty-three million,' he groaned. He sounded disgusted. He was disgusted. He would have felt better if the sum had been half. He would have felt less of a failure. Now he'd spend the rest of his life thinking of what might have been.

'Twenty-three fucking million!' he repeated between clenched teeth.

Such obvious anger unsettled Roos. For a second he was tempted to go all the way up to the twenty-five million and get the business over and done with, but experience stopped him in time. Instead, he said modestly, 'Just an estimate, of course. I follow your thinking. You're relying on the TV exposure, I can understand that. There's no doubt it will help, perhaps more than I allowed for.' After appearing to consider for a moment, his face brightened. 'You could be right. Once we go to auction we might get twenty-three and a half, even twenty-*four* million.'

Todd lowered his gaze and stared at him.

Roos laughed nervously. 'That's the thing about auctions. Sometimes even professionals get carried away. But what we need to do now is get cracking. Eh? We want a *real* figure, not one plucked from thin air.'

Todd blinked. Until then he had been absorbed more with his own worries than what Roos was saying. But now his attention was caught by Roos's sudden nervousness. There was a note in Roos's voice which he recognized. He heard echoes of himself in Majorca trying to persuade Carrier. An echo of desperation.

Roos pushed the contract another inch across the table. 'Would you like some more coffee?' he asked and half-rose from his seat.

Todd looked up from the document. With Roos leaning towards him, their faces were close enough for him to see a sheen on the man's forehead. He was surprised. Questions jumped into his mind. *He's wearing that fancy silk suit, yet he's sweating. Why? I don't even feel warm.*

'Coffee?' Roos repeated, but he was looking at the contract, not the coffee pot.

As Todd followed Roos's eyes, instincts honed over the years came into play. Most of his life had been spent selling cars. He was a good salesman. And suddenly he knew *exactly* why Roos was sweating. *This guy's afraid of losing a sale.*

He was so startled that he felt confused. To give himself time to think, he glanced at his watch. 'Er . . . no coffee, thanks. I better not.' He stared at Roos. Another thought occurred with searing clarity. *If he's got a sale he must have a buyer.* Thoughts were exploding like rockets in his mind. *He's already got a buyer for Paloma Blanca.*

'Sure?' asked Roos, this time pointing to the coffee pot.

Convinced he had guessed right, Todd shook his head. 'Er . . . no thanks. I really ought to be going. Why don't we discuss this some more at the Hilton?'

With a look of disappointment, Roos eased back across the table.

'You really ought to come with me,' said Todd. 'The press conference will give you a better idea of what we're selling.' He focused on Roos's eyes. 'You never know, you might decide you're not interested.'

'I'm sure I won't,' Roos said lightly, but his quick smile failed to disguise the dismay in his eyes.

Todd's heart threatened to leap out of his chest. *The crafty bastard's got a buyer! For twenty-three million!* He was too excited to know what to do. He had closed thousands of deals but never like this. This was not the straightforward sale of a car. With a new Jaguar he would stress pride of ownership, the status bestowed upon the owner, reliability, craftsmanship, a hundred and one other factors. He would be acting out a little play in which he was the salesman and the customer was the buyer who needed to be coaxed. But Roos was acting in a different play and Todd was so confused and elated that he could no longer sit still. He stood up. He picked up the contract. He looked at it. Glancing up he saw the anticipation in Roos's eyes. So he folded the printed pages and slipped them into his pocket. 'No point signing it now,' he explained. 'You see, it . . . er . . . might not be needed. I won't know until later.'

'Won't know?' Roos exclaimed, concern flooding into his face. He rose to his feet. 'Why's that?'

The alarm was unmistakable. Todd paused. He had arrived shattered and defeated, but now of the two of them he was looking the more confident. The balance of power had shifted. In fact Roos was beginning to bluster. 'I don't understand –'

Todd gambled. 'I've already had one offer for Paloma Blanca,' he said. 'And I'm expecting another at the press conference.'

Roos dropped into his chair with a thump. He could scarcely believe what he had heard. He had boasted to his clients: 'No one even knows this is coming to the market.' It had been part of his spiel. Now – to hear of an offer! 'What happened to your exclusive buying rights?' his clients would ask angrily. The consequences even went beyond the loss of his million-pound fee. His reputation was at risk. There would be no more million-pound fees. Swallowing hard, he took a deep breath and, when he did find his voice, it rose in disbelief. 'You've been to another agent?'

'No, no, these people are hoteliers.'

'And they've made you an offer?'

'I'll say they have.'

'But you haven't accepted?' Roos asked quickly, betraying himself yet again.

'Not yet,' Todd admitted cheerfully. 'But today's the big day.'

Roos stood up again and hurried round the table. He put a hand on Todd's arm to delay him. 'Surely you don't have to rush off? We need to discuss –'

'Mr Roos, I've been trying to get you for two weeks.'

Tightening his grip on Todd's arm, Roos demanded, 'So how much have they offered? These hoteliers,' he said, trying to sound contemptuous.

'I can't tell you that.'

'Was it twenty-three million?' Roos blurted out. 'Do you realize what I'm offering? Twenty-three million pounds.'

Todd looked at him. 'Is that a firm offer?'

Roos released Todd's arm. He bit his tongue. Startled by talk of another buyer, he'd said more than he'd intended. He had planned to reach his price in instalments. He had imagined calling Todd a dozen times during January and February, inching the price upwards as a consequence of negotiations he would pretend to be conducting. He liked clients to think he worked hard for his money. It was not unknown for grateful clients to make him a generous gift at the conclusion of a sale, tax free on top of his fee. Now, having spoken out of turn, he tried to recover lost ground. 'That's the sort of sale I think I can achieve after this concert,' he said. 'And after all this TV exposure. I did say that. I did say eventually.'

Hopes raised were now dashed.

'Not now?' Todd asked, trying to conceal his dismay. He tried to bluff by taking another step towards the door.

The bluff failed.

'Of course you can't expect a price like that now,' Roos retorted. 'Paloma Blanca will be booked out after the coverage you're talking about. We all know that. That's what you're selling. But you can't expect it before, can you? Suppose Barzini falls under a bus? Suppose you don't get this TV exposure?'

Lost for answers, Todd felt his heart sink.

'I told you,' said Roos, trying to regain his earlier advantage. 'You can't rush these things.'

Todd stared at him. For a few glorious seconds he had dared hope. Now with one valid and irrefutable objection, Roos had ruined any chance of a sale today.

Roos said, 'Now what I suggest is –'

'Wait a minute,' Todd interrupted, thinking desperately. 'If the concert gets cancelled I'll give you a discount.'

'A discount?'

'Why not?' Seizing the idea, Todd clung to it for dear life. After a pause he continued, 'If the concert doesn't take place or . . .' he tried to remember Mike Thompson's schedule '. . . or if it's not screened in . . . say at least five countries, I'll give you a discount. That's fair, isn't it?'

Roos blinked as he absorbed the idea.

Recovering from his setback, Todd grinned. 'I'll knock five million off the price. That's what I'll sign today. A firm agreement, with two figures on it.' He looked at Roos in triumph. 'Nothing wrong with that, is there?'

Roos sat down in the chair which Todd had vacated. 'I've never known a deal like this,' he said softly, but even as he spoke he could feel a quickening interest. A deal today would be in his interests as well. It would be a record to button everything up in one day. Neither Arlsruher nor Wormack had ever made over a million pounds in a single day. It would be something to boast about at the partners' meetings. He looked at

Todd. 'What you're saying is twenty-three million if the concert takes place and eighteen million if it –'

'No,' Todd interrupted cheerfully. 'I didn't say that. I expect the figures will be bigger. Depends what offers I get at the Hilton.'

Roos looked at him.

'I'm selling Paloma Blanca today, Mr Roos.'

Roos felt his stomach turn over. 'I'll be there,' he said quickly. 'But I'll have to make a few calls first.'

Todd turned away to hide his excitement. 'You know where to find me,' he said as he opened the door.

Roos called after him. 'Don't sign anything until I get there. Okay? I want your word on that. I'll be there as soon as I can.'

Todd scarcely noticed the reception hall downstairs. When he arrived he had been taken aback by its grandeur, yet on his departure he saw only the plate glass doors which led to the street. Outside, he sucked in the damp air and almost tripped as he ran down the steps. Feverish with excitement, he looked around for Herbert. In a futile attempt to see across the square, he raised himself up on his toes. He craned his neck. He looked left and peered right, and failing to find Herbert, set off for the Hilton. He ran, then walked, then ran another few yards. Red-faced and breathless, he was into Curzon Street by the time Herbert drew alongside, tooting the horn and waving through the open front window. 'Bloody hell, Boss. Hang on a minute!'

Too breathless to answer, he threw himself into the back seat.

'I did flash my lights,' Herbert complained.

Wheezing and puffing, Todd gasped, 'Okay, I missed you that's all.'

'Where to? The Hilton?'

Todd nodded, recovering, but still gasping for breath. He glanced at his watch. Twelve-thirty exactly. He was late. So what? It was worth being late. He'd be late for anything for twenty-three million. *Twenty-three million! Five million profit! We're safe!* He imagined their faces when he told them.

Perspiring from excitement and his rush down the street, he

took out his handkerchief and patted his forehead. He straightened his tie and brushed a speck from his jacket.

The rain which had threatened earlier started to fall. Inside the car it was as if the sun had come out.

'You're looking better,' said Herbert as he switched on the wipers. 'How you feeling?'

'All right,' Todd nodded and once started seemed unable to stop. 'I'm okay, I'm all right, Herbert, I'm fine, I'm feeling just fine.'

'You had me worried earlier,' said Herbert as he edged the car into the Park Lane traffic. 'And what about that bloke back at the office?'

'Fuck him.'

Herbert grinned. 'That's the spirit. Fuck him!'

But Todd wondered if they could? He was terrified that news of the receiver would get out. He wondered how Manny was coping? Bowing his head, he stared down at himself. His chest and his paunch were still heaving. He realized he was praying – *Please God, we've got a chance after all, let Manny have bought us some time. Even forty-eight hours could make all the difference . . .*

Then the short journey was behind them and they were there, pulling into the rear entrance of the Hilton with the commissionaire hurrying forward to open the door.

'Good luck, Boss,' said Herbert, turning to look over his shoulder.

'Thanks,' he said, and suddenly he wanted to say something about all the years they'd been together and the way Herbert had never let him down and how grateful he was – but all he could manage was a grin. 'We're not beaten yet, Herbert. We're not beaten yet.'

Once through the doors, he could hear the music from the foot of the stairs. And the signs were all over the place; huge banners proclaiming *Barzini at Paloma Blanca* in gold letters on a ruby red background. Taking a deep breath, he ran up the stairs, hoping to find Manny, only to run into the most incredible crush of people with drinks in their hands, all talking and laughing at once. The excited hubbub of conversation was loud enough to drown even the music in the background. Deep in earnest discussion, Mike Thompson looked up, saw him and waved. Startled, Todd managed to raise a hand in response. Across the room he saw Sophie holding a man's glass for him while he juggled with cigarettes and a lighter. He could see Don Antonio with his head thrown back roaring with laughter. He caught sight of Hank, but Hank had his back towards him, talking to Carrier. Anxiously he searched the faces for Manny.

Manny was not to be seen.

As he looked around he felt a glow of pride in Katrina as he realized what she had accomplished. Until then he had been too busy even to imagine 500 people in the same room. Now, seeing this crush, he fairly gawped. He swivelled his neck to take in the huge photographs of Paloma Blanca and the big pictures of Enrico Barzini, who smiled down with beaming good humour. He caught sight of Charlie's red hair in the distance. A passing waiter offered him a glass of champagne from a tray, which he took without thinking. Then he was distracted by a tug at his elbow. He turned to find Gloria beside him. 'Isn't this fantastic?' she asked, dimpling prettily. 'It's a full turnout. In fact we've even got some we hadn't bargained for.'

He saw one at that moment. Shouldering his way through the crush, coming towards him and scarcely ten yards away, was one of Moroni's thugs. His temper flared as he recognized the tallest of the men who'd been at the house. The man was smiling and turned to reveal Lapiere ploughing along in his wake.

'Monsieur Todd!' exclaimed Lapiere, arriving with hand outstretched. 'I must congratulate you. Everyone is here. I've just been talking to *Le Figaro*.'

Todd scarcely heard him. 'What's he doing here?' he demanded angrily. He looked up at the big man. 'Get out, or I'll have you thrown out!'

Before the man could respond, Lapiere put a hand on Todd's wrist. 'You have something to give me today?'

Despite the gentle tone, the threat was unmistakable.

'You won't get it like this,' Todd retorted. 'Get him out, or you won't get it at all.' He might have said more but he felt a hand on his elbow. He turned back to Gloria, only to find Hank had taken her place. Forgetting all about Lapiere and the big man beside him, he grabbed Hank by the arm. 'Hank! Thank goodness! We've got to talk –'

'Carrier's here.'

Earlier the most important thing in life was for Carrier to be at the press conference. Now Todd propelled Hank backwards into a corner. 'Forget Carrier. Have you seen Manny Shiner? Listen, I've just had the most fantastic meeting . . .' He stopped and looked over his shoulder, aware of other people. 'Jesus! We need somewhere to talk.'

Guiding him by his elbow, Hank led him into a small office containing a few chairs and a desk littered with press releases. Todd slammed the door in his hurry. Then he leaned against it to prevent anyone coming in. In a torrent of words he poured out everything that had happened with Roos, and by the time he had finished Hank was as excited as he was.

'Twenty-three million!'

'The crafty sod's got a buyer lined up. He was phoning him when I left. That's why he was out on the site the other month. Now he's shit scared of losing the sale.'

'*Two* buyers!' Hank threw his hands into the air. 'Carrier's still screaming about this auction, but he's here to do business. He wants a firm deal today.'

Todd laughed as he remembered his frantic thoughts of three hours before. He had guessed right. 'So he can have one, but we'll still have our auction. We'll have it today. You deal with Carrier and I'll take Roos when he gets here. Keep them apart but let them know they're in competition. We offer them the same deal with the discount of five million –' he broke off, interrupted by the door being pushed hard into his back.

He turned and wrenched the door open and saw Katrina, but Katrina as he had never seen her before. 'Jesus Christ!' he exclaimed. She was wearing her blue suit. He liked her blue suit. He had *always* liked it, but last time he had seen it she had worn something beneath it.

'Where have you been?' she exclaimed.

'With Roos,' he said to her cleavage. 'Have you seen Manny?'

'The presentation starts in ten minutes,' she scolded.

'Here's Manny now,' said Hank, peering through the open door.

And there was Manny, looking hot and bothered as he elbowed his way through the crush. As he caught Todd's anxious look, he winked and turned to reveal another figure behind him. 'You remember Mr Drury,' he said smoothly, turning to allow the banker to join them.

Todd recovered himself enough to stick out his hand. 'Mr Drury. Good of you to come.'

'Pleased to be here,' said Drury. 'A big day for you, I imagine.'

'You don't know the half of it,' Todd said with feeling, but he was looking at Manny. Failing to read his expression, he introduced Drury to Hank and Katrina, and then hurriedly excused himself. 'May I leave you with Hank and my wife for five minutes? I need a quick word with Manny.'

With which he took Manny's arm and steered him out of the office and back into the crowd.

'It's okay with the re—' Manny began and lowered his voice to a whisper. 'I put the fire out.'

Ready to collapse with relief and excitement, Todd hugged him. 'You're a genius. How did you —'

'I lied. How else? A crook I've become.' He pulled a face at Todd's expression. 'Me and Abe Katzman. I got Abe on the phone and called in a big favour. Abe pretended to Atkinson that he was considering making us a big loan, but it was all off if there was any bad publicity . . .'

Even the qualification that Atkinson would delay matters for only twenty-four hours failed to extinguish Todd's euphoria. With his arm around Manny's shoulders he pulled him towards the top of the staircase. People thronged on all sides. Under his breath he cursed leaving the sanctuary of the office, but it would have been churlish to ask Drury to leave. 'We need somewhere quiet,' he said urgently and scarcely had he spoken when he saw a waiter emerge from a door. Dragging Manny with him, he hurried over and peered into a small storeroom, cluttered with boxes and conference chairs stacked in one corner. Pushing

425

Manny across the threshold, he thrust a twenty-pound note into the man's hand. 'Stand guard a minute, will you?'

Then he shut the door in the man's face, and turned to Manny. 'I've had the most incredible offer! Wait until you hear this.'

Manny's eyes widened as he listened. He opened his mouth and closed it again. He put his hand inside his jacket and began to massage his heart.

Without even pausing for breath, Todd grabbed a chair from the stack and set it on the floor.

Manny sank down gratefully, his gaze glued to Todd's face. 'This is for real?' he asked when he could get a word in, questions in his eyes and prayers in his voice. 'Roos has a client? You have this in writing?'

'I think we can get it. He'll be here any minute. And Hank's working on Carrier.' Todd sucked in a breath and looked at Manny in triumph. 'This is the good news you wanted, Manny. This is it!'

Manny clutched his hand, and then they were embracing, holding each other's shoulders, patting each other's backs, so that nearly a minute passed before either of them could say anything. Todd was the first to speak. 'Will Drury play ball?'

'Would he be here for nothing? But we need the offer today –'

'I'll get it today –'

'In writing –'

'Yes, yes,' Todd interrupted rashly, busy calculating his cash requirements. Along with the receiver, he would dearly love to pay Charlie. She would be safe. The worry would go from her eyes. Adding the figures all over again, he discounted Moroni, Moroni could wait until after the concert. 'I need ten million,' he said. 'First thing in the morning. Drury should go for that, shouldn't he? The worst way we get eighteen million. He'll have plenty of cover –'

'Hey,' Manny objected. 'Steady a minute. You don't even know who Roos is acting for. Tell me the name of his client and I'll get you an answer.'

'I bet it's one of the big corporations.'

'So get me their name and I'll get you the money.'

Todd's mind reeled at what had to be done. There was so little time. 'Bernie should be here somewhere. Have you seen him?'

Manny regarded him with dazed eyes. 'Bernie who?'

'Bernie Francis. My lawyer. You've met him. For Christ's sake! You know Bernie.' In his impatience, he shook Manny by the shoulders. 'Look, find Bernie and get him to knock an agreement together. Or he might have a standard form back at his office. He'll know what's best, but you'd better help him, you know what we need.' Todd's mind was leaping past one problem and on to the next. 'Leave the names and figures blank. We'll fill those in later. If there's any typing needed, Katrina will do it, unless the hotel –'

A knock sounded at the door. Cursing the interruption, Todd hesitated and then pulled the door open, expecting to see the waiter and instead finding Charlie. His face lit up. He dragged her through the opening and hugged her, wanting to tell her the wonderful news, wanting to say he could pay her tomorrow, that she was safe and had no need to worry, but Manny was there and Manny knew nothing of Charlie's involvement.

'You're on stage in five minutes,' Charlie protested breathlessly, prising his hands from her waist. 'Katrina's going frantic looking for you. It was only by chance that I saw you come in here.' Her brow creased as she looked from Manny to the crates and boxes stacked against the far wall. 'What are you doing here anyway?' Without waiting for an answer, she was dragging him through the door. 'Oh, Toddy, come on,' she said insistently as they emerged into the reception lobby which was beginning to empty of people. Then she was making him stand still while she straightened his tie and brushed a speck from his shoulder. 'Have you got your speech ready?' she asked sternly.

The last thing on his mind was his speech. He felt like the driver of an express train running slap bang stop into the buffers. With a dazed look on his face, he began patting his pockets in search of his notes.

'Don't worry,' she said. 'Just say a few words of welcome. Introduce Mike and Don Antonio and Hank, and let Mike take it from there. He's got everything organized.'

'Okay,' he said gratefully, looking at the crowd filing into the conference room. Beyond them he could see other people taking their seats. And wherever he looked he could see the banners with the gold letters on their ruby red background. *Barzini at Paloma Blanca*!

'Good luck,' Charlie whispered, squeezing his arm.

He nodded and held up crossed fingers.

He felt ten feet tall as he strode down the aisle. He no longer felt like a loser. With his heart thumping with excitement he felt like a conquering hero. When he stood up at the lectern he dispensed with his notes. Who needed notes? In the mood he was in he could have addressed the combined Houses of Parliament. So he spoke well. He even made jokes. He conveyed a sense of occasion. And when he handed over to Mike Thompson he was rewarded with a long round of applause.

And Mike was good. Fluent and amusing, he was an accomplished performer who carried the audience along with him.

So Todd sat back and enjoyed it. Flanked by Hank and Don Antonio, he beamed down from the platform. He laughed at Mike's jokes. He listened respectfully when the lights dimmed and Enrico Barzini appeared on the screen to talk about the concert. He watched with proud admiration when Mike's five-minute film clip of Paloma Blanca was shown.

And twenty minutes went by.

Then half an hour.

From time to time Gloria opened the door at the back of the room and ushered in a late arrival – but none of them included Philippe Roos.

Todd began to fidget. He saw Carrier sitting in the front row. He saw Lapiere. He could see Katrina sitting next to Drury, who kept turning to look boggle-eyed down her cleavage. Manny and Bernie were huddled together. From his vantage point up on the stage Todd could see the entire audience. But Roos was not there.

The presentation was timed to last forty-five minutes.

Todd was overcome by a sudden fear of jumping the gun. What if Roos didn't turn up? Or what if he turned up and said there was no deal? What if . . . ?

His heart sank.

He hadn't liked Roos. In fact his feelings were stronger, he had disliked Roos. He hadn't trusted him. In fact he wouldn't trust Roos with . . .

Roos came through the lobby knowing he had to buy Paloma Blanca to save his own reputation. His ears were still burning from his telephone call to New York. Clients dislike making decisions in a hurry, and they had left Roos in no doubt of the displeasure he had caused. Things would have been even worse for him had Barzini's hugely successful New York season not prompted the papers there to publish a piece on his concert at Paloma Blanca – but Roos had lost face and he knew it.

Now he intended to make good. Armed with firm authority to bid up to twenty-eight million sterling – 'but not one cent before all this television coverage' – he was determined to buy Paloma Blanca for the twenty-five million he had thought of in the first place. Then he would boast to his clients that he had 'saved' them a cool three million pounds. Once again he would bask in their approval. Not to mention earning a record fee in the process.

At the top of the stairs, he hurried across the reception hall, past the huge photographs of Barzini and Paloma Blanca, guessing everyone to be behind the big double doors on the far side, and he was half-way there when he was accosted by a woman.

'Good afternoon,' said Gloria. 'May I help you?'

'The name's Roos,' he said, looking less at her than at the clipboard in her hands.

A great burst of applause came from the other side of the doors.

Roos tapped a foot impatiently as the woman turned a page on the clipboard. He said, 'I was with Mr Todd earlier this morning.'

Gloria found his name on her list. 'Ah yes, Mr Roos, but I think you're just too late for the presentation.' Before she could say more the double doors opened and people began to stream out into the reception hall. Roos was staggered by the number.

He had imagined a few dozen, not hundreds of people, and one look at their faces told him they had been highly impressed. Watching them distracted him from what the woman was saying, but he registered that a buffet lunch was about to be served across the hall, and would he like her to get him a drink? He was about to answer when he saw Todd being buttonholed by someone with a recognizable face. Roos frowned and then it came to him. Carrier! Carrier from the Bella Vista in Majorca! Of course. So Carrier was Todd's mysterious hotelier. Scornfully Roos remembered how Carrier had struggled to raise the money for the Bella Vista. Carrier wasn't in the same league.

'Ah!' Todd exclaimed, relieved and elated to see Roos. He advanced with hand outstretched. 'I believe you two know each other?'

Their reactions could not have been more different, for while Roos managed a tight-lipped smile, Carrier actually blanched beneath his Mediterranean tan.

Not that the two men were together for long, for scarcely had they shaken hands when Hank arrived to take Carrier off to the dining-room.

'Catch up with you later,' Todd called after them before turning to Roos. 'We've an office over here where we can talk in private,' he said leading the way and then turning to usher Roos over the threshold. 'Sit yourself down.'

Neither was as confident as he pretended. Roos feigned nonchalance by studying the pictures of Paloma Blanca on the wall. 'Was that your hotelier?' he snorted dismissively as he sat down. 'Carrier's small beer. He ain't got the bread to play in this league.'

'I don't believe you know his partner,' Todd countered as he went to the other side of the table. 'Juan Gonzales? The wine grower? He owns half of Spain.'

Like boxers they sparred for an advantage. Each jolted the other. Todd's remark about Gonzales unsettled Roos more than he made out, yet he was making Todd nervous with his apparent indifference. Todd was wondering if he had been too quick to count his chickens.

A judge would have scored them equal on points.

430

If only they had known how much they had in common. Roos *had* to buy Paloma Blanca. Todd *had* to sell it. Moroni would have been amused to see them together. The irony of the situation would have appealed to him, for having put Todd in jeopardy he had unwittingly sent Roos to his rescue. Moroni would have rubbed his hands at the joke. He would even have said, 'Is'sa my nature to help people.' And Leo would have dined out on the story for years.

But Todd knew nothing of Roos's meeting in Montmartre . . .

And Roos knew nothing of Moroni's threats to Todd . . .

Elsewhere in the hotel Katrina was typing as fast as her fingers allowed. With Bernie Francis on one side dictating amendments to a standard agreement, she had Charlie on the other side checking for accuracy. From time to time they exchanged excited glances, for although figures were excluded from what she was typing, Manny had told Katrina the sums involved, and she had told Charlie, and they had hugged each other, saying with their eyes what they were afraid to put into words. *Is it possible? An agreement today? For twenty-three million?*

In the dining-room at a corner table, between mouthfuls of chicken and coleslaw, Manny was working on Drury. 'My guess is Roos is acting for a big corporation. Some outfit that's A1 with Dun and Bradstreet all over the world. So if we assume we're right about that we can take the next step . . .'

Across the room, Hank was saying to Carrier. 'This is what you wanted, José. A deal today. But you'll have to go a hell of a sight higher . . .'

And at a huge table, bedecked with flowers in the centre of the room, Mike Thompson was regaling journalists with tales of filming all over the world. 'Sure, I've been all over, but I have to tell you, I've never seen a more beautiful spot than Paloma Blanca. It'll look terrific on screen.'

Close by, with the unmistakable poise of a successful model, Sophie was looking at the man from the *Sunday Times* from beneath lowered eyelashes. 'Don't you think this man's a genius?' she purred, turning to Don Antonio sitting beside her.

While, circulating among the tables, Gloria was making sure

431

glasses were full and that everyone was enjoying themselves. And they were, with the exception of José Carrier, who was having a thoroughly miserable time. Half an hour later he was on his way back from the telephone. He had been pleading with Juan Gonzales for more money.

Hank watched him sit down at the table. 'Well? What's it to be, José? It's time for me to go and see Toddy. I need your final offer.'

Carrier looked the most miserable man in the room. People were laughing and talking and raising their glasses on all sides of him, but he was cocooned in his own private hell. He had been so *sure* of becoming the owner of Paloma Blanca. He had arrived in London totally confident. Before leaving Madrid, he had told Gonzales, 'We'll get it for seventeen, eighteen at the most.' Juan had not been pleased to receive his phone call.

'Well?' Hank persisted.

Carrier wiped his damp hands on the napkin. 'Twenty-four,' he said, with a grimace of pain. 'We'll go up to twenty-four million.'

Hank rose from the table. 'This is your last chance, José. You could still lose out. Can you go higher?'

Shaking his head, Carrier moaned like an animal in pain.

'I'll be right back,' said Hank, setting off for the lobby.

Todd was emerging from the office. Seeing Hank, he pointed to the staircase and they both hurried down the flight of stairs, only to meet Katrina and Charlie on the way up. The four of them gathered on the half-landing.

'Well?' Todd demanded, looking at Hank. 'What you got?'

'Twenty-four million. And you?'

'Twenty-five!'

They looked at each other with faces suffused with joy and excitement. Without knowing it they were clutching each other, Todd's hand was on Hank's shoulder, Hank's arm had encircled Charlie's waist, Katrina almost dropped the agreements.

It was Hank who spoke first. 'Carrier's at his limit,' he said breathlessly. 'He'd swap his soul for Paloma Blanca, but my guess is Gonzales won't go any higher.'

They were all looking at Todd, waiting for his reaction when

432

Manny appeared at the top of the stairs. He hurried down to join them. 'Well?' he demanded, his gaze going from one face to the other. He sank down on the stairs when they told him. It was a moment before he could speak. And then came the questions. 'So who's Roos acting for? Can he sign on their behalf?'

'He won't reveal their name yet, but he says they're one of the biggest groups in the world. They'll fax their authority through if we accept his offer.'

Manny extended a hand and Todd helped him up. They looked at each other for a moment. Then Manny said, 'So? You going to gossip all day? I thought you were a salesman?'

Suddenly the others were all nodding. Hank slapped his shoulder, Katrina leaned forward and kissed him, and Charlie was dazzling him with a smile reminiscent of the first time he had met her with Leo. It seemed so long ago, so much had happened.

As he turned and went back up the stairs, he remembered Leo saying, *I've still got faith, old boy.*

The memory was so strong that it was as if Leo was at his side, more than ever as he hurried past the dining-room and caught sight of Lapiere at a table just inside the open doors. *I'll give you the lawyer's address in Paris if you like,* Leo had said. And here was the lawyer in London. With his thugs, for Todd now recognized Lapiere's other companions. He stopped, then hurried over to the table. 'Two points,' he said, leaning over and putting his mouth close to Lapiere's ear. 'One, I'll have these goons arrested for stealing my food, and second tell your boss I'll be taking a discount.'

Lapiere twisted around with a look of amazement.

Todd said, 'He gave me until April. I'll be paying a month early and taking a discount. You'd better call him and tell him.'

'But —' Lapiere began, but Todd was already on his way out of the dining-room, and then through the doors and into the reception hall, with such a determined expression on his face that Gloria, meeting him at the office door, exclaimed, 'My word, you're looking fierce. I just brought some drinks over for you and your guest. I thought you'd still be with him.'

'I am now,' he said, taking the tray from her hands and

backing through the door. 'Thanks, Gloria,' he grinned, and the grin was still on his face as he turned to Roos.

How was Roos to know it was a grin of thanks? To Roos it looked like a grin of victory. His heart sank. 'Well?' he said anxiously.

And in that split second Todd knew that even more money was on the table!

'You were right,' he said. 'Twenty-five was too much for Carrier.'

Roos smiled with relief and reached for his glass. 'I told you –'

'But Gonzales is one of the wealthiest men in Europe. I did warn you.'

The smile died in Roos's eyes. 'He's ready to pay *more* than twenty-five million?'

'And there's no agent's commission if I deal with them.'

Thoroughly agitated, Roos jumped up and shut the door as if to prevent Todd from leaving. 'More than twenty-five million?' he repeated. He groaned as he imagined his clients' reaction. They would never deal with Arlsruher, Wormack and Roos again. In terror, he asked, 'Have you *signed* anything with Carrier?'

Todd flourished the papers he had taken from Katrina. 'I've got the agreement. It's ready for signing.'

Roos reached out and snatched the agreement. He glanced at it quickly, relieved to see it was unsigned. He pushed Todd down into a chair. 'Can't we settle this between us, without all this dashing back and forth . . .' he waved a hand towards the closed door behind him. 'I'm not an unreasonable man. I'll go a bit higher.' He looked into Todd's eyes. 'Maybe quite a bit higher.' Swallowing hard, he hated himself for what he was about to do. He had never gone to his maximum before. He forced himself to speak. 'If I give you a figure I want your word that we'll clinch a deal now. Right here. No more haggling. What d'you say?'

'Depends on the figure.'

'Okay, okay, but this is it. Right? I can't go a penny more. This is the bottom line below the bottom line. Understand?'

Todd looked at him.

'Suppose I was to say twenty-eight million?' he said, watching Todd's face. 'Would that clinch it? Twenty-eight million, with the same discount if things don't work out with this concert.' He thrust out his hand. 'Twenty-eight million with the concert, twenty-three million without it?'

Todd felt weak. Even without the concert they would make five million. With it, he and Hank would make five million each.

'What d'you say, Mr Todd?'

'There's still this fee. Seems to me you're acting for the buyer in this —'

'Forget my fee,' Roos said for the first time in his life, but the words were out before he could stop them.

'Okay,' said Todd, pointing at the telephone. 'I suggest you call them, and I'll have the hotel put a fax machine in here.' He pointed at the agreement. 'You happy with that?'

Roos ran his finger down the page, his eyes flying along the lines of type. Then he turned over and did the same to the second sheet. 'Looks okay. Ah, wait a minute . . .' He frowned. 'The date for the exchange of contracts needs to be filled in. It just says after the concert —'

'I've been thinking about that. The concert finishes at ten-thirty. How about we have a little party to celebrate afterwards? Your clients must come as our guests. They'd like that, wouldn't they? They can meet Enrico Barzini, do the whole bit, and we'll do the completion at midnight.'

CHAPTER FOURTEEN

EXCITEMENT HAD BEEN GROWING in Majorca ever since December, and nowhere was the tension greater than at Paloma Blanca itself. For seventy days and nights the builders had raced the clock, with every twenty-four hours bringing another emergency. Plans were altered and adjusted; compromises were made, although none of them showed. They were hidden away behind locked doors. Like the entire second floor of the main hotel. Seen from the outside the spacious terraces led through wide Moorish archways into luxurious suites. Except that the suites were not luxurious. They were empty shells with rough plastered walls and unfinished floors. But on the floor above one hundred suites had been finished, and as dawn broke on the great day they were occupied by musicians and singers, cameramen and recording technicians, most of whom had been there for the best part of three weeks.

As far as the eye could see, or was allowed to see, every public room had been finished. The huge terrace overlooking the sea was finished. So were the manicured grounds; except that where one day would be tennis courts and secluded pools, were now seats for the lucky 4000 who would attend the great concert. The stage and the backdrops were finished. The orchestra pit, built on a raft inside the Olympic-size swimming pool, was finished. Mike Thompson's control room was finished. And not only was the marina finished, it was full. Yachts, dressed overall, lined every jetty and crammed every waterway.

The kitchens in the yacht club buzzed with the sounds of chefs and commis chefs and kitchen porters and waiters as they prepared for the big day.

Paloma Blanca was in business – a mixture of hotel, film set, television station, recording studio and concert arena in which the inhabitants were living in a state of increasing tension. For one glorious night Majorca was to become the cultural centre of Europe with the concert being beamed live to France and Germany, Holland and Belgium, Italy, Switzerland, Spain and the United Kingdom. And the understandable nervousness which affects all artists when giving a performance, especially one to be seen by millions of people, was generating an excitement which spread far beyond Paloma Blanca.

It could be felt all over the island – from Andraitx to Cap-depera, from Deya to Salinas – and on the streets of Palma as Herbert drove Katrina out to the airport.

Banners and bunting ran from one end of the Maritime Promenade Gabriel Roca to the other. People wearing *Barzini at Paloma Blanca* sweatshirts were reading about Barzini in their morning papers as they breakfasted in cafés adorned by *Barzini at Paloma Blanca* posters. Barzini's voice soared on the fresh morning air, amplified from loudspeakers outside every music and record shop in the city.

'Blimey,' Herbert chortled. 'The Spanish Tourist Board should give you a medal for this lot.'

Katrina giggled. 'I think they have in their way.'

A stream of officials had journeyed out from Madrid to see Paloma Blanca for themselves. The Ministry of Cultural Affairs had hosted a reception for Barzini when he and Ossie had arrived at the beginning of the week. A press office had been established, staffed by four linguists who were helping to respond to media enquiries from all over the world. And Katrina had been run off her feet – liaising with Mike Thompson, organizing photographs, arranging interviews, visits to Paloma Blanca, meeting VIPs at the airport. Charlie had flown out every week to help, but, restricted by her contract with Bob Levit, could remain only from Thursdays until Sundays. And then on top of everything else Roos had arrived with the new owners who, after wanting to check everything at first hand, had been caught up in the excitement along with everyone else.

Herbert grinned. 'It's like a carnival, ain't it? Sort of Mardi Gras. With everyone happy.'

He had arrived two weeks before, driving across France and down to Barcelona to catch the ferry, with Gloria beside him talking non-stop all the way from London. It was Gloria who was now back at their temporary office – suite 102 at Paloma Blanca – holding the fort with Charlie while Katrina went to the airport.

'Let's hope they stay happy.' Katrina held up crossed fingers. 'Everything's ready. The maestro's pleased with rehearsals. The film men like what they've got –'

'And the Guv'nor's like a dog with two tails. Know what I reckon?' Herbert cocked his head. 'I ain't seen him like this since we started at Kilburn.'

It was true. Todd had become all things to all men. To Enrico Barzini and the artists, he was the most conscientious, most hospitable organizer they had ever encountered. Whatever they wanted, they got. So did Mike Thompson's film crew, who had never worked a better location. Notorious for being demanding about food, the yacht club was at their disposal morning, noon and night; with Hank's team from the Crow's Nest ensuring they had no cause for complaint. And with Paloma Blanca busy and happy, Todd never stopped selling. Sweatshirts, souvenir posters and programmes had appeared in the shops, and with Ossie to help him, biographies, records, CDs and tapes of Barzini had flooded the island.

Every school choir was competing in a contest to commemorate *Barzini at Paloma Blanca*.

Local operatic societies were reporting an influx of new members.

And in his good-humoured chairing of the daily press conferences, Todd had become everyone's favourite. His face was in the local papers even more often than leading politicians. In Majorca at least, Señor Todd had become *someone*.

Katrina laughed. 'I don't think he's slept in five weeks.'

Herbert grinned. 'Who needs sleep? That's what he used to say in the old days. Still, not long now, is it? It all happens tonight.' He looked at her in the mirror. 'So who we meeting this morning? Must be someone important.'

She knew what he meant. For two weeks he had been ferrying

438

people back and forth between the airport and Paloma Blanca, and only rarely did she accompany him. She hesitated. 'As a matter of fact it's my father's lawyer, but I don't want Toddy to know until this evening. It's a surprise.'

'Ah.'

His voice conveyed enough unspoken questions to make her feel uncomfortable. 'I've booked him into the hotel in Paguera, so we'll take him there from the airport. Okay? And I want you to pick him up tonight for the concert.'

'You're the boss,' he grinned. 'You know, I met your father a few times. Drove him out to Heathrow now and then. He was a smashing old character. He'd have loved all this. Just up his street.' He threw her a quick look. 'He'd have been dead proud of you.'

Katrina opened her mouth to reply – to say she had changed, that she could understand now what had made her father tick, that she might even have liked him – but before she could say anything Herbert interrupted. 'Hells bells! Look at this lot!'

Coming towards them on the other side of the road was a heaving mass of coaches and taxis and private cars, all on their way from the airport.

'Yesterday was bedlam,' said Herbert, looking in awe at the long queue of traffic. 'But this beats everything. By God! The world and his brother's coming to this concert.'

'Encore!' people shouted, excitedly waving their programmes. 'Encore!'

Applauding as one, 4000 people rose to their feet to create a crescendo of sound which rolled and reverberated around the lantern-lit hillsides.

On stage, a perspiring Enrico Barzini beckoned members of the chorus and ushered them forward to the footlights.

The crowd clapped more furiously than ever, beating their hands together in a positive frenzy, creating such a noise that ears buzzed and rang and sang with such volume that even standing next to each other people could not hear their neighbours.

In the control room, Mike Thompson cued camera three.

The cries rang out with growing insistence, louder all the time until the noise became a thunderous roar with the entire audience stamping their feet and shouting: 'Encore! Encore!'

Constantine Leopardi, the conductor, turned on his podium in front of the orchestra, bowed low from the waist and let the approving roar wash over him. Like Barzini on stage, his smiling face was gleaming with sweat.

The shouts exploded in the night sky, soaring up through the pines and the palms and above the almond trees on the hillsides.

In response to a wave from Leopardi's baton, the ranks of musicians rose to their feet.

In the control room, with his gaze still glued to his screens, Thompson wagged a cautionary finger at his first assistant. 'How they doing in the marina?'

'Hank's arrived. He says they're ready.'

'Tell him six minutes to the fireworks.'

In the marina, breathless from hurrying the hundred yards from his seat, Hank positioned himself with the camera crew next to the yacht club and looked out over the serried ranks of yachts. Every boat was ablaze with lights from stem to stern, as were the other boats further out in the bay.

Hundreds of boats; ocean-going yachts, power boats and cruisers, with the crews aboard all awaiting his signal.

Behind him, he could hear the roar of the crowd subside for a moment, then the excited murmur rose again to an expectant hubbub of anticipation.

As he looked along the jetty to the huge scaffolding erected for the fireworks, he felt a tingle of pride, not just for himself but for them all – Toddy, Katrina, Charlie, Don Antonio. Their work and the work of so many others had created Paloma Blanca, and the reality exceeded even his most Technicolor dreams.

Suddenly the sounds of the audience were interrupted by a vibrant fanfare of trumpets. Golden notes shimmered and rose and hung like skylarks on the night air before the orchestra burst into the opening bars of the Toreador's Song from *Carmen*. There came a huge answering roar from the crowd, great shouts of approval, fading within moments as the orchestra

440

got under way and the audience became caught up in the trium-phant tempo of Bizet's music.

Hank felt triumphant along with everyone else. And excited. Turning he found himself looking into Charlie's shining green eyes. He grinned. 'Ain't it great?'

'Fantastic! The whole thing! Barzini, the atmosphere; there's never been a night like it.' Taking his elbow, she drew him up the steps into the yacht club, shutting the glass door behind them to lessen the noise.

'I must be out there,' he protested.

'In a minute,' she said, curling a hand behind his neck and bringing his mouth down to her lips.

'Hey?' he gasped when she released him. 'What's that for?'

'I couldn't think of the right words,' she laughed. 'Even thanks a million sounds silly and flippant when it *is* a million . . . I mean . . .' catching her breath, she shook her head in bewilderment. 'Oh, God! See? Who knows what I *do* mean tonight? Me, lost for words? I wouldn't have believed it. I'm *never* lost for words –'

'Take it easy,' he laughed as a look of realization came into his face. As soon as the deal was struck, they had decided to give Charlie a million from their profit.

'Take it easy!' Charlie echoed. 'How can I? I'm still bowled over,' she exclaimed, grasping both his hands. 'Seriously, it's the most incredibly generous –'

'You weren't supposed to know until the party.'

'Katrina told me before the concert. She couldn't keep the secret any longer. I tried to find you earlier . . .' Gulping for breath, she looked at him with shining eyes. 'So I came as soon as I could, and what do I find? You looking sad.'

'Me?'

'Yes you were. You were staring at the marina with a sad look on your face.'

'Never,' he denied, shaking his head.

'Stop trying to kid me. What's wrong? Would it help if I loaned you some money?'

He laughed and hugged her. 'I was saying goodbye, I

suppose,' he said. 'Not just to all this, but . . .' he hesitated. 'I sold Max the Crow's Nest yesterday. Did you know?'

'No! No one told me. Oh, Hank, why?'

He shrugged, almost embarrassed. 'I dunno. I guess fourteen years is long enough. Majorca's been good to me, but the place won't be the same from now on.'

'You're leaving?'

He nodded. 'Reckon so.'

'Where are you going? Back to the States?'

He shook his head. 'No point. The past is a different place. Where I grew up ain't there no more.' He smiled. 'I think I'll buy myself a new boat and look around for a bit. Some guy was telling me about a place down in the Seychelles. He said it might be for sale.'

Sudden understanding lit her eyes. 'You're going to try again, aren't you? You're still looking for Paloma Blanca.'

He grinned like a small boy revealing a secret. 'Maybe. What about you? What are your plans?'

'Are you kidding?' She shook her head. 'I'm still catching my breath about this money. I mean, I'm loaded! I'm a million-airess. Do they still say that?'

He laughed. 'Why not?'

'Maybe people think it's sexist? Anyway, I've got to get tonight over first.' She grinned. 'I could end up in jail.'

He looked at her. 'You're still telling Levit?'

Even though Todd had repaid her the six million plus interest the day after Roos had signed the agreement, Charlie's sense of guilt had lingered on.

She saw the doubt in his eyes. 'Don't worry. Bob's bound to be a bit shocked, but if I explain everything he'll be okay.'

'I hope you know what you're doing. If he cuts up rough, I can always borrow a boat. We could slip out of harbour under cover of darkness.'

A look came into her eyes as if tempted, but before she could reply one of the cameramen banged on the glass door. He pointed at his watch.

Taking her arm, Hank grinned as he steered her towards the door. 'Time for the fireworks.'

'I'm coming, and don't worry. Nothing, just nothing, can spoil tonight.'

Charlie was right. After the fireworks came the party, and the festivities seemed set to last until dawn. At one-thirty in the morning, the crowds on the terrace showed no signs of leaving. Emerging from the crush, Katrina had just started up the main staircase when Hank caught her arm. 'You seen Charlie?'

'I've been looking all over for you. We're meeting in the office. Come on.'

'Has she told Levit?'

'She and Toddy are with him now.'

'But I thought –' He broke off, interrupted by people descending the staircase. 'She said she didn't want us there.'

'Toddy wouldn't take no for an answer.' She laughed and, looking down at the vast room, saw Sophie and waved to her. 'God, what an incredible night!' Impulsively, she hugged him. 'We did it, Hank! We did it!' When he was slow to smile, she said, 'Charlie will be all right.'

'I should have gone as well –'

'Put that man down,' shouted Todd, taking the stairs two at a time. Flushed and breathless, he wagged a finger at Katrina. 'I saw that –'

'Where's Charlie?' Hank interrupted.

Todd grinned. 'Don't worry, she's not in leg irons.' Taking Katrina's arm so that she walked between them, he led them on to the office. 'She'll be up in a minute,' he said as he threw open the door. 'Set the glasses up, Hank.'

'But what happened?'

Closing the door to keep out the noise, he leaned back against it. 'Levit's fine. He said rules are meant to be broken in exceptional circumstances, and these were the most exceptional he'd ever heard of.'

'I'll be damned!' Hank stared at him. 'All that worry –'

'So Charlie could have told him after all?' Katrina exclaimed as she flopped down on to the sofa.

'I didn't say that,' Todd chuckled. 'Levit got his money back, plus a good dollop of interest. What he really meant was, it's okay if it all comes right in the end.'

'And it has, hasn't it?' asked Katrina, turning to Hank who was standing at the bar.

Lifting a bottle of champagne from the ice bucket, he grinned at Todd. 'Cheers, ole buddy. Do we open this now, or wait for Charlie?'

'She'll be here in a second. We were working our way across to the stairs when we bumped into your admirer.' Todd looked at Katrina. 'That guy Ossie. Cheeky sod! D'you know what he said? What a remarkable woman I married! One in a million, he said.'

'Oh, that's just his way,' she laughed. 'It's mixing with the theatrical crowd. They're all over the top. Don't take any notice.'

Suddenly the door burst open and Charlie flung herself over the threshold. 'Ta ra!' she trumpeted above the noise of the party. 'Wow, what a madhouse out there!' Shutting the door, she grinned at Hank. 'I trust you're opening that to celebrate my freedom.' Kissing Todd on the way past, she pirouetted into the centre of the room. 'I'm footloose, fancy free, and over twenty-one, God dammit!' Breathlessly, she plumped herself down next to Katrina. 'But better than that, thanks to you lot, I'm filthy, stinking rich!'

Katrina could contain herself no longer. 'Rich?' she echoed, tossing her head. 'You want to know rich?'

They all looked at her with questions in their eyes.

'Leo's estate has been settled!'

'It has?' Todd gulped, sounding astonished. 'No one told me.'

'I've hardly seen you all day.'

'Settled?' he repeated blankly, staring at her.

They were all staring at her. Hank paused with his thumb under the champagne cork.

'Rochère came to the concert,' Katrina explained, looking at Todd. 'He's here now.'

'He did? He is? I haven't seen him.'

Taking a deep breath, Katrina said, 'Leo left me four million pounds.'

'Wow!' exclaimed Charlie.

'You're kidding!' said Hank.

'Bloody hell,' said Todd, sounding awed as he slumped into the chair by the door.

Hank released the cork and champagne frothed out over his hand before he could reach the glasses. Charlie sprang to his rescue, rushing to the bar and setting flutes on a tray.

Todd and Katrina remained where they were, exchanging looks, Todd in a daze and Katrina beside herself with excitement.

Carrying the glasses round on the tray, Charlie gave one to Todd, who accepted it without saying a word. In fact, it was a moment or two before anyone spoke. Charlie was the first to break the silence.

'Four million!' she whispered, passing Katrina her glass. 'Good heavens above, Katrina! That's seriously rich. What are you going to do with it all?'

With her gaze fixed on her husband, Katrina said, 'Hank was telling me about some land in the Seychelles. Why don't we all go to see it?'

As Hank caught her eye, a look of delight came to his face. 'That's an idea. And this time we'd start off with the right sort of money −'

'Great!' Charlie interrupted, her green eyes shining with excitement.

'And we've learned a hell of a lot,' said Todd.

For a moment they exchanged glances, then Todd rose to his feet. 'I propose a toast,' he said, raising his glass. 'To Leo.'

'And his daughter,' said Charlie.

'Who knows?' Katrina laughed. 'Perhaps even to our new Paloma Blanca!'